Far From My Father's House

Elizabeth Gill

Quercus

First published in Great Britain in 2015 by

Quercus
55 Baker Street
7th Floor, South Block
London W1U 8EW

A CIP catalogue record for this book is available
from the British Library

PB ISBN 978 1 78429 990 3
EBOOK ISBN 978 1 78206 174 8

10 9 8 7 6 5 4 3 2 1

Printed and bound in Great Britain by Clays Ltd, St Ives plc

Typeset by CC Book Production

In memory of my wonderful mother, Pat Rippon

Prologue

1915

In the end Letty waited for the right time, when Will had gone up the very top fields to see to the sheep, shouting his dog to go with him, and she called Hannah in from where she was feeding the hens in the yard.

The little kitchen was full of the smell of newly baked bread. They had not needed new bread making that day but she always made bread when she was anxious and she had never been more anxious than she was now.

Hannah looked pale. She was beautiful. Letty had always known without exaggeration how beautiful her daughter was, the thick golden hair, the bright blue eyes, the skin which browned in the summer sun. She was tall and slender with graceful limbs, a happy smile and she was all her parents had.

Letty had dreamed of Hannah married to a good man somewhere in the dale, giving them grandchildren. She had dreamed of afternoons over the teacups with the babies, of somebody who would take care of Hannah because the girl was shy. She rarely ventured far from home except to church on Sundays, and Letty happily saw the young men trying not to stare. One day one of them would walk up the steep hill from the village, open the gates on the way, up to the little hillside farm where Hannah had been born and then Hannah would know the happiness of a good marriage. There was nothing more her mother wished.

But now the dreams were fading. Now Letty didn't know what to say. Hannah had of late become withdrawn and silent and in the early mornings while her father slept the older woman had heard her get up and go outside and retch into the long grass beside the stone wall. Hannah ate nothing.

'I want you to tell me,' Letty said. She needed to be angry, to have at least some explanation so that the anger would have a place to go.

'Tell you what?'

'I want you to tell me who the man is.'

'There is no man.'

'But there has been, hasn't there? There must have

been or you could hardly be having his child!' She felt impatient. She wanted to shout, maybe even slap Hannah for having destroyed the dream before it had taken wing.

Hannah looked down.

'I didn't think you knew,' she said.

'Your father doesn't know but he will have to. There's no way you can keep a secret like that.'

'I thought I might, at least for a while. I haven't done anything wrong.' That was a blow. If Hannah had done nothing wrong . . . Letty took a deep breath and tried to keep her voice steady.

'Is it something that can be put right?'

Hannah shook her head.

'There's nothing to be done,' she said.

'If you tell me who it was—'

'I can't.' Hannah sank down on to the little stool before the kitchen fire. She didn't cry though her mother thought she was going to.

'If it was just a mistake – everybody but God makes them . . .' her mother said but Hannah was shaking her head definitely.

'I was on my way back from the village when he came by on his horse. I didn't think anything about it. He got down from the horse and tied its reins around the gate in the middle field. There was nobody. He got hold of me. I didn't scream at first but even when I screamed and screamed until I couldn't scream any more nobody came. He thought it was funny. He laughed quite a lot. He put me down and did – he did things to me. When it was over he tried to give me some money. He said if I told anybody he'd have us put out.'

'Oh, Hannah, I wish you'd said. I wish you'd told us. Why keep such a burden to yourself?'

'Father would have killed him. I couldn't. I didn't think this would happen. I thought if I pretended it had never happened everything would be all right. I thought you couldn't be expecting when it had only happened once.'

'That's an old wives' tale,' her mother said wearily. 'What shall we tell your father?'

'What I told you. That I didn't know him, that it happened in the dark when I was walking home. That's what we'll tell him.'

Letty took the girl into her arms. The dream was shattered now and it seemed there was no one to pay the price but them.

One

1929

It was when he went to live at Grayswell that the children, remembering from school, called him Blake. When he lived with his grandparents they called him Davy. Blake could not remember a time when he did not work. He could barely remember a time when he could not take the horse and have half the bottom field cut in the July morning before the seven o'clock bus went down the dale, carrying the men to the quarry.

The only other people on the little hillfarm were his grandparents and a hard living it was. They seemed to him so very old. He could not imagine how they would have managed without him. His grandmother was always calling him from the yard and his grandfather was always calling him from the field and he feared that some day he would break right in two because there was not enough of him to go round. At night by the fire his grandmother would hug him to her.

'You're all we've got,' she would say.

His mother lay up in the churchyard not far from the waterfall. Not that far from the farm, you could almost see the house from the churchyard but it was a long, long way, Blake thought, when somebody was dead. All he could see to indicate his mother's presence was a small wooden cross with her name, Hannah Blake, and her years, 1898–1916. There was nothing left of her anywhere. Except for him it was as if she had never existed. There were no photographs of her, no possessions. His grandparents didn't talk about her unless he asked and even then not much, and it seemed to hurt them so he tried not to ask though he would have liked to have known more about her. He only asked once about his father but they said that they knew nothing.

When Blake lay in bed at night he thought a lot about his parents. He was even comforted by the fact that he must have had a father, even the calves and the lambs had them, it was biologically impossible not to have but as far as he knew there was no sign of any man who might have been anything to him.

One day the summer that Blake was thirteen he had begun cutting the low pasture early. He kept going until he was finished and as he walked the horse back up the fields he heard his grandmother's voice as usual from the yard. 'Davy! Davy, your breakfast's getting cold!' The words never varied and they were never less than a relief. He was very hungry by now and his grandmother was the kind of woman who should have had a large family – though how they would have supported them is difficult to say – because she loved to cook. She liked nothing better than seeing people around her table. There would be thick slices of bacon and fresh eggs and plenty of bread because his grandmother had made bread only yesterday. She made bread two or three times a week and with such loving care that it always tasted wonderful.

It was some time before he reached the house and she was still fussing about the breakfast getting cold though she was only just ladling it from the pan, knowing exactly what he had been doing and how long it would have taken him and the amount of time it took to come back up the fields and make everything right before he walked into the kitchen.

It was not a big house but its kitchen was a big room and there was also a tiny parlour at the front. There were bedrooms above it and housing for the animals next to it and Blake could not have liked a room more. It was always warm. He and his grandfather kept the fire well supplied with wood for cooking and washing. The kitchen was his grandmother's kingdom, just as the outside and the barns were his grandfather's.

His grandmother looked up sharply now.

'Have you washed your hands?'

She always said that too. Blake smiled and did so at the kitchen sink.

'Where's your grandfather?'

'I don't know. Up top I expect. He said he was going to see how the heifer was getting on.'

His grandfather liked to make sure that every animal on the small farm was safe and well each day and he had a heifer due to calve.

'He should have been back by now.'

Blake knew that trying to soothe her would do no good so, not thinking of the smell of bacon he was leaving behind, he put on boots again and his jacket and set off up the fields behind the farm, trudging up the deep cart-rutted track, climbing over the gates instead of opening them and enjoying the walk in spite of his hunger. It was a good day in late July. Summer was wonderful at the farm and though the winter had been a hard one it had not been dismal. His grandmother made all kinds of country wines throughout the season and kept a stock of them in the pantry. His grandfather laughed and said that dandelion wine gave you backdoor trot but the truth was that her wines were very good. Blake well remembered her elderflower wine which had gone into a second fermentation and become what she called her elderflower champagne. It was the best thing that Blake had ever tasted, the bubbles like bitter honey. She made birch sap wine and beetroot wine – the colour was rich and deep – and she made honeysuckle wine from the honeysuckle which twined itself around the tiny wooden bridge in the front garden. There was elderberry, which was almost black and it sometimes fermented again like raspberry froth, and gorse, which they had sworn never to make again because their fingers had bled trying to pick the flowers.

Blake kept his mind on these things as he trudged up the steep fields. He ignored the view because it was a thousand times old to him, even though he loved it better than any place on earth; he just thought about Christmas and chicken and sitting around the fire, reading and playing cards and being in the warmth while the wind did its best to batter down the walls of the old farm. The stone buildings had been well put together and Blake trusted them. He remembered going to bed on Christmas night with a hot brick in his bed and listening to the soft voices of his grandparents in the next room and thinking of how much he loved them. This last thought made him move faster. He was almost there now but he couldn't see his grandfather. He jumped over the gate in the very top field – it was his grandfather's favourite because the view from there was the best, all the fields laid out before him and the grey farms, and way, way below at the bottom of the valley was the river running silver.

The cows were at the far side of the field. In the corner there was what looked like a bundle of something, dark and strangely twisted and when he got nearer Blake's head told him what his heart had already feared.

He had never met disaster and grief head on before but he saw it now. His grandfather was dead. He didn't doubt it. There were no moments of almost relief when he thought that perhaps the old man had fallen or lost his wind. It was the way that he was lying. Blake didn't have to have seen it before to know that it was death but in a way, he thought, he had seen it before. He had seen animals die and it was really no different. It was an ending, it was a defeat, it was a kind of awful triumph over the man that his grandfather had been, it was a horrible simple wiping out of something complex and intricate and well-loved. Blake got down beside him and started to cry and all he could think was that his grandfather had died alone and that he could have been there with him and comforted and possibly even helped him. For his grandfather to die alone seemed the worst thing about it and then he thought that he had to go back down and tell his grandmother. He knew what this meant for her: no one to talk to in bed for the rest of her life, no one to share the memories with from childhood because they had known one another since they were babies. It meant that the past was over and maybe even the future for her. He couldn't go down, he couldn't move. He didn't ever want to move again. The summer wind blew warm across the field where his grandfather lay and Blake cried.

That autumn his grandmother didn't even attempt to get him to go to school. She had done so in the past even though Blake hated it and would have done anything to get out of it, and because they needed him he had often succeeded. Things were different now. She could not manage without him, indeed they could barely manage even though he worked from light to dark and sometimes beyond that.

It was strange. He had thought that the long, winter nights would have been more difficult than the summer and early autumn after his grandfather's death but it was easier somehow, as though the darkness gave the little house a blanket to hide behind. Nothing could have been more difficult than that August. The light rarely went from the sky and he had no peace and no sleep and he knew that his grandmother did not sleep either. He heard her moving around, going downstairs, the stairs creaking under her weight. Day and night they drank tea. It was enough to put you off for good. She was in the kind of shock which meant that she worked all the time and because it was so light and because he did not sleep he was up at four and outside and it was just as well because there was no one to help him now. She could not do the heavy work though she did everything she could. They had to keep the farm. The farm and all the other farms around it belonged to Joseph Harlington, who lived in Southgate Hall at the top of the valley. He was not an unkind man, he had said they could keep the farm as long as they could work it but both Blake and his grandmother were terrified that somehow they should lose it. When Blake did sleep he had nightmares about being put from the land and other dreams, better ones in which his grandfather came back. Night after night when he slept his grandfather returned to the farm. Waking up was so cruel, in the silent dawn with only his grandmother for company. He had thought that he knew loss because of his mother but he didn't remember her. The old man had been as precious to him as breathing. Each breath hurt.

On the nights when he did not dream that his grandfather returned – or even sometimes on the same night – he dreamed of losing the farm, of being turned out though how it should happen he could not imagine. The daytime was bearable and between them they managed the work, and his grandmother gave to him and he imagined that he gave to her a little sanity as the days shortened and cooled and the darkness brought the comfort of the fire and food and wine, which his grandmother now deemed essential at the end of each day. Blake was grateful for the darkness when it came, for the dawn which broke his nightmares, for the days which were never quite as bad as he imagined they were going to be. The worst had happened and there was some kind of comfort in that, at least it could not happen again. Only once could he find his grandfather dead. Each day he did not have to face that again so each day was better than the worst day of his life.

Mr Ward, the teacher at the school, sent books so that it would look as if Blake was doing schoolwork but he rarely did. Mr Ward was a farmer's son and he knew that if Blake was to keep the farm he had to work it but he knew also that Blake was meant to be at school.

That Christmas was the first difficult Christmas of Blake's life and even that was not as bad as he had thought it would be. Nothing could ever have been as bad as he imagined.

Two days after Christmas the vicar, Mr Lawrence, came out to the fields where Blake was giving hay to the sheep. He was comforting himself with the thought of the hay. After his grandfather had died he had worked hard to make sure that there would be winter feed for the animals and when the first frosts came he had snagged turnips so that there would be nourishment for the ewes in lamb. Work was good. Work was easy compared to everything else. It made you feel human again.

Mr Lawrence stood, watching him, smiling, and then he said, 'Can't you persuade your grandmother to move into the village, David?'

Blake eyed him uneasily.

'Why?' he said.

'It would be better for her. You can't manage this and your lessons.'

'We get by,' Blake said.

'Your education is important.'

'So is the farm.'

'Mr Harlington will give you a house in the village.'

It was then that Blake decided he had never liked the vicar.

'My great-grandfather had this farm, my grandfather died here. Nobody's taking it from me.'

'Nobody's trying to take it from you, David—'

'No? So what's all this talk about a house in the village? My grandmother doesn't want to move. This is our home.'

'You're just a boy.'

'I don't need you to tell me what I am. Now you get off my land.'

'David—'

'Get off it, and don't mention this to my grandmother. She's had enough to worry about these past months,' and Blake turned and walked away.

It was not easy being rude to the vicar and afterwards he doubted the wisdom of it but at the time it felt good and he needed to feel like that, to hit out at somebody and something for what had happened. It did seem slightly unfair to take it out on the vicar. Mr Lawrence was an easy target, he was clumsy and stupid, but he had asked for it and Blake was more than willing to do whatever was necessary to ensure that he and his grandmother could go on living at Sunniside. The name seemed all wrong now. The sun was gone from the farm, there was nothing but endurance and the kind of love which kept his grandmother baking bread three times a week even though there was only the two of them to eat it. He didn't know how long it would be before he pointed out to her that she was still cooking and baking for three. She didn't seem to know how to do anything else.

After Christmas the weather suddenly turned worse. It was too cold to snow, the frosts were bitter and relentless. He urged his grandmother to stay inside, told her that he would take care of everything, but there was so much to do that she would not linger indoors if he needed help. She began to cough and though he tried to keep her warm and look after her the cough grew worse until not only was he doing all the outside work but having to come in and start there. At first she kept on as best she could with the house and the cooking, and she did the small jobs that she had always done like feeding the hens and seeing to the dogs and cats. After a while she was sitting down every time he came in and then she was lying asleep on the sofa because she did not sleep at night for the coughing fits. Blake went to the village for the doctor but even though he came and gave her something she did not get better. He put her to bed. She didn't object and she would have, he knew, had she been able. She got worse. She was hot and didn't know where she was and she kept talking to him like he was his grandfather. The only peace she seemed to have was when he pretended to be his grandfather. Then she would smile and nod and go back to sleep for a while. Blake got the doctor again. He sat with her all night and most of the day except for the feeding of the animals. The night and the room were cold and he came to dread the nights because she no longer knew who he was or who she was and when the doctor came again he said that Blake's grandmother should be in hospital.

She wouldn't go. She wept and pleaded and it made her cough all the more.

'I'm not leaving the farm. If I leave it I'll never come back, I know I won't. I'm not leaving the farm and I'm not leaving you.'

They brought an ambulance for her. It came as near to the farm as it could. The frost had turned soft and the track was deep with mud where the puddles looked like broken glass. The ambulance men didn't want to get their vehicle stuck so they carried her on a stretcher the last quarter mile. Blake wanted to go with her but there was nobody to look after the farm. He managed the journey the following afternoon after a long bus ride down the dale and into Wolsingham.

When he enquired after her they sent him along narrow corridors to the ward but as he reached the entrance the nurse took him aside into a little room and told him that his grandmother had died during the night.

'There was no way to contact you,' she said.

There was suddenly nothing to do and nobody to be with. His grandmother had died without him. Was he never to say goodbye to anyone?

That night the wind howled around the small farm. Blake slept with the old dog, Bessie, on his bed and a small cat on the pillow above his head and he looked up into the darkness and saw what would happen. They would take everything from him now, the house, the barns, the fields, the animals. He huddled closer to Bessie but he couldn't sleep. He had never been here alone before. It was as if the whole world had died. The little house was freezing, the wind moaned. Bessie went to sleep. Her body was not even moving, she was so peaceful. She didn't know what had happened though she had spent a lot of time that first late summer looking for his grandfather, watching for him by the door, waiting for his footsteps. She had never been his grandmother's dog so at least she would not wait for the old lady to come back. She slept now, curled into a circle as though there was no beginning and no end, as though life was perfect.

Two

Since she had been a little girl, Annie's mother had told her about Ireland. It had always been her favourite story, until her mother tired of telling it.

'You've heard it a hundred times from your grandma,' Rose would say.

'I know. That's why I like to hear it,' Annie would say, snuggling down into her bed with Madge almost asleep nearby.

Rose would settle herself at the end of the bed and stare across at the wallpaper and then she would begin.

'Once upon a time there was a family in Ireland. They weren't considered by some to be a rich family but they were titled, they had breeding. They had a great big house with hundreds of acres of land and they had horses and carriages. The ladies didn't work and the gentlemen fished and shot and rode to hounds and looked after their land like big farms and the ladies played the piano and drew and planned dances and dinners and shopping in the towns with their friends.

'The son of the house was very handsome but he would not marry any of the pretty ladies he was introduced to and the family could have done with a fortune and some of the ladies who had fortunes would have had him.

'Now in the house there was a parlour maid and she was called Mary and Mary was the prettiest girl that he had ever seen, and they fell in love and he wanted to marry her. When his family found out about this and he refused to give her up they told him to leave the house and never come back and they would never hear his name again and they would never see him. And being stubborn as well as handsome he would not give up his Mary so they ran away to England and were married. He never went back and he never saw his family again and he and Mary never had any money because he had been taught no trade and he found it hard to learn but learn he did eventually. They settled in England and they were very happy.'

Annie frowned because Rose had finished the story early.

'They had a little girl – Grandma.'

'Yes.' Rose tucked her in.

'And Great-grandpa died, didn't he, a long time ago?'

'Yes,' Rose said and she kissed Annie and went back down the stairs, the brass rods clinking under the weight of her feet. Madge was already asleep, she knew the story well. Annie never tired of hearing it. Her great-grandmother had married a lord. In time she too would marry one. She snuggled down into the bedclothes for warmth. The farm was quiet now. Sometimes when it was very quiet she would think that she could hear the river but it was only wishful thinking. The river was at the very bottom of the valley, down beyond the bottom pastures and even on a still night you could not hear it because mostly it ran shallow over flat stones. They had plodged there and built dams since they were very small. Annie's brother, Tommy, had recently begun playing the cornet and he went down into the fields near the river because his mother couldn't bear the noise and there he would sit practising with the cows all around him, he said, appreciating the music.

Tommy had left school, he was fifteen. He helped his father around the farm though he also took out the post. He wanted to be a joiner but there was no way that would happen, there was so much to do.

Annie was still at school but she would leave that

summer. Madge was almost twelve and little Elsie was ten.

Their farm was called Grayswell. Annie loved the name. In fact she loved everything about the farm. They had not always lived there. She had been born in their first house, two rooms above the joiner's shop in the village. She thought that was maybe where Tommy had got the idea that he wanted to be a joiner because he had been born to the sound of Jackie Stephenson's saw and plane and hammer as Jackie made the coffins down below.

The farm had been their grandfather's, at least tenanted by their grandfather. The Harlingtons owned nearly all the farms in the valley and on the valleysides, apart from the odd one like Western Isle, which was owned by Charles Vane and his family. The Vanes were rich. Alistair Vane went away to school and was only seen in the holidays riding his sleek horse.

Annie wondered sleepily who Gray had been and when he had found the well.

Blake didn't know how to leave the farm. Mr Hodgson, Mr Harlington's assistant, had come to the farm and officially told Blake that he must leave because there were new tenants. Everything that belonged to him would be sold and he would have the money. Blake privately doubted this would amount to much. The new tenants were to be Mr and Mrs Austin and somehow over his head they had agreed to take everything, including Bessie. That was the worst thing of all, having to leave Bessie, but Blake didn't know where he was going. Bessie belonged here at the farm, she knew the land, she would be unhappy anywhere else. He probably would not be allowed to keep her at some orphanage or whatever. Blake had privately resolved to run away at the first opportunity. The only good thing about it was the fact that Mr and Mrs Austin seemed like nice people and had taken to Bessie and she had taken to them so she would help them because nobody knew the farm or the sheep like the old dog.

Blake didn't listen to anything so he didn't hear about arrangements being made for him until the day when Jack Lowe arrived at the farm. Blake knew all the farmers in the dale. He knew Mr Lowe's children from school but only just because he went to school so infrequently. Jack was tall and red-haired. He walked into the barn where Blake was working, not right in, just stuck his head around the door and Blake stopped and regarded him carefully.

'Now,' Jack said. He didn't say any more until Blake nodded in acknowledgement and then, 'I want a word with you.'

Blake walked out of the barn into the sunlight.

'Come for summat, have you?' he said.

Jack said nothing to that.

'It's all sold,' Blake said.

'I know. It isn't about that. What are you going to do?'

'I don't know.'

'Do you have anybody to go to?'

'I'll find somewhere.'

'You could come to us.'

Blake eyed him suspiciously.

'Why?' he said.

'You could help.'

'Work on the farm?'

'You do know how to do that, don't you?' Jack said, smiling a little. 'And you could go to school.'

'I don't go to school.'

'You'd have to.'

Blake looked hard at Jack Lowe and wondered what reason the man had for offering to take him in. It was unpaid help of course but they had to put up with him and feed him and give him a room or at least a bed.

'Are you my father?'

Jack went on looking at him and shook his head.

'Does Mrs Lowe want me there?'

'She seemed to think it would be all right.'

'You've already got four children. What do you need with another?'

Jack didn't answer straight away and Blake watched him carefully to see the answer in his eyes before he said anything but it was difficult.

'I know you have to leave the farm but there seems no reason to me why you should leave the dale.'

'There seems no reason to me why I should leave the farm.'

'I'm sure there doesn't,' Jack said. 'Will you think about it?'

Blake wasn't going to. When Jack Lowe had gone he worked at twice the speed, he was so angry. The next day he had another visitor, Mr Lawrence, the vicar.

The snow was all gone by then but it was bitterly cold on the hillside and Mr Lawrence's cheeks were purple with cold and broken veins. It was almost teatime and Blake should have asked the man inside but he didn't. He liked keeping Mr Lawrence in the freezing yard, knowing that the animals were warm.

'You'll have to leave soon, David,' he said, his voice partly torn away by the wind. 'I know it will be difficult for you but Mrs Lawrence and myself would be glad to give you refuge at the vicarage.'

He made Blake want to laugh somehow. Mr Lawrence

couldn't contain the triumph in his voice and he thought himself more godly for offering a place in that bloody awful old house. Blake had been in it once and had never seen such a cheerless building in his life. It smelled of mould and mice and rancid fat, and as for Mrs Lawrence . . . Blake had tried to imagine Mr and Mrs Lawrence in bed together and couldn't bear the thought. Mrs Lawrence had what he imagined were large, wobbling thighs and big drooping breasts and Mr Lawrence probably said his prayers at the bedside. Watching Mr Lawrence now Blake suddenly thought that Jack Lowe's offer was a good one. After all, he didn't have to stay there if he didn't like it. There was nothing to keep him anywhere now and when he was fourteen in the summer he would be free.

'It's very kind of you,' he said, 'but Mr Lowe's already asked me to go and stay there.'

The vicar actually looked relieved, Blake thought.

Experience of difficult things didn't make it any easier, Blake discovered, the day that he left. Finding his grandfather dead in the field, watching the ambulance taking his grandmother out of sight, none of that made leaving any easier. It made it all harder; it was like an act of betrayal, as though something in the stone buildings and the newly green fields was still his grandparents. Blake never forgot the sight of Bessie standing just outside the door. He wondered whether she would wait for him to come back as she had waited for his grandfather, and if she remembered that his grandfather had never come back again and if that would help when he never did. He watched until it was all out of sight and he knew that however many times he saw the place again it would never be home any more, that other people would live there and dim the memories of his grandparents and himself and their life together on the little hillfarm.

Three

Annie found them all gathered in the parlour when she came back from her ride. Every morning either before school or at weekends she took her black horse, Shard, and rode a long way. It was, she thought, the only way she could face the rest of the day because she hated school and she hated the work there was always to do. She would have liked to have helped her father outside but her mother maintained that she had to do the housework. Annie would rather have milked half a dozen cows than wash a floor. She had her own cows to milk as it was but they were a pleasure compared to washing the big kitchen floor. Her mother washed the stone flags with buttermilk to make them shine. There was also the dairying to be done, the cream to be separated from the milk each day and the toing and froing up and down the stone cellar steps, and worst of all the butter had to be made. Sometimes it seemed to her to take forever and if her mother wasn't well, which she sometimes wasn't, or if she was busy Annie had to walk to the station with fifty pounds of butter, take the train to Stanhope and walk to the shop which was quite a long way from the station. The buttermilk which was left over was given to the calves. There was always another job to do, no matter how many you had already done and at the end of the day the cows had to be milked.

'They can't milk themselves,' her father used to say.

For the family to be gathered in the parlour before breakfast meant that something important was happening. They were all sitting down too except her father and it was such an unusual sight for her family to be seated doing nothing that she stood in the doorway and stared.

'Come in,' her father said. 'We were waiting for you. I've got something to tell you.'

Annie glanced across at her small, brown-haired mother for some clue as to what was happening but her mother was sitting with her head down so there was no help there. She sat.

'You know that David Blake's grandparents have died,' her father said. 'David has nowhere to go. Now we could do with another pair of hands around here. I've suggested to him that he should come here—'

'Like Prudence?' ten-year-old Elsie asked. Prudence had been their servant girl.

'Yes, like that except that he'll have to go to school for a little while until he's fourteen, which won't be long—'

'Mr Ward says Blake should have been at the grammar school,' Madge announced.

'He never goes to school. He knows nothing,' Tommy scorned. 'I don't see why he has to come and live here. He could work here and live somewhere else.'

'If he does that he has to be paid,' Annie said. 'Isn't that right?'

'Something like that,' her father said.

'Well, he's not sleeping with me,' Tommy said. 'He could sleep in the attic, keep the rats company.'

'There are no rats in the attic,' Rose said shortly.

'Prudence didn't sleep in the attic,' Madge said.

'He isn't a very nice boy,' Annie said.

'He can have the little room next to yours.'

'It's hardly big enough for a bed. Do we have to eat with him?'

'He'll be here some time next week,' Jack said.

Nobody said much over breakfast. Afterwards Annie helped her mother to wash the dishes.

'Why can't Blake stay where he is?' she asked.

'Because he's too young to run the farm.'

'I don't understand why he has to come here.'

'He doesn't have to come here—'

'Then why are we having him? He can't be the only boy in the dale who was ever left to fend for himself and Daddy didn't bring them in to live with us.'

Her mother didn't answer and Annie didn't dare go on somehow. She knew Blake from school because they were about the same age but he was not talkative, especially to girls; he didn't like being there – at least they had that in common – and he was nearly always missing.

As soon as her mother would allow she escaped outside. It was a bright spring morning. She tried to remember what life had been like when she was small and Prudence lived with them. It could hardly be like that having a boy to stay. Still, if he had lived on a farm all his life at least he would know how to go on and there would be less for the rest of them to do.

Alistair Vane was home for Easter. It was not his choice. He had been asked by friends to go and spend the holidays with them in London but the directive from his parents had been clear: he was to go north for Easter to where the weather would be freezing cold and there would be nothing to do and nobody to do it with.

The journey from his school in North Yorkshire

took hours, changing trains, standing around on draughty platforms, but when he finally reached the dale it was impossible not to feel something. He had grown up here and his family had lived at Western Isle for generations. There had been a time when he was happy among the farms and fields here when he was a child. That the happiness had gone was not the fault of the winding river or the budding trees. There were lambs in the fields unsteady on their legs or dancing about together and the best thing of all was that the dale was so unchanging. It looked exactly as it had done all his life.

No one was waiting for him when he got off the train at the tiny village station so he left his luggage there and walked the half-mile to the house. It was quite dark by then but he knew every inch of the road.

There was no one even to answer the door but when he reached the hall his mother was halfway down the stairs.

'Darling. I thought it was tomorrow,' she said.

Alistair loved to come home and hated it. Every time he did so part of him said that it would be like the old days when his grandparents had been alive. It was almost a different house then. Since that time his parents had spent a great deal of money changing everything. They had ripped out fireplaces and put in the very latest designs. Everything was modern and sparse. There were telephones in every room, three large bathrooms. The drawing room looked as though no one ever sat there; there was nothing in it, no books, no dogs, it was cream, everything was colourless, there were lots of tiles, the bookshelves had been ripped from the downstairs rooms. In the huge garage outside were expensive cars, an Alvis sportscar in which his father roared up and down the tiny winding dales roads and a Lanchester 40, a huge beast of a car which his mother drove precariously and grandly when most other people in the area had no car at all.

Part of him was bored and wished to be away, wished for something, for anything exciting, to be with friends, to try new things and new places and new times. He was all guilt and responsibility; he wanted to be there, he wanted to be away. When he was at school he wanted to be at home here in the dales where he had been born and when he was here he wanted to be away to he knew not quite what, just that he had lost the best times when he was small and his parents were young. He didn't know what had gone, only that there was some kind of vacuum in its wake, some emptiness that ached, some possibility, some future that was no more. He hated the way the days piled up behind him. The future all misty like the river in the early morning.

There were a dozen horses in the stables, exercised regularly. When he was here riding was Alistair's greatest pleasure especially now when the weather was getting warmer. Every morning of the holidays he left the house early, hours before anybody else but the servants was about, and he rode in the quiet about the dale enjoying the peace. He began to think that there was something to coming back here for the holiday. In the afternoons he walked his father's labradors across the fields and occasionally he called in to see Tommy. They were almost the same age.

As his mother came down the stairs towards him now, smiling, Alistair went to her.

'We're having a dinner party tonight, darling,' she said. 'You will find yourself something to do, won't you?'

Alistair nodded and smiled and said that he would. He knew exactly what he would do, he would go down to the river and do some sketching until the light faded. His parents would never know, they would be too busy eating, drinking and smoking with their guests.

Jack Lowe's farm was the kind of place, Blake thought as he arrived, that every man would want to farm. It was low down near the river so that the grass was good and the soil was rich. There were no small stony fields such as his grandfather's place had had, no places where you couldn't put cattle because the grass was only good enough for sheep.

The house was big, it had four bedrooms and down-stairs there was a back kitchen and then a big kitchen with a fire, stairs leading out of the room and a parlour next to it. There was also a garden, small but well-tended by Mrs Lowe. The garden had a sundial.

The buildings were big and had stout doors. The yard was cobbled and in a big L-shape with the buildings all around it. From the upstairs windows you could see the river in the valley bottom. Blake envied the Lowe family their farm so much that he could hardly breathe for it.

When he arrived – in the doctor's car – the children disappeared and it was left to Mr and Mrs Lowe to greet him. Mrs Lowe showed him his room upstairs. Blake couldn't remember having seen her before; she was small and very thin with neat brown hair and a sing-song accent which betrayed that she had not been born in the dales. The room was much smaller than the one he had had at home. Blake had brought nothing with him but a few clothes, which were all he had. The money from the sale of the animals had been put in the post office for him. He could think of nothing he needed. Mrs Lowe made tea and Blake politely sat in the back kitchen with her and drank it and ate a scone but although the scone was perfectly made he could hardly swallow, it stuck dryly to the roof of his mouth. Afterwards Mr Lowe took him around the farm and showed him where everything was and then Blake helped him with the evening milking.

The children were there for supper. They said little. Blake said nothing. Eating was beyond him. When he finally escaped up the stairs to bed he pulled back the covers only to find that someone had soaked the bed with water. He turned the feather mattress over and lay down just as he was. The night was cool. He blew out the candle. It was the first night he had ever spent away from Sunniside. Mr and Mrs Lowe were talking softly downstairs just like his grandparents had done. Blake closed his eyes against the darkness.

The next morning Blake was up early to help with the milking. Mr Lowe thanked him for what he did and Blake was glad. He liked milking cows, as long as they didn't stand on him or push him into the wall. A cow could crush you and some of them had nasty habits but the cows he was given to milk were patient and stood still. He liked the warm smell of them and the way that they let down their milk easily so that it frothed into the bucket. Annie did some milking too but she didn't speak to him so he said nothing to her, he just got on with the work.

When he was about to go in to breakfast some time later and was alone in the byre Tommy walked in. He was bigger and older than Blake.

'Sleep all right, did you?'

Blake ignored him and the tightening feeling at the realisation that Tommy didn't like him or want him there for some reason.

'You're only a servant here. You should speak when you're spoken to.'

Blake didn't even look at him and Tommy went to him and got hold of him and pushed him up against the wall.

'Let go of me.'

'Why, what are you going to do about it?' Tommy banged his head off the wall.

'Leave him alone, Tommy, or I'll tell Dad.' Annie's voice was clear and level as she paused in the doorway. When he didn't obey her she walked across the byre to them and glared at her brother. 'What is the matter with you?' she said.

Tommy gave Blake another nasty shove and then released him and walked quickly out of the byre.

'He's always been the only boy,' Annie said. 'Mam says the breakfast's getting cold.'

It reminded Blake so much of his grandmother that he thought he could hear her voice calling him inside: 'Davy, Davy, hurry up.'

'I don't want any,' Blake said and turned away.

Annie went but only a minute or two later Mrs Lowe's small figure was framed in the byre doorway.

'Ham and eggs is nasty cold,' she said, 'and if you don't eat it now you'll get it for your dinner.'

Blake looked at her determined little figure and smiled.

'Huh,' she said, 'your face'll crack next,' and Blake followed her in to breakfast.

That night the other side of Blake's mattress was drenched so that he wouldn't have been able to sleep on it at all but he didn't get as far as thinking about sleeping. He went out of his room and down the hall and burst in on Tommy, who was half-dressed and turned the other way. By the time Tommy had turned back Blake had launched himself at him and they ended up on the cold linoleum floor, struggling. Blake vaguely heard the girls in the doorway and then Madge, who ran to the head of the stairs, crying, 'Daddy, Daddy, the boys are fighting! Come quick!'

And then he was being pulled off Tommy and on to his feet. Jack held them apart.

'What is going on?'

'Blake wet the bed and blamed it on me,' Tommy said, recovering quickly.

'I did not!'

'Whoa, whoa.' Jack had to hold Blake off Tommy again.

'He did it two nights running.'

'Liar!'

Jack dragged Tommy off to Blake's room and there with Tommy still held he examined the bed. Then he stared at Tommy.

'Why?' he said.

Tommy looked down.

'Why behave like a child?' Jack said.

Tommy said nothing.

Jack looked at him for a long time and then he released Tommy.

'Leave him alone. Next time you do anything like that I'll take you out to the barn and thrash you,' he said to Tommy before he went.

Tommy glared at Blake before he went off to his bedroom.

Mrs Lowe changed the mattress and the bedding, her

brow creased into a frown all the while. Annie helped her. Blake stood about. When her mother had gone Annie lingered for a moment or two.

'Can you ride a horse?'

'Of course I can.'

'Of course?' and Annie whisked herself out of the room.

Blake wasn't nearly as miserable the second night. His bed was warm and dry and the feathers in the mattress came up around and hugged him. The sound of the voices down below urged him to believe he was at home. He could go back and live in the past and know only sweet dreams until the morning.

Four

There wasn't as much work to do now that Blake was there and Tommy went off most afternoons with his friend Frank Harlington. Frank's father had the big house in the area and owned most of the farms. Frank went away to school but he was at home now for the holidays. He was much the same age as Tommy and they had known one another all their lives.

'You're not supposed to go and leave Blake to do everything,' Annie protested the second day that this happened.

'He's a servant. That's what servants are for,' Tommy replied, pulling on his coat and walking out into the yard.

'No, it isn't and you know that.'

'And who are you, his mother?'

'He's younger than you. He can't manage all afternoon on his own with Daddy away at the mart.'

'If you like him so much you help him then,' Tommy said.

'I don't like him . . .' She stopped because Tommy was walking away and not listening and Blake was probably within earshot. 'Tommy!'

Madge came up behind her.

'We could tell Mam.'

'No, and don't you. Daddy would belt our Tommy for it,' and she went off up the yard and left Madge standing in the doorway.

There was a lot to do. Blake accepted her presence without a word as they worked and when the long afternoon was finally over she was frustrated at his silence and said to his back, 'Don't thank me then.'

'What do you want thanking for? It's your farm.'

'If it hadn't been for me you'd have had all this to do on your own, or were you going to tell Daddy?'

He didn't have time to reply. There were voices in the yard and soon Tommy and Frank came into the barn.

'Well, who's a good little helper then?' Tommy said. 'I think she fancies him.'

'Shut up!' Annie said but Tommy went over and chucked her under the chin and when she lashed out at him he hit her round the head. Blake grabbed him even while Frank stood there and Tommy, taken by surprise, went down on to the cold stone floor, winded and knocked. From there he eyed Blake, and as he did so Frank went up behind Blake and hit him and he and Frank pulled Blake down on to the floor and held him and thumped and kicked him.

As they did so Annie heard a noise and ran outside. Alistair Vane was walking into the yard. Annie ran to him.

'Come and help,' she said breathlessly and Alistair went after her into the barn.

Alistair had walked down to Grayswell because he was bored. He had thought he might see Tommy or help Jack with something or even be invited into the kitchen for tea and ginger cake. He had whistled up his father's labradors and made his way slowly across the fields.

When he reached the yard at Grayswell there was nobody around but Annie Lowe ran out towards him and when she called to him he followed her into the big barn.

Tommy and Frank Harlington had some fair-haired boy down on the floor and were thumping him. They had him helpless. Annie looked appealingly at Alistair.

Alistair didn't recognise the boy, who was curled up as small as he could be, but he could see light hair and brown skin. Worst of all the boy was silent. Tommy and

Frank stopped hitting him as Alistair said mildly, 'Really, Tommy, what are you doing?'

'I'm just teaching Blake his place, that's all,' and Tommy brought his fist across Blake's face so hard that Alistair had to check himself from going forward. He had seen a lot of bullying at school.

'He's only a boy,' Alistair said.

'He thinks he's too good to be a servant,' Frank said. 'And everybody knows what his mother was. He doesn't even have a man's name, only his mother's.'

Blake was struggling wildly. Frank got hold of him by the hair so that Alistair could see his face. 'Look how pretty he is. He should've been a lass.'

Alistair looked straight into the helpless blue eyes and remembered how awful school was. The blood was running down Blake's mouth from his nose.

'I think he's had enough.'

'Who asked you?' Tommy said.

Alistair sighed. He was beginning to wish that he had stayed at home. He hadn't been that bored. He looked irritatedly at Blake. He could probably better Tommy but Tommy and Frank together would be too much. Tommy's eyes widened.

'You wouldn't?' he said. 'For him?' and he laughed. 'Fancy that, do you?'

Alistair hadn't been angry for weeks. At school it was best not to.

'Leave him alone.'

Tommy and Frank let go of Blake and got to their feet.

'You're going to be sorry you didn't stay at home,' Tommy said.

'Tommy, I already am sorry but I'm not going to stand here and let you half-kill him.'

'Think you can fight both of us at once?'

Behind them Blake unfolded and got quietly to his feet.

'I won't have to,' Alistair said. Beside him Annie Lowe appeared with a hay fork.

Tommy glanced around him.

'I don't think Goldilocks is worth it,' he said and made a scornful exit from the barn. Frank followed him. Blake stood stemming the blood from his nose with his knuckles.

'I'm going to tell Dad,' Annie said, putting down the hay fork.

'No, you aren't,' Blake said immediately.

'It'll only make things worse, Annie,' Alistair said.

Blake walked out and didn't come back. Jack questioned Tommy and Annie closely but neither of them said anything. Blake hadn't come back when the night was dark and cool and everybody went to bed. Jack left the doors unlocked.

Annie didn't sleep. She felt so responsible for what had happened. After a long time she dozed and then awoke suddenly. She had the feeling that he was somewhere close. She put a jumper over her nightdress, put on socks and shoes and slid from the house. The night was cold but clear. There was a moon. She crossed the yard into the big barn and peered up into the shadows of the hayloft.

'Blake, are you there? Blake?'

When there was no reply she climbed the ladder. It was still but she was not afraid. She could never be afraid at Grayswell. For years now in the dark nights tramps had come knocking on the door and she had lit their way in here and given them what her mother could afford as supper.

It was not quite dark. The moon let in light, the shadows varied. He was sitting in the corner with his back against the wall and his knees drawn up to his chest. He didn't say anything to her and Annie didn't know what to say at first. His silence was somehow so quelling.

'Daddy left the doors open for you.'

Blake didn't answer. Annie was sure she looked stupid standing there in a long nightdress and socks and shoes and her old green jumper.

'How did you know I was here?' he said finally.

'Did you have somewhere else to go?'

'I did think about running away—'

'Oh, Blake, I'm sorry—'

'I daren't start running, I might never stop.'

Emboldened by his unsteady voice Annie ventured nearer. She sat down beside him. It wasn't warm in the hayloft and she could see why he had chosen that corner. The hay was all over the place and quite comfortable if you didn't mind the odd piece sticking into your back. It was warmer there and the smell was good.

'Who taught you to hit people like that?'

'My grandfather. Pity he didn't teach me to take them on two at a time.'

'They're bigger than you and older,' Annie said helpfully.

'Did you tell your dad?'

'You said not to. Dad and Mam are worried about you.'

'Going off before I did the milking, you mean?'

'That's not fair. There have been plenty of other boys they could have taken in but they didn't.'

'Do you know why they took me?'

'Don't you?'

Blake shook his head.

'Maybe we're related,' Annie said.

'If it had been that simple they would have told us.'

'I suppose so.'

He didn't seem inclined to talk any further. Even though it was dark she could see the bruises on his face and guessed there were others in other places.

'I don't know what Daddy will say when he sees you. He'll probably guess what happened. I'm sorry, Blake.'

'It wasn't your fault.'

'I should have had more sense than to go on at Tommy. I didn't think. I didn't know you would . . . Tommy's got used to being the only boy, you see. Why don't you come in?'

'No. You go in.'

'Please come in, Blake. I'll let you ride Shard tomorrow if you do. Please. I can't sleep thinking of you out here in the cold.'

'Are you freezing?'

'Perished.'

He smiled at her and agreed and they went inside. Blake bolted the doors after him and they crept upstairs. It took Annie a long time to get to sleep after that because the room was cold and so was her bed. For the first time in her life she wished there was somebody warm to cuddle up to. Her toes and fingers would not warm up.

She slept late the next morning. Nobody called her and by the time she came downstairs her mother was frying breakfast.

'So the boys were fighting, that's why Blake took off?' her mother said.

'Who said?'

Rose looked patiently at her.

'Nobody said. Tommy has a black eye and Blake has bruises.'

'I don't know.'

When her father came in for his breakfast she said, 'Daddy, could you give Blake a little bit of time to himself today?'

'No, I couldn't.'

'I promised him that he could ride Shard.'

Her father looked surprised, as well he might, she thought. She never let anyone ride her horse.

'He has yesterday to make up for and the fact that he won't tell me what happened.'

'Just half an hour.'

'Not even five minutes.'

'Please, Daddy.'

'No.'

'Does he have to work all the time?'

'He gets his meals and a bed for it – and the pleasure of our company, of course.'

'It's not fair.'

'Life isn't. It's more than a lot of lads have. Much more than he might have had.'

'But he's . . .'

'But he's what?'

'Nothing. If I help him can he have time off? I'll milk his cows for him.'

'You did that last night. He can milk his own cows.'

'When will you give him some time off?'

'That's enough, Annie,' Rose said sharply. 'Go and do some work and leave your father to have his breakfast in peace. You're two hours behind now.'

'But—'

'Out!' her mother said.

Frank turned up the following day, shame-faced. He offered her a sheepdog puppy when they were born in a few weeks time and Alistair came over and asked her if she would like to go riding with him. She was very flattered by this because Alistair had ignored her up till now. She accepted both though her mother insisted that the dog be kept outside with all the other dogs when it came. Going riding with Alistair was good too. Tommy had stopped speaking to her because he was now having to work alongside Blake and she was left free to go off, and she enjoyed the morning riding. It was the warmest day they had had and she was slightly in awe of Alistair. He had a tall grey horse which she liked but it would have been too big for her, she reasoned, and she liked Shard better than any horse in the world. They stopped on the hillside late in the morning and let the horses crop the grass and she sat down there happily with the dale spread out before her in grey and green and silver.

'Don't you love this?' she said, waving a hand over the fields and buildings and the trees and river. 'Do you miss it when you're at school?'

'No.'

Annie was astonished.

'You don't like living here?'

'Nothing ever happens here; it's a backwater. I can't wait to get away.'

'But you are away most of the time.'

'It's not that I don't like being here, it's just that I want other things.'

'Like what?' Annie said.

'I want to be an artist, you know, to paint. I want to go to Paris and live in a city and have excitement.'

'Do you really? I didn't know that. What about the farm?'

Alistair was silent for a few seconds.

'There's only you,' Annie said.

'That's what my father keeps saying. He says farmers don't paint.'

'But that's not true. My grandfather did. He was a miller to begin with and then he farmed. We have his paintings hanging in the house of the dale and the cattle he had, they were caillies and he carved the big stone dog that stands by our gate. Do you take art at school?'

'No, I'm not allowed.' Annie heard the flinty tone come into his voice.

'Why not?'

'My father won't let me do painting so I don't take it any more.'

Annie didn't know much about his parents other than the fact that his grandfather had been deemed a clever man in the dale and had good cattle and that his father and mother spent a great deal of money. Her father had prophesied that the Vanes would come to a bad end going on like that with their ostentatious cars and their dinner parties. Her mother had said nothing. Annie thought that sometimes her mother envied Mrs Vane her brightly coloured car and many dresses, her jewellery and her glamour.

'What did your father say about the fight?' Alistair said.

'Lots,' Annie said. 'Tommy's awful to Blake.'

'That's not very surprising.'

'Isn't it? Why?'

Alistair stared into the distance and frowned.

'Probably because you like him.'

'I don't really like him it's just that . . . he doesn't have anything. No parents, no home.'

'I'm not sure that's a reason to like anybody. You said he hit Tommy for you. You like that?'

'Well, yes.'

'I'll hit Tommy for you any time.'

Annie laughed.

'Will you?' she said, looking into his blue eyes, and he leaned over and kissed her very gently and slowly on the mouth. Annie was entranced.

When they got back and he had gone home Annie looked at herself in the mirror in her bedroom like she had never looked before and she was astonished at the face which looked back at her. She was not quite fourteen. She had thick black curly hair and wide brown eyes. Her skin was milky and her neck was long and her wrists were slender. Her mother had often told her that she was just like her Irish ancestors, whereas Madge was brown-haired and Elsie was red-haired like her father. Annie liked being different but she wouldn't have hurt them by letting them know, and in a way she thought they were both just as good-looking as she was because Madge was so slender and fine-boned and Elsie was dainty. Then Annie laughed at herself for her conceit and stopped looking in the mirror but she was pleased that Alistair Vane had kissed her. It made her feel grown-up.

Once upon a time there had been a fairy tale, Alistair Vane could almost remember it. The farm that had belonged to his family for hundreds of years was set in the kind of place where people dreamed of living and when he had been a child there had been a happiness which was there no longer.

There had been a stable full of big working horses, Clydesdales for the fields. There had been women to help in the house and men and boys outside. His grandfather had owned a big car, had ridden to hounds, had taught him over those long childhood days how to fish and ride and shoot, his grandmother had spent the evenings playing card games with him and reading him stories and they had talked to him about the future, or so it seemed to him. But they had died and it was as if the future had become the past without anyone recognising its passing. His father complained loudly and continued to complain that his grandfather had left death duties because there was no will.

They were still better off than most people in the dale. For a start the farm was theirs and it was on good land and there was a lot of it, it was bigger than most of the other farms. The farm was built in a square, the house making up one side and the buildings the other three. Nobody seemed to know how old the farmhouse was, tenth or eleventh century. It was a good house, with stone mullioned windows, and pretty, with a garden in front where there were sloping lawns and big cherry trees and an orchard beyond that with a tiny stream and a rickety bridge. There were kitchen gardens too and at either side of the house dovecots where tumblers had fascinated him with their wonderful flying. In the evenings, as they came down the road towards the farm in his grandfather's big car, the doves would come to meet them and fly down like an escort tumbling white and sunkissed at the day's end. Alistair thought that God must have touched his home, such a place it was.

It was changed now. Every modern convenience was

theirs and in the evenings while he retreated to his room his father and mother entertained the local doctors and business people, the solicitors and the better off, and the smell of roasting meat wafted up the stairs towards him until Alistair felt sick. The cars would arrive, their big lights illuminating the yard, the women with their high voices and their laughter, the men with their low voices and their enthusiasm. He remembered being younger and being brought down to say goodnight, the smell of gin and tonic and cigarettes on his mother's breath, the women with their perfumed necks and jewellery, the men standing with their drinks by the big fire. There was never a cat or a dog inside the house. All the old familiar paintings had been relegated to the attics. There were drinks in strange-shaped bottles, green liquid and orange and brown which he knew the guests drank with their coffee. When it was late and the people went home livelier than when they came for the alcohol they had consumed he would lie awake and wonder how many days it was until he should go back to school. Strange to think that there was a kind of peace there; at least he could sometimes get away to draw in peace. It meant getting into trouble for missing games or chapel but after a while they had stopped punishing him for doing that. He was good at his school work and that compensated.

He would go to university, he would get away and when he had some decent kind of education behind him he could do anything.

After Easter Blake and Annie went back to school for their last term. They both hated it. Madge and Elsie went off together early but Blake and Annie lingered until the last minute and then walked slowly up the road to the village.

'Good of you to join us,' said Mr Ward when they finally arrived some ten minutes late.

It was strange to Blake to go to and from Grayswell to school along the main road in the bottom of the valley, rather than coming down the hill from Sunniside and then toiling back up thankfully at the end of the day. He tried not even to look in that direction. The Austin children, two of them, also came to school, a girl and a boy both a lot younger than him. They seemed so carefree, so settled. They talked about Bessie as though she was their dog. Blake was glad for her sake.

The schoolwork was easy and boring and Mr Ward shook his head and said for the umpteenth time that Blake should have taken the scholarship and been at the grammar school. Blake had not been there for the tests but he knew that it would have been no good. His grandparents could never have afforded either the uniform or for his attention to be that diverted. They had needed him and he was glad that he had been able to help them while they needed him. It was a lot more important than things like books. Mr Ward thought it something special that he could recall what he read, that his memory was good, that the mathematics were easy to him. Blake thought Mr Ward was a poor creature for a farmer's son. What on earth was he doing sitting in classrooms on fine days like these when he could have been outside producing something rather than trying to instil knowledge into silly little minds?

Weekends and holidays were the best times. Blake worked with Mr Lowe and when Tommy started speaking to him occasionally everything seemed to come all right as long as he didn't get in Tommy's way or try to act like one of the family when Tommy was there. The rest of the time it wasn't bad. Mr Lowe seemed more and more pleased with him and he was unstinting in his praise so that Blake worked harder than ever. Mrs Lowe sat Blake next to her husband and herself at mealtimes as though he was another adult and Blake began to eat heartily because her cooking was almost as good as his grandmother's had been. She told him that she had worked in a bakery when she lived at home. Her home was at

Seaton Town near Sunderland. Her father had been a miner there and after she left school she helped in the local bakery. It was obvious that she had learned a great deal there. The crust on her rabbit pie tasted better than anything Blake had had before and her cakes and bread made the whole house smell wonderful.

At night sometimes Tommy still put frogs into his bed or worms or cowpats, but only dry ones because Tommy was rather afraid that his mother would find out and Blake had discovered that Mrs Lowe had a temper. You stayed well clear of her when things were not going as she wanted or she shouted.

One day when Mr Lowe came in in a bad mood and grumbled about the dinner she had put in front of him she picked the whole plateful up off the table and threw it through the small open window. It sailed clean over the yard wall and smashed into the byre opposite.

'There's your dinner,' she said and walked out and Mr Lowe never said a word.

The girls helped in the house. Annie tried to get out of it and since she was a good help outside, especially with the milking, her parents let her get away with it. Elsie and Madge helped in the house. Their mother said that Madge was as good as any housekeeper. She had been taught to cook from an early age and her mother could go and leave her in the kitchen now to make the dinner, only popping in from time to time to make sure that everything was all right.

One night early that summer when Blake had got used to being there he heard a noise in the middle of the night coming from the girls' room and he lit a candle and wandered through. It was a warm night but dark because it had rained and rained. Madge stood with a lit candle by the window. She was a sight in her long nightgown, like a ghost reflected in the window. Elsie was asleep but Annie, who slept in a single bed beside them, was out on top of the covers and when Blake ventured into the room she put her finger to her lips and clasped hold of his arm and drew him down on to the bed.

'Don't say anything,' she whispered, 'not out loud anyroad.'

'What's she doing?'

'She's asleep. She does it a lot.'

'Shouldn't you tell your Mam and Dad?'

'You would,' she said scathingly but she regarded Madge with concern. 'She did this all last winter. It made her chilblains worse and they were that bad she could hardly straighten her fingers.'

'Hold that,' Blake said, shoving the candle at her, and he went cautiously to the window and said to Madge, 'It's time to go back to bed now,' and as he spoke she turned around blankly and blew out the candle and put it down and climbed back into bed.

Annie's brown eyes sparkled as she held the candle.

'She won't remember. You won't tell her?'

Elsie whimpered in her sleep.

'It's all right, Else,' Annie said. And to Blake, 'I suppose you think that makes you clever?'

'No, but it makes me cleverer than you,' Blake said and retrieved the candle from her. He did not miss the grin she gave him. He was almost happy when he went to bed.

Best of all that summer Blake liked the haytiming, the hot days, the food and tea which Mrs Lowe and Elsie brought to the fields, the broad-backed horse and the smell of the hay and the work done and the sun setting and the big suppers which Mrs Lowe set out in the large kitchen for all the workers. By then Blake was a head taller than Mrs Lowe and to Tommy's dismay as big as him.

When he and Tommy were working together they became better friends. Tommy had stopped picking on him by then partly because he had got used to him and partly because Tommy was now more aware of being older. It was beneath his dignity to fight with Blake.

Frank was home from school and came to help in the fields. Annie's best friend, Clara Evans, came as well. She lived up on the hillside and had been a neighbour of Blake's when he lived there though he had rarely seen her. She was an only child and Annie envied her her pretty clothes.

She and Blake had left school now but instead of the freedom which she had hoped to gain she had to go daily to Alistair's house to help with the milking and dairying. Annie didn't mind the milking or going to the house but she was ashamed that she had to go out to work for the money. She had tried arguing with her father but it didn't make any difference. He had insisted. Alistair wasn't there in the autumn when she began working at his farm and she was glad of it. She didn't want him to see her there as though she was a servant.

She came to understand why Alistair didn't like being there. His father was a perfectionist and he expected other people to be like that too. The house was always spotlessly clean and the cars were washed daily. He came every day to the dairy to check that there too nothing was amiss and as far as he was concerned something always was. It was hard work keeping to his standards and also he was rude, he shouted at Annie. He was so big and so dark and so angry that he frightened her. She wondered what it had been like for Alistair growing up there with a father like that.

The house was colourless and everything was new and expensive, everything had to be polished, Annie heard the maids say, and the three huge bathrooms had to have fresh towels and be cleaned every day. There were great vases of flowers which Mrs Vane constantly attended to and changed and the cook laboured in the kitchen to turn out perfect meals for the constant stream of guests.

Annie didn't get fed when she was there, she didn't even get invited beyond the kitchen or the dairy but the cook was a kind woman, and since Mr Vane rarely went into the kitchen as long as nothing was wrong the cook would sit Annie and the maids down at the kitchen table whenever she could and give them newly baked bread with jam, lemon curd tarts and cups of strong tea. She never dared give Annie any main meals or any meat because Mr Vane would have known instantly. Annie thought that he was the meanest person she had ever met and told her mother so. They paid her as little as they could, knowing that work was difficult to find. Annie proudly took every penny home to her mother, who received it thankfully.

As the Christmas holidays drew nearer she worried

about being at Western Isle as the dairymaid and one Sunday afternoon when the others were sitting around the fire because it was cold she walked down to the river by herself and stood watching the grey water running over the cold stones.

She was there a while before she sensed that she wasn't alone and when she looked up Blake was walking down the field towards her. It was late afternoon now and the light had almost gone.

'Is the tea ready?' she greeted him. She loved Sunday afternoons even though Monday lurked after them. Her mother always made Sunday tea special even though they had already had a big dinner. There would be ham-and-egg pie and custard tart and little diamond-shaped sandwiches and maybe tinned peaches and cream with bread and butter.

'She doesn't want you out in the dark,' he said.

Annie tossed her head.

'What on earth does she think is going to happen to me here? It's the last place God made.'

'I thought you loved the dale.'

'I used to. It's boring now. Don't you get bored?'

'Everything I care about is here.'

'You haven't got anything,' she said flatly. Alistair would have coloured up and retreated at such scorn.

'Try not to be so obvious,' Blake said. 'What are you doing down here by yourself?'

'Nothing. I can't think at home, there's too many of us.'

'Think about what?'

'It's none of your business, Blake.'

'Walk back up with me then before it gets completely dark.'

'I'm not a child. What does my mother think I'm going to do, fall in?' But she turned with him and began walking slowly.

Part of the reason for coming out had been so that she could walk back up the fields watching the buildings which made up the farm, seeing the cream light which spilled out across the field directly in front of the house, knowing that the people she loved best in all the world were gathered there around the fire and that her mother and Elsie and Madge would have been back and forth between the little back kitchen and the front one until the table was covered with good things to eat.

She walked towards the house knowing that she would be out of the cold and into the warmth within minutes, that the fire would be blazing high up the chimney from their own wood. The tea would be brewing in the big pot, the cutlery winking in the firelight. Sunday afternoon was the best time of all and it was magical now, walking slowly with Blake. She wished that she could hold the moment, have it go on being that time, capture it somehow so that she didn't have to go on or back but just be almost home, almost warm, almost full of custard tart and strawberry jam and peaches. In the almost-dark the birds were silenced and Blake was walking more slowly than he usually did but she wanted to prolong the moment and he didn't seem to mind. He didn't say anything either. He didn't ask any more questions. He wasn't irritating like Tommy would have been or a nuisance like Madge or Elsie, he was just there and the moment of happiness was captured for ever.

Five

By the time Madge left school they needed her to go out and work too and she went to Frank's house to help with the general housework. Annie knew that her mother could have done with at least one of them at home but they needed the money. Times were hard.

Her grandmother and aunt lived in a small house in the village and her father had to keep them. Her aunt was continually ill and sometimes her father grumbled about the doctor's bills. Her mother worried about how much it cost to keep his mother and sister and Annie knew that her grandma didn't like her mother because she was not backward in coming forward about it.

Sometimes Annie had to go and see her grandmother. Her mother did not encourage her to go but her father asked her and although she didn't like the old woman or her dark little house or her Aunt Myra, who did nothing but sit around the fire knitting or reading, Annie felt obliged to go. She usually took Elsie with her because her grandma seemed to like Elsie (which was unusual because she liked nobody else) though only then because she said that Elsie looked like her and was a true Lowe. She claimed that the rest of the family looked like their mother except for Tommy of course because he was the only boy. Tommy could do nothing wrong.

'I don't know why your father married your mother,' her grandmother said on one such occasion, a rainy autumn afternoon when the turning leaves dripped wetly in the small garden and the hills were blotted out with mist.

'There were plenty of nice girls around here who would have married him. He was always very popular, was your father. Nice chapel girls they were too.'

Another reason that her grandma didn't like her mother was because she was a Roman Catholic. Annie remembered her mother saying that her other grandma, Mary Ann, had come from Seaton Town to see them and said, 'Never mind, Rose, there not being a Catholic church. You can send them to the parish church. It's the next best thing.'

And to the parish church they went in spite of how Jack's mother had objected. Annie thought that secretly her mother was pleased to send them there just to spite her, her grandmother being what folk called 'chepel'. In her worst time her grandmother had called her mother 'that common little nowt' because Rose's father had been a pitman over on the coast. The local people thought that pitmen were another breed, not quite human somehow. Rose's father had died when she was a very little girl and her mother, Mary Ann, had married again and sometimes Ralph and Mary Ann came to the farm. They stayed overnight on these occasions. Annie liked Mary Ann. She had had six children, most of whom were scattered and whom Annie had never seen.

Ralph was kind and funny and would play silly games. He was big and dark. He was a pitman as well. Annie thought if pitmen were like Ralph there couldn't be much wrong with them but her grandmother had never come to the farm to meet Ralph so she didn't know.

Ralph and Mary Ann used to hold hands when they went for a walk up the road to the village. Annie thought if her grandmother had known such a thing she would have been spluttering with jealousy since her husband had died long since and according to Jack they had never got on. Annie secretly thought that one of the reasons her father had married her mother was because his mother didn't like her.

'When he married your mother he put us out,' her grandmother declared.

Sometimes Annie wondered why her father should be obliged to keep so many people. No wonder she and Madge had to go out and work.

That autumn her aunt died. Annie found it difficult to be sorry, she was only glad that the doctor's bills had ceased. Her father worked so hard and got no thanks for it but then sometimes when she wandered into the kitchen she caught her father kissing her mother or holding her, just smiling, so maybe that was thanks enough.

Madge liked working for the Harlingtons just as much as Annie disliked the farm work at Alistair's house. She came home with tales of Mr and Mrs Harlington.

'She drinks so much that she has to go to bed in the afternoons,' Madge said.

The Hall was a curious place, the biggest house that Annie had ever seen, and living so close – it was just across the field and up the hill – they had all spent a lot of time there when they were younger before Frank went away to school and afterwards in the school holidays.

Like Alistair Frank was an only child. He lived there with his parents and his father's two old aunts. The aunts wore dark brown clothes, skirts with big pleats and shapeless sweaters and they smelled to Annie of another century. They would tell her stories of when they were girls, of the parties, the picnics and the musical evenings. She could not understand why they had never married, they seemed no more ugly than anyone else and even plain women married – there were plenty of those everywhere – but when she had tried politely to enquire they said it was because they had no money, their father had drunk it away.

Annie knew that there had once been another estate further down the country and a house in London. But those had gone.

Mr Harlington did little work. He walked his spaniels in the afternoons with a gun broken over his arm and the villagers bowed or curtsied or acknowledged him in some other way as their superior. Mrs Harlington did even less. She talked to the cook and she wrote letters in her little sunlit room in the mornings. She took tea with the aunts in the afternoons and occasionally went visiting friends, driving precariously in their old car.

Annie liked the house and she could see why Madge liked being there. It was shabby in a nice sort of way with a fire in the hall where the spaniels slept when they couldn't persuade anybody to take them for a walk. Old Mrs Donaldson from the village was their cook and nice smells permeated the whole house all day, and there were dark pictures on the walls of hopeful-looking people. Madge was given her meals and those who ventured near in mid-morning or afternoon were greeted with enthusiasm in the kitchen and given spice cake and hot tea. Often much of the food which went to the dining room came back uneaten and Mrs Donaldson shook her head over people with small appetites.

The rooms smelled of books and tobacco and sherry, which Frank's aunts drank in minute quantities. His father drank brandy and his mother drank anything, but they drank a lot. Many of Frank's parents' days were spent in fuddled glee. All they had left now was the Hall and the farms in the valley.

It seemed to Annie that the Harlingtons had no idea of how other people lived. Mr Harlington did nothing. He sat mostly in the library and read books which had probably never been read before or maybe he just dozed and drank and thought of how things might have been. There was an air of decay around the house, like an ending of some kind was taking place, as though something was over. The house was very shabby. Things were not replaced. Broken machinery was left in corners. Fences were falling down. The gardens were growing wild. That Christmas when Frank came home Madge seemed to be at the house more and more.

'I don't know,' Rose said, taking scones from the oven one Sunday afternoon. 'She's not supposed to be there this afternoon.'

Rose and Annie were alone in the kitchen making tea. Madge was supposed to come back after helping to wash the dinner dishes at about two o'clock.

'Maybe they had something on,' she said.

'And maybe they didn't,' her mother said, gingerly putting the scones on to a wire rack to cool.

'What do you mean?'

Her mother shot her a telling look.

'I think Madge has taken a shine to young Frank. If we could afford it I'd have her back at home. Goodness knows I could do with her here. I'm trying to find her something else.'

'Frank? Frank wouldn't look at Madge.'

'Why wouldn't he? She's coming up fifteen and she has that way of looking at men through her eyelashes that gives me the collywobbles.'

Annie half-wanted to laugh but she knew that her mother was serious. She was also a little bit jealous. She didn't particularly like Frank but she didn't want him to like her sister better than he liked her.

'It's dangerous, Annie. I wish there was something I could do.'

73

'Frank's not dangerous,' Annie said, laughing.

'He might be if he knew Madge liked him. His family aren't rich like they used to be but they still own most of the dale including this place. I don't want Madge mixed up in anything like that. This is our home.'

'If you take her away from there Mr Harlington would probably be offended. They pay better than the Vanes pay me so he wouldn't think you had a good reason and she likes being there.'

'Yes, I noticed,' her mother said.

Annie looked critically at Frank the next time she saw him. He walked his dogs around to the farm almost every day and it was only a few days later. Annie had her dog with her and he patted Rufus and smiled and Annie thought, yes, she could see how Madge might like him. He was almost finished school, talking about university, and he had breeding. He was tall and slender and wore shabby expensive clothes. He had warm brown eyes and a shy smile, and he spoke well without a local accent. He had grace in his walk and bearing, his hands were fine from never doing any work and there was that sadness about him she knew came from the way he loved his parents which would appeal to a girl like Madge.

'People who drink too much don't care about food,'

he had confided to Annie. 'It spoils the pleasure of the alcohol.'

He knew too much about things like that for somebody his age, Annie thought, shuddering. She was glad that her parents didn't go on like that or like Alistair's. No wonder Alistair and Frank liked to come to the small farm where there was little money but kind people who were trying hard, to her mother's meals made with love and her mother singing in the kitchen.

It was not always like that of course; they fought quite a lot being so many of the. Her mother had a quick Irish temper and her father a slow dales one which made for some lively battles, and she and Madge being of an age fought and sometimes even Elsie joined in, throwing things without thought. Blake never fought but then he was never entirely one of the family and when arguments started he would go to his tiny bedroom and read. Sometimes Annie sat up there with him on the single bed and talked. She didn't think it was anything important, not like when she talked to Alistair, who was now into politics and music and art, and it was not gossip such as she talked with the family and obviously it was not the same things as she talked about with other girls. It was just general stuff about the farm and the horses and the day-to-day things. As the year progressed it got colder and colder in Blake's room but they went on sitting there in the evening until her mother said, 'I think you ought to come downstairs to talk to Blake.'

'Why?'

'I just think you should.'

'We can't talk the same with Elsie and Madge there.'

Tommy wasn't often in the house. He was in the local silver band by now and went off to concerts and practices and sometimes he went to the pub in the village – unbeknown, she hoped, to her parents.

'You ought not to go and sit in his room with him, Annie.'

'I'd like to know why.'

Her mother looked at her like she was being particularly stupid.

'Because you're both growing up,' she said.

Annie was instantly cross.

'It's not like that,' she said. 'How could it be? Blake's like Tommy.'

'No, he isn't,' her mother said and when Annie thought about it afterwards she knew that her mother was right. She wouldn't have spent five minutes sitting on Tommy's bed talking to him and Tommy wouldn't have wanted her to. So after that she didn't go to Blake's room any more but it was getting so cold up there that

Blake retreated to the back room to do his reading while
the others sat in the big kitchen during the evening. Her
mother apparently had no objection to her sitting with
Blake in the little back room by the range, drinking tea
and watching the flames lick green and blue around the
wood, glad of the comfort of being inside while the wind
howled its way in and out of the buildings which made
up the farm.

It was the hardest winter that Annie had ever known.
Getting up in the icy darkness and going to the Vanes
and working there in the cold and then helping her
father outside much of the time made Annie miserable.
The ice rarely gave way and when it did there was deep
snow. Her father and Blake spent much of their time
looking for sheep and even when the spring came and
the lambs were born the weather was unrelenting. Her
father brought the sheep as near the farm as he could
and those he was concerned about inside, but when the
weather should have softened and there should have
been nothing more than the odd lambing storm it was
bitterly cold and her father and Blake rarely went to
bed for days at a time because the work was so hard
and she had to do extra because they had so much
more to do.

When Alistair came home from school for Easter she

resented the fact that he had so little to do. His father employed sufficient help so that his only son could be a gentleman, Annie had heard him say often enough, and when Alistair complained about school and exams Annie turned on him.

'You've never done a decent day's work in your life,' she declared and went off home to begin again. She expected that he would follow her there and apologise but he didn't and he didn't come the next day either. She didn't see him when she went there to work and to her dismay he did not invite her to the small dance which was being held at the village hall the following Saturday night, when it looked as though there would be nothing to do because the lambing was finished and the weather had finally warmed. She had waited all week for him to ask her and when Madge came home on the Friday and announced that she was going with Frank and that Alistair was taking Clara, Annie ran up to her room and threw herself on the bed, crying.

Blake found her there.

'You're not meant to come in here,' Annie said, cross that he had walked in when she had no control over herself.

'What's the matter?'

'Nothing. Nothing you can do anything about anyway.'

'Don't be so prickly,' Blake said, sitting down beside her on the big bed which Madge and Elsie shared.

'I wanted to go to the dance.'

'What dance?'

'Do you ever think about anything except the farm? The one at the village hall. I was nasty to Alistair last week and he's taking Clara.'

'Alistair?'

'Yes. And Frank's taking Madge.'

'Does your father know?'

'She lied and said she was going with some of the other girls. Is Tommy going?'

'He never mentioned it.'

'And you're not going, of course, are you? The barn roof might fall in if you leave the place for half an hour and you can't dance anyway.'

'Why were you nasty to Alistair?'

'I didn't mean to be, it was just that we've worked so hard and he does nothing but go to school and then he actually complained about how much work he had. I was tired and fed up and I just couldn't stand it.'

'But you want to go to the dance with him.'

'Well . . . I just wanted to go. We don't get to go far and we've worked so hard and I wanted to get dressed up and go out.'

'I'll take you.'

'You don't want to go. You didn't mention it. It wouldn't be fair.'

'You want to go, don't you? Say yes quick before I change my mind.'

Annie looked doubtfully at him.

'Do you dance?' she said.

'Of course.'

'You always say of course you can do everything.'

'I can.'

'When did you learn?'

'When I was little. My grandmother loved to dance. She taught me.'

'Your grandparents taught you to do a lot of things.'

'I was all they had.'

Madge wore yellow to the dance, which suited her. Clara wore pink, which did not, and Annie wore a blue dress which was so much prettier than Clara's that she almost forgave Alistair for not having asked her to the dance. Madge went with her friends and met Frank there. Tommy spent the evening in the pub getting drunk. Annie was apprehensive about going with Blake because it wasn't what she had wanted to do, but she soon discovered that the fun of being at a dance was having a partner who could dance well and to her surprise he did. Also, and she hadn't noticed lately, he was so tall now that he looked older than he was. He held her lightly but guided her properly and it was such a pleasure dancing with him that when she danced with Frank she missed the guiding hand, the sure feet, the confidence. She was happy to go back to dancing with him. She even forgot about Alistair asking Clara instead of her and when the supper was announced and Blake went off to find her a plate and Alistair was somehow beside her she wasn't as pleased as she had thought she might be when he asked her for the dance after supper.

'What about Clara?' she said.

'Clara dances rather as I think a sack of potatoes might.'

She knew that he did not mean to be unkind, that he only said it to make her laugh but she could see Clara from where she stood and Clara was alone so she didn't laugh. She just said, 'I promised the next dance to Blake.'

'Whatever for? Annie, he's your farm labourer.'

'Yes, and I'm your dairymaid,' Annie said and she followed Blake off to the table where the food was laid out so splendidly. 'Are you managing?' she asked.

He handed her a plate heaped with food. Annie was very hungry.

'Let's go outside,' she said and he didn't say how cold it was or that everybody else was here in the warmth. He followed her outside and it was then that she knew she had been right. The night was shiny with stars, and she had her first ever gin and tonic in her hand in a tall thin glass so that the bubbles went on bubbling. It was dark out there and the food smelled better against the cold and he gave her his jacket to sit on.

'You'll be frozen,' she said.

'No, I won't. Sit down.'

'It won't do it any good.'

'It's your dad's old one. Who cares?'

'Is it? It looked all right.'

Later Alistair came to her when Blake had gone to get her a drink of lemonade.

'Will you come riding with me tomorrow?'

'Why don't you go riding with Clara, you seem to like her company well enough,' Annie said and moved away. She thought he was following her and went right out of the way outside but Alistair was still there.

'Why can't you be nice to me?' he said. 'You know I like you.'

'I'm as nice as you deserve.'

'Dance with me then.'

'I promised Blake.'

'You like him, don't you?'

Annie had never considered this.

'I neither like nor dislike him,' she said. 'He's just there and he'll be wondering where I am.'

She made as if to move and he got hold of her arm.

'You'd better let go,' she said flatly.

'Or what? You'll set your tame watchdog on me? All right then, I will take Clara riding and to hell with you,' and he walked off back into the hall.

Annie wasn't very happy. She stayed outside so long that Blake came looking for her. She was sitting on a low wall with her head down. He went over and sat beside her and put his arm around her shoulders.

'Have you had enough? Do you want to go home now?'

'In a minute.'

Blake took off his jacket and put it around her and she looked up. Afterwards she could never quite work out why but at the time it seemed natural to lift her face and kiss him. She thought that it would be like kissing Alistair had been but it wasn't. For a start he already had an arm around her over the jacket and that stopped it from being a brief casual thing. Also he hadn't initiated it and surprising somebody by kissing them had an exciting element to Annie. And then he didn't let go. He tightened the hold he had on her and drew her nearer. His lips were warm and sweet and being close against him was even better than Annie had imagined being close would be. Annie stopped thinking and just did what she wanted to do, which was to put one hand into the straight fair hair at the back of his neck and invite the kind of assault on her mouth that brought from her a little sigh of pleasure.

The sound of voices in the doorway brought her back to reality and she drew away and he let her. People were leaving, talking and laughing. She listened to the noise until they had gone down the road which led into the village.

'I think I'd like to go home now,' she said woodenly and she slid down from the wall.

'Annie—'

'I just want to go home.'

All the way there neither of them said anything and when she finally thankfully reached the house Annie fled. She didn't even say goodnight and when she was safely in bed she lay there and wished and wished that she hadn't done it or that he had been Alistair or that she had had enough sense to come home straight after supper. She wished it was before the dance. Things had seemed so simple then and now they weren't.

She didn't sleep and therefore slept in the next morning. Luckily it was Sunday but her mother was not well pleased that she didn't appear until the middle of the morning when everybody else had either gone to church or was doing something useful. She set Annie to peeling potatoes and all Annie could think was that she would have to face Blake across the dinner table.

She couldn't eat and afterwards would have escaped to her room but that her mother made her do the washing up and when it was finally done Annie fled again, out of the house and down the fields to the river.

After a while of just sitting there in what was trying to be a warm day she felt calmer. An hour or so later she didn't even hear Blake until he was right there. Even so she managed a face the colour of poppies before she turned away.

'I want to be by myself.'

'I know you do. I'm not staying. I don't want you to be upset, that's all.'

'I'm not upset.'

'Yes, you are. It was only a kiss. It was just the – the night and the dancing and the gin and the fact that we worked too hard and ... it was like being let out. It doesn't matter at all if you don't want it to.'

'It did matter,' Annie said quickly. 'I didn't think, I

didn't know . . . When Alistair kissed me it wasn't anything like that at all.'

'Like what?'

'Like that. Like . . . I didn't want to go to the dance with you. I wanted to go with Alistair.'

'I know.'

'You dance too well,' she said.

'We had long winters at Sunniside.'

'I want it never to happen again.'

'All right,' Blake said.

The following day when she went to work Alistair appeared in the dairy and since they were alone she turned to him and said, 'I'm sorry I was nasty to you.'

Alistair smiled.

'Clara fell off the horse,' he said.

Six

The autumn that Frank went off to university his mother died. She drove her car into a wall one afternoon when she was drunk. His father's response was to drink even more and Frank declared to Annie that he was glad to get away. Madge was not glad. She cried on and off for days after he had gone.

On Sunday afternoons Annie often walked over to meet Madge at the Hall since she went there every day because Mr Harlington wanted her to. Sometimes Blake went with Annie and now that Mr Harlington had dispensed with help in the house except for Madge they ended up bringing in wood and coal, washing dishes, helping with anything which might make things comfortable but it was so neglected there, so dusty now, Mr Harlington contenting himself with drinking whisky during the afternoons by the fire and the two old aunts dozing so that it was past help, Annie thought.

Mr Harlington had one thing which encouraged Blake to go. He kept two horses in the stables, one for himself and one for Frank, and when Blake talked enthusiastically about them Mr Harlington encouraged him to go there and ride them. There was a stable lad to feed them and muck out and Blake went to help sometimes until Jack told him he was not to go. There was a row about it which surprised Annie since Blake rarely put up a fight about anything but after the first Monday that Blake went there to help Jack stopped him in the big kitchen.

'You've got enough to do here without helping the Harlingtons.'

'All they've got is a stable lad.'

'They've got a great deal that we've never had, including this place. They don't need your help.'

'I wanted to do it.'

'Yes, well, I'm telling you you're not. He doesn't pay you for going there so what use is it?'

'I feel sorry for him.'

Jack glared at Blake just as Annie walked in.

'You feel sorry for Joe Harlington? What's he ever done for you except put you out of your house?'

'I like the horses—'

'I'm telling you, lad. You don't set foot in Harlington's

yard again,' and Jack turned and walked out, passing Annie without a word.

'What was all that about?' she asked.

'I don't know. Mr Harlington promised me I could ride his horse.'

Annie whistled.

'He's a beauty too. Daddy will never give you the time off.'

Blake said nothing. After dinner, a good time to approach her father, when he was full of meat, potatoes and crumble with custard, Annie followed him out to the fields.

'What do you want, miss?' he growled, stopping when he saw her.

'Mr Harlington has said that Blake can ride Black Boy. Don't you think he's entitled to a bit of time for himself?'

'Blake doesn't need you to fight his battles. I just don't want that man taking advantage. He's done Blake enough harm.'

'What do you mean?'

'I mean if they'd given the lad a bit of help for a year or so he could have kept that farm, but people like that, they never think about other folk.'

'Blake doesn't have a horse.'

'I know that.'

'Please.'

'Ah, you'd turn stone to mush you would,' her father said.

After that Annie and Blake went riding nearly every day. Frank came back at Christmas and they went out, the three of them. One evening when Frank had come over to the farm he and Annie were talking in the back kitchen, at first just about general things, then about Madge, who was baby-sitting in the village, and then Frank began complaining.

'I'm perfectly capable of exercising the horses. I don't know why my father wants Blake there.'

'You aren't here most of the time.'

'There is a stable boy. We don't need another.'

'Blake's not a stable boy.'

'It's the same thing. I don't really care to go riding with the servants.'

'That's not very nice, Frank.' Frank, she reflected, was a very bitter young man since his mother had died and he didn't care who he took it out on.

'I don't know what to say to him,' Frank said. 'He's nobody. He's just somebody's bastard.'

'Frank, if my mother hears you use a word like that in this house you'll be an ex-visitor.'

'Do you know who he is?'

'What do you mean?'

'I mean do you know who his father is?'

'Nobody knows.'

'I do. Charles Vane.'

Annie wanted to shiver.

'That's not true,' she said.

'Yes, it is. I heard my father say so when he was drunk. Drunk people always tell the truth. He's a Vane, that's who he is, or rather isn't.'

Frank stopped there and Annie heard or rather sensed somebody outside the door in the darkness of the passage.

'Oh, go away, Frank, why don't you?' she said.

Frank went, fumbling in the darkness for the back door and Annie walked through the big kitchen where her parents were sitting and up the stairs. She didn't knock or ask if she could come into his room, she just opened the door and walked in. There was no light when she had closed the door.

'Blake, are you in here?' she said, narrowing her eyes to try and see him. 'I think Tommy's gone to the pub again. If he gets drunk Dad will find out. Come and help me. Blake?'

She could just make out where he was sitting on the bed.

'It isn't true,' he said roughly.

Annie gave a sigh of horror that her notion was confirmed and Blake had been about to walk into the kitchen and heard them talking about him.

'It couldn't be true,' she said.

'Are you sure?'

'Frank's a fool.'

Even without touching him she could feel his distress.

'What if it is true, what if Alistair's father is mine? That would make us brothers.' He sounded as though this was the worst thing that could possibly happen.

'Alistair's not that bad,' she said.

'It's not that. It would make him my older brother. It would mean . . .'

And then she understood.

'So it can't possibly be true. Alistair's parents were married when you were born.'

'Do you think my mother went with a married man?'

'No. Frank was just talking, just . . . he hasn't been right since his mother died, you know he hasn't. He's hurt and he wants to hurt other people.'

There was an intake of faltering breath from Blake. She couldn't be sure since she had never heard him cry before. She certainly didn't want it to happen now. She sat down as close as she could and took him into her arms. He fastened both arms around her and from the front of her cardigan said in muffled tones, 'You really don't think it's true?'

'I really don't think so.' She stroked his hair, silently cursing Frank.

'Why would Mr Harlington say it if it wasn't?'

That was a harder one to be reassuring about. Annie frowned in the darkness.

'He probably never said it,' she countered.

'If it is true it means that he never wanted me, never liked me, would have let me go into a home when my grandparents died but Alistair . . . Alistair has everything.'

There was no point in arguing with that, Annie thought. Alistair certainly had everything – except good parents, and this wasn't a choice moment to start comparing those. She was just beginning to think that perhaps she ought to move Blake from where he was comfortably settled against her breasts when he let her loose and moved back.

'Let's go and find Tommy,' he said.

They trudged up the road in the dark.

'Do you think I look like Alistair?'

'No.'

'We've both got blue eyes.'

'So has half the nation.'

'They're rich.'

'They're not very happy. Mrs Vane has a face like a wet fortnight and Tommy says Mr Vane's too mean to shit.'

She meant Blake to laugh but he didn't.

'Just think if he is my father. He's such a horrible man. He's the last man I'd want. I'd rather have Mr Harlington.'

'Oh, I don't think you would. Frank thinks he'll be orphaned within a year or two. He'll be left with those two dreadful old ladies.'

'They'll never die,' Blake said.

'I don't think they were ever alive.'

He did laugh at that, a little. Annie was grateful.

'Don't worry,' she said.

'I'm not. I'm just worried about how we're going to get Tommy in without your dad seeing him.'

When they reached the village there was a lot of noise coming from the pub. Annie stopped.

'Do you think we should?' she said.

'I'll go. You stay here.'

'Dad hates drink. If Tommy's drunk—'

'Just give me a few minutes.'

Blake had only ever been in the pub to bring the odd drink outside for them. The landlord didn't care whether you were underage or not. Tommy wasn't though and was quite entitled to be there even if his father wouldn't have said so. The inside of the pub was warm and noisy and comforting and Tommy was there, singing by the bar. Blake wasn't very happy about that. Half a mile was a long way with somebody drunk, he felt sure, and if Tommy sang how would they ever get him home without Jack finding out? How would they get him into the house?

Tommy didn't want to come home. He had his cornet with him and was all set to give a rendering of anything anybody suggested.

'You've been an age,' Annie said when he finally managed to drag Tommy out, minus his cornet. He left that with the landlord.

'Dad'll kill him,' Annie said, 'and if he doesn't Mam will. She hates drink more than anything because of Grandpa Ralph.'

'Ralph doesn't drink.'

'He used to. Mam has a horror of it. Whatever are we going to do with him?' she added as Tommy collapsed neatly into the road.

Blake managed to get Tommy back on to his feet, and between them they walked him the half-mile to the farm. It was quite late by then but Rose and Jack were still up.

'Distract them,' Blake said.

'What?'

'You know. Tell them you thought you heard a noise in the barn.'

'They're going to believe me, aren't they?'

'Make them believe you. Go on.'

Annie went inside and shortly afterwards came back out with her parents. Tommy groaned just then and Blake clamped a hand over his mouth and dragged him into the house and up the stairs and into his room.

'You don't deserve this,' he said, pulling off Tommy's clothes. Annie quietly opened the door. 'Don't come in. I'm getting him undressed.'

'It's nothing I haven't seen before, you know. Stop being daft and I'll give you a hand.'

'No, you won't. If your dad finds out there'll be trouble.'

'Are you sure you can manage?'

'Positive.'

'Thanks, Blake.' She paused in the doorway. 'We're going riding tomorrow, aren't we, just you and me?'

Blake thought they were the sweetest words he had ever heard in his life.

Seven

The school had tried to talk Alistair's parents into letting him go to university but nothing made any difference and somehow in the deepest part of his mind he had known all the time that he would not be allowed to go. He had wanted to escape from his parents and school and most of all from Western Isle so that he could come back to it. It was like having the prison door closed behind you and it was not all of his parents' making. He had lain in bed at night at school when the dorm got as quiet as it was going to get and thought about the farm and the dale and how much he loved it and he thought about Annie Lowe whom he could never entirely get out of his mind but it was not enough. And worst of all was the fact that he had the ability to go to college. It didn't have to be to do art – although that would have been the best – but just to get away. Even if he had to do agriculture or some kind of science, which he detested, anything would have done, just to know that he was not going to wake up in his bedroom at Western Isle for the rest of his life and feel the weight of the responsibility. That, in the end, was the only thing which stopped him from running away. He felt that if he left something terrible would happen to that place which had for so long been his family's. He could not let his father destroy whatever was left and he felt that as long as he was there somehow it could not entirely be destroyed.

'A farmer doesn't need to go to college,' his father said when he came home from school. 'You can learn everything from me. The best college you could have is this place. Besides, your mother and I haven't had you here for years. Don't you think we'd like you to be here, to take part in the farm? I can teach you to do the books, the accounts, to see how the farm is run because it will be yours one day.'

'I want to be able to do other things,' Alistair said.

'This isn't that ridiculous arty idea again, is it?' his father said patiently. 'You know, Alistair, it's a case of each man to his job and each man can only do one job properly. Now if you had not been my only child that would have been different perhaps, but you are the only one and this farm is your inheritance. You're lucky; many

many people would give anything for a place like this, for opportunity and prosperity such as you have. I don't understand why it isn't enough for you and it hurts me. Our ancestors sweated over this land so that we could have it and bring up our families here and enjoy it. Are you rejecting that?'

'No—'

'Well then?'

His father was not usually this reasonable. Alistair thought he liked him better when he shouted. When he was reasonable it was difficult to argue without seeming immature and selfish and also his mother hated them to argue. He felt like a traitor to Western Isle and to his parents but the longing to get away increased.

After he finished school there was nothing to look forward to, there was not even the change that school had been. Frank went to Oxford. Alistair envied him so much that it was difficult to talk to him even though Frank's mother had died and he felt sorry because Frank's home circumstances were as bad as his own. He wanted to go to Grayswell more but he felt guilty so at first he went nowhere, he stayed at home and did as his father asked and his mother wanted and they smiled at him and there was peace of a kind but it was so frustrating. Because he did not say anything they seemed to think that there was nothing wrong, that the things which mattered to him were of no importance. In a kind of solitary defiance Alistair began to use one of the attic rooms as a studio. The light was better there than anywhere else and he drew and painted what was around him, not just Western Isle in all its moods and colours but the other farms, the fields, the animals, the people, the river, the hills and the trees. He painted the little market towns and the sheep sales, the pubs and the marts and the women shopping in the streets and the children playing in the parks. The painting stopped him from leaving. That and the idea of Annie were the only things which prevented him from running away, and the reality of waking in the morning to the silver river and the slow sun on the stones of the farm buildings, the hens running about the yard, the cows in the thick meadow grass and that his grandfather's spirit wanted him to look after the place. After all, there was nobody else to do it.

Eight

Blake paused as he ventured to the back door. There was a car parked by the gates. It was no ordinary car, it was an MG sports car, bright green and the top was down. The young man sitting in the driving seat was looking up at Annie, who was perched on the gate, and they were laughing. Blake didn't linger. He walked up to the stables and collected Black Boy and then he went back and saddled up Annie's horse. Annie sauntered in.

'Who was that?' Blake asked.

'Paul Monmouth. You know him. His father has the shops. He's got the most-beautiful car. He asked me to go to the pictures with him on Saturday night to see Douglas Fairbanks and Maria Alba in *Mr Robinson Crusoe.*'

No more was said but any pleasure Blake might have felt was gone. He did not think that he had ever felt jealousy before but perhaps that was just because there had been no cause. He could not understand why he should feel so miserable because Annie had been asked out by somebody.

The riding made him feel better. He was glad that Frank was not with them and Annie galloped, her hair flying in the wind. She laughed and jumped a fallen tree and went on and Blake went after her. He put Paul Monmouth from his mind. Why should thoughts like that spoil the time he had with Annie? She wanted to be there with him and he knew that she would not tolerate people's jealousy. Blake fought with himself about it and on Saturday night when she came downstairs looking better than ever in a blue taffeta dress with a bolero, which her mother had carefully made for her, she did a pirouette in the big kitchen at the bottom of the stairs in front of her mother and father and Blake. Her father said she looked very nice, her mother smiled approval. Blake said nothing. Madge was going out too; he hardly noticed her. Mrs Lowe answered the door and Blake could hear Paul Monmouth's confident tones as he came into the room, extending his hand to Mr Lowe and saying that he would have Annie back not a second after eleven o'clock. When they had gone Mr and Mrs Lowe spent five minutes on how much they liked him and then he went back to his book and she to her knitting and the quietness was resumed around the fire.

By eleven o'clock Blake had gone to bed. The others were out but Annie came back on time and soon afterwards she crept into his bedroom and whispered, 'We're still going riding in the morning, aren't we?'

A warm glow fell on Blake like a quilt. He turned over towards her as she stood in the doorway.

'Did you have a good time?'

'Wonderful. You'd love his car. He bought me two gin and tonics. They have such a lot of money, Blake, you wouldn't believe. Six o'clock,' she reminded him and went out.

That morning they jumped the fallen tree three times and raced across the fields and he won. Back in the stables at the Hall Annie was laughing so much that she nearly fell off her horse. He caught hold of her by the waist. The stable was full of sunlight, her black hair had a silver sheen, her hands were slender on his shoulders, her breath was sweet. He put her on to her feet but he didn't let go of her. He fastened both arms around her, pulled her to him and kissed her. As first he could taste the hesitancy on her but it didn't last. Even though her hands didn't encourage him her mouth did and so did her body. Then she pulled back and he let go and she banged into the wall just behind her.

'You said you wouldn't do that again.'

'You wanted me to.'

'I did not.'

Blake said nothing and after a moment she looked up sheepishly at him.

'I did want you to . . . but I wish you wouldn't.'

'Because I haven't got a sports car?'

'We're living in the same house.'

'What's wrong with that?'

'Everything.'

'But you like me.'

'Of course I like you. I know you better than everybody else and we . . . we get on.'

'You like Paul Monmouth better?'

'No.' Annie shifted her feet about. 'It's different, that's all.'

Blake slid his hands around her waist and drew her away from the wall. She made a half-hearted attempt to stop him and then he was kissing her, one hand in her hair to turn her face up to his. Blake didn't know how to stop once she was returning the kisses and pressing against him. He wanted her more than he had ever wanted anything in his life and it was only when she hesitated again and tried to turn her mouth away and made her hands sharp against him that he let go of her.

Her lips were dark red from the kisses, her face was slightly flushed and her eyes had darkened too. She stood back against the wall.

'You're in my way,' she said.

'Yes, I know.' He brought his hands down on either side of her and leaned forward and kissed all the way down her throat and then her neck and then he reached and undid the top button on her blouse and Annie stopped him.

'No. No, Blake, don't. Don't.'

'I love you.'

'No.'

She got herself past him and out of the stable and ran.

They saw each other all day after that at the farm and at mealtimes. She didn't speak to him or look at him. That evening she went out again with Paul Monmouth. She was not late back but everyone had gone to bed. Since Blake was about Jack had asked him to lock up when she came home. He heard the car and her light tones, heard her unlatch the door and tread softly into the big kitchen. He wished that he had gone to bed early so that they wouldn't be alone now.

'Did you have a nice time?'

He didn't wait for her reply, he went and put in the bolts but with some difficulty because his hands were shaking. When he went back into the room she was standing by the fire.

'I want to talk to you, Blake. I feel like this is my fault.'

'What is your fault?'

'What happened today.'

'It obviously didn't matter to you. You still went out with Paul Monmouth.'

'The one has nothing to do with the other.'

'No? How do you think I felt watching you go out like that?'

'I have to.'

'Why?'

She looked clearly at him.

'I have to go out with people. I have to find some-body to marry, what else am I going to do? I'm almost eighteen. I'm just a – just a farm girl in a backwater. I don't have an education. If I'm not careful I'll live and die here, having half a dozen children and scrubbing floors until my back aches. Do you think I want that?'

Blake stared at her.

'I can't stay at Grayswell forever,' Annie said. 'I wish I could, I love the place better than anywhere on earth but Tommy will marry and have children. There won't be room here for me.'

'Don't you care about me?'

'I do care about you, Blake, yes, but what's the good of it? I can let you put your hands on me, I can let you take me to bed and then what? I get pregnant, we have to get married. Then we're stuck. Where would we live and on what? You don't really think I want that.'

'I can work.'

'At what? You don't know anything except farming, you don't have any kind of qualifications. You won't even be able to stay here if you marry. There's no room. Madge and Elsie and me, we have to find husbands. Paul Monmouth has money—'

'No—'

'You're not very realistic. My father doesn't even pay you.'

'I don't want him to pay me. He took me in. God knows where I would have been otherwise.'

'That may be enough now. It won't be later. You should leave and go somewhere and find work—'

'That would be a fine way to repay your father and mother for all the kindness they've shown me. They need me, they can't afford to pay somebody, you know that.'

'You've worked all these years. You don't owe them

anything and they wouldn't expect it.'

'God, that's selfish. I can't leave here.'

'You have to. It's the only thing you can do, otherwise you'll spend the rest of your life as a farmhand and no girl will ever want you because you have nothing to offer.'

'And that's how you see me?'

There was silence, complete silence. Even the fire didn't crackle.

'I thought . . . I thought you wanted me,' Blake said softly.

'Blake—'

'No money, no family, no name. I still thought you wanted me. Whatever made me think so?'

'It's not that.'

'What is it then?'

She looked at him like she was about to cry. Her face had flushed and her eyes were huge.

'You're never going to be like Paul Monmouth, no matter how hard you work or what you do; you have no background and no education. If you worked from now until doomsday you'd never be like that. He goes to university, his family have money. They have a lovely house with a great big garden and his sister plays the piano and sings and they have serviettes with every meal and—'

'Oh, serviettes,' Blake said. 'I suppose you let him kiss

you before you got out of the car. You let him kiss you because he has serviettes.'

'Do shut up about it, Blake, I did not.'

'Oh yes you did, because he has a sports car and a sister who plays the piano—'

'You shut up!'

'It's all that matters to you, isn't it?'

She didn't answer and Blake heard himself shout.

'Well, isn't it?'

He was getting frightened now of the way that he felt. The anger was like a barely containable fire and the more he tried to suppress it the worse it got. He wanted to take the strides necessary across the room and get hold of her and hit her. He had to keep telling himself that he would knock her over if he did that. He had to keep telling himself that it wasn't worth doing.

'You horrible grasping little bitch.'

She was white-faced and her eyes were even bigger. She looked like a farm cat, ready to spit but her eyes were bright with tears.

'Do you think I want to spend the rest of my life here?' she said.

'There's nothing wrong with it.'

'Everything's wrong with it. I want a nice house with a garden for my children to play in. I want a car and some decent clothes and I want a china cabinet and a piano and to talk to people who know things.'

'You wouldn't have anything to say to people who know things,' Blake shot back and she was across the room in seconds. She tried to hit him and he grabbed her. He put her up against the door and looked into her white face and angry frightened eyes.

'I'm going to make you sorry,' he said softly. 'You go ahead and marry Paul Monmouth and have a piano and serviettes and a nice garden but I will never ever forgive you for it because you love me.'

The tears began to fall now, her mouth started to tremble.

'I don't love you,' she sobbed and she raised a fist and ineffectually hit Blake on the shoulder. When he let go of her she fell back and bounced off the door. He went off upstairs to bed and she was still crying.

Nine

'I want to go away,' Blake said.

It was early morning and he and Jack were by themselves outside and he didn't want to go away, he never wanted to leave. He had spent the night thinking about how much he never wanted to go and about how he would never speak to Annie again because he hated her and now he had to say it.

Mr Lowe turned around in surprise as well he might, Blake thought, that he should find such ingratitude.

'Go away,' he repeated. 'Where to?'

'I don't know where to, just somewhere else, that's all.'

'But why?'

'I need to make my way. I know that you've been kind to me but I can't stop here. Tommy will get the farm and the girls will get married.'

'That's a long way off. I need you here, Blake, I can't manage without you.'

Blake didn't know what to say to that.

'I'll start and pay you a little—'

'It's not that.'

'What is it then?'

Mrs Lowe called them in to breakfast just then. In the big kitchen there was nobody but the three of them.

'Blake wants to leave, he's not happy here.'

'That's not true,' Blake objected.

'It must be true, you don't want to stay here with us.'

'I do,' Blake managed.

'I thought you were content—'

'Jack. Eat your breakfast,' Rose said.

He looked up and she returned the look just as Blake got up from the table, scraping back his chair and saying, 'I don't want any,' before he bolted from the room.

Rose waited until he had gone and then she said, 'Let him go.'

'You mean let him leave? Rose, I can't afford to pay a man to do what he does and I can't manage without him.'

'I think you're going to have to.'

'Why?'

'Because if he stays here we're going to have problems with Annie.'

Jack frowned.

'You what?' he said. 'What, with him? God Almighty, Rose. He's a nice enough lad but . . . You don't think he's—'

'No, I don't but I think it would be a good idea if he went away.'

That afternoon Blake was mending a wall between Grayswell and Western Isle and he was in the field at the far side when Charles Vane strolled down.

'What the hell are you doing on my land?' he said gruffly. 'Isn't Grayswell big enough for you?'

'I'm just trying to keep your sheep out of the field. If you rebuilt your walls occasionally I wouldn't be on your land.'

'You cheeky young bastard. Who taught you to speak to your betters like that?' Charles looked up as Jack reached them. 'The lad needs a good hiding,' Charles Vane said. He went off and Jack and Blake finished rebuilding the wall. As they walked back up the field Blake said, 'Is he my father?'

'What?' Jack stared at him. 'Whatever made you think that?'

'I just wondered. Is he?'

'As far as I know you haven't got a father.'

'I must have somewhere. You knew my mother. Surely—'

'I know nothing about it.'

'She was very young. She can't have known that many men.'

'She could have had half the dale for all I know.'

Blake turned on him.

'Don't you say things like that about my mother!'

'I didn't mean it like that, lad. I just meant that I never heard of her being with anybody.'

Blake asked Rose too when they got back.

'Did you know my mother?'

'Not very well. I wasn't here that long before I married Jack. I used to be in the post office then. I lived with the Harrisons. Mrs Harrison was a friend of my mother's.'

'Is Charles Vane my father?'

Rose looked sharply at him.

'Not that I know of,' she said. 'Whoever told you such a thing? Charles Vane was married when . . . when your mother died. He married Iris years before you were born. What made you ask that?'

'Frank says Charles Vane is my father.'

'And how would he know?'

'He overheard his father say so when he was drunk.'

'When men are drunk you can't trust anything they say. Sometimes you can't when they're sober. I don't know anything for certain. I don't think anybody does but there was nothing wrong with your mother. Everybody makes mistakes.'

'Except that around here you aren't ever allowed to forget them.'

'Your mother was a good respectable girl. She wouldn't have had anything to with a married man, especially a nasty piece of work like Charles Vane.'

'If she was so good and respectable how come she became pregnant and nobody knew about it?'

'I don't know. I never saw her with a man or a lad either. She hardly ever went out.'

It occurred to Blake later that if his mother had taken up with a man she wasn't married to people would have known, unless it was just that Mr and Mrs Lowe didn't like to talk about such a thing, but then he thought also would his grandparents have loved him quite so much if he had been the product of a disgraceful affair?

He went to bed that night and tortured himself with the idea that Charles Vane might actually have forced his mother. What other explanation could there be?

Tommy walked into his room when it was very late.

'You're not really going away?' he said.

'I have to.'

'And what are Dad and I supposed to do without you?

I'll have to give up the post and work all the time here now and we need the money.'

'I can't help it. You'll get the farm.'

'I suppose you think you're entitled to a share in it?'

'No, I don't think that.'

'Then what?'

'I don't have any choice.'

He hoped there would be. He hoped that a morning would come and there would be an event or a letter which would prevent his going away, that Annie would say she had not meant it, she cared for him, she didn't want him to go but none of this happened. He had never felt selfish before but he did now. He saw the worried look on Mrs Lowe's face because they couldn't afford to have anyone else to help on the farm.

The next morning after breakfast she called him back. The others had scattered and she was about to begin the clearing away.

'What would you think to going over to the coast where my family lives? You could stay with them to begin with and there might be work. I could write to my mother and see. What do you think?'

Blake had not had a single good idea since declaring that he was going away and this seemed to him feasible except for one thing. He did not know how he could ever go away from here. He had never been away and now it seemed like too much somehow. All of a sudden he wanted to be here like he had never wanted to before, he couldn't leave. There was Elsie with her ginger curls and bonny laugh, Madge dreamy and quiet and Tommy playing awful tunes on his cornet with the cows gathered around him in the low pasture and most of all there was Annie. Blake couldn't get past Annie; he thought that he never would.

She came to him when he had gone away down by the river so that he didn't have to be with anybody. It was the middle of Sunday afternoon, a bright warm day. She came upon him suddenly on soft feet and Blake was surprised and sat up and didn't know what to say. The leaves on the trees had changed colour by now and the days were short but warm.

'I thought we might have taken the horses out,' she said.

'I don't think so.'

'You don't have to be like this,' Annie said.

'Yes, I do.'

'I didn't mean what I said. I didn't think you'd go.'

'You thought I'd stay here and watch you marry Paul Monmouth or somebody else who has good table manners?'

'That's not fair, Blake.'

'No, it isn't, is it?' he said and he got up and would have gone away from her out of her sight to have her out of his except that she got hold of him. It wasn't a good hold, she wasn't that big. He could have torn himself from her physically except that he couldn't because they had barely touched, and it was that not touching that came to Blake in the ungodly hours of the night when it seemed to him that the chaos they talked of in church had a hold on everything. In those hours he thought of Annie so close, just through the wall. Sometimes he put his fingertips to the wall thinking that it made him closer to her because it was the nearest he would ever get. If he listened hard he could hear her breathing, at least he thought it was her, her warm constant breath. It had never occurred to him that they might be married, just as it had never occurred to him that they might be parted. He just wanted to go on like this, being young and working on the farm and going out riding the horses with Annie, sitting across the table from her and listening to her talk and her laughter and knowing that she cared. It was enough. He didn't even have to touch her, but it was too hard to know that he would never be able to touch her, that he could not go on sitting over the table from her, that everything would change, that he could not hold on to this part of his life which had become so dear. He was afraid each second of it altering and it brought him to the kind of rage he had never experienced until lately. So when she stopped him there down by the river he wanted to throw her off like he had never done, to throw her off and go away and be invisible and for her to know that it was all her fault. The trouble was that he knew it was not her fault. Finding nobody to blame made him want to shout and throw things and hit people. Nobody was to blame that he had got up in the early mornings as a small child and known that his grandmother would be weeping at the loss of his mother and her dreams. Nobody was to blame that he loved Annie so much. He couldn't hurt her now even though he wanted to because her father and mother had given him a life here. Nobody was to blame that he had to leave this place he loved so much and the girl that he wanted. He could never come back here because if he did then he might find somebody to blame and then he would know that he had been mistaken about himself and he was worth nothing. He shrugged her off as gently as he could considering how he felt and walked back to the farm with her following, crying, and that was the worst part of all, he thought afterwards when he had gone. He thought that nothing in his life would ever be that hard again.

Ten

Blake had always thought that he was at home in the country, that he would be content always to stay there and he would have been. It seemed to him that things went on there as they ought to and that he would hate life anywhere else but the minute that he stepped on to the beach at Seaton Town he knew a different kind of homecoming.

It was late autumn by then and there was a stiff breeze. The waves were flinging themselves over the harbour walls, the limestone cliffs were high, the beach was sandy away from the town, the water moved with the wind on it and he felt a kind of exhilaration, an excitement which he had never known before. There were ships in the harbour too and he had discovered that he liked to potter about down there, seeing the comings and goings at the coal staithes, hearing the accents and the languages which were new. The men had different-coloured skins and different kinds of clothes and he felt the excitement. He loved the noise and the people and all the buildings and seeing the ships away over on the horizon.

He was by himself, had gone for a walk away from the house where Annie's grandmother and step-grandfather had been so kind. Blake had not expected to be so well-received, he was nothing to them, but they seemed so pleased to see him. He did not feel at a loss, that had passed and this was as different as it could be with the cars and railways and shops. It was so busy and Blake had thought that he would find it overwhelming and too strange but he didn't. Already he felt as though he had lived there for quite a long time.

Ralph and Blake had tramped the streets in search of work. Blake had said that he didn't want to go down the pit and Ralph had laughed. He worked in the pit office now.

'You'd never stand it,' he said. 'Not that there's work to be had. There isn't.'

Blake had not been surprised to find that there was nothing for him to do. From the beginning he had not been hopeful, thinking only of getting away and it was easier being away from Annie altogether than seeing her every day, especially watching her go out with Paul

Monmouth. He didn't think about her any less but the ache eased when there were other things to think about and other people to see. Also, although Ralph and Mary Ann had a much smaller house than he was used to, there was now nobody but them in it. Their family all had their own houses, they had married and gone. At first it occurred to Blake that it could be like his life alone with his grandparents but it was not like that at all.

In the first place the pit town was as different as it could be from the countryside and it took him weeks to get used to the dirt and the smell and all the people, the close way that everybody lived and the way that there was never silence. He couldn't sleep to begin with and he even hated it for the first few days, but Ralph and Mary Ann were so kind and the people around him all spoke to him even when they had no idea who he was. The pit people, introduced to him by Ralph, took him to them in a way which Blake had not expected just because he was living there. He thought they were the kindest people he had ever met and that this was because the work was so hard and so dangerous, they were all for each other and caring.

Also he had his own room but he was not required to get up at daybreak and work until dark and that felt strangely free at first. He had his money from the post office so he could afford to take a holiday and still pay Mary Ann and Ralph for keeping him. He took long walks on the beach and through the town and looked for work but jobs were impossible to find and Blake was discouraged and saw himself having to go back to the farm without a future.

In the end he decided to go to classes and get himself some kind of an education, this having been one thing which Annie had taunted him about, so for the first year that he was away he studied and was encouraged because he worked hard and the teachers liked him.

The job situation was no better in Sunderland. Ralph had told him that many skilled and younger men had left the area because things in the shipyards were so bad and Blake thought hard about leaving the area altogether. The town seemed to him so noisy but Ralph disabused him of this idea. The clatter and bang of work from the shipyards was absent and after going to the employment exchanges the men hung around the streets. Some of the shipyards were closed. Grass grew up around the gates.

But to Blake Sunderland was exciting and it was where he went when the money ran out and he could no longer afford to do nothing but study. He lingered there in the East End enjoying the mass of people and the crowded streets. He spent a little money that he had on him, crossing the river by ferry for a ha'penny, buying ice-cream in Grey Street and sitting in a pub in Villiers Street when a customer who had been put out threw a brick through the window. Those sitting near complained of the brick in their beer.

At night he wandered there, watching the people; the streets were filled with bars and when it was late the young men, worse for beer, took to fighting in Villiers and Coronation Streets. He didn't go into the tempting cinemas or the shops or public houses from which in the early evenings a lot of noise and laughter came. He knew no one but he liked being there and one night as he was passing the Market Tavern there was a sudden commotion. The door opened and a young man was thrown out. Blake didn't have time to get out of the way; instead he put up both hands and was able to stop the young man from falling full length upon the pavement, which he would otherwise have done. He was, Blake estimated, holding up his weight, very drunk indeed.

'I am most awfully sorry,' he said, 'you must allow me to apologise and forgive me.'

He had a posh accent, something Blake thought odd in that area.

He would have slid on to the pavement but for Blake's hold on him. The young man, about the same age as he was, smiled unsteadily into his eyes and Blake was reminded of Tommy and how much he missed everyone.

'Can you drive me home?'

'No, I don't think I can,' Blake said.

'Why ever not?'

'I haven't a car. Don't you have any friends?' Blake looked vaguely in the direction of the pub.

'I came here to forget my so-called friends, in particular a lady. She is called Winifred Carlton. Perhaps you know her?'

'I can't say I do,' Blake said. 'Do you live in the town?'

'Ashbrooke.'

Blake got him to what the young man assured him was the correct tram stop but when the tram came the conductor said, 'He's not getting on here. Not like that.'

'Can he if I get on with him?'

'I suppose,' the conductor conceded and off they went.

It was an unusual experience for Blake to be in the company of someone most happily drunk. Tommy usually ended up crying. And in spite of having to hold up the young man, who swayed as they went, Blake enjoyed it. They went through streets he did not know and into the better part of the town and when the young man indicated they got off and walked a short way.

It was dark so when they stopped outside an impressive set of gates Blake was sure that the young man must be mistaken.

'You think I don't know my own house? I'm not that drunk,' he said.

Blake would have left him there but the fresh air seemed to make him worse, so he helped him through the gates and up the long drive, which had trees at either side, to an impressive and unusual-looking house of great size. In several places the roof came to points with arched windows beneath and there were jutting windows with great stone surrounds. Blake thought it was too big for anyone to live in, bigger even than the Hall where the Harlingtons lived. Blake found the main door and knocked hard but nothing happened and then he saw a bell and pushed that and after a short while the door opened and a girl stood there. She was the prettiest girl that Blake had ever seen, not conventionally beautiful like Annie but sparkling somehow. He put it down to her fine expensive clothes, which were stunning on her. She wore cream in varying shades, totally impractical, and she had brown eyes and copper-coloured hair and she wore lipstick.

'Oh, he hasn't done it again?' she said, and turning away slightly she shouted, 'Daddy, Simon's drunk.'

'You pig,' her brother said steadily, for Blake knew that only a sister would give you away like that and where he came from even sisters didn't always, but when the biggest man he had ever seen came out of some room further along the hall Blake could see why she had not hesitated. He must have been about six foot four and towered above everyone. He was heavily built and wore a suit and he had a beard and a lot of thick white hair.

'You scoundrel, when are you going to learn?' he admonished Simon and then he turned on Blake a pair of warm smiling brown eyes, like velvet. 'Well, young man,' he said, 'and are you drunk too?'

The girl closed the front door behind Blake.

'I don't drink,' Blake said.

'Not a drop? Not one of these Methodists, are you?'

'No. Church of England.'

The big man threw back his head and roared with laughter for some reason.

'In that case you'd better bring some tea to the sitting room, Irene.'

Blake protested. Simon staggered off upstairs but Blake was ushered into a big room, cosy with a fire, and after a short while Irene came in with a tea tray herself, which Blake had not expected. Didn't rich people have servants? He had always thought that they would, like the Harlingtons and Vanes. On the tray were small sandwiches and a large fruit cake and since he had eaten nothing since early that morning Blake had several sandwiches and two pieces of fruit cake before he remembered his manners.

Having explained hesitantly that he didn't know the son of the family even before the tea tray arrived, Blake was surprised to be the recipient of such hospitality. But from the beginning he felt a sympathy for the family because the mother did not appear and Blake assumed from then that there was no mother and he knew all about that.

'I am Sylvester Richmond,' the man said, 'and what is your name?'

'Blake. David Blake. People don't call me by my first name.'

'Don't they? Why not?'

'I don't know. Most of them just don't.'

'It seems a perfectly good name. Perhaps you don't like it?'

Blake had never thought about this.

'You're not from here?' Mr Richmond said.

'No. I come from a farm in the country. I'm staying with a family in Seaton Town while I look for work.'

'That could be difficult.'

'It is.'

After Irene came back with the tea Blake sneaked several looks at her. She really was very pretty but nothing like Annie. Annie would never have sat around pouring tea like that into red and gold cups with saucers but it suited Irene. He thought that she was the first real lady he had ever met and though there were women in the dale who thought they were ladies none of them had Irene's combination of looks, grace, soft voice and gentle smile. The firelight made her skin glow and the cream colours of her clothes were pleasing. That she was so different from Annie only made him want Annie more somehow and for the first time then, in the comfort of the biggest room he had ever seen, Blake was unbearably homesick for the farm and would have given much to hear Annie's voice as she came in from the yard. The thought of Black Boy made him more miserable than ever. He wondered who was riding the big black horse he had been so fond of. Blake excused himself as soon as he could. It was a long walk home now that he no longer had any money but before he went Mr Richmond said to him, 'Come to dinner on Sunday.'

'Dinner?'

'Yes, you know, that wonderful meal in the middle of the day with Yorkshire puddings. One o'clock and don't be late.'

*

Blake would have given much to have stayed at home. He didn't understand why he had been invited and to his dismay there were other people, men in expensive suits and women in clothes like the ones Irene wore and they were all dressed up. He felt out of place even though Irene greeted him warmly at the door and Mr Richmond smiled on him.

Over dinner, in the huge dining room where the cloth was starched white linen, the cutlery was silver, the plates all matched and the chandelier glittered horribly somehow in the sunshine, the woman sitting opposite, who was about the same age as Mrs Lowe, watched him for a long time in a way that made him feel very uncomfortable and then she smiled and said, 'And so, David, I understand that you come from the country, that your people are farmers.'

Every instinct shrieked at Blake to lie.

'No.'

'I understood that they were.'

'I don't have any family.'

'Orphaned? Oh, my dear, how perfectly dreadful for you,' and she leaned across the table and patted his hand.

'I'd watch it if I were you,' Simon said a bit later, 'or Marjorie Philips will have her hands down your trousers.'

'What?'

'If she invites you to tea say no unless you like middle-aged women.'

'You must come to tea,' Marjorie said, moving towards him with her coffee cup, but Irene was too fast for her.

'Come and see the conservatory,' she said, pulling at his sleeve.

It was too hot in the conservatory. They left their coffee cups and retreated to the shade in the gardens where there was a seat which went all the way round a huge oak tree.

'I'm sorry about Marjorie. We have to invite her sometimes. Her husband is in shipping. You must come to lunch again. I won't ask her next time.'

Later there was tea and cake and more talk. Blake was about to leave when Mr Richmond invited him into the library. It overlooked generous lawns and had big bookshelves, comfortable-looking leather chairs and a desk. The room was warm. Evening sun glowed in at the window.

'I come in here for peace and tell everybody I'm working,' Sylvester said. 'Brandy?'

'No, thank you.'

'Port?'

'No.'

'You really must learn how to drink, David. Gentlemen ought to know how.'

'I'm not a gentleman.'

Mr Richmond looked carefully at him.

'That's an interesting point. Do you think a man has to be born a gentleman or do you think he can become one?'

'I'm not sure it has anything to do with wealth or name.'

Mr Richmond smiled on him and went over and poured from a crystal decanter a dark brown liquid into huge round glasses.

'There you are, take it. Sniff it, think about it.'

'What is it?'

'It's brandy of course. A gentleman doesn't like port. He may drink it if he has to for politeness' sake but believe me only brandy hits the spot. Drink it. You're being polite.'

Blake took a sip, choked and then as it went down, warm and smoothly, decided that it wasn't so bad.

'What's it like?'

'It tastes like syrup of figs. It doesn't have the same effect, does it?'

Mr Richmond laughed.

'That's the best brandy in Sunderland,' he said. 'So, what are you planning to do with your life?'

'I don't know, sir, I really don't know. I've studied very hard and I'd like to do something worth doing. I want to make something of myself. I didn't leave the farm for nothing.'

Mr Richmond frowned into his glass for a second or two and then he looked straight at Blake.

'If you come to the offices at the shipyard on Monday I'll see what can be done.'

Blake looked at him.

'The shipyard?' he said.

'Yes, lad. You do know it? Richmond and Dixon. Times are hard and jobs are difficult to come by.'

'But I don't know anything about ships.'

'Here's your chance to learn. It's going to get easier, you know.'

'What is?' asked Blake, rather lost.

'Work in the shipyards. There's going to be a war.'

'You're the only person I know that thinks so, Mr Richmond.'

'The government thinks so, my boy, in spite of what they say, and the orders are beginning to trickle in.'

The shipyard offices were a nightmare to Blake. Many was the time during the first few months that he wished himself back at the farm. His hands were already soft from not working, but for the hard skin where he was holding a pen. The inactivity and lack of fresh air made him want to stick his head out of the window and he was only glad that he had taken the time for some learning before he arrived here because Mr Vincent, who headed the offices, told him his figurework was awful, his writing worse and sent him on so many errands that Blake was convinced he was going to lose the job even though he knew that he wasn't as bad as Mr Vincent said. Worst of all Ralph and Mary Ann were impressed that he had found what they called 'an office job'. Blake hated every minute of it for the first few weeks and then things changed.

Mr Richmond decided he had sufficient ability to study engineering and after that it was all classes and meetings and following people around, learning things.

One evening, when Blake had been there for many months and seen nothing of Mr Richmond except through work and even less of Simon, Simon stuck his head around the office door just as Blake was about to finish for the evening and go home. He grinned and beckoned. Blake went to him. He was, after all, the boss's son, even if he did not work and spent all day riding around in a sports car, drinking in various places and escorting young women to parties.

'Having a good time, are you?'

'You have no idea.'

'Oh yes, I have. My father tried to make me into an engineer. I've never been so bored in my life. Are we going out for a pint tonight?'

'I don't drink, Simon.'

'It's time you did. Come on.'

'I can't,' Blake said awkwardly.

'Why not?'

'I'm saving my money.'

Simon stared. He looked a bit like his sister, Blake decided.

'Whatever for?' he said.

'Because I need to.'

Simon looked hard at him.

'Do you know something, David? You're in danger of becoming the dullest person I ever met. Oh, and my sister says are you coming to lunch on Sunday?'

Eleven

For a long time after he went away Annie hated Blake. Every time she thought of him the anger rose redly before her eyes and she spent time thinking up awful fates which she hoped would be his. He wrote very occasionally to her parents but her pride did not let her ask about these brief letters or read them and her parents, oddly she thought, said little about him other than that he had found work at the shipyards and was still living with her grandparents. The one time when Mary Ann came to stay during the first year Blake was not working and Mary Ann only mentioned him briefly.

That first winter was a long one for them all. Her father could not afford to take on anyone to replace Blake and Annie found herself working as hard as a man and hating it and cursing him for leaving when they needed him so badly. She told herself that she didn't understand why he had left, that there had been no need, that she had never told him or given him to think that she cared about him. Why did he have to be so stupid? The rain never stopped, the fields were sodden. Mud and stones came down from the top fields and flooded the road past the farm. It almost reached the back door and they were glad that there was a big step up into the house, otherwise the water might have gone in the back door, through the house and out the front and left the sundial surrounded.

She had never been as uncomfortable as she was that winter. The wind tore around the house and everything was dark and gloomy. The draughts were icy gusts in the barns, the cattle huddled together, her father complained because there was not enough hay for the animals. He talked of the sheep getting footrot and some of them did, because the water stood in great pools in the fields, and early in the year the lambing was the worst it had ever been with snowstorms. It felt to Annie as though she was going to spend the rest of her life getting up in the dark and going to bed in the dark and being cold and wet and exhausted.

Madge spent more and more time at the Hall, where Mr Harlington and the two old aunts seemed to have accepted her as one of the family.

Sometimes Annie saw Alistair. He was spending as

much time as he could away from Western Isle and his father's ideas. He learned to do the farm accounts and to supervise the general day to day. His father wanted him to go to Houghall Agricultural College but Alistair refused. When he could, he and Tommy would take off in Alistair's new car – his father's guilty gift to him when he was not allowed to go away – and tour the pubs in the dale. On Saturday nights they went dancing. Sometimes it was almost morning when Tommy came home and his father was not pleased with him.

Annie went out with Paul Monmouth for a while almost out of defiance after Blake had gone. She revelled in his detached stone house, the garden where his mother grew roses, the way that his father wore suits. When you walked in the sound of Mozart filtered through from the music room, the smell of good food wafted into the hall from the kitchen. His mother played bridge, his father played chess, his sister was engaged to a doctor.

Paul talked to her about his ambitions to expand the family shops and Annie thought that it sounded good but the night that Paul Monmouth kissed her she realised that she didn't love him, that she was bored with his talk about his father's business, that his sister was silly, that his mother thought of nothing but her family, nothing in the real world. She was glad when he dropped her at the white gates that night. It was clear with a moon and not very late but cold and the stone dog stood out vividly beside the gate. When she got inside her parents were sitting talking quietly by the fire and she thought that she knew for the first time what it had been like for Blake when he left Sunniside. She wanted never to go away from here, not for good, and that was when she began missing Blake, admitting to herself that she didn't hate him, that she only wanted to be here with him. She wished that he would come back. There was nothing lost, he had no job, and then Mary Ann wrote and said that Blake had been taken on at the shipyard office. Annie couldn't see Blake as a clerk but she realised then that she had no business and no right to ask him to come back to the farm.

She began to go out with other young men. Paul was not deceived. He noticed her inattention, that he was not foremost with her and he did everything that he could to bind her to him. There were flowers and chocolates and small presents. He took her dancing and to the cinema. He was punctual and courteous, he was rich and eligible. In vain did Annie try to love him. Every time she went to his house for dinner or tea and there were linen squares for her lap she smiled over Blake and his sharp retorts about the serviettes. Paul's mother, being correct, called them napkins. It made Annie unhappy thinking about Blake and how her ambitious plans with Paul had come to nothing. The farm would never be the same somehow; it was all so boring without Blake and as time went on even with the winter long over the need for him grew worse.

Madge was seeing Frank when he was at home but doing her best to hide the meetings from her parents. Annie still went to Western Isle and here she saw Alistair daily. His father was always shouting at him and Alistair was miserable.

One afternoon about eighteen months after Blake had gone Alistair wandered into the dairy where she was about to finish work and go home.

'Are you going to the dance?' It was Saturday.

'No,' Annie said.

'Why not?'

'Nobody's asked me.'

'Paul would ask you.'

'I don't want to go with him.'

'I thought you liked him. I thought, for a while, that you might marry him. Isn't that your type?'

'What type?'

'Cultured, well-dressed—'

'No, that's not my type,' Annie said crossly.

'Maybe you'd go with me then.'

She couldn't help smiling at that.

'I might, if you would promise not to get drunk.'

'I never get drunk.'

'Last time I went out with you and Tommy it was the most embarrassing night of my life.'

'Tommy's taking Clara.'

'I think he likes her,' Annie said, secretly pleased because Clara was still her best friend.

'And I know Madge is going with Frank because he told me.'

'All right.'

'I'll pick you up.'

'Just to the gate. I don't want my parents to know.'

Alistair looked as if he would have liked to say something about that but he didn't.

'Eight o'clock,' he said over his shoulder.

They went to the pub first, it was the custom. Annie liked pubs. She had developed a taste for gin and tonic and she was glad to be with Tommy and Clara, Madge and Frank and Alistair. Being with people you knew made it so much more fun.

Things had not been fun since Blake had left, she thought, but they were now. And she needed fun. Now she was almost happy. Alistair was too frustrated at being stuck at Western Isle to be any fun usually but that night for some reason it was different. In the first place she had slightly too much to drink and for once Alistair didn't talk about the farm or his parents or problems. They came out of the pub laughing and went into the hall to dance.

She danced with Alistair and with Frank and then with other young men. By the end of the evening Annie was happy like she had not been in a long time. Alistair had his car and was taking her home but when they were driving along the road at the top side of the valley she said suddenly, 'Pull over. I want to see the dale.'

It was late but not dark. The lights twinkled in the farmhouses, the shadows showed up the square neatness of the fields. Annie got out of the car. Alistair got out of the other side and came round to where she was standing leaning against the car.

'I love this place. I could never love anywhere more.'

'How do you know, you haven't been anywhere yet?'

'Do you hate being at home?' Annie said softly.

'It feels like a prison. If I didn't have to be there it would be all right. I wouldn't mind. Western Isle's my home but because of my father it feels like a gaol.'

'Poor Alistair.'

'I'm not poor. Perhaps I'd be better off if I were – at

least I wouldn't have any responsibilities. Then I could leave.'

Annie put a hand on his shoulder and as she did so he leaned over and kissed her. It was not as first kisses should be somehow, Annie thought, it was as though they had started halfway through and although he had once kissed her years since that had been just a touch of lips. She didn't normally object to a kiss when young men took her to a dance – usually the kiss was a goodnight one but this wasn't. He got hold of her and because his hands and mouth were gentle there was nothing to object to. Most young men were clumsy with inexperience but Alistair wasn't. She found herself in his arms, wasn't quite sure how she had got there but she knew one thing. She didn't want the kiss to end.

'Do you do that a lot?' she said, finally breaking away.

'What a suspicious mind. Who on earth with?'

'I don't know. You go out in the evenings.'

'What is this, the Inquisition?'

'You taste nice.'

'I should think it's gin and tonic.'

'You haven't been drinking gin and tonic.'

'No, but you have. Shall I take you home?'

'Do it again.'

'Annie—'

'Don't argue. Kiss me.'

It was even better the second time. After that they went home.

Late that night when she and Madge had gone to bed and Elsie was asleep Madge turned over in the darkness and said, 'Frank's asked me to marry him.'

'What?'

'Don't shriek, Dad will hear.'

'You can't marry him.'

'Why not?'

'He hasn't finished university yet.'

'He's going to come and see Dad. I want to marry him, Annie, it's all I'm ever going to want.'

Annie lay awake long after Madge slept, thinking how lucky Madge was, knowing exactly what she wanted. There was a chance she would get it too. How could her father turn down the family who owned his farm?

That Monday morning Charles Vane had gone to the mart. Annie knew that Alistair would be in the study so as soon as she could get away without being seen she tiptoed along the hall through the house and noiselessly opened the study door. He was sitting with his back to her, writing.

'Alistair!' she whispered. 'Is it all right if I come in?'

He stopped writing and turned around.

'You don't have to whisper. Close the door.'

Annie did so.

'I just wanted to say I was sorry about Saturday.'

'Sorry about what?'

'I think I had too much to drink.'

'Oh, that.' Alistair got up and Annie could not help but think how nice and tall he was.

'I—' Annie could feel herself blushing.

'Don't worry about it. It's all right, really.'

'Are you sure?' Annie's face was fiery. She wanted to get back to the dairy before her face burned to ashes.

'I'm sure.' He smiled at her and Annie smiled back hastily and fled.

When Frank saw her father one bright spring Sunday not long before he went back to Oxford he came out of the parlour with a set mouth and flushed cheeks and after Madge was called in there she came out crying.

Annie and Tommy sat on the big white gates at the roadside to stay out of the way.

'I thought he would have agreed,' she said.

'You didn't really think so.'

'Why shouldn't he?'

'With Frank's history? His mother and father drinking like that and they're in debt.'

'Mr Harlington owns the valley. How can you say that they have nothing?'

'Because it's true. If Frank's father is ever in his right mind for long enough he'll realise that he has to sell the farms. I've heard Dad say so, and I'll say this for him – he'll be right. He always is about things like that.'

Later when she was alone with her mother in the kitchen making the tea Annie asked carefully, 'Aren't you going to let Madge marry Frank?'

Her mother didn't look at her. She only said shortly, 'Madge is too young to be thinking about marrying anybody.'

'But she loves him.'

'Stuff and nonsense,' her mother said. 'Frank's hardly out of short trousers himself. What does either of them know about marriage? Marriage is a serious business, my girl, and if it's to work it needs more than all this poppycock about love. Now go and set the table.'

Annie dared say nothing more but in the quiet of the night when Madge had finally stopped weeping she listened to her sister say, 'I'll go to bed with him and when I'm pregnant they'll have to let me marry him.'

'Oh, Madge, you can't do that. If you just wait a little—'

'I can't wait. I don't want to wait and there's no reason why we should.'

'They'll come round to it when they get used to the idea.'

Madge choked on her tears.

'Daddy says I'm not to see Frank any more. He says that I'm too young and that Frank would make me unhappy. I don't see how he knows.'

Madge cried so much and was so miserable over Frank that her parents eventually gave in but not until Frank's father appeared at the farm, sober and grave, and spent two hours sitting by the parlour fire with Rose and Jack.

'What made you change your minds?' Annie asked her mother when Madge had gone back to the Hall with her father-in-law to be, taking with her a face so shiny it would have been good competition for the moon, Annie thought.

Rose hesitated over the teacups she was stacking to wash and then said stoutly, 'Madge will be mistress at the Hall. Mr Harlington – Joe – is going to make sure that they're happy. He's very fond of Madge. I wasn't very old when I met your father, you know.'

'But you were so against it.'

Rose looked at her.

'It isn't what we wanted but Madge wants to marry him so badly and I know what that's like and when I met your father my mother said nothing but good things. I remembered that.'

'And Dad?'

'He's still not very happy about it. You're all his little girls, you know.'

That summer Annie stopped going out with half a dozen different young men and stayed at home. When she was not at Western Isle she worked hard on the farm, helped her mother and refused all invitations. Finally one Saturday evening when she was sitting in the garden among the roses Alistair turned up. She hadn't seen him for weeks except at work.

'How are things?' she said.

'You should know. You're there most of the time,' he said, sitting down some way off. She saw him often at Western Isle but they barely spoke any more.

'You should leave home,' she said.

'What's the use? It isn't that I hate Western Isle and I can see my father's point. My family have worked hard to have such a farm. It isn't that I don't want it, it's just that I know it isn't what I'm supposed to be doing, and when I can't do the work I want to do I feel so useless and dissatisfied.'

Annie was quite surprised. Alistair was not given to explaining his feelings.

'Why don't we go to the dance up at Alston?' she said.

He looked surprised. He had stopped asking Annie out, having been turned down twice, she had been so embarrassed at her own behaviour.

'I didn't think you wanted to go anywhere. Paul's practically gone into a decline. You never see anybody. It's because of David Blake, isn't it?'

'He's been gone for ever. How could it be because of him?'

'I don't know.'

'I wanted him to go away.'

'Did you, why?'

'He could never be anything here.'

'And now he's a clerk in a shipping office. Dizzy heights,' Alistair said.

'At least he's got a job, which is more than a lot of people.'

'I hope it's a job he likes,' Alistair said, getting up.

It was a perfect June evening. For once they were alone. Tommy and Clara had gone off somewhere else and Madge was meeting Frank. They didn't see anyone they knew and it was rather pleasant just to dance. Alistair didn't talk much, the one long speech seemed to have exhausted his verbal capacity, but Annie didn't want speech, she was content to dance and listen to the music and be in his arms.

When it was late they came out. It was a lovely night, not dark, quite still. The sheep were crying in the fields below, the houses were grey dots on the hillside, the fields were shadowed squares in the quiet and the sky was clear and pale and graced with a star or two.

'I don't know how you could ever bear to leave this,' she said.

'I probably wouldn't want to leave it if I knew that I could. Just now it's like a prison with a pleasant view.' Annie smiled over that and turned to him and she caught a look or an angle that was familiar. She waited and nothing happened.

'Aren't you going to kiss me?'

'You never want me to kiss you. You've kept well away from me for weeks.'

'I do now.'

So he did, very slowly and carefully as though she was about to change her mind. Annie's body went into shock. There was something about it that was all Blake. She broke away, shaking, and stared at him.

'See?' he said.

'Alistair—'

'Oh, let's go home, I'm tired of playing games.'

'It isn't a game. I wasn't, it's just that . . .' but he was already in the car, slamming the door. He didn't speak all the way back, pulled up sharply at her gate, 'Get out.'

'Alistair—'

'Just get out, will you?'

Annie did so. She ran into the house. She could hear the car as it tore away. She said a hasty goodnight to her parents and went to bed. The other two girls were asleep. She lay there and thought. Frank had been right, Blake's mother had gone with a married man. She had gone with Charles Vane but Alistair didn't know. She thought about the kiss and how sweet it was. She turned in towards the pillow, trying not to think.

Alistair didn't spare the car. He threw it around the tiny roads, not caring if anything should get in the way, not minding if there should be an accident.

When he got home to Western Isle there were cars in the yard, sleek expensive cars. His father and mother were having a dinner party. He had forgotten. He hated their social life, the way that they mixed with the best people in the area, the best being the people who had professions or money.

He didn't go straight in; he wished that he could stay outside until everyone had gone. He went around for a while to the duckpond and walked around there and through the rose gardens and over the bridge which led into a big orchard where plum and pear and apple trees grew in profusion. To one side was a kitchen garden. From the front he could see the light in the middle of the house on the landing where there was a big round window like a bicycle wheel. Inside, he thought in disgust, the house had everything, a sumptuous drawing room, a dining room which could seat twenty people, big kitchen and dairy and various small rooms leading off, a music room and a billiard room and a library and a study and bedrooms and bathrooms and long halls. It had seemed to him when he was a child that his parents should have had other children to fill the house but his mother couldn't have any more after him. That was why he felt the responsibility so much, why he couldn't walk out even when his father had told him that he was to stay there. He felt somehow that it was his fault there was no one else to bear the name and ease the burden. He would have to stay here and carry on as though he didn't hate the place now.

From the drawing room came the sounds of laughter. His father's friends drinking brandy, his mother's friends drinking coffee and bragging about their children. Of late his mother had begun inviting various families who had girls of about his own age or a little younger. People whom she thought were suitable. She did not think Annie suitable because she had no money and was their dairy-maid. That was why he had stopped talking to Annie when she was at Western Isle. He didn't want his parents to find out how much he cared about her. He wasn't sure now whether he wanted her to know either. He had watched her with Blake. She cared more for a penniless farm boy than she cared for anyone else but Blake was not here. He had thought for a while that she would fall in love with Paul Monmouth but she had not done so.

He walked through the hall and was about to climb the stairs when his mother opened the door of the drawing room and came into the hall.

'So there you are,' she said, looking questioningly at him.

'Well, I think it's me,' he said.

'You aren't funny. Where have you been?'

'Out.'

'I know that. Where?'

'Nowhere in particular.'

'I asked you to stay here. I invited particular people here tonight and I asked you to stay in.'

'I forgot.'

'How could you possibly forget?'

'Probably because I wanted to,' Alistair said. 'Mother, I wish that you would stop inviting girls here for me to meet. I'm not interested in them.'

His mother came to the foot of the stairs.

'You'd better get interested in them,' she said, 'because if we have any more nonsense about Annie Lowe she'll be looking for another job. Really, Alistair, I thought you had more sense than to pay attention to one of the servants,' and his mother turned around and went back into the drawing room.

He climbed the stairs. It was quiet up there. The old walls were so thick that you couldn't hear any noise from the drawing room. The windows were open to the sweet smell of the roses in the garden. In the distance was the river and way over to the side, though you couldn't see it from there, was Grayswell. He didn't understand the way that Annie was behaving.

He sought her out the next morning when she was alone in the dairy.

'Are you still angry with me?'

'I wasn't angry with you.' She looked anxiously at him. 'You were the one who was angry.'

'But you pushed me away.'

'Alistair!' his father roared from the house.

'I think you'd better go,' she said.

'What were you doing in the dairy?' his father demanded when he reached the study.

'Talking to Annie.'

'She isn't here to talk, she gets paid to work. We have the accounts to do.' His father threw him a glance. 'You look tired. Must you go out drinking every night?'

'I wasn't drinking.'

'That Lowe boy is a bad influence on you. Why can't you choose people like yourself to mix with?' and his father, grumbling, got down to work.

Alistair stopped listening. It wasn't difficult, he did it all the time now.

Twelve

It seemed to Blake a long time before he realised that the design and creation of a ship was something that he might understand. At first it was so far outside of his experience that even just to be there under the shadow of such mighty goings on unnerved him and then gradually everything began to take on a different shape in his mind. The rise and fall of the shipbuilding world became all his concern. Simon laughed at him; he hated business and did everything he could to get Blake away from the office. This wasn't easy. Long before the others came in and after they went home Blake was there. He had no other interest. He stopped travelling to Ralph and Mary Ann's house and found a room in a respectable house where he could walk to and from work. All he did was eat and sleep there. He didn't know anybody except his landlady, he didn't want to know anyone. Blake had decided what he wanted. If he could become properly established here at the shipyard, if he could become an engineer then in time he could go back to the dale and ask Annie to marry him. He would be a man with a profession then, with some kind of a future, and she could come here to Sunderland and they would rent a nice house with a garden out the front and a yard at the back and they would marry and settle down and have children.

The dream was so real to him that he worked harder and harder and saved every penny. He began to go often to the Richmond household for his Sunday lunch and he became fond of Sylvester Richmond, who treated him almost as he treated Simon.

'You can stop calling me "sir",' Sylvester said. 'We're not at the office. And not "Mr Richmond" either. It sounds so stuffy. I think you might be an engineer given time.'

'I consider myself lucky to have the chance.'

'You are very lucky, my boy.'

Irene always seemed pleased to see Blake, though she grumbled that he and her father talked of nothing but the shipyard.

A young man called Robert Denham came over sometimes too, more often in the afternoons because Sylvester did not want Robert there for meals, he said.

'Huh. Young Denham. Haunts the place. A solicitor. I hate lawyers and everything to do with the law. His father's a solicitor too. Couldn't they think of anything better for him to do? Solicitors are like leeches, they live off other people's blood, sometimes literally, I think. And he talks too much about the law.'

'Not half as much as you and David go on about ships,' Irene said.

'It's a dead bore,' Simon said.

'It's a pity you don't take a leaf out of David's book,' his father said and Simon pulled a face at Blake across the table.

That summer on Sunday afternoons it was pleasant to sit in the garden and drink tea with Sylvester – Sylvester always put brandy in his tea, a habit which made his daughter shudder. They would sit under the trees in the garden and Blake would listen to Sylvester on his favourite subject, Richmond and Dixon, its origins, its growth, its problems, the men, the ships, the future. And Robert would ask Irene to walk around the garden, which she did, listening to him as they went with her head slightly inclined towards him.

Robert didn't talk much to Blake, just general polite conversation. Blake could talk freely to Sylvester. It was his greatest pleasure to know that a man so far above him would treat him as if he knew something when in fact he did not, but he could ask the stupidest questions and Sylvester answered him patiently because shipbuilding was his passion and he told Blake that to find someone who would talk endlessly about it was better than a gold mine.

'We've gone through a long depression, lad, it's made the twenties look like a bloody picnic,' he said, one summer afternoon, 'but I think we're almost through it now.'

'Are you going to talk ships with Daddy all afternoon?' Irene protested. 'The sun is shining and I want to go for a walk.'

Robert was not there that Sunday. He had gone away with his family.

'Nobody's stopping you,' Simon said.

'David, please,' she coaxed and in the end he left her father to coffee and a cigar and walked.

'I am not going anywhere near the harbour. You'll bore me to death with detail,' she said, as they left down the front steps of the house.

'Where then, Mowbray Park?'

'Yes.' She put her hand through his arm and they walked slowly. 'I'm glad Daddy has somebody to talk to.'

Blake laughed.

'He's just being polite. He has people to talk to about ships every day at work, he doesn't need me. I'm the newest humblest engineer he's got. I know nothing.'

'I think he just likes you,' she said.

'Probably because I don't know enough to argue with him.'

'You don't give yourself any credit but then he does get tired of the way that Simon goes on.'

'Simon won't be happy until he's allowed to go into the army.'

'That won't ever happen.'

'It will if there's a war.'

'He'll be needed here more than ever if there is. Daddy would never let him go.'

'Irene, he has no natural ability. Not even as much as I have and that's not saying a great deal.'

'You love it,' she said. 'That's the difference.'

Blake did not understand his continuing relationship with the Richmond family. He could not see what they got out of it. He knew nothing, though after his first few visits he made sure that he had a better idea of politics and world news because Sylvester was the kind of man who grilled you on these things if he thought that you had not seen a newspaper all week. Luckily there were newspapers in the office or Blake would have remained in ignorance. Also he asked Blake's opinion on books and loaned him them and expected him to read them swiftly and with understanding. It was rather like school as school had never been because Sylvester's mind was more alive than any Blake had ever met before.

Simon was always trying to persuade Blake to go out drinking and with girls. He stopped even trying to pretend that he was doing any work. He was the only person Blake knew who was praying for war. Because his father would not hear of the army he went out nightly and got drunk, knowing how much Sylvester hated stupid idle people.

'Why don't you ever go out?' Simon asked, one evening that autumn.

'Because I need the money.'

'What on earth for?'

'There's a girl—'

'Oh, I knew it would be that. Don't tell me. You want enough money to go back and marry her. She's probably a milkmaid. Pardon me while I'm sick.'

'I love her, Simon. I'm going to marry her but I have to be something first.'

He thought that in another year or so he would be making enough so that Annie could come to him. He even wrote to her, just a light letter, telling her what

Sunderland was like, about her grandparents, whom he still saw sometimes, about the occasional visit to the cinema.

She would be able to work too, at least at first until there was a child and that might take a year or two. They wouldn't need much. He wanted to see her so badly that he lay with his eyes closed at night and conjured her face. He tried not to think of what the farm was like without him, it hurt too much, but he grew used to being away, the bustle and activity, the people, the shops and the sea and he came to know the area and to be at home there. He thought that perhaps for his sake Annie might be persuaded to leave her beloved country and her horse and come to him there and marry him. He pictured them in a room neat and cosy with a fire and a bed and some books. He thought of her sweet face and her laughter.

She didn't write back. He thought that perhaps the letter had been lost in the post. He did get a letter from her mother with scarcely any mention of Annie.

Blake knew by now that, in spite of what Sylvester said about Robert Denham, he would be very glad to have the young man marry Irene. He came from a good family. He lived in a big house. He had a father who was a solicitor and a mother whose family were doctors and he had a car and a profession and a brother and a sister. Most of all Blake envied him the brother and sister and had tried to be polite and not to ask too much but he imagined Robert Denham going home to his family on winter evenings, to fires and food and conversation, not to a tiny freezing bedroom, Mrs Southwark's variable cooking and a cold bed in the dark silence. Blake was no better pleased to find that Irene did not ignore him for Robert, rather the other way round. He had tried to stop going to the Richmonds' so much. He was sometimes invited to Seaton Town to have Sunday dinner with Ralph and Mary Ann and he was relieved to go there but he liked the Richmonds so much, not just their house and their fine dinners, he liked Simon as though he was a brother and Irene was as dear to him as Madge and Elsie and made a good substitute and most of all there was the tall broad kind man that his childhood had lacked. Sylvester Richmond meant more to Blake than anyone in the world save Annie and though his past was not spoken of he was at home among the dinnerplates with Sylvester talking about shipping and carving great lumps of beef and encouraging everybody to eat too much. He called Blake 'my boy' and 'my lad', clapping him on the back when they met and encouraging him to drink and scoffing at his political ideas even if a week before he had agreed with them, just for the enjoyment of an argument. He wished that Irene would not look at him with those sparkling eyes. Her father, he knew, would have died rather than let her marry a nobody and Blake did not want to lose Sylvester in such a way. It had never occurred to Sylvester that she might like Blake better than she should. Until lately it had not occurred to Blake either that she hated his going rather than Robert's, that she liked his conversation better, that she would play silly games with him for hours and laugh across the table at him. There was no room in his life for Irene and no place in hers for him and he did not want to hurt her.

Annie got drunk at the party. Alistair watched her drinking great quantities of punch until she was pink-faced and giggling. The party was at Paul Monmouth's home and Alistair had not expected to see her there after the way she had treated Paul. Now the evening was late and he was standing across the room from her with Tommy.

'What is your sister doing?'

'She'll be to carry out,' Tommy prophesied.

'I've never seen her drink like this. Is she all right?'

Tommy had to think about it.

'She's been a bit fed up lately,' he said. 'And if Monmouth thinks he's taking her home when she's in that state he can think again,' and Tommy went over and took her by the arm.

'I'll take her home,' Alistair said.

'Are you sure?'

'Positive. You look after Clara.'

It was a wet night. She slipped when she got out the door so it was lucky that he had hold of her arm. She sang all the way back. When he stopped the car outside the gate she turned to him and said, 'I love you.'

'No, you don't. You're just drunk.'

'I've always loved you. It's the way that you kiss.' She leaned over. Alistair leaned back away from the alcohol fumes.

'Come on,' he said and he got out and opened the door and helped her across the yard. Her father opened the door.

'It wasn't me,' Alistair said instantly.

'I didn't suppose it was. Thank you for bringing her home.'

Alistair said goodnight and went off but her words went round and round in his head. Why had she said that she loved him? Oh yes, she was drunk, but why? And had she always loved him? And last time he had kissed her she had pushed him away abruptly and gone so it couldn't be the kisses.

*

The next day she came to Western Isle and found him in the stables, stroking his horse and talking to it. He heard her come in but he didn't turn around, thinking that it was probably his father, but when she paused in the doorway he turned and she was standing in a pool of sunlight, looking more beautiful than ever before, and smiling at him.

'I'm sorry,' she said.

'Do you have a hangover?'

'I did have this morning. It was nothing compared to the earache I had when my father had finished shouting at me. How are you?'

'Fine.'

She went across to him but Alistair turned back to the horse. He didn't want to see her or talk to her.

'Don't be cross, Alistair.'

'I'm not cross, it's just that . . . I wish you wouldn't pretend that you care about me when you don't. It isn't easy to take.'

'I do care about you.'

'No.'

'I do.'

'It's Blake that you like, it always was.' And then he realised, quite suddenly like when you saw the solution when you were doing a crossword, and he turned sharply and looked at her. 'You thought I was him last night.'

'No, I didn't,' Annie said quickly. 'Why should I think such a thing?'

'I don't know.'

'It was just that . . . I hadn't been kissed in so long until that night when you stopped the car up on the top road and . . . I thought I was never going to want to again until you started kissing me. I got a shock, that's all. I thought I . . .'

'What?'

'I thought I loved him but if I did then I wouldn't feel how I feel about you.'

'How do you feel about me?'

She put her arms around his neck and kissed him on the mouth. Alistair didn't realise until then how often he had imagined them together like this. He tightened his hold on her and kissed and kissed her, thinking all the time that she would pull away but she didn't and when he finally thought it was enough and would have let her go she put herself back into his arms and hid her face against him. He held her close to him like he had held no one before, nor ever been held. It was more than man and woman, more than family somehow. It was a special knowledge, secret and close.

'I hate the way things are,' she said finally without moving away far.

'So do I.'

'We could make it different.' She moved back more now to look into his face.

'I can't leave Western Isle. I can't ever.'

'Because of your father?'

'Not just because of him, because of all kinds of things. I can't ever just walk out on it. I would feel as though I was betraying something important. It'll be mine, you see, and I can't let my father down no matter what. He's still my father, he'll always be that.'

Annie looked up into his face and smiled.

'I love you. Just you. Not Blake and not Paul Monmouth and nobody else in the whole world, just you,' she said.

'Are you sure?'

'I've never been more sure of anything in my life.'

'Annie . . .'

'What?'

'Will you marry me?'

Thirteen

Blake had a letter from Rose to say that Frank and Madge were to be married. She didn't say much so Blake gathered that it wasn't what she and Jack wanted. She asked him to come home. He had been gone for such a long time, two years, and he wanted to go back so much that he wrote to her and said he would.

He told Irene about the proposed holiday. Sylvester had granted him a week.

'How lovely for you,' she said.

It was a fine autumn afternoon. Robert Denham was for once talking to her father and she and Blake sat under the big oak tree in the warm sunshine.

'I'll miss you, you know,' she said, smiling at him.

'I'll only be gone a week.'

'You will be back for dinner the following Sunday. Promise me.'

She looked at him and there was no mistaking the sparkle in her eyes, the invitation on her lips.

'Irene . . . there's a girl at home.'

The sparkle went; she looked down and then back up, smiling dimly.

'And you haven't seen her in all this time. How awful for you. You must miss her very much.'

He would miss Irene too when he went but he did not want her to look at him with those sparkling eyes.

'I'll be back on Sunday,' he said. 'Give Robert my regards.'

All the way home the train beat a comforting rhythm. It was the Friday, Madge and Frank were to be married the following day. The sun shone. It shone on the sea as he left the coast, on the river in Durham and on the fields as he approached the dale and he thought that it had never looked better. The homesickness faded into a warm glow of homecoming and when Blake fairly tumbled off the train in the village and into Rose's arms he was all smiles and gladness. Jack was there too. They walked him home between them. Blake stood for a few moments just up the road where the farm buildings came into view, the white gates and the old stone dog and the farmhouse itself, and he wanted to run but he couldn't.

Across the cobbles and up the step into the yard and

up another step and down into the gloom of the hall. Nothing had changed, his heart sang, it was all there waiting for him just as it had been and would be. They were gathered in the big kitchen and the tea was laid on the table. Tommy looking exactly the same, Elsie grown up and with her hair short, Madge arm in arm with Frank and Annie standing nearest the fire.

She was more beautiful than he had remembered, wearing a simple blue dress – her favourite colour – smiling a little uncertainly at him. Blake tried not to stare, to act naturally in front of the others.

And then he was among them and it was as if he had not been away except that they teased him about his posh suit and asked a hundred questions about his new life.

They sat down to tea and it was the best tea ever, a big cooked ham, custard pies, beef sandwiches, sausage rolls, pease pudding, pickles, jam tarts, little cakes and endless cups of tea from the big brown teapot. It made Blake more sure than ever that he didn't want to go back to Mrs Southwark's soda bread and grey cheese scones.

After tea all Blake wanted was to have Annie to himself but it wasn't possible. Traditionally the groom was to take the young men out and it was taken for granted that he would go with them. Frank drove down the dale to Stanhope and there they were joined by several other of his friends, including Alistair Vane. Both Alistair and Frank treated him in a very friendly fashion, asking about the shipyard and buying drinks.

Everybody teased Frank about his marriage but Frank said that he was a very happy man and turned to Blake and said, 'So what are the girls in Sunderland like?'

'I don't know. I've never had anything to do with them.'

Alistair laughed shortly.

'What, in two years?'

They were several drinks into the evening now. Around him a silence fell. Frank and Tommy and Alistair looked at one another and then Frank started to talk about London where he was taking Madge on honeymoon. Blake went to the bar for more drinks and everybody talked.

They walked down the main street to another pub, singing, Tommy with his arm around Blake, stopping to climb into somebody's front garden to do a little dance on their lawn. When they came out of there they walked up to the ford and threw Frank in and ran races to the far side. When Blake was back at the farm it was this memory that brought a smile to his lips before he went to sleep, he and Alistair sitting in the middle of the ford by moonlight, singing 'Here Comes the Bride'.

*

He slept late and awoke with surprise to find himself at home at the farm with a headache but very happy. From his window in the same tiny room he had always had, he could see the yard and the buildings and the old stone dog beside the gate. His headache soon went and he ate breakfast and ventured out into the yard to help. The wedding was to be at the little parish church in the village and for some time there was a lot of activity upstairs and giggling and the rustling of dresses before Mrs Lowe came downstairs with Annie and Elsie, dressed alike in dark pink. When Blake saw Annie he wished that it was their wedding day, she looked so lovely, smiling at him, and he still had not had any private talk with her.

There was no chance of that. Madge went up the aisle on her father's arm in white beaming her happiness and came back on Frank's arm looking even more happy and there were photographs outside the church. Frank's father was sober for once, and his old aunts were dressed in pastel shades. The reception was to be at the Hall and it was obvious to Blake that the place had been what Rose called 'turned out'. It was in all its shabby magnificence a wonderful house. The old furniture was polished to a high shine, the big dining room with its stained-glass windows let coloured sunbeams on to the polished floor. The long tables were covered in white cloths. Rose and the girls had been baking and cooking and there were big sides of beef and ham and pork, pies and tarts and puddings. Blackberries had been garnered from the hedgerows and mushrooms from the fields. There were dishes of yellow butter and great jugs of cream and Mr Harlington had raided his cellar for champagne and good claret and brandy. Blake wished Sylvester could have been there.

From that room there was the view over the valley, the village with its stone houses, the bridge, the church, the pub, the churchyard, the school, the fields, the farms, the bottom road and the river.

Blake found Annie beside the window and said in her ear, 'I want to talk to you.'

She jumped and turned and looked nervously into his eyes.

'Yes,' she said, smiling, and then Alistair came over. Blake frowned at him. Couldn't he give them five minutes together?

There were more photographs in the gardens and then they all sat down to eat and Blake was not near Annie so that he couldn't talk to her; she was being polite to Frank's aunts and Mr Harlington, who to Blake's great surprise still wasn't drunk, having dispensed champagne with a generous hand to all his guests and then abstained on the grounds that he didn't like the stuff. Blake didn't care much for it either, it was too insubstantial somehow and the bubbles got in the way.

Later, Madge and Frank having been waved away to begin their journey to London, the Lowes and their friends drifted back to the farm where Rose made tea and sandwiches. Blake was surprised to find that he could be hungry again. There was plenty of conversation and Tommy's friends from the silver band entertained in the garden though it was a little crowded by the time they were all outside. In the parlour Annie seemed somehow to linger with Alistair Vane and there came a coldness on Blake, watching them. He recognised it from way back when his grandfather and grandmother had died and he had lost the farm. People talked to him. He tried to make sense of what they were saying. They were eating and drinking again but Blake had had enough alcohol and more than enough food and wanted nothing.

Later still when the silver band had gone home and the evening was filled with peace and most people had gone, Blake stood by the sundial in the garden. The leaves on the trees were going yellow, the grass was rough, the sun had gone and a cold wind picked up the few leaves on the path and played with them. It grew dark; the cream light spilled across the front of the house and left the garden in shadow.

'Blake . . .'

He had known she was there even before she said his name and even though he was turned the other way. He had heard the rustle of her lovely dress.

'I wanted to explain to you—'

'There's no need. I already know.'

He didn't even turn around. Her presence made no difference to the truth and nothing mattered now. Before when things had gone wrong, even when he thought that he had lost everything, there had still been in him some kind of hope, some resilience which told him that he would be happy again, that he would recover, there was always something at the back of his mind that carried him through, a knowledge that the best of his life had not happened, but he didn't have that any more. He would never wake up in the morning again and know that the best thing in his life was still there. He knew now that was what had carried him through the difficult times in Sunderland, that he had left and gone through it all for her and now it had all been for nothing.

'How could you know?'

Blake shrugged.

'You didn't write to me, you didn't come to meet me at the station, you didn't come to me when I walked into the house. I should have known then. Of course I did know really. You told me before I went away that you would marry somebody else. You are going to marry him?'

'Yes.' It was almost a sob.

Blake turned reluctantly and looked at her. She was so beautiful. She was not his, she was never going to be his and there was a part of him which had always known it. How could he ever have imagined otherwise? He could see now – how could he not have noticed before? – that she had a ring on her finger. It matched the stars which were even now beginning to glow faintly above them, the cold diamond on her left hand. It was like a perfect chip of ice, the dew under the horses' hooves, the rain caught on a branch.

'Happy families?' Blake said. 'Mrs Vane, the farmer's wife?'

'It wasn't like that. I know I said that things like that mattered but it wasn't like that in the end.'

Blake thought about telling her about his job but there was no point now. He had let them go on thinking he was nothing more than a clerk, firstly because he wasn't sure that he would ever make an engineer and then because he wanted it to be a surprise. And even then he had hesitated. The future was always so uncertain. Now it wouldn't even make ammunition.

'So you fell passionately in love with Alistair Vane? I don't believe it.'

'He's not like you think he is.'

'Isn't he? Then how is he? He's rich, of course. He has a big farm, a herd of fine cattle and hundreds of acres. Is that what you gave me up for, a paltry place in this godforsaken hole and some cows? Do you know that there is a world out there where the dale ends? This is not a heaven.'

'I know that.'

'Do you? You're going to be gaoled here now for the rest of your life.'

Annie glared at him.

'I love him!' she declared.

'No, you don't. You don't love him—'

'You weren't here,' she said loudly. 'You weren't here and everything got changed around in my mind.'

'Is that right? Or was it just that you got bored with Paul Monmouth and his serviettes?'

'I hate the way you say things!'

'Why didn't you wait? I was going to come back here and ask you to marry me—'

'I couldn't help it.'

'You could help it with me though, couldn't you? Because I'm not a Vane, because I don't have a great big farm and a car and people to fawn on me.'

'That's not true—'

'Why couldn't you wait?'

'I was tired of waiting,' Annie said in a low voice. 'I love Alistair.'

'No!' Blake got hold of her and shook her. 'You can't love him. You love me.'

'No, I don't. Let go of me. Let go!'

Blake did and she fell back.

Jack stepped into the garden, closely followed by a rather worse-for-drink Tommy.

'What is all the noise?' he said.

'Nothing. It's nothing,' Blake said. 'It's finished now.'

'You've made Annie cry,' Jack said, scrutinising his daughter's face.

'I'm sorry, I didn't mean to.'

'They're getting married at Christmas,' Tommy said triumphantly and Annie turned and lifted her long skirts and ran back into the house. 'You didn't really think she was going to marry you?'

'That's enough, Tommy,' Jack said and he looked kindly at Blake.

'You should be pleased. One daughter married well and another about to,' Blake said.

'I am pleased.'

'Good name, good family—'

Tommy laughed.

'I don't know that I'd want to put up with Alistair's father though he does have his good points.'

'Does he?' Blake said. 'I never noticed.'

'Tommy, have you thought about giving your brain a rest and going to bed?' his father suggested.

'He's giving them Sunniside as a wedding present.'

'Sunniside?'

'Frank's father sold it. He needs the money and they need somewhere to live. The Austins moved out a while back. Didn't you know?'

Nobody spoke. Jack looked down. Tommy glanced first at one and then at the other.

'Go to bed, Tommy,' his father said softly.

'He had to know, didn't he? It isn't a secret. Charlie Vane's not a bad man, he's just a bit sharp sometimes, that's all.'

'Go to bed.'

Tommy stared at his father for a few seconds and then he went. Jack looked steadily at Blake.

'I'm sorry.'

'Sorry? Why should you be sorry?'

'About the – about the farm.'

'It's all right. It doesn't matter to me any more. It's just a little hillfarm. It was never mine.'

Blake went to bed. Jack went off to the kitchen where Rose was alone finishing the last of the clearing up. He only had to look at her.

'Does Blake know?'

'Yes.'

'All of it?'

'Most of it.'

Rose put up her chin.

'She's made a good choice. Alistair's a fine young man and Sunniside will be a pretty place for them to live. What a day.' She went over and kissed him. 'I know Frank wasn't what we wanted for Madge but I have a feeling things will turn out well. She's so happy and if his father doesn't go and drink everything away they should be all right.'

'He behaved very well today and the Hall looked wonderful, thanks to you.'

'Madge will make a very good mistress for the Hall and if Mr Harlington can stay sober he might even live to see his grandchildren,' Rose said and they put out the lights and went upstairs to bed.

Fourteen

Alistair's father had not wanted them to get married. It had made Annie all the more determined. In her presence he had shouted and called her 'the bloody dairymaid' and said that she was common and beneath them. Alistair had said nothing. He had learned over the years that shouting back only made things worse and Annie wondered if one of the reasons why he wanted to marry her was because he had known that his father would object. She did wonder at first how she would ever learn to live with Charles Vane when he was her father-in-law. Was he going to go on as though she was the muck behind the tractor and he was some lord of the earth? For comfort she and Alistair spent a lot of time up at the Hall. She envied Madge her happiness.

The old man had stopped drinking, Madge had hidden the cellar keys with his permission and the Hall was like a different place now. Frank had taught Madge to drive and she taxied his aunties around. She had got them into a bridge club and they went to tea with their newly found friends. She worked hard in the old house and every time Annie went there good smells came from the kitchen. Sometimes Annie went and helped with the housework because there was so much of it and they couldn't afford any help.

Mr Harlington had actually begun to work outside and now rode every morning for hours, greeting tenants he had scarcely seen for years. It was as though a light had fallen on the house.

Frank had gained a first class honours degree that summer and began work, teaching mathematics at the local grammar school. Unlike Charles Vane, Mr Harlington did not think it was beneath his son to work. He said that he was proud of Frank's achievements and glad that he was making his own money. Annie secretly believed that Frank hated having to teach and make money but he was so happy at home and glad he could help that he put up with the teaching job.

She had seen the way Madge ran to the door when she heard his car turn in at the big gates. She would run outside, regardless of the weather, and hurl herself into his arms the moment he got out of the car.

She had told Annie that there were huge debts run up because of the death duties when Frank's grandfather drank himself into an early grave. Annie thought she had never seen people so happy when so financially encumbered.

Annie was excited at the idea of not having to live either with Alistair's parents or her own. She had never imagined that they would have their own house so soon. Alistair's home was modern and elegant but it held no appeal and she had thought that they would live at Western Isle when they were married.

Mr and Mrs Vane had finally accepted that Alistair would marry her and she had tried to think positively about being there but she did not understand how she would ever feel like more than a servant. She would keep edging towards the dairy and worry about the cows and – horrible thought – would they expect her to go on doing such things? Alistair assured her that they wouldn't and he laughed but Annie didn't think any of it was funny.

Some parts were good. He taught her to drive his car and although it wasn't as easy as it looked she soon got the idea and Alistair began to complain because she had his car all the time.

Annie knew that her parents were very pleased about her marriage; her mother was now happy to have daughters married to two of the most eligible men in the dale though she didn't like the Vanes as people.

'You mustn't let him bully you, Annie,' she said though how Annie was to stop Charles Vane from doing to her what he did to everybody was not immediately apparent.

Annie hated going there. Mrs Vane made her feel shabby and if they had tea Annie dropped her teaspoon on the floor or spilt tea into her saucer. Mr Vane made her feel as though she ought to creep back to the dairy and get on with her work. She no longer worked there, she stayed at home and helped her mother and for the first time in her life was grateful for domesticity. Her home had become a refuge. Some days she didn't want to get up at all, just hide under the bedclothes and pretend that she wasn't going to marry Alistair or anybody else.

So the news that his father was buying them the little hillfarm was such a relief that all Annie wanted to do was go up there and claim it as hers.

It was a bright warm day. They had got up early and gone riding together and Alistair had come back to her mother's hearty Sunday breakfast. Sunday had a special feel to it, tranquil and slow. They went to the little village church and there Annie thought about her wedding day and how happy she would be wearing the white dress which her mother had promised her. She would be Mrs

Alistair Vane. She glanced sideways at him while she sang the last hymn; he was so tall and dark beside her and he was hers. She couldn't believe it. She couldn't think now that she had ever cared for Blake. It had been nothing but a childhood thing associated with memories. She thought of Blake teaching her to tickle trout in the summer river, carrying her home when she fell off her horse and hurt her leg. She thought of sitting by the fire with him reading and talking, walking up the fields in the twilight, riding home in the sunset slowly with the dale all around.

She dropped her hymnbook and bit her lip. He was not her farm boy any longer, some tall stranger in a suit with the same grey-blue eyes that Alistair turned on her now as she glanced at him before picking up her hymn-book with trembling hands.

Blake was hurt now, irreparably perhaps, and there was a part of her that had wanted to run after him, shouting.

When the service was over she walked out with Alistair into the fine morning and she knew that she had been right. Her future was here with him and her family. She couldn't leave them and Blake didn't belong here any more, he had no place.

They had their Sunday dinner and then she and Alistair drove most of the way to Sunniside until the track got too bad to take the car and then they left it and walked up the deeply rutted track, opening the gates as they went.

The Austins had, for some reason, not lived there long. The gates were heavy and fastened with string. The fields were neglected and overgrown. There had been no tenant at Sunniside for some time. When they came in sight of the little hillfarm she stopped and looked at it. Blake's family had lived there for generations. His name was all over the churchyard. She thought of seeing Hannah Blake's grave which was politely put away in one corner of the graveyard but it stood out in her mind's eye. Hannah Blake who died at Sunniside, it said.

The small buildings were covered in sunlight. Annie thought of the girl dying there, she had been very young, dying of childbed fever or whatever it was, of having no husband and no future and of the disgrace of expecting a child when she had no man. She thought of Hannah growing Blake inside her, knowing how the people of the dale shunned such things. She thought of how Blake had gone away from the dale without saying goodbye to her and she stopped within sight of the house and thought how lucky she was compared to Hannah Blake and whether this had been a mistake. Alistair stopped too.

'It's a long pull up the hill,' he said. 'I'm going to have something done about that road. It's no good if we can't bring cars up.'

The little house was empty in a certain way, it was more than just vacant. There were ashes in the grate. Annie didn't think much of Mrs Austin's housekeeping. Blake's grandmother would have had a spotless house. The rooms were covered in dust, the windows were thick with cobwebs and streaked with rain. The garden beside the house where Blake's grandfather had grown produce was covered in weeds and out the back she found Bessie's grave with a small stone marker and her name scratched on it.

'Too many memories?' Alistair said, coming up behind her.

She smiled brightly at him.

'I was never here,' she said.

'Neither was I. I don't think Blake ever had any friends.'

'He was always working,' Annie said.

'Annie . . .'

'What?'

He looked straight at her and then hesitated. 'Nothing.'

'Don't say nothing like that. Tell me.'

'You don't regret it, do you, saying you'd marry me?'

Annie felt such a rush of love for him that she laughed.

'Of course I regret it, you're so little and ugly and simple-minded and impossible—'

He grabbed her and kissed her. Alistair Vane's kisses were, Annie always thought, one of the reasons why God had created the world, they were so essentially wonderful.

'But really, Annie,' he insisted.

'Really, I love you so much I think I'm probably going to die from being so happy.'

They pulled the insides out of the little house. It made Alistair shudder to think of it. The workmen trod all over the garden and broke a branch off one of the fruit trees so that he had to go around anxiously preventing more damage, sectioning off Bessie's grave and the other trees. He didn't say anything to Annie because for once she and his father were in agreement: the house must be brought up to date. Alistair thought of Western Isle and determined not to let that happen here.

There was a generator for the electricity, a new Rayburn was put into the kitchen. The old fireplaces were ripped out, the floors were pulled up and relaid. The walls were replastered. There was a brand-new bathroom made by breaking in two the room where Alistair felt sure Blake had been born and Hannah had probably died.

The rooms were redecorated until there were more flowers inside the house than there could have been outside in the last hundred years. A bright new tiled fireplace gleamed in the little parlour.

Alistair decided that he'd had enough when she wanted in the house the kind of comfortless angled furniture he had at home. She was just like his father, she had no eye at all.

'But Western Isle is like that,' Annie said.

'I know it is.'

They went out and bought a few good pieces of oak furniture.

'I think you have taste,' she admitted as they surveyed the big bedroom.

'It's more than could be said of some of us.'

Annie pretended to hit him and he gathered her into his arms and kissed her all over her neck.

'Want to try the bed?'

'No, I don't.'

But he picked her up and carried her the few steps to it and put her down there without letting go and he pressed on her the kind of kisses which he knew Annie couldn't say no to. She dragged her mouth free eventually and he stopped and released her.

'I love you,' he told her. 'I think I've loved you all my life.'

'As long as you love me all the rest of your life that's what I care for.'

'I will,' he said.

Fifteen

The Sunday that Blake was not there it rained in Sunderland. Irene minded the rain. She minded everything when he was not there. She wished that she could have feigned an illness and stayed in bed but her father would have had none of that so she got up as usual and helped with the Sunday dinner, went to church with her father in the morning and went on as though nothing was the matter when in fact everything was.

Irene had spent a lot of time denying to herself that she liked Blake as anything more than a friend. She knew very well that he was not the kind of person her father would have wanted her to care for. She was not surprised that her father encouraged him to come to the house because from time to time he had taken to unsuitable people and encouraged them. He would not have thought that there was anything about Blake which attracted her.

In the first place he had no money, in the second he had no background of any kind. He had a rough accent, his clothes were worn, his manners were just average, he had no address and no confidence. He had looks of course but her father would not see that or the indefinable something which women liked. She did not think her father acknowledged that such things went on, not since her mother had died.

The trouble was that Blake had got better right from the start because he was intelligent. He learned quickly and not just work but how to dress neatly and modestly, how to talk to her father (and thereafter other people) and from being in their house he had learned about food and drink, manners and clothes, about books and newspapers and music and art, and there were some things he didn't have to learn, his dark eyes, his smile and his bearing did the rest for him. She knew that her father had watched Blake improve and was glad with his progress, pleased that he had helped and happy to find somebody who would be what Simon would not be, willing to learn and to take part both at home and at the shipyard. Blake was the son that Sylvester wanted, she thought, though he would not have believed that. She also knew how fond of her father Blake had become. Her father did not see that she yearned for Blake's company and she rather hoped that Blake could not see it, especially now when he had gone home to ask the girl to marry him. She knew that he had, just by the look on his face. She had cried a lot that week though late and privately. To her father Blake was nothing more than a family friend, somebody to be entertaining on Sundays and to be relied on at work. He liked Blake's influence on Simon because he rarely drank and never to excess and he seemed capable of keeping Simon out of trouble.

That Sunday Robert came to lunch and the rain stopped so that during the afternoon they went out into the garden. Robert was in a particularly good mood and chatted easily. She was glad he was there because Blake left such a space to her and she chatted back and comforted herself that next Sunday he would be there. Her father stayed inside and Simon had gone she didn't know where.

'I'd like to talk to you, Irene,' Robert said.

'I thought we were talking.' She smiled at him. The garden was lovely in autumn with its leaves all turning different colours. There had been a frost the night before and the grass was still wet, showing like diamonds in the afternoon sunshine. She liked autumn best, the idea of fires and dark nights and Christmas. She thought of Christmas Day, the big tree in the hall, sitting down at the table with her father and Simon and Blake—

'Particularly,' Robert was saying. 'I don't see you alone often. I think you already know what I want to say. I've mentioned it to your father and he laughed at me for being formal but I wanted it that way. I want you to marry me, Irene. I love you and I think you'll make me the perfect wife.'

Irene stared at him.

'What?' she said.

Robert looked startled.

'It's a shock to you? I thought you knew how I felt. We've spent so much time together recently. You do feel the same way? You must.'

She had a ridiculous impulse to be like heroines in old-fashioned novels and tell him that it was very sudden except that somehow it wasn't. She had always known that Robert liked her, it was just that when Blake was there he was somehow in shadow and nothing to do with her and she had not wanted to know that Robert had a particular regard for her since she could not care for him.

'No,' she said.

Robert gave a half-smile.

'But you do feel something for me, I know you do. I wouldn't have spent so much time here if I had thought any different. I know you like me and we have so much in common. You enjoy my company and I have such a lot to offer you, everything, Irene. Shall we go and tell your father that we're engaged and go on from there and get to know one another a little better and then—?'

'Robert, I couldn't,' she said.

He frowned and she saw that it was impossible for him to imagine that she had no regard for him. How could she not? He was tall and good-looking and well-connected. He had brains and money and a good family. He was charming and competent and a dozen girls she knew would have given anything to have landed him, girls who were beautiful and accomplished and agreeable.

'You couldn't? What kind of an answer is that?'

'Robert, I like you very well, you know that I do, as a friend. I could never think of you as anything else.'

He didn't say anything for a moment or two and she wished that they were not quite so alone in the garden; it was awkward.

'I don't understand this,' he said. 'Are you telling me that you didn't encourage me?'

'I didn't know that I had.'

'Your father knows it and so does your brother. How is it that you claim not to?'

'I'm sorry. I didn't intend to make you angry.'

'Perhaps there's someone else?' Robert said stiffly.

Irene thought of how warmly Blake had spoken of

the girl he was going back to and how much she had been hurt and she shook her head.

'There's nobody,' she said.

Robert's eyes had taken on a rather ugly hard stare.

'It's David Blake,' he said.

'David is engaged to be married,' Irene said. This was embroidery, she knew, but by now it would be true. 'He's had the same girl since they were children together. He comes here because my father enjoys his company. It doesn't have to be someone else just because I don't care about you, does it?'

'What other reason could you have?'

'I'm quite happy with my life as it is.'

'Every woman wants a husband.'

'A husband like you?' Irene said scornfully and she ran back into the house and up the stairs and stayed there until teatime.

When she came down her father called her into the drawing room and by his face she knew that Robert had told him what had happened.

'I'm very disappointed in you,' he said. 'I understand that you turned young Denham down.'

'Whatever made you think that I wanted to marry him?'

'He's a nice enough lad for a lawyer, he thinks a lot

about you and you seem to like him well enough. Or is there another reason?'

'I don't understand. I do like him. That doesn't mean to say that I want to marry him.'

'He thinks that young David is the cause of this.'

'Nothing of the kind. David has gone home to ask his girl to marry him.'

'Has he indeed? I knew nothing about it. It seems to me that you've grown very fond of him.'

'I'm not especially fond of him,' Irene lied. 'I like them both but I don't like anyone sufficiently to marry him. Are you wanting to be rid of me?'

'I want to see you happy, established. If you didn't like Robert Denham why keep him hanging around like that? It doesn't seem a very kind thing to do.'

'I didn't realise—'

'And what did you think he came here for, the exercise?'

Irene was astonished at her father's anger. Had he really expected her to say yes? He looked so disappointed.

'What else do you intend doing with your life?' he asked her roughly.

Irene hadn't thought about that.

'I'm quite happy here with you and Simon, running the house. Don't you want me to do that? I've done it ever since mother died. I—'

'I can get a housekeeper to do that.'

Irene said nothing more for a few moments and then, 'I can go out and find some work—'

'Women of your calibre don't work, Irene. They marry and have children, that's what they do best. Young Denham is perfect for you. I can't imagine why you turned him down. I can't imagine what you were thinking of,' and her father walked out of the room and left her there.

On Tuesday Irene went shopping in the town and she thought that she saw Blake from a distance. She ran across the road and followed him around a corner and was sure that it was him. She ran on and caught up and then, a little breathless, she grabbed him by the arm so that he stopped.

'I thought you were away for a week,' she said.

Blake stopped and when he looked at her Irene realised immediately that something was very wrong though she was not quite sure what betrayed him. He was like someone who had been laid low with bad flu and was just out of bed, pale and dull-eyed and slow.

'I came back,' he said unnecessarily.

'You don't look well. What is the matter?'

'My lodging is just around the corner. I have to go.'

'I'll go with you.'

'No.'

'David, you look awful. Let me come with you.'

He didn't argue but she wasn't glad that she had gone. She hadn't realised that he lived in such a place. It wasn't the worst area of town, it had a kind of desperate respectability. The house was brown inside and the sitting room where he took her burned a meagre fire, had grey curtains and linoleum and dusty plants and dark pictures. It made Irene want to run back out into the street. She tried not to think what his room was like. The fire smoked and the day beyond the window was dull and she had never been in such a cheerless room in her life.

'I think you should be in bed,' she said.

'There's nothing the matter with me. Would you like some tea?'

'No. No, thank you. Come home with me and we'll have supper.'

He refused at first but Irene persuaded him. Her father was just coming back from work when they arrived and for the first time ever her father frowned darkly when he saw Blake and Irene knew that she had made an important error. Irene worked hard at conversation but only Simon helped and when Blake left as soon as he could after the meal she saw him down the path and grabbed his arm and said, 'I wish you would tell me what happened.'

'There's nothing to tell. Go in, you'll get soaked.'

It was raining hard now.

'I know that something has happened. Is it your family?'

'It's nothing.'

'David, I'm your friend. You can tell me.'

'If you don't go in your father will do more than scowl at me. Go on,' and Blake pushed her gently towards the door and strode off into the evening so that she had no choice but to go inside. Her father was shouting to her from the study and when she went in he was standing there in front of a blazing fire. Irene could not help noticing as though for the first time the leatherbound books, the oak desk, the thick velvet curtains. It looked so rich compared to the room that Blake had invited her into earlier that day.

'I don't want that young man here any more,' her father said, 'and you are not to see him again.'

'But—'

'I don't want to hear an argument about it, Irene. If you disobey me I shall send you to stay with your aunt.'

Her aunt had a school in Newcastle. It was not a

prospect that anyone of sensibility could look forward to with pleasure, Irene thought.

'What is he to think?'

'I don't care what he thinks,' her father said. 'Now go to bed.'

The following afternoon she went again to his lodging and this time was ushered upstairs by the woman who helped his landlady.

It was the barest room that Irene had ever seen, nothing but a bed, a chair and a small cupboard. The window frame was rotten, the window overlooked a yard and other buildings and it was dark. It was bitterly cold too and foisty-smelling as though there had never been a fire anywhere near it. He had been sitting on the bed, reading, but got up as she opened the door and said as soon as the woman had gone, 'You shouldn't be here.'

'Why shouldn't I?'

'If Mrs Southwark comes back I'll be thrown out for having you in my room.'

'I don't think that would be such a great loss,' Irene said, looking distastefully around her.

'No, of course it wouldn't be to you.'

'Can't you really afford anything better than this?'

'I was saving my money.'

'You don't look any better.'

'Irene, do you know a polite way to tell a young woman to mind her own business?'

'How was the wedding?' Irene sat down in the one chair and almost got back up again immediately, it was so uncomfortable. She wondered how the bed was and then blushed at herself.

'None of it is anything to do with you and if your father finds out you were here I'll be out of a job.'

'Your job and your room. Dear me, what havoc.' Irene went on looking at him and then plunged on because she had done a lot of thinking since the day before. 'She's not going to marry you, is she, the girl you wanted?'

He wandered around the room like somebody penniless at a fair and then he said, 'It was nothing new. She told me before I left that she wouldn't.'

'And you thought you could make her change her mind.'

'I thought she cared for me. I thought she would wait. I have a job now. I don't know why I thought it, it was stupid. I have nothing to give anybody, as you can see.'

'But you will have if you go on working like you have done. My father speaks very highly of you. He doesn't do that of just anybody. I've heard him say that you'll do very well, you just need a little time to learn and to work.'

'I don't have any time. She's engaged to somebody else. They're planning to be married at Christmas and her parents are pleased. His family have money. They've bought them a small farm.'

'I'm sorry.'

He smiled at her. Irene wanted to take him into her arms but didn't know how.

'I'll be all right,' he said. 'Irene, you really must go, your father wouldn't like you being here, you know he wouldn't.'

'He wouldn't like you being here either if he could see the place.'

Blake persuaded her out of the door. Irene hated leaving him there.

Early and late that week Irene went to his lodging but he was never there. It was not until the following Sunday afternoon that she saw him and then he insisted on seeing her outside. It was cold but clear. They went to the park and Irene sat down on a bench there and when he saw that she was going to walk no further he sat down too.

'You've been out all week.'

'I wish you would stop coming to the house,' he said.

'Why?'

'My landlady doesn't like it. I don't want to have to find new lodgings.'

'I never see you.'

'Irene, you're not supposed to see me. What would your father say?'

'He didn't mind all these months when you've been coming to the house.'

'That was different.'

'No, it wasn't.'

He looked at her and Irene looked down.

'That's not true,' he said. 'Your father doesn't want me there any more. What's happened?'

'I refused to marry Robert Denham.'

'Why?'

'Because I don't care about him,' Irene said and pulled her hat further down over her eyes.

'Poor Robert.'

'Poor Robert nothing. I didn't realise he was so arrogant and conceited. He thought all he had to do was ask. He's never taken me anywhere, he's never even sent me a bunch of flowers. What does he think I am, a piece of furniture?'

Blake said nothing. Irene looked at him.

'Did you assume that she was going to, whatever her name is?'

'I suppose I just wanted her so badly.'

'That's not fair either, you know, to assume that a woman wants you.'

'I thought she loved me.'

'Well, she obviously doesn't, does she?'

'No, she doesn't.'

'Oh, David, I'm sorry.' Irene forgot that she was in public and put her arms around him and to her delight he held her there but only for a few moments.

'Don't be sorry. It'll be all right,' he said. 'You must go home now.'

That evening her father called her into his study and there was a look on his face which Irene had never seen before.

'So,' he said, 'there was a good reason why you didn't want to marry young Denham. Why didn't you tell me?'

'Tell you what?'

'That you cared for another lad.'

Irene couldn't think what to say or where to look.

'How did you find out?' she said.

'I had a report that you were seen at his lodgings and in the street with him and that you were embracing him in the park this afternoon. Such a lack of taste, my dear.'

'Oh, that,' Irene said.

'It is true?'

'Yes, it's true. I care for him very much but he doesn't care for me. He went home to marry his girl and she's become engaged to someone else. That was comfort this afternoon, not passion.'

'How could you learn to care for a man like that?'

'Do you mean because he's poor?'

'He's a working-class nobody, Irene.'

'How strange, I thought you had some regard for him yourself.'

'That was before I learned that he wanted my money.'

'Your money?'

'You said yourself that he cared nothing for you but he has a good deal to gain by the connection, has he not, now that he knows of your regard?'

Irene sunk her pride.

'He knew about my feelings for him long before and did nothing.'

'Did you tell him?'

'I didn't need to tell him,' Irene said.

Sixteen

When Blake went into work the following day he was dismissed. He was given the money owed to him and thrown out and not just metaphorically, two burly men were there to see him off the premises and into the street, bruised and knocked and left lying in the dust, and it mattered. It was not just the money, it was not just the work, it was not just the place or the not knowing what to do next, it was not even just Simon and Irene. Most of all it was Sylvester Richmond who mattered. It proved to Blake that the man who meant so much to him had never cared for him but only treated him as light entertainment for Sundays and for a workman who was worth nothing. And suddenly all the anger which had not been given room over the years found it – against the Harlingtons for putting him off the farm, against Charles Vane for denying him a name and a family and a home, against the

Lowes for him not marrying Annie and against Sylvester Richmond for trying to take away the future. The anger filled Blake and ousted every other feeling. He swore to have revenge against them all, to give them back what they had done to him, to make them aware, to make them sorry. He lay there momentarily outside Richmond and Dixon's front gates and promised himself to have his day with them all.

He didn't know what to do after that. He looked for work but so did hundreds of other people and when the interested ones could not be provided with any reference they lost interest and Blake had nowhere to go. He saw Simon in the street that first week. Simon looked as if he would have given much to have avoided the meeting but they came face to face on an empty pavement one evening and Simon hesitated, looked embarrassed and finally stopped.

'I'm sorry,' he said.

'What did I do?' Blake demanded.

'You made up to my sister.'

'I did nothing of the bloody kind.'

'Yes, you did. You were seen with her, at your lodgings, in the street, kissing her in the park.'

'I don't care anything for your sister and she knows it.'

'My father thinks differently.'

'Your father wants to think differently,' Blake said from between his teeth.

'Then you should do better than to kiss her in public.'

'I didn't kiss her. Did he really think that I would go behind his back? He doesn't think much of me, does he?'

'No, he doesn't. Why should he?'

'Because he knows me quite well by now. I thought that would have been sufficient.'

'My father gave you a leg up when you needed one. He doesn't owe you anything.'

'He owes me common courtesy and the right to explain myself before he kicks me out.'

'You're not going to get that.'

'You tell him then that if he thinks he can do this to me and get away with it he's wrong—'

Simon laughed. 'Don't be stupid, there's nothing you can do.'

'You just wait,' Blake said and he walked past Simon and went on up the road.

After two weeks Blake hadn't found any work. The money he had saved was coming in handy after all, he thought ruefully. He was sitting in his room reading one evening when Mrs Southwark came up and sniffily told him that there was a man in the front hall asking for him. Blake went down and saw the tall figure of Ralph standing there.

'Get your things,' he said, 'you're coming home with me.'

'Ralph—'

'Don't waste your breath arguing. I was told not to go back without you and I won't. Howay then.'

There wasn't much to take, just his clothes and a few books.

He paid Mrs Southwark what he owed her and heard her complaining from her front door all the way down the misty street.

When he reached their house he stepped up into Mary Ann's kitchen and there she was, smiling, and there was also the most wonderful smell of beef stew.

'There you are,' she said, coming forward and taking him into her arms and all the hurt and resentment and loneliness dissolved. Blake gave in and buried his face against her.

'Oh, Mary Ann,' he said, 'I've made such a mess of things.'

Mary Ann held him close.

'Never fret, my precious,' she said. 'Folk always do sooner or later. You're not alone.'

She fed Blake one of the best meals of his life and

sent him to bed and he slept well into the next day. After that Ralph provided him with the appropriate clothes and took him to the pit and they set him to work.

It was such a surprise to Blake, not just because he had been using his head and not his body for so long but because even when he had done farmwork from dawn to dark and beyond it was not as hard as this. Nothing, he concluded, could ever be as hard as this.

The pit was a shock: the Hutton Seam, three or four miles in with poor roadways, the air hot, stifling and bad, the dust a fine film two or three inches thick, like walking on a carpet of it, the small oil lamps getting lower and lower as the lack of air became worse. The seam was three feet high; men lay at full stretch in the darkness.

At first all he could see was shadows and all that could be seen of the men for dust and sweat was the whites of their eyes.

It was weeks and weeks before he got used to it but there were compensations. For a start there was the kind of comradeship which Blake had never met before. They didn't seem to care that he was an outsider with a different accent. When he worked in such conditions and did his best he was one of them right from the start. The job was too hard to be done without the certainty that every man in the pit was looking after every other man. He soon picked up their language, mostly from his friend, William Bedford, who showed him what to do. Blake soon got to know Will's patient tones when he wasn't getting something right.

'Why, Davy man, what are you doin'?'

'Nowt. What for?'

'Give's it over here, man, and I'll show you. Like this, man, like this.'

Will had called him Davy from the first and Blake didn't like to correct him. It reminded him of his grandparents and how happy he had been then.

There was always comfort too because at the end of the shift no matter when it was Mary Ann was there. The food was good and plentiful, the house was shining clean, the clothes were washed and ironed, the water was hot and ready and she was kind and welcoming and these things made the work bearable. In some ways life was easier than it had been at the shipyard because he had never gone home to a woman then, he had not realised the value of marriage. He began to make good money too and tipped it up fortnightly to Mary Ann even though she objected and told him that she didn't need it all and insisted on giving him a fair proportion back.

'Keep some. Save,' she said.

'Later. I want you to have it now. If it hadn't been for you and Ralph I don't know what I would have done.'

'One of these days you'll want a wife and then you'll need your money.'

'I don't want a wife.'

'Get away. A bonny lad like you. Just give them time, some lass'll have you round her little finger.'

Blake tried not to think about Annie. He thought that Ralph and Mary Ann must have known something of what had happened because they did not mention her in his presence. There seemed no chance now that he would ever have the kind of job which would make him respectable to her and in any case it didn't matter. She claimed to love Alistair Vane and they were soon to be married. Blake wasn't looking forward to Christmas.

One Saturday night late that autumn when Blake had made a rare trip into Sunderland with several other pit lads he saw Simon in one of the pubs. Simon had obviously had a few drinks by then. He came over and clapped Blake on the back and offered to buy him a drink and the others sat him down and welcomed him. In company Blake was determined to be polite and asked after his father and then Irene.

'My father's fine. He and Irene quarrelled. Didn't you

know? I suppose you wouldn't. He sent her to live with my Aunt Martin.' Simon pulled a face.

'Put her out?'

'Might as well have done. Aunt Martin's a witch. Runs a school up in Newcastle.'

'What would Irene do there?'

'I don't know. Behave herself I imagine. He wasn't very pleased with her about you.'

'She didn't do anything.'

'Well, you would say that, wouldn't you?' Simon grinned.

'How could your father do that?'

'I expect he doesn't like deceit. So you're a pitman now, are you? How are the mighty fallen?'

Next to Blake was Will.

'I think he's drunk,' he observed.

'You're a shrewd judge of men, Will,' Blake said, putting an arm around his shoulders.

Blake thought a lot about Irene after that night. He could not imagine that she had been sent away. He thought of her unhappy and when he saw Simon again, which he did just before Christmas, he asked for the aunt's address. It was not that he intended doing anything about it, he just wanted to know. He was having enough trouble with women as it was. The pit lasses knew by now that he was not married and everywhere Blake went, from church to the town, they were there and he wanted nothing to do with any of them.

Mary Ann tried in vain to get him interested. She invited various ones to tea even though he begged her not to. To him they were all just not Annie and to his surprise they were also not Irene.

He thought of her dressed in fine clothes, running down the stairs, sitting with him in the garden. He thought of her pretty hats and her soft hands, of her playing the piano and reading books and supervising the servants in her father's house and he wondered what kind of a place she had gone to and he thought that it could not be so very bad. Perhaps by now she had changed her mind and agreed to marry Robert Denham or some gentleman like him. It was more than likely. Irene was the ideal gentleman's wife. She knew how to hire servants and order dinner, he thought, smiling. And then he wondered what kind of a woman her aunt was and whether she had made many friends and he convinced himself that she was perfectly happy. She would probably be better off away from her father. He thought of her dancing at parties with men who knew about musical evenings and supper and things like that. Irene was probably having a wonderful time.

Simon seemed disinclined to give Blake his sister's address so Blake took him up a back alley by his shirt-front and convinced him that it wasn't worth what Will called 'a good clout in the gob'.

'Learn to fight down the pit, did you?' Simon sneered.

'Want to find out?' Blake shoved him back hard against the wall and banged his head off it. 'I thought you were going to be a soldier. Don't you know how to use your fists?'

'I'm a gentleman. I wouldn't dirty my hands on you.'

'Have you heard from Irene?'

'I don't write to her.'

'Well, that's nice.'

'She's only a woman.'

'You lump of horseshit,' Blake said.

'My father didn't send her there to have a good time.'

'Like that, is it? The address?'

When Simon didn't answer Blake hauled him away from the wall and pulled back a bunched hand and Simon told him what he wanted to know. Just for plain satisfaction Blake got him down in the back lane and pushed his face into a big dirty puddle and he told Simon that muck always finds its own level.

Seventeen

Irene's Aunt Martin had never married. There were tall tales at the school that Aunt Martin's fiancé had been killed in the Great War and that she was one of the two million women who couldn't find a husband.

Irene was secretly convinced that even if there had been a surplus of men when Aunt Martin was young she would still have had problems. She must have been pretty once but it was gone now. She was a tiny thin-figured woman with a sharp red face, a small mouth and lank grey hair. When Aunt Martin was amused, which was not often, she uttered a high pitched noise which turned her face purple. Aunt Martin had a temper so fearsome that Irene shuddered at the idea of going to stay with her even for a short while.

During and after the fight with her father Irene had wondered through tears whether there was somewhere else she could go and finally came to the conclusion that she was ill-equipped to go alone into the world. All she had that belonged to her were her clothes, her books and a string of pearls which had been her mother's. This made her feel so frightened that she went to her Aunt Martin's but she was resolved to stay there no longer than she had to.

Aunt Martin was not one of those clever women who used their brains and did not have time or desire for marriage. Her school had been born of necessity because she had no money.

She lived in a drab draughty house in a quiet street on the edge of the city and there she took in boarders. They must have been, Irene thought, the kind of girls whose parents were too busy for them but hadn't enough money to send them anywhere they would be kindly and intelligently taught. Here they spent long hours sewing in silence, being taught manners and plain cooking and a little French and music.

The house was dark and cold and in December icy draughts swept across the brown linoleum in the halls. Aunt Martin greeted Irene in a stuffy little room at the front of the house with the words, 'So, your father wants rid of you? Nice behaviour, miss, for a girl of your breeding. He wrote and told me all about it.'

Irene immediately resolved to leave Aunt Martin's house as soon as possible but that night when she lay in her bed in the tiny room which she had been allotted she didn't see a way out of the situation and that was the hardest thing of all. Aunt Martin would give her no money. She knew nobody here. If she left there was nothing but the streets and it was almost winter. She knew what happened to women who broke the rules. There were poor streets in the East End of Sunderland where the children had no shoes and the women wore filthy tattered clothes. Irene was so frightened by these prospects for her future that she couldn't sleep and overslept the six o'clock bell.

She was told to see to the girls and she did try from that very first day to make their lives more pleasant but it was a hard task considering that her aunt spent as little as possible. The weather was bitterly cold, the fires in the rooms were meagre, Irene was not allowed to go out. She spent her days straining her eyes in the dim light, sewing and trying to correct the girls' mistakes before her aunt should see them.

She forgot what being warm was like, she forgot leisure and good food. Her aunt ate alone in the little front room. She ate with the girls in a room off the kitchen and the food was neither plentiful nor interesting. The tea was invariably lukewarm and Irene had got to the stage where she dared not question anything. At night before she slept she let a picture of David Blake flood her mind and even then she found difficulty in gaining any happiness from it because she knew that he had lost his job. She didn't know where he was or what had happened to him and she knew for certain that he was unhappy because of the girl who would not have him. Irene could not imagine how the girl could not have wanted him – she had wanted nothing in her life as much – and the days and nights dragged more and more slowly. She clung to the idea that her father would send for her before Christmas but he did not. Even though she wrote, asking penitently to come home, there was no reply. She wrote to Simon to see if he could do anything but though she watched from the upstairs window each morning there was never a letter. It was almost as though she didn't exist.

Irene soon realised that there would be no merry-making in her aunt's house. She dreaded the thought of being left there in the echoing darkness with her aunt and the one or two boarders who did not go home.

The festive season was almost there. The shops had in them coloured decorations and the bigger shops had shiny gifts. In the churches people were practising carols.

This was the only time Irene went out, on a Sunday morning to church. She found herself thinking of what last Christmas had been like when she had presided over wonderful meals in her father's house. When every room had roaring fires, when she had a maid to herself, the running of the household, the ordering of delicious food and drink. When she could do almost exactly what she wanted, go out shopping, walk in the parks, read by the fire, have music and conversation and comfort. She thought of Robert Denham and how perhaps she had made a mistake. She even thought of writing to her father and telling him that she had changed her mind and would marry Robert. Not that Robert would have her now but anything, anything at all to get out of this place.

The snow fell beyond her window. She thought of taking walks in the country with the holly berries and the icy ponds. Simon did not write or come to see her. He had been her last hope and even though she wrote again both to her father and to Simon there was no letter from home.

The girls went away, the house was silent, the wind blew down the halls, the trees in the garden were black and bare, the nights were bright with stars, the windows were frosted with patterns.

Two days before Christmas, early in the afternoon,

when she was huddled before a tiny fire with the two girls who were left, trying vainly to cheer them by reading them *A Christmas Carol*, her aunt's little maid, Sally, came up the stairs.

'You've got a visitor,' she said, looking surprised. 'A man.'

Irene stared at her for a few moments. It had to be Simon, she thought in delight.

'A young man?'

Sally blushed.

'Yes,' she said.

It must be Simon. Her heart lifted. She put down the book. Her father had relented and she would go home for Christmas, maybe even for good. She wouldn't have to stay here in this awful cold house with her miserable aunt any longer. She had known in her heart that it would be so and she could go back to Sunderland and there she would be a model daughter. She would never ever defy her father again. She would never leave any more.

She ran out of the room and along the hall. She stopped at the top of the straight flight of stairs. The young man who stood in the hall was not her well-dressed brother and at first she didn't recognise him because he didn't look up. Her heart twisted with hurt. It was a mistake, it was nothing to do with her, it was nothing to do with her father or Simon. She would not go home for Christmas. She would stay here maybe for always. They didn't care about her after all. They had not sent for her, not thought about her even now. They didn't love her.

And then he looked up and even by the ill-light in the hall she could see the straight fair hair. He was wearing a suit and had a cap in his hands and she saw the blue eyes and the tentative smile and the day suddenly took wings.

'David.'

She held herself back. She made herself stay there for seconds and then come slowly down the stairs. She made herself act like a lady. She put out her hand when she reached the bottom of the stairs, hoping that her feelings were not showing on her by now carefully schooled features. She must pretend that she was pleased to see him but not delighted. He must not know that he was her last thought at night and her first in the morning. He must not suspect that she loved him.

'How very nice to see you,' she said as he took her hand. 'What are you doing here?'

'I just wanted to know how you were getting on.'

'I'm very well.' Irene was not deceived. Unless he actually lived somewhere near he could scarcely have been passing her door. She badly wanted to invite him into one of the downstairs rooms and give him tea but she couldn't and as she hesitated he said, 'Will you come out and I'll buy you some tea?'

Her aunt, Irene thought swiftly, was not at home and she had little to lose so she put on her coat and went with him. He took her to what was, she well knew though she had never been to it, the best teashop in town and she was much too polite to suggest to him that it was out of his reach. Instead she revelled in the warmth, the mahogany, the brass, the waitresses in their black and white uniforms, the starched white cloths and the silver cutlery. He didn't look out of place there, he didn't even look nervous. He smiled so well at the waitress that he got everything he wanted instantly and Irene sat back in her chair and thought that he had changed. There was a cool reserve which stilled her lips.

When the sandwiches and scones and cakes and tea arrived she fell on them and only recovered her manners when she saw him watching her curiously from the other side of the table.

'I didn't eat much lunch,' she excused herself.

And then she saw the girl she was in the mirror behind him and knew that he was undeceived. She had lost weight and more than that. She looked down so that whatever he did not perceive he would not read from her eyes.

'I thought you might have gone home for Christmas.'

'So did I. My father hasn't forgiven me.'

'For what?' The words were brutally plain. Irene poured out more tea and didn't answer. 'Irene, what are you doing here?'

'I'm having tea with you.' She bit her lip over the flippant reply and looked carefully at him. 'I can't be long. My aunt mustn't know that I went out. Have a scone.'

'I don't want a scone.'

She put down the plate she had picked up and offered him, and then she said, 'I'm sure you think it's very feeble of me but I don't know what else to do. I have to stay here.'

'Until when?'

'Until my father lets me go home.'

'And then what?'

'I don't know.' Irene thought desperately. She hadn't imagined beyond the desire to go home. Perhaps there would be another man like Robert Denham. Perhaps there would not. Perhaps she would end up like her Aunt Martin, sour and red-faced with a pepperpot by the bed in case some man attacked her.

'Your father has no right to treat you like this.'

Irene managed a smile. 'You're going to go and tell him that, are you?'

'He had me thrown out.'

'Yes, I imagine he did.'

'For nothing.'

'I expect he thought it was something.'

'I'm going to have my day with him.' And that was when Irene understood the difference. Her father could not have called David Blake 'my lad' or 'my boy' any more. He was not.

Suddenly she didn't want her chocolate cake or her tea but neither did she want to leave and go back to her Aunt Martin's. There was nothing else to do. Blake paid the bill and they went out into the cold wet street. They walked in silence; he seemed so tall and so remote that Irene couldn't think of a thing to say and when they were back and standing outside her aunt's front gate her heart twisted for all the things she couldn't tell him.

'I'd like to invite you in,' she said, 'but I can't.'

And then her aunt opened the door and came out into the street.

'And what on earth do you think you're doing, miss?' she said.

'This is David Blake, Aunt. David, my Aunt Martin. David used to work for my father—'

'Yes, I've heard all about him.' She gave Blake a look

that would have felled trees and then turned to Irene. 'Get inside,' she said.

Irene would have gone too, shaking, but a grip descended on her wrist.

'You're not going back in there,' he said.

Her aunt glared. 'I'll call the police,' she said.

'Call them. You have no right to keep Irene here.'

For the first time ever Irene saw her aunt falter.

'David, I have to.'

'No, you don't.'

'I have nowhere else to go.'

'You can come with me.'

'You don't understand—'

'I understand very well. You don't really want to go back in there?'

Irene hesitated.

'Have you left anything of value?'

Irene was already wearing her pearls. She shook her head.

'Come on then.'

It was like a dream. Her aunt stood there, shouting, her face getting redder and redder. He took her by the hand and walked her away and Irene, like someone she wasn't, went with him.

It began to snow. He walked quickly. His hand kept hers warm. She pushed the other into her pocket.

'Where are you taking me?'

'Don't tell me you wanted to stay there? You look ill.'

'I'm not ill. I just hate it but I can't walk out with nowhere to go and I can't stay with you.'

'Don't worry, I'm lodging with friends. They'll have you.'

'David, it isn't respectable.'

'This is the real world now, Irene. It isn't very respectable and it's the only thing you can do. Now come on, I'm getting soaked.'

It was one of the strangest afternoons of Irene's life and parts of it were rather pleasant. They travelled back to Sunderland and Irene was full of cake and tea and warmer than she had been. He looked after her. He held her hand. Nobody had ever looked after her before that. Nobody had ever needed to. She had always had her father's protection, his money, his status, his house. Since leaving there she had felt vulnerable and alone but she didn't feel like that any more, she felt grown-up in a way in which she never had and proud as though David Blake was her young man or even her husband and though he was not there was no harm in a pretence that he did not know about. She thought that other people would think so too and it brought a smile to her cold lips.

They left Sunderland; she felt the wrench, she thought of her father and what he would be doing. She strained her eyes in the station for sight of Simon or anyone she knew. She wished she could even have gone to within a street or so of her home. She had never wanted to be there so badly.

They went on to Seaton Town. Irene had never been there before and was becoming more and more anxious about going there now.

'They live in Seaton? Are they the people you stayed with when you first came here?'

'Yes.'

'Are you working there now?'

'Yes.'

'I thought Ralph worked at a mine.'

'He does.'

They were walking through the snowy streets of the town now. Irene thought that she had never been anywhere more ugly. She wanted to turn and run. The houses, she estimated, were worse than her aunt's for being in dark narrow streets. They looked little and mean. She stopped and he turned impatiently and stopped too.

'Is that what you're doing, working down a mine?'

'I had to do something. There wasn't a lot of choice.'

She was suddenly very tired; the initial excitement had worn off and he walked so fast all the time. She began to wonder if anything could be worse than what she had come from. She knew nothing of miners, only that people considered them a breed alone and maybe not quite human, digging in the earth like moles. Her father despised them for troublemakers and when she looked at Blake now she could see that he was one of them.

'Don't worry,' he said. 'It'll be all right. Are you tired? It's not much further,' and he smiled at her and put her hand through his arm.

She thought of her father and Simon and all the things she had taken for granted in her life and her steps slowed. She thought of this young man whom she thought she had known and now realised she didn't and she was frightened.

He led her down the back street, unmade and muddy, where the houses had outside toilets and tiny yards and about halfway down he stopped and opened a little gate. Up the yard and in by the back door and into the warmth and light. There was the delicious smell of dinner just eaten. The people there, a man and woman, seemed surprised to see her but they were not hostile, in fact they were hospitable as though they had been expecting her.

Mary Ann took her wet coat and urged her near to the fire until Irene was warm enough to move back. They sat her down at the table with them and put good food in front of her and Irene was at once ravenously hungry. Mary Ann refilled her plate as soon as it was empty. She had hot tea and a comfortable seat and later there was a bedroom all to herself on the front so that it overlooked the street. The lights from the other houses beamed companionably as the curtains were closed and although the bedroom was cold the bed itself had been warmed for her. The sheets were fleecy and smelled clean and the bed was a mass of feathers. It was not long before Irene fell into a happy dreamless sleep.

Mary Ann barely allowed the door to close before she said softly, 'What do you mean by bringing that lass here?'

'She had nowhere to go,' Blake said.

'She must have come from somewhere,' Mary Ann said reasonably. Blake smiled at that.

'Her father put her out. She was staying with some old aunt in Newcastle. You should have seen it. I couldn't leave her there.'

'What did her father put her out for?' Ralph said.

'Because she . . . because I . . .' Blake hesitated. 'This isn't going to sound good however I put it.'

'I had a feeling it wasn't.'

'And her a lady,' Mary Ann said. 'Oh, Blake.'

'They wanted her to marry some man she didn't like and when she wouldn't her father got hold of the wrong end of the stick and thought there was something between us.'

'Was it the wrong end of the stick?' Mary Ann said.

Blake looked at her.

'I never cared for anybody but Annie and she wouldn't have me.'

Mary Ann glanced at Ralph and shifted.

'I know,' she said.

'I thought you did but then you took me in and after that I wasn't sure. Irene's nice. I couldn't just leave her. I'll find her somewhere to go; this was just until I could think what to do. I didn't mean to put on you but I couldn't think of anything else.'

'The trouble is that she's a lady,' Mary Ann said.

'I'll pay for her.'

'You already pay enough. Does she have other family?'

'Not that I know of. I can ask her tomorrow.'

He went to bed.

Mary Ann listened to his feet on the steep stairs and then she turned to her husband.

'What do you think, Ralph?' she said.

'I think somebody had better show her how to be a pitman's wife, quick,' Ralph said.

Eighteen

Alistair's father got drunk on their wedding day. Annie was cross, she had wanted it to be perfect and it wasn't. Tommy had quarrelled with Clara and since Clara was her bridesmaid and Tommy was Alistair's best man it didn't help that they weren't speaking. Her other bridesmaids were her sisters and they both looked lovely in dark cream. Annie just hoped that she could be as happy as Frank and Madge so obviously were. She felt so humble starting her married life on a little hillfarm when Madge, her younger sister, had the Hall. Madge was not reticent when it came to talking about how much work there was at the Hall, how you were never done, but Annie did not mistake her sister's complaints for unhappiness. The two old aunts and Mr Harlington smiled all day on Annie's wedding and she knew that the smiles were not for her. Madge was not like her, she was not afraid to be happy for fear of what might happen. Madge loved Frank wholeheartedly whereas Annie was always aware that Blake had taken a small part of her affection.

When she walked down the aisle of the small village church on her father's arm Annie felt so near to everything which mattered, only a breath away from Grayswell and Sunniside. Only two minutes' walk from her beloved river, only five minutes from Western Isle with the village behind her and the hills on either side, the waterfall just beyond. She knew that she would never love anywhere like she loved this place and that in order to survive she needed to be here.

All the family that she loved, all the friends that she had were gathered in the small church where she had been brought for her christening, her confirmation, her first communion. She had played around the churchyard as a child. It felt so right to be married here. She was wonderfully, gloriously happy.

She hadn't been able to resist Frank and Madge's invitation to have her reception at the Hall but she had worked hard so that they would not have to do too much and to her delight the day had a covering of snow, not too much to make the arrival of the guests a problem, just enough so that the photographs would be dramatic and the Hall would look exciting rather than shabby. The sky was a perfect blue. She hugged Madge in the kitchen at the Hall and thanked her and Madge told her not to be silly. Her mother came in and Elsie and even the aunts to help and when Annie looked over the valley and saw the village and the churchyard and the hill she thought that she had never been so happy or so lucky.

Charles Vane did not speak to anyone. He sat and drank and since he had paid for the drink nobody could say anything and Annie knew that he had been more than generous in giving them Sunniside so she kept a smile on her lips and determined that he should not spoil their happiness.

They were going to Blackpool for a week the following day but Annie had not wanted to go and leave her friends that day especially since Mr Harlington had said that they could have a dance in the evening at the Hall.

During the afternoon and early evening the sky changed until it was thick and still and snow began to fall and by the time Alistair suggested that they should go home to Sunniside there was a covering an inch deep.

The little house had looked so welcoming when Annie had last seen it but it was in darkness now except for the snow on its roof and around its buildings. A wind was getting up too and when they were safely inside and

Alistair had put a match to the fires Annie shivered for how cool the little rooms were.

She was not at all afraid about her wedding night. Rose had, very sensibly as usual, Annie thought, smiling, told her.

'Don't expect miracles. The important thing is that you care for each other. Alistair's not very old. He probably doesn't know any more than you do. Bed is something that gets better. Just be kind and it will be all right.'

Her very new husband had turned into somebody she didn't recognise since they had come home. He burned his fingers on a match, dropped the box and scattered the contents all over the kitchen floor and then stood around like somebody very embarrassed. She guessed that his parents hadn't been kind to him about this. His father had probably been awful to him.

Annie wasn't quite sure what to say or do to make things easier. They were so very alone in the house. From the front windows she could pick out other farms across the valley but their nearest neighbour was several fields away. She almost wished now that she had let Alistair make love to her when he had wanted to the last time they were here together. It was strange, she thought, how situations changed. Now they were meant to be close he looked as if he would have been happier running away down the fields.

The snow was getting worse with the wind behind it. She pulled the curtains shut in the sitting room and then turned around to where he was standing in front of the fire.

'We might not get to Blackpool tomorrow, if this keeps going.'

'I'll get you there,' he said.

'Would you like some tea?'

'No, thanks.'

'It would give us something to do.'

He stood for another moment with his back to her and then turned, smiling a little.

'All right,' he said.

Annie went off into the kitchen and he followed her after a moment.

'I didn't think it was going to be like this,' he said. 'I've been waiting for years to have you to myself and now I feel so stupid.'

'Years?' she said.

'For ever.'

'Really, Alistair? You didn't tell me.'

'You didn't want to know. Blake was always in the way.'

Annie went to him and kissed him briefly.

'I never cared for him like I care for you,' she said and he took her into his arms and as he did so the wind fairly screamed around the house.

They drank their tea and sat by the fire until the house had warmed up a bit and then they went to bed. Annie thought it would be uncomfortable and embarrassing and difficult but when he took her into his arms it was as though the little house wrapped itself around them and shut out the sound of the storm and the rest of the world. It was as though the place had come to life again with their lovemaking. She had never slept in a bed with anyone else and Alistair seemed to take up so much space that she couldn't sleep. The room grew alarmingly cool and eventually when he was turned away from her, which she was grateful for because when he was turned towards her she found herself matching her breathing with his, she put an arm around him and cuddled in against his back and that was how finally she went to sleep.

In the night when Annie turned over she thought that she could hear a woman's voice faint from the back door in the kitchen down below.

'Davy. Davy.'

When she awoke Alistair was gone and it was daylight behind the curtains. She got up and went to the window and her heart fell when she saw the snow. It covered everything inches deep and there were great drifts against the barns.

She pulled on a dressing-gown and went downstairs and he was dressed and standing with the back door open and there was a huge drift which overnight had blown in there.

'We're not going to get to Blackpool, are we?'

'Not today,' he said.

'Why don't you come back to bed?'

'I ought to dig us a way out.'

'Whatever for? We've got a mile of track. It would take a week. Come back to bed.'

'I thought you wanted to go to Blackpool.'

Annie started to laugh.

'I don't care about Blackpool but if you don't take me back to bed this minute you'll wish you were there or anywhere else in the world.'

His face was cold but his kisses weren't.

'I didn't like to stay in bed. I wasn't sure whether I'd hurt you and—'

'Alistair, I worship and adore you. How many more times. Please, take me back to bed. I want you.'

It was the best day of Annie's life. They stayed in bed all day, only getting up at teatime when the light was completely gone. They sat by the fire and ate from the supplies which Annie had got in for when they came home. These were mostly tinned or dried but she didn't care.

The snow was so bad that they spent the week at home and it could not have been better. Completely cut off from the world they built a snowman and had a snowball fight and kept the fires burning brightly so that the little house would be thoroughly warm. By the end of the week Annie thought that she was twice as much in love as she had been when they were married. She had got this right. Alistair Vane was kind and unselfish. He made her feel as though she was the only person or thing in the world that mattered to him, he made her feel so womanly, so vital and free. She discovered the freedom of being able to grab somebody any time she liked and not be rejected, to know that he didn't have moods but was always ready for a game or laughter or comfort and he knew how she wanted to be loved, when to insist and when to let go and he made the magic. Love, Annie thought, had turned her world around.

At the beginning of the following week when he had to go back to work the snow was not so bad, so he had no excuse but he went late and came back early. Annie spent all day firstly struggling with the shopping and then cooking but they didn't eat. When he came home they went to bed.

Lying in his arms in the middle of the evening Annie said, 'I don't think I could have done this in your parents' house.'

'What, gone to bed at teatime? It would have looked a bit odd.'

'No, I mean gone to bed with you at all.'

'My father would probably have come into the bedroom and told me I was getting it all wrong.'

Annie laughed.

'I don't understand why you're so unlike him. You're intelligent and sensitive and kind and softly spoken—'

'This couldn't be prejudice, could it?'

'You know, Alistair, we don't have to stay here if you don't want to.'

'I thought you loved the dale.'

'I love you.'

'But you do want to stay. Besides, I wouldn't let him win.'

'What do you mean?'

'One day Western Isle is going to be again the kind of place that it should be with people who care for it properly. It's mine and I'm going to have it.'

'P'raps not that sensitive,' Annie said.

Alistair grinned.

'Maybe not,' he said.

Nineteen

When Irene awoke her first morning in Seaton Town she did not even imagine that she was at her aunt's, she was too comfortable for that. She remembered that it was Sunday, she remembered that it was Christmas Eve. She turned over, luxuriating in the warmth of her bed, and then she realised that she was in the pitman's house and she opened her eyes and got hastily out of bed.

The kettle was singing by the time she made her way down the treacherously steep stairs. Mary Ann turned smiling from the fire. Irene didn't know what to say.

'I'm sorry to have put you to such trouble and at Christmas too.'

A polite woman would have said that it was no trouble, leaving Irene feeling no better, but Mary Ann came over and said, 'You need a cup of tea, lass. Sit yourself down and don't fret.'

When the tea was poured Mary Ann sat with her.

'Now,' she said, 'they're both out. I want you to tell me what happened.'

'There isn't much to tell. My father wanted me to marry Robert Denham and I didn't want to. He took it for granted that I would and he became very upset about it when I refused.'

'Why didn't you want to wed him?'

'He's very nice of course but . . .'

'He wasn't as nice as a certain pit lad we won't name.'

Irene blushed but she said stoutly, 'David's not a pit lad.'

'He is now, my girl—'

'He was going to be an engineer. He was good too—'

'I wouldn't get your hopes up. He's lucky to have work at all.'

'I know.'

'This Robert Denham,' Mary Ann said slowly, 'a gentleman, was he?'

'Yes.'

'Money?'

'Oh yes, lots of that.'

'A job?'

'He's a solicitor.'

'Nice family?'

'Very nice.'

'And you turned him down for a lad who had no name, no family, no job, no money and didn't even care about you? Eh, lass, you want your head read.'

'I couldn't help it. I knew David didn't care about me, he told me about his girl at home. He went back to ask her to marry him and she was already engaged to somebody else.'

'Aye, I know. That's my granddaughter. Her parents would never have let her marry him.'

'But he had a good job and—'

'He lost it.'

'That was because of me. When my father found out that I wouldn't marry Robert because of David he threw him out. It was my fault he lost his job.'

'And your father sent you away?'

'To stay with my aunt in Newcastle. I was very unhappy there but I had nowhere else to go.'

'So you asked Blake to bring you here?'

'No, I wouldn't have done that. It was his idea. He took me out for tea and then my aunt saw us outside and he could see what she was like. He wouldn't let me go back in.'

'You love Blake?'

'He doesn't care about me, Mrs McLaughlan. You said yourself—'

'I think in the circumstances you'd better call me Mary Ann. You're obviously no better than the rest of us. There's a saying that goes something like: "be careful what you wish for, the gods might grant it."'

'I wish they would. I'd take the chance. Will you help me?'

'To learn to graft like a pitman's wife and be our Irene? Are you sure?'

'I want him,' Irene said.

She went to church with them. Irene had never been inside a Catholic church and was surprised at how ornate it was and how full and she was glad to be there. The ground outside was icy. Back at the house she helped with the dinner and it was a better dinner, Irene thought critically, than her father's cook turned out on a Sunday.

She helped to wash up and afterwards she took a walk with Blake on the sands. There was no snow or ice there, just a bitter wind coming off the sea and the waves crashing over the harbour. The wind twisted the sand into peculiar shapes and when she and Blake ventured on to the pier the sea spray stung her face.

He was very quiet. He had never been noisy but he was quieter than he had been when she had known him in Sunderland.

'Ralph and Mary Ann will go to midnight Mass but we don't have to go,' Blake said.

'I'd like to go. Do they sing carols?'

'I don't know. I was never there.'

'Aren't you a Catholic?'

'No. I always tell people that I'm Church of England but it isn't true. I'm nothing really. I was never christened. My mother wasn't married and it was a big disgrace. Even after she died a lot of people never spoke to my grandparents again. I don't think it was considered polite for me to go to church. It might have upset respectable people. Mind you, the bloody vicar was always at the farm. Maybe he thought I could be saved.' Blake grinned at the thought of Mr Lawrence.

'Is that why people don't call you by your christian name?'

'I don't know. My grandparents used to call me Davy.'

'I think it's the nicest name in the world,' Irene said. 'Do you let other people use it?'

'I might,' Blake said.

Mary Ann found her an old dress and a pinny when the men went to work and she showed Irene how to cook. Irene burned herself half a dozen times that first week and had dark patches on her hands and arms. There was such a lot to do and Mary Ann's standards were high. Never had Irene thought about having servants but she wished now that she had not taken her prosperity for granted. She was only glad that Mary Ann and Ralph did not have a house twice as big. The floors had to be scrubbed, the meals had to be ready, there were vegetables to peel and meat to pore over and clothes to wash and brasses to clean and furniture to polish.

Every Friday Mary Ann did what she called 'turning the house out'. The rugs were lifted on to the washing line and beaten, the floors were swept, the whole house received what Irene had known only as spring cleaning before now. Monday was washing day. In bad weather like now the clothes could not be hung outside and were put around the fire filling the whole house with steam and making the place damp and cool because the fire was too occupied with them to heat the room. There was baking day and breadmaking day and there was the shopping to be done.

They went together to do the shopping and Mary Ann introduced Irene to her neighbours. It was most women's only social life. Men went out in the evening but women were at home with the children, the darning and the fire. Irene tried not to sound different from these people but she couldn't help her accent and they couldn't help the way that they stared.

'Ooh, aren't you posh?' Esther said the first time that they met. Esther was Will's lass. Will was the lad that Blake worked with and since they were friends Irene tried hard to be friends with Esther but it wasn't easy. Esther had never read a book or heard a piece of music or seen a painting or had a new dress. Her mam bought her dresses 'off the market' as Esther called it.

Irene was lucky. People who went to church or chapel did have a social life as there were different things on at the church during the week and sometimes she went with Mary Ann. Occasionally one of the neighbours dropped in for a cup of tea and there was the chat after church on a Sunday. Other than that it was all work. Irene had never worked so hard in her life. Blake was on different shifts different weeks and somebody had to get up and look after him. The water had to be hot, the meal had to be ready when he came in and when he went out his clothes had to be prepared and put out and his bait put up. Irene began to think that pitmen were the most exacting men in the world. A dirty fingermark or a burned scone was a disaster here.

The houses had thin walls and she could not get used to the idea that there was never silence. If she had had time she would have gone to the beach for the quiet but there was always too much to do and people would have thought it strange that she wanted to spend time alone. Blake worked so hard that he did not seem to appreciate her efforts and Irene was shocked at how little money there was. It went on necessities and there was no more for anything else and now she knew that Robert Denham had been a gentleman. The men here wasted no time with flattery or polite walks. If there was time on a Sunday and the weather was fine, which it rarely was, she and Blake could take a walk in the country or on the beach. This was all the recreation they had together. Nobody had a car or ventured away much; it was too expensive and every day was a work day except Saturday afternoon and Sunday. Irene began to long for a new dress, a book to read from her father's library and the time to read it, an afternoon sitting by the fire talking about art and music. She longed to go to a concert or to hold a conversation which was not about work or other people. She tried to make friends but she had no gossip, she sounded so different, she had been educated up to a point. Even if there was free time Blake spent it with Will and with Will there would be Esther, Irene could not even pretend to have anything in common with Esther except that they now looked alike. Their hands were red and sore with work, their complexions pale from not being outside.

One Saturday that winter Irene burned the stew and made it bitter. She knew that there was no room for waste. Any kind of meat was expensive to them. She ran upstairs into her room and burst into tears in spite of Mary Ann's protestations.

A minute or two later she heard footsteps on the stairs and Blake knocked lightly, opened the door and said from there, 'Can I come in?'

Irene, sitting on the bed, facing away from him, scrubbed at the tears.

'I'm sorry about the dinner,' she said. 'Mary Ann must think me very stupid.'

'She doesn't think that at all. She's very fond of you. Everybody has to learn.' He sat down on the bed and though she knew that he was watching her Irene didn't look at him. 'Do you hate it?'

He caught her offguard with the soft question.

'Yes,' Irene said and the tears fell even harder though she had not meant to say that and not meant to cry. It was just such a relief to be able to tell somebody. 'I don't mean it. I don't hate it—'

'It's all right. It's all right to hate it.'

Irene shook her head but the tears didn't stop. 'It isn't nearly as bad as Aunt Martin's. It's just that . . .'

'It's so hard.'

'Yes. How did you get used to it?'

'I didn't really. There just wasn't any other way.'

'Couldn't you go back to the country?'

'There's nothing to go back to any more. I don't belong there. I have nobody.'

'Neither have I.'

'You'll be able to go back eventually.'

'I don't want to go now. They obviously don't care about me. You brought me from Aunt Martin's because you're kind and you could see how it was.'

'To this,' he said, looking around the small freezing room. Outside the back lane was covered in frost.

'It's a lot better than what I had. It's a lot better than Aunt Martin's and Mary Ann and Ralph are very kind.'

'Wash your face then. If she thinks you've cried she'll be upset.'

Irene went over and poured some water from the jug into the basin and washed and dried her face and tidied her hair. She felt much better after that. She even managed a smile.

'Crying helps.'

'Come downstairs to the fire,' he said. 'I would bet you any money that Mary Ann's made you a cup of tea.'

*

William Bedford was not the most handsome man in the world, Irene decided when she met him, but he was certainly one of the kindest. He was a typical Durham pitman, short and broad-shouldered with brown hair and a north-east Durham accent, but from the moment they met Irene liked him. He stood back in amazement in the street when Blake introduced them and said, 'Irene, you must be the bonniest lass in the whole world. Can I take you for a walk on Sunday?'

Irene laughed and shook her head.

'Why, has this lad got a claim on you?'

'No, he hasn't.'

'Howay then.'

'What about your Esther?' Blake reminded him.

'Oh aye, I forgot about Esther,' he said and winked.

Sometimes on Sundays they went out with Will and Esther and when the fine weather came they went walking on the beach and Esther and Irene took off their shoes and stockings and paddled in the water.

It was fun. Irene hadn't had much fun in her life. One such afternoon when they had all been paddling in the water Blake and Will had gone up to the top of the beach where the sand was soft and she and Esther had walked along a little way, their feet in the water. When they came back Will was sitting up, smoking a cigarette but Blake was lying down with his eyes closed. Irene plumped down beside him.

'You haven't gone to sleep?' she said.

'Too many hard shifts this week,' Will said.

'He had a lie-in this morning. Didn't you, lazy-bones?'

He opened his eyes, sat up and made as if to grab hold of her and Irene yelled and got up and ran. She ran along the beach and around the corner but she was laughing so much that she couldn't run very fast and he caught her, lifted her off her feet in both arms and took her down to the water's edge and pretended to throw her in until she was clinging to him and laughing and protesting. No one had ever taken such liberties before and Irene knew that as a young lady she should have been horrified but she wasn't. And then he bent down and kissed her. Irene had never been kissed before. Her upbringing prompted her to protest, to say something, to try to get away but she didn't. Nothing in her life had prepared her for the experience. Robert Denham would never have done such a thing, he would have talked and tried to persuade her, perhaps even asked her permission. Irene liked the way that Blake kissed her; there was nothing tentative about it. She couldn't bring herself to stop him, she just lay there in his arms and learned how to kiss him.

Afterwards when he let her go and put her down and they went back around the corner to where Will and Esther were sitting up the beach, talking, Irene was rather ashamed of herself and later when she walked back with Blake she didn't know how silent she was until he said, 'What's the matter?'

Irene stopped, blushed and didn't look at him.

'Nothing. Why should anything be the matter?'

'You haven't opened your mouth in ten minutes and that must be a record for you, and you've got a face the colour of strawberry jam.'

'I've caught the sun, that's all.'

'No, you haven't, you little fibber.'

'It's none of your business, David Blake,' she said and walked off. Blake followed, laughing.

'What's funny?'

'You sounded just like a pit lass.'

'It's what I am.'

Irene walked off and he followed her back up to town. That night Irene worried about what she had done and in the end when they went upstairs to bed she knocked on the door of his room.

'David, I want to talk to you.'

He opened the door and Irene went in and then she said quickly, 'I don't want you to think . . .'

'I didn't think it, Irene.'

She looked gratefully at him.

'You don't know what I'm going to say yet.'

'Yes, I do.'

Irene stared at him. 'I just felt so awful afterwards.'

'Why?'

'It was the first time.'

'Robert Denham never kissed you?'

'No.'

'Well, no wonder you didn't want to marry him. Don't worry about it, Irene. It was only a kiss.'

Irene didn't know what to say to that so she just nodded and went to her own room and thought about him holding her so carefully down by the water and his mouth so gentle and warm.

After a while when even Mary Ann thought Irene had nothing left to learn about housework she said to her, 'I think I've found you a little job.'

'What sort of a job?'

'At the corner shop on Bamburgh Street. Would you like that?'

'Yes, I think I would.'

'Are you any good at adding up?'

Irene said gravely that she was.

'Mrs Patten's got a bad leg. She could do with a nice lass to help her.'

Irene put on her coat and went straight round to see Mrs Patten and she got the job. Irene had never before felt the satisfaction of job-finding. The little shop on the corner was suddenly a place full of promise. It would get her out of the house, she would meet different people and Mrs Patten's shop was so neat and organised just as Irene would have organised it if she had had the chance. The jars of sweets stood in a row, and the various bottles shone in the light. The shelves were free of dust, there was a curtain which partitioned the shop from the rest of the house and behind the counter were potatoes and vegetables and all kinds of household items. Mrs Patten told Irene how much she would earn and Irene fairly danced home.

Mary Ann was very pleased. They had a cup of tea to celebrate and when the men came home Irene couldn't wait to tell them. Ralph seemed pleased but Blake said nothing much and later that evening when Mary Ann and Ralph went off to a do at the church, much to Ralph's disgust, Irene looked straight at Blake as he sat by the fire and said, 'You might at least have been pleased for me.'

'I am pleased for you.'

'But?'

'You shouldn't have to go out and work.'

'I can keep myself if I do.'

'You shouldn't have to.'

'You would rather that you kept me, would you?'

Blake looked at her. 'You're a lady, Irene.'

'That's lovely for us all then, isn't it? I'm supposed to sit here on my backside—'

'That isn't what I meant.'

'Isn't it?'

'Your language certainly isn't very ladylike.'

'Well, you just listen to this. It's nothing to do with you what my language is like and if I want to go out and work and bring some money in, the least you could do is be pleased for me!' Irene ran out of the room and up the stairs.

It wasn't long before she heard him come upstairs and say, 'I'm sorry.'

'So you should be.'

'I just wanted to look after you for a while. It made me feel less guilty, I think.'

'There's no reason for you to feel guilty. I want to help. Mary Ann and Ralph are so kind.'

'I didn't mean to spoil it for you, Irene. I just kept remembering how things were.'

'They aren't like that any more.'

'Because of me—'

'It wasn't because of you.' Irene wrenched open the bedroom door. 'It wasn't because of you. Sooner or later I was going to break out of being a lady and do something my father didn't like. It was inevitable. I couldn't have married Robert Denham or anyone like that. He didn't see me as a person, just as a wife.'

'Isn't a wife a person?'

'Not that kind of wife, there to arrange flowers and look nice and stand back admiring the husband.'

'I see.'

'I thought you would eventually.'

'Just one thing.'

'What?'

'If you have to come home late in the dark you'll let Ralph or me walk you.'

'Of course I will,' she said, smiling.

Twenty

That spring Annie became pregnant. Alistair's father was delighted and boasted about the baby to anyone who would listen. Annie said little to her sister about the baby because she knew that Frank and Madge would have loved a child but her family was pleased and her mother hugged her.

Charles Vane was convinced that the child would be a boy, an heir for Western Isle, and went on and on about it until Annie became worried that her child might not be a son.

She spent a great deal of time alone after they were married. Alistair's father seemed to need him always at Western Isle, mostly, Alistair said, because his father went to the various marts and spent all day getting drunk with his friends, but Annie was lonely and often walked over to Grayswell. There she heard her parents discussing the fact that Mr Harlington might sell them the farm. He needed the money. Her father, however, was having no luck in borrowing. As Alistair was the person who now did the books for Western Isle she said to him one warm evening, 'Do you think there is any way your father might be persuaded to lend my father the money he needs to buy Grayswell?'

'I wondered when we would get to that. My father doesn't have any money. As a matter of fact we're in debt and have been for some time.'

'In debt? How's that? I always thought . . .'

'He can't afford the way that he lives. He hasn't farmed well enough to be extravagant and he's been extravagant for years now.'

'But he bought us this.'

Alistair sighed.

'I didn't want to tell you. The bank loaned him the money. He insisted on buying it.'

'But why, when he doesn't have any money? My father works hard and they won't lend him what he needs.'

'I don't know. If he would let me run things, alter things, it wouldn't be so bad but he won't. He thinks he knows best about everything. He goes on buying expensive cars and new machinery and antiques for the house, paying too much money for everything. My grandfather was a shrewd man but my father's just the opposite. I think that's why he drinks so much. It's easier than facing his responsibilities. He'll get like old Harlington shortly. At least Frank has some qualifications. He can make a living.'

It was not until then that Annie realised how fond she had become of the little farm. It seemed truly theirs now. She and Madge sat on warm days in the tiny garden where Blake's grandfather had grown produce for the house. There was an ancient plum tree there and an apple tree. She dreamed of making jam in the autumn. Her mother sometimes came for a cup of tea and Annie had coaxed from the oven the most wonderful pies and bread. The house had lost its cold feel. She and Alistair had laughed and talked and made love there. She had decorated the rooms and bought several pieces of pretty furniture. The sitting room had vases of spring flowers now and the fruit trees were filled with blossom. They had a sheepdog and a lazy tabby. She had even ventured to the stream which ran down the hill to put her feet in its clear cold water. The idea of having to go to Western Isle and live with Alistair's parents was not a happy one. She liked having her kitchen, her privacy, somewhere of their very own.

The feeling of insecurity did not go away. Charles

continued spending money which they did not have while not giving Alistair the freedom to run Western Isle as he wanted to and make some money.

As well as this things were not good at Grayswell. Her father and mother badly wanted the farm. Her father's family had farmed there for many years and if they were to be given the opportunity to buy it they wanted to make sure that they were able so they were saving every penny.

Tommy and Clara were married in the summer and Annie's parents seemed more anxious than ever that their dream to own Grayswell should come true but they had no money and Frank's father had not indicated that he would sell the farm yet, but they knew that it would happen eventually.

Annie wished that Madge were pregnant as well and that they could have had their babies together. It was more important than ever now that war seemed to get closer every day. Rose prophesied that Hitler was going to try and take over the world no matter how much he might pretend not to. When Annie and Alistair went to the pictures and saw the newsreels she was always so glad to come back outside and know that everything was peaceful in the dale and to feel that it might always be so.

That summer as the baby grew inside her Annie lay in

the garden, dreaming of the wonderful times they would have together when it was born. She thought of names and knitted small clothes. Alistair was rarely at home, there was so much to do at Western Isle during the warm weather. She missed him so much that sometimes she ventured down to the farm but not often. The Vanes had not forgiven her for marrying their son and made it clear that she was not welcome there. They always made her feel as though she was interrupting something important and one afternoon when her mother-in-law was giving tea to a friend they sat and talked for over an hour, ignoring Annie until she got up and left and toiled back up the hill to the quiet comfort of Sunniside.

Twenty-one

Esther and Will were married that summer and had their own house. It was of more interest to Irene than any big house had been in her other life. It had two rooms upstairs and two down, a tiny scullery, a yard and nothing more. Irene would have given anything for such a house of her own and she helped Esther to scrub it out during the first week it was theirs and to furnish it as best they could out of what little money there was, but one thing was certain. There was no cleaner house in the county. She found a freedom too in this house that she had not in Mary Ann and Ralph's home, just because Esther and Will were her age. Often Blake walked to the shop in the early evening and they went on to have supper with Will and Esther. Esther, like most pitmen's wives, was a good cook and Irene looked forward to these evenings spent around Esther and Will's kitchen fire.

They talked after supper. Sometimes Will and Blake went out to have a pint of beer while the women washed up and Irene liked these times. She and Esther had grown much closer and now they had so much in common. They sat talking by the kitchen fire and then later sometimes played cards or silly games, most of which were suggested by Will.

Often if Blake was on the late shift Will would go to the shop and walk Irene home. Sometimes he bought Black Bullets in the shop and gave them to her. Other times he brought flowers for her. Irene was convinced that he stole these from other people's gardens. Once they were even Sweet William. It made Irene laugh. He also flattered her, telling her how bonny she was and how she would make somebody a good wife.

'Aren't you going to marry Davy then?' Will said one night as he walked her back.

'Has he said something?' Irene asked eagerly.

'No. He never talks about owt, nowt important anyroad,' Will said.

'There's another girl,' Irene said. 'He's loved her all his life and she married somebody else.'

'I thought . . . I might be wrong but I thought he might have kissed you one day on the beach.'

'He did.' Irene tried to laugh. 'He mustn't have liked it, he never did it again.'

Will stopped.

'You're a wonderful lass, Irene, and you mustn't think like that. It's just that he – he doesn't find things easy. It took me ages to get him to be friends, like he doesn't sort of know how to make friends with people and that's a lot easier than getting a lass to love you.'

'You don't seem to find it hard.'

'Ah no, but I'm a funny bugger, me,' Will said and laughed and squeezed her waist. 'Dinna worry none, Irene, it'll be right.'

'I hope so. I want a house like you and Esther have and – and . . .'

'Now don't start on about babies, Irene, I haven't got that far yet,' Will said and Irene laughed.

'Have a Black Bullet,' she said, taking the sticky white bag from her coat pocket.

By the end of the autumn Esther was pregnant and Will went about with a big smile on his face. Esther showed Irene how to knit and she knitted bootees for the baby.

'Very nice,' Blake said gravely when she showed them to him.

'I'm very proud of these. They're my first attempt.'

They walked up to Esther and Will's house with the bootees and afterwards since the night was fine they walked through the town and on to the front and the pier. It was late October but the waves were slow-moving and small and the few ships in the harbour bobbed a little. When they reached the end of the pier Blake turned and looked at her.

'I wondered . . .' he said, 'if you might like to get married.'

It was, Irene thought later and savagely, quite the most inelegant proposal that any girl had ever had.

'What?' was all she managed.

'I thought you might like your own house; it would be better and we could . . .'

'We could what?'

Blake looked past her, though there was nothing special to look at, just the sea. He didn't say anything else. Irene would have walked away and left him there but he stopped her. He put both hands on her waist and then he kissed her. Irene pushed him away. She was angry now.

'You don't care about me, you never did—'

'Yes, I do.'

'Since when? You kissed me once down on the beach in the summer. I wouldn't marry you if you were the last lad in Seaton. Just because Will has a wife and a baby coming and a house of his own—'

'It isn't because of that.'

'What then?'

'I just couldn't . . . I just wanted . . .'

Irene walked away very quickly and left him there.

One evening when she and Mary Ann were in on their own together Mary Ann sat down by the fire with her and looked across at her and said, 'What's up, lass?'

'Nothing. At least . . . I don't think so.'

'But something's happened?'

Irene put down the sock she was inexpertly trying to darn and said, 'David asked me to marry him.'

'Oh.'

'It was the way he did it, Mary Ann, like he was asking for four ounces of wine gums. He doesn't love me. I thought in time that he might come to, that my wanting him to might make the difference but it didn't.'

'So why did he ask you then?'

'Because of Will and Esther, because they're so happy and have a house and a baby due.'

'Seems like a good enough reason to me. People have married for worse. But you said no.'

'If he'd put it differently . . . but he didn't.'

'Well, if he does it again you could try saying yes.'

'I can't.'

'What for?'

'I told you, he doesn't care about me. He still cares about your blessed granddaughter.'

'She's expecting her child any time and Blake needs a wife and a future. He may not love you now, Irene, but you could make him love you if you married him. You're a good bonny lass and clever and once you married him and had a bairn ... He's loyal and responsible and he uses his wits. If you don't marry him somebody else will and then you'll lose everything.'

'I could marry Geoffrey.'

Geoffrey was a young man with a car who worked in Sunderland and called in at the shop every morning. He had asked Irene to go out with him on several occasions.

'Yes, you possibly could but you don't care for him like you care for the other and you wouldn't be happy.'

Irene went out with Geoffrey several times over the following few weeks. She and Blake scarcely spoke. If he was in when Geoffrey arrived he was even civil to him. Irene didn't understand until Christmas came and Mary Ann slyly invited her lodgers to kiss under the mistletoe at the beginning of a modest party she was holding for the neighbours. Just the touch of his lips convinced

Irene. It was the least passionate kiss in the world, since Mary Ann and Ralph and half a dozen other people were there, but during those weeks Geoffrey had kissed her several times and not once had it felt like this. Later they went to midnight Mass – it was Christmas Eve – and on the way back snow began to fall and they lingered, letting Ralph and Mary Ann get further and further ahead but he didn't stop and offer to kiss her. Irene was so frustrated that she wanted to hit him.

That Christmas it snowed. Will built a snowman in the yard, stuck some mistletoe on his head and insisted on Irene kissing the snowman. Esther made her first Christmas cake when she had morning sickness with the result that it was so disgusting they had to give it to the seagulls. Will was reluctant even to do that, he said it would give them bellyache. They had a party and played charades and lottery and on New Year's Eve, when they were both rather drunk, Will dragged Irene behind the pantry door and kissed her so hard that she wished he would do it again and swore the next day not to drink any more sherry.

It had been a good party, Blake and Will arm-in-arm singing, and Blake more relaxed than Irene had seen him in a long time.

In the New Year Blake and Will were always on the

same shift, going out together, Blake whistling some tune, calling for Will on his way. Every Saturday night they went out and came back happy and at the weekends took short cold walks by the stormy sea, coming back to the house, a big fire, teacakes and blackberry jam.

One afternoon in early February, a bleak cold day, the pit siren went late in the afternoon. Irene had to stay there and look after the shop because Mrs Patten was not well and had gone to bed but after a short while, Ralph, white-faced, came into the empty shop and Irene's heart dropped.

'It's not David?'

'No, it's Will.'

Mrs Patten said that she should just close the shop and go so Irene did, her hands shaking. She put on her coat and Ralph walked with her along the dark narrow street.

'Is he bad?'

'They didn't think so at first but aye, he's not so good. They took him to hospital.'

Irene wanted to go to the hospital with Esther but Ralph wouldn't let her because he said that Esther's parents and Will's parents were there and she would only be in the way so they went home. She hadn't really thought of it as home until then. She had never imagined that a little pit house could seem so comforting, or was it Mary

Ann McLaughlan's arms where she took her wet face and shocked body for refuge?

'Where's David?' she asked eventually.

'I don't know.'

They sat around waiting for news. Mary Ann would have given Irene some tea if she would have eaten it. In the end they went to bed, they had work to go to the next day but Irene lay, straining her ears for any sound.

She got up and went to work as usual but Mrs Patten sent her home after dinner because she was so tired and upset and there was not much to do.

As soon as she walked in the door she knew that things were worse. Ralph was not at the pit, he had come home, and he and Mary Ann turned and looked at her.

'What is it?' she said.

Mary Ann glanced patiently at her husband.

'Will died this morning,' he said.

'No. No, he can't have.'

Mary Ann took her coat and gave her tea with lots of sugar and Irene sat down by the fire before she thought.

'Where's David?'

'He went out.'

'Where?'

'I don't know where. He didn't say and I didn't ask.'

'I think I should go and find him.'

'Just leave him alone. He'll come round,' Mary Ann advised.

Blake came back when it was late and Irene had given in and gone to bed.

He went to work the next day just as ever and the day after and Irene thought of how he usually went out cheerful, calling in for Will. She thought of him having to go down without Will to the very place where Will had been so badly hurt and of having to stay there for a full shift and most of all having to come back out on his own and not to have Will to jostle or shove good-naturedly up the road. No plans would be made to have a drink later or for walks at the weekend.

On the day of the funeral he even ate his tea and then went out and came back late, singing loudly. That fortnight he drank his pay. Irene had never seen anybody get so consistently drunk. Even Simon had never been that bad. He was late to work, he didn't eat. Mary Ann and Ralph said nothing and when Irene would have the older woman stopped her.

'Give him time,' she said.

The following fortnight Blake was never late for work, didn't go drinking once and gave his pay to Mary Ann, apologising. But the fun was gone from their lives, all the light. He was silent. When he wasn't at work he sat in his room, reading, so he said when asked. Irene had the uncomfortable feeling that he never turned a page.

Irene went out with Geoffrey since it was the only way she could get out. She had been to see Esther but the girl was surrounded by family and Irene felt pushed out. Geoffrey took her to the pictures. He came into the house when he picked her up and had a word with Ralph and Mary Ann. When she came back they had gone to bed but Blake was there. Geoffrey didn't linger. He kissed her goodnight and left. Blake was sitting by the kitchen fire. Irene couldn't decide whether he was drunk or not since he didn't talk to her. She went to bed.

The next day he didn't go to work, he didn't even get out of bed and on the following two days he got up but didn't speak to anybody or eat. He left the house and didn't come back until it was late and had been dark and cold for hours.

Ralph wanted to talk to him.

'If he doesn't get himself back to normal soon they'll get rid of him,' he said, 'and there are no jobs.'

Irene thought about Will and Esther. She couldn't believe that everything was spoiled, that the happiness was gone. She thought of paddling in the sea in the summer and of the fun they had had after Esther and Will were married. Esther had had to give up the house now that Will was dead. Irene avoided going anywhere near the street where they had lived, she couldn't bear it. She missed Will so much that it made her angry. Nothing good ever lasted and Esther was getting bigger with their child.

On the Sunday Mary Ann and Ralph went to evening Mass and when Blake came in for his tea only Irene was there.

'There is something to eat presumably, is there?' he said.

'Of course there is.' There was broth and ham sandwiches. Mary Ann had made the broth the day before and left the sandwiches in case he should come home.

Irene watched him eat and then she said, 'Are you going to work tomorrow?'

Blake looked sharply at her. 'Why?'

'Ralph says that if you don't go soon they'll get rid of you.'

'Aren't you seeing Geoffrey tonight?'

'Not on Sundays.'

'Oh, right. He has a job to go to.'

'He's an engineer in Sunderland.'

'Lucky Geoffrey.'

'David, you've got to go to work—'

'I heard you the first time, Irene. What difference does

it make to you anyway? You keep yourself. You're independent. You don't have to worry about whether I go to work.'

'I understand how you feel. I know how much you miss Will. I miss him too. You've lost something you can't get back no matter how much you try.'

'He was the best friend I ever had. I thought . . . I thought we might be given enough time together so that it would stop being a luxury, so that I would stop holding on to each second for fear there wouldn't be another. And I was right, I was right to be afraid.'

Irene tried to think of something to say but couldn't. And then she tried to take him into her arms but he pushed her gently away.

'You stick with Geoffrey, Irene. He can get you out of here. It's more than I can do for you.'

Irene stared at him.

'Do you really think that having turned down a catch like Robert Denham I would accept Geoffrey?'

'You should,' Blake said and he got up to go upstairs. He stopped at the bottom of the stairs and looked at her. 'How many times have you wished you hadn't turned Robert Denham down?'

'Almost every day,' Irene said softly. 'I didn't realise how things really were, that it was all I could expect. I thought I was entitled to more. I thought everybody was entitled to love and be loved.'

Blake left her there. When he had gone Irene began to cry. It was the first time she had cried since Will's accident. She had been so shocked and so hurt that there didn't seem to be any room for tears. She followed him upstairs and went quietly into her room. The crying wasn't a problem, she had learned to cry soundlessly at her aunt's. It was so cold up there but she needed the privacy somehow. She sat down on the bed, unable to stand up any longer, she felt so tired. It was a big bed, three of Mary Ann's children had slept in it. Her bedroom was over the kitchen and was warmer than the other one though there wasn't much evidence of it now.

She huddled in against the covers for comfort as well as for warmth. When the door opened she stilled her shuddering body and tried to remove the tears with the covers. Blake always knocked before he walked in. This time he didn't. Irene pretended he wasn't there, even when he sat down on the bed. He leaned over and kissed her damp face. She turned further away. He kissed the top of her head and the back of her neck and he put a hand on her back, gradually sliding it down to her waist. He turned her over towards him.

'Come here,' he said.

Irene went there, blotched face, misery and all. She hid her face against his shoulder which gave the tears leave to begin again. The more she cried the more he kissed her so it seemed politic to let the tears run but gradually the misery began to shift and the tears to dry as he stroked her hair and kissed her face and murmured little half-sentences of comfort. She became warmer, happier.

'I'm sorry, I'm sorry,' he said softly, 'I didn't mean to be nasty to you.'

'You weren't.'

'Yes, I was. I hate Geoffrey.'

Irene couldn't help but smile.

'You don't have to hate Geoffrey.'

'Don't I?'

'No.'

He smiled into her eyes. 'I don't think I've got any kind of a future, Irene.'

'I've given up on things like the future. I don't care. Now will do.'

'What if you had to stay here for always?'

'Is that the problem?' Irene said. 'You're going to let me die an old maid in case I have to stay here? I didn't realise you were such an idiot.'

'You were brought up to be a lady, Irene.'

'If you don't shut up and kiss me I'm going to forget

about being a lady and . . . I don't want to be a lady, I just want . . . I just want you. Don't make me say things I shouldn't.'

Blake didn't. He kissed her. Irene was even happier then. She liked the kisses, she especially liked the way that he put his hands under her jumper and on to the bare warmth of her skin. Her upbringing tried to get into the way here and tell her that no gentleman would have done such a thing and Irene knew that it didn't count since he wasn't a gentleman. Her upbringing also reminded her that she should have stopped him from sliding his hands past her underwear, loosening it and then putting his hands and eventually his mouth on to her breasts. Luckily by then Irene couldn't think straight so that didn't count either. After that her upbringing fought a losing battle. He put his hands and mouth all over her, he took her skirt off her, he pulled down her knickers. Irene was soon totally lost as a lady but she thought that possibly she made up for it as a woman. She felt like one big rosy glow, like she was the only woman in the whole world. She wasn't cold at all in that freezing little room, naked against him, skin to skin, it was wonderful. She loved every second of what he did to her and what he encouraged her to do to him. Ralph and Mary Ann did not come back. In an idle moment much later Irene did chance to think of them and was glad that they had discovered something so entertaining to do that evening that they weren't there to discover their lodgers in bed together. She just hoped that the neighbours couldn't hear what was going on. Crying out with delight was something she wasn't prepared to contain.

It was very late by the time Ralph and Mary Ann came home and by then Irene and Blake were quiet in each other's arms and half-asleep. Irene could not understand therefore the following morning late, when she was helping Mary Ann with the dinner, why Mary Ann looked askance at her. Irene had almost chopped off a finger with a kitchen knife and thrown out the vegetables instead of the peelings by then.

'I hope he's asked you to marry him, young woman. I'd hate to see you go down the aisle fat with your first like any common little pit lass.'

Irene blushed scarlet.

'Well, has he?' Mary Ann insisted.

Irene nodded. Mary Ann hugged her.

'When's the day to be?' she asked.

'Soon,' Irene said.

Irene had always imagined that her wedding day would be lavish, that she would be married in a long white gown, wear a veil and have half a dozen bridesmaids, the girls she went to school with. She had thought that there would be a big church and a reception at a top hotel, that all their family and friends would come to wish her well, that she would have a honeymoon in Paris, dozens of exciting gifts and a house rather like her father's house with its own set of gates, a drive, lovely gardens and that there would be welcoming fires in the drawing room and a library and servants and there she would make a home comfortable for the gentleman she had married. The vision became a little blurred then because there had never been a gentleman she cared about anywhere near as much as she cared about David Blake.

They had been given a house of their own and though it was in a dark narrow street she knew that she would much prefer living alone with him and to her surprise things were easier than she had thought.

Mary Ann made her a lovely white dress for her wedding and Mary Ann and Ralph organised a reception in the church hall.

It was a perfect spring Saturday when they were married. Ralph gave her away and all the people had made or bought small presents and suddenly these meant just as much as expensive canteens of cutlery and Wedgwood dinner services would have because she realised that she was part of the community now. Mary Ann had chosen the bridesmaids and made their dresses but she privately told Irene that she outshone not only the other girls but any bride she had ever seen. The sea was as blue as a summer's morning, the waves broke gently on the shore, the church was decorated with wild flowers and everything at the reception had been homemade and there was plenty of it.

There would be no holiday, just the Saturday night and the Sunday since Blake was on early shift but when they were alone, when the day was over and they had all their new things around them and the good wishes of her neighbours were still in her mind, Irene looked back over the day and thought it was one of the best she had ever spent, even without her father and Simon.

She knew that the families on either side of her would help if she needed them, the fire was burning brightly in her kitchen and her sitting room for once and she had the man that she had wanted. Robert Denham with all his education, money and background had never looked half as inviting as the young man who grabbed her by the waist and whispered in her ear, 'I love you, Irene, let's go to bed.'

'What, now?'

'Yes.'

'Won't the neighbours be scandalised?'

'I don't care. We've only got tonight.'

'Right then,' Irene said.

In spite of Will's death that was one of the happiest summers of Irene's life though she was poorer now than she had ever been. Blake was not quiet and difficult any more even though she knew how much he hated working down the pit and how much he missed Will. Sometimes he went drinking but not often because it brought back memories. He seemed content to sit at home by the fire with her but occasionally he went out for the conversation of other men.

Irene and Mary Ann went shopping together and Mary Ann urged her to buy good secondhand dresses and together they unpicked them and sewed them so that Irene went to church on Sundays looking what Mary Ann called 'as fine as a new pin'. Mary Ann's mother had been a dressmaker. Her husband had died when Mary Ann was small and her mother had made a living for them. She showed Irene all kinds of useful things about sewing which Irene had not known before or ever needed.

Irene was glad too that Mary Ann had shown her how to cook and bake and how to look after a house and a pitman. Her house was perfect, her pastry was light, the smell of her dinners drove people to put their heads around the open back door in approval but best of all was Blake, who came home to her at different hours of the day and night depending on his shifts. Sundays were wonderful. On sunny summer afternoons they went for long walks on the beach but Irene preferred the days that rained because they bolted the doors and went to bed. She learned to love the sound of rain running down the windows.

Twenty-two

Annie's baby was a girl. Charles Vane was so disappointed that he didn't even come to Sunniside to see the child but Alistair's mother came and Annie realised that her mother-in-law was in fact delighted with the baby. She sat down with Rose and they congratulated themselves that she was the most beautiful baby ever born.

When Annie went to Western Isle all Charles Vane said to her was that he expected the next child would be a boy. She had not expected Alistair's reaction.

'It's none of your damned business,' he said, 'and don't you speak that way to my wife.'

'I'll speak to her how I choose,' his father said angrily. 'She was just the damned dairymaid.'

Alistair got to his feet and Annie was horrified. She thought he was going to hit his father.

'Alistair!'

That stopped him but he turned around to her, said, 'We're going,' and walked out.

Annie got up, the baby in her arms, stuttered something to his mother and went after him as best she could. He was already starting up the car in the yard.

'That's it,' he said as she got in. 'I've put up with him all these years and I'm sick of it.'

'Alistair, he didn't mean anything.'

'How can you say that?'

'He's always been like that and . . . you can't blame him for wanting a grandson. Western Isle is all he's ever cared about.'

'I don't understand how people can care more about buildings and pieces of land than they do about people,' Alistair said, wrenching at the steering wheel as they took the track up to Sunniside.

'Things are difficult. He's doing his best to keep the place together. He wants it for you and then for your son—'

'He's not here to want things for other people. He's not bloody well immortal,' Alistair said.

When they got back to the house Annie soothed her daughter to sleep and then she went back downstairs and poured him a glass of whisky and took it in to where he was sitting on the sofa in front of the newly stoked-up fire.

'Here,' she said, sliding down beside him.

He took the glass from her hands.

'Why didn't your mother have any more children? Couldn't she?'

'She used to ride to hounds. She had a riding accident. He always said that was the cause. I suppose they had to blame something. Maybe it was him. He always goes on and on about wanting more children, he couldn't even be kind to the one he had. It's always been the farm first and everything else afterwards with him and now we're in debt because he thinks he's so important. If we ever lose the farm it'll be his fault.'

'Lose it?'

He didn't look at her.

'I keep trying to tell him not to spend money but he doesn't listen. We don't have it to spend.'

'Why don't we sell this place?'

He looked at her then.

'And live with them? I couldn't.'

'Can we afford to go on paying the bank what we owe them in interest?'

'Nobody's going to buy it anyway, not the way that things are going. I'll be glad when there's a war. At least I'll be able to get away from here.'

Annie was so hurt that she said nothing.

'When I think of the things I could have done with my life—' he said.

'But you love Western Isle—'

'Annie, I'm not going to have Western Isle if things don't get better. I'm not going to have anything and I'm not qualified to do anything else.'

'That doesn't mean you have to talk about going and getting yourself killed!'

'I didn't mean it like that.' He took her into his arms.

'I'd have to stay here if you joined up.'

'You could go to your parents.'

'Don't talk about it.' Annie hid her face against him. 'You probably won't get called up anyhow. You're needed here on the farm.'

'You could do that,' he said.

'What, run the farms?'

'Why not?'

'What about the baby?' Even as she spoke she could hear Susan start to cry. She ran upstairs and picked her up and held the child very close to her. The wind had got up. She went and pulled the curtains across. There was not a single light to be seen, the fog had come down so thickly across the hillside and in the valley. She rocked Susan in her arms until the baby fell asleep again and then put her down gently into her cot. It seemed strange to her that her child should have been born in the same house as Blake and the awful thought came to her: what if her child had to grow up like Blake without a father? It was so horrifying to her that when Alistair came to bed which he did soon afterwards she flew into his arms.

'I'm so frightened,' she said.

'There's nothing to be frightened of here unless it's a few ghosts all with Blake's scowl.'

She tried to laugh but couldn't. They went to bed and made love for the first time since Susan had been born and Annie thought then that it was too real not to have a future. It was what life was all about, being in love, being in bed here with the night all outside and the baby sleeping peacefully in her cot. Nothing could destroy that, it was the most important thing of all. Alistair was right, his father cared for things which didn't matter but she thought about the future, Alistair and Susan and herself living at Western Isle and using it as a home and providing it with laughter. And there would be other children too to fill the rooms and run down the fields and chase each other around the trees in the orchard.

She drifted into sleep. In her dreams she could see a fair-haired girl running up the hill and a tall-legged horse following. A man, dark like Alistair (was it Alistair?), getting off the horse and running after her and catching her. He was laughing. She didn't think that the girl was laughing, she wasn't, she was afraid, she was— Annie awoke covered in sweat to find the baby screaming and Alistair stirring beside her.

Twenty-three

One summer day when Blake came in off the foreshift there was a car parked in the back lane outside his house, and it was no ordinary car, it was a big shiny silver Bentley. It looked completely out of place, almost comical, and the local children had gathered around to stare at the size and the sheen. It filled most of the street. No one he knew except Sylvester Richmond could have afforded such a car and since they had had nothing to do with him for so long he could not believe that Irene's father had come to visit them.

He went up the back yard and into the house and there was Sylvester sitting by the kitchen fire looking very big in the small room. Blake could have smiled. Not even for her father would his wife have opened the front door or put him in the front room to show that he was special. She was a true pitman's wife was Irene these days.

'We have a visitor,' she said, getting up from the table as Blake came in.

Sylvester was sitting sideways at the table looking as out of place as anybody Blake had ever seen in his life. He was such a big man that he dwarfed the room and Blake had forgotten or had just not seen in so long the very expensive clothes which he wore. Everything in the room took on a shabbiness which it had lacked until now.

'Good afternoon, David,' he said, getting up as Blake stepped into the house.

'What do you want?' Blake said.

Sylvester flushed at the lack of respect and perhaps from embarrassment, Blake thought.

'Do I have to want something? You married my daughter and in spite of my objections. A pretty pass you've brought her to here.'

'I don't think that's any of your business,' Blake said.

'Perhaps you'd like to go and sit in the front room, Father?' Irene said politely.

'What?'

'Until David is washed and changed,' and he allowed her to usher him into the front room and close the door.

'What does he want?' Blake asked softly.

'I don't know. He's only just arrived. I wouldn't have let him in but I got such a shock I didn't know what to do.'

'Don't worry, you don't have to do anything.'

When Blake had washed and changed she called Sylvester back into the room. Luckily it was Friday. Irene always baked on a Friday and although Blake thought that Sylvester would have been happier not to eat he did dig into a still-warm ham-and-egg pie and Blake didn't blame him. Irene's pastry was the nearest thing to heaven. He also meekly accepted a cup of tea and said little. Irene ate nothing. Blake squeezed her hand under the table and she smiled at him. Things were harder than ever workwise but the house was spotless, the fire was generous and the food was good.

'Simon has joined the army,' Sylvester said after the silence had gone on for a long time with nothing but the scrape of knives and plates to punctuate it. 'I begged him not to but he wouldn't listen. All that nonsense. There's about to be a war. He'll only get himself killed.' He glanced at Blake. 'Will you go into the army?'

'I expect so, yes.'

Sylvester paused, looking down at his empty plate.

'There's no one to help me run the shipyard,' he said.

Blake looked sharply at him.

'You're not talking to me, are you? I know nothing about shipyards.'

'You could have done.'

'Yes, I could have done but I don't.'

'You're not much more than a lad. You could learn.'

'I'm not interested.'

'You mean you like mining?'

'No, I don't like it but it pays and there's nothing else.'

'Shipyards are booming with the threat of war.'

'So will everything else, I expect.'

'I need help.'

'You have help. You have a board of directors, a good manager, engineers, draughtsmen—'

'I meant somebody from my family, somebody to talk to. Simon was never any good. You had ability, lots of it.'

'You weren't interested in my ability.'

'I'm interested in it now. You can't mean to make my daughter live here for ever.'

'I'm not making her do anything.'

Irene got up from where she was sitting and went over and from behind Blake's chair she put her arms around his neck so that she was facing her father. Blake ran a thumb over the inside of her wrist.

Sylvester watched them for a moment or two and then looked down.

'I have nobody,' he said finally, 'nobody and nothing. All I've got is that great big house. I want you to come back. I want you to help me, David.'

'I told you. I'm not an engineer. I have no training. I can't help you.'

'You have good instincts. You were the best engineer ever in that office and then you went and spoiled it.'

'I spoiled it?'

Sylvester looked him straight in the eyes.

'If it hadn't been for you my daughter would have married a gentleman. She's far too good for you and you know it. What do you expect? You should be grateful I came here and offered you so much. You could have everything.'

'I don't want it,' Blake said.

Later, when Sylvester had gone, Irene went upstairs to bed but he couldn't go after her. He and Irene had found a kind of peace during the short time that they had been married. She liked having her own house, he knew, she liked being here with him and they had grown used to the way of living and to one another, even though sometimes it was anything but easy, and now her father had spoiled that hard-won peace. Blake looked up when she came down the stairs in her nightdress.

'Aren't you coming to bed?' she said.

'No.'

'Do you want to talk about this, David?'

'No.'

Irene stayed where she was for a few seconds and then she went back upstairs and after a little while he followed her. He wasn't sure whether she was asleep but she didn't move so he turned away from her and closed his eyes and lay still for a long time listening to the silence.

The following week Irene burned the dinner twice, left the washing outside in the rain, produced almost inedible custard tarts and burst into tears twice for what Blake didn't consider a reason. The second time he sat her down by the kitchen fire.

'I think we should talk about it,' he said.

'There's nothing to talk about. My father behaved unforgivably and I'm not going back at a time of his choosing after what he did to us.'

'But you're upset about it. I don't think I can go on eating pastry that tastes like pitprops.'

Irene laughed a little through the tears.

'You're very rude,' she said.

'Irene, I fear for my teeth. My grandmother made me eat lots of carrots and turnips when I was little to get them like this. I don't want to break them on your pies.'

Irene laughed and he took her into his arms and then down on to his knee.

'I just can't stop thinking about him,' she said. 'He's

sixty, you know. He was older than my mother. It's old to run a shipyard by yourself.'

'He doesn't run it by himself.'

'You know what I mean.'

'No, I don't. If Simon hadn't gone off to fight the war he wouldn't be coming near us. He doesn't want us, not really. He threw us out. He doesn't like me. We're not going back there—'

'Are you dictating to me, David Blake?'

'You want to go back?'

'No, but—'

'I'm not going back there,' and he shoved her off his knee and went as if to move past her.

'Don't you walk out of the room when I'm fighting with you, David.'

'There's nothing more to be said.'

'Yes, there is.'

'Do you want to go back? I thought you liked being here with me?'

'David, he's my father.'

'He put you out. He sent you to live with that miserable old bitch—'

'Don't swear. He's still my father.'

'And I'm still your husband and we're not going.'

'You unreasonable, pig-headed . . .'

'Yes?'

Irene said nothing but her face was pink with temper. They rarely argued.

'I wouldn't be any use to him,' Blake said. 'I wasn't allowed to study and learn about the shipyard—'

'That's what rankles, isn't it?' Irene was on her feet now and almost shouting. 'You won't go back because my father didn't give you the chance and you loved the yard.'

'I didn't!'

'He's giving you the chance now.'

'Oh yes, now, after all he's done to us. If we went back there we'd have to put up with his moods and his whims. He could throw us out again. I won't be nice to him for something I can gain.'

'Not even for half a shipyard?'

'Not for the whole bloody world!'

'That doesn't sound like a principle to me, that sounds very much like stubborn stupidity.'

'You what?'

There was a short silence before Blake added, 'Does that mean you'll go without me?'

'No. I love you but that doesn't stop him from being my father.'

'I wouldn't know about things like that.'

'Yes, you would. You cared a lot about him and he hurt you, I know that he did but you shouldn't let that influence your judgement now.'

'I thought he cared about me,' Blake said flatly, 'but he didn't and when I think about it now it seems incredible to me that I should actually have thought that he might. Now all he wants me there for is his shipyard.'

'I don't think that's quite true.'

'Irene, you always think the best of people even when they've done awful things to you.'

'He's my father and I love him.'

'So if I threatened you and shouted at you and threw you out and then came and wanted you you'd say, "He's my husband and I care about him"?'

Irene didn't answer.

'I hope you wouldn't.'

'He wanted me to marry Robert.'

Blake was silent for a few moments and then he said, 'You want to go back, don't you?'

'I feel so awful about it.'

'Did he feel awful when he put you out and for something you hadn't done?'

'I had done something. I had disappointed him.'

'And you think that isn't the fate of all parents?'

'Don't go clever on me, you know exactly what I mean.

I don't like not seeing my father and Simon and not being part of the family. It doesn't feel right to me. I can't help that. It's got nothing to do with how they treated me. Blood's just that, there's nothing you can do about it, the ties are there. I have the opportunity now to put that right. You wouldn't have me say no?'

'Why can't you accept that it's your father who's at fault here, that no matter how much guilt you feel it's your father who's done the wrong thing? Your guilt is directed at yourself when really it's anger that you should have for your father. When he takes his clothes off he's nothing but a man and he makes mistakes every day of his life just like other men and he made a mistake with you.'

'He didn't want me to marry you, that's all, and he knew that I loved you. He tried to prevent it, that's all he did. Now it's done and he can't prevent it but we could try again differently.'

'Your father can't try differently, Irene, he's too old and too selfish.'

'I loved him once and he loved me. Nothing can change that,' Irene said.

Twenty-four

Gradually Irene became downhearted. At first it only showed in her cooking but as the days turned into weeks and they did not mention her father she became tired and listless. She took to going for long walks on the beach when the weather was good and sometimes when it wasn't with the result that she caught a heavy cold and was ill enough to stay in bed. Her cough lingered. She had nothing to say when he came home; she would pretend to read and stare into space. Blake decided that things had gone too far. He suggested to her that they should go and see her father and she agreed.

They went the following Sunday when they were sure of finding Sylvester at home. Blake had forgotten what that area was like, how prosperous some people still were, and the house was a shock. It was so big. The gardens around it were lavish with flowers, the lawns were lush and green and perfectly cut. Sylvester was sitting in the garden in a wicker chair with a table in front of him on which were a jug and glasses. When she saw him Irene's face broke into the biggest smile that Blake thought he had ever seen and Sylvester got up and caught her into his arms. Blake looked at his father-in-law across Irene's head and did not miss the gleam of triumph in Sylvester's eyes.

They sat down and drank whisky and soda with ice and lemon and Blake tried not to look around him too much. The garden air was heady with roses and the big trees all around the outside walls were heavy with leaves.

'Such a beautiful day you chose to visit. You should have let me know. You could have come for dinner.'

As it was they had tea in the garden. Blake looked at the array of food, the tiny salmon sandwiches, the rich fruit cake, the china tea in the cups that you could see your fingers through and he despaired of ever getting Irene away from this place.

A maid waited on them. Blake noticed how ordinary Irene's dress looked and how shabby his suit against Sylvester's and after tea they went into the house and he could see Irene's hungry eyes taking in the house she had been driven away from.

She said nothing on the way home. Blake was meant

to go to bed, he was on the early shift, but he couldn't sleep. She never came to the door to greet him when he came home now, she rarely turned to him in bed, there was no show of affection. Sylvester, he thought grimly, had destroyed their peace. When Irene finally came to bed he turned over towards her.

'If you really want to go home we'll go.'

'No.'

He thought of walking back into the smell of the pit town and then of Sylvester's garden. He thought of what he could do if he was given the chance. How one day he might even be able to build the kind of ships that he liked.

'You can't want to stay here, Irene.'

'I'm not going anywhere without you.'

He pulled her to him and hugged her.

'I want to go too.'

'You don't want to live with my father.'

'I'll do it for half a shipyard.'

'You're a fibber, David Blake. I don't want you to be unhappy.'

'I couldn't be unhappy anywhere you were,' Blake said.

Going back to Sunderland as Irene's husband was just that. He should have been called Mr Richmond, Blake reflected over the first few days. He panicked. The house seemed bigger than ever, it was like a mountain, and the old man was no easier than Blake had thought he would be. Never had a miner's cottage seemed so comforting and to his dismay Irene stopped being a miner's wife the minute she stepped back into her father's house and became a lady. She was somebody else, ordering dinner, seeing to the house and the servants. Once again she wore the clothes of a rich young woman. Blake was intimidated. To come to this house as a visitor on a Sunday was one thing. To live there in luxurious rooms, to be waited on, to have to dress accordingly was another. And if the house was a mountain the shipyard was Everest. He didn't just doubt himself there, he wanted to run away, and to go along with Sylvester to the office each day was the most difficult thing he had ever done. He fell into bed exhausted at night, his own bed, vast and empty. Irene had her own room and if he walked in there was always somebody doing her hair or putting her clothes away or undressing her.

Sylvester's Bentley was the nearest thing to a ship Blake had ever seen that didn't float, the house was filled with expensive furniture, the gardens were perfect, ladies came to tea in the afternoons and people were invited to dine in the evenings where there was an array of knives and forks that would have defeated a gourmet and all the right things were said and done.

In particular there was Irene's best friend, Pauline Kington. They had gone to school together and Irene confided to Blake that the only thing about her wedding day that she regretted was that Pauline had not been her bridesmaid. Pauline, a pretty blonde woman, had a lot in common with Irene. Her father too owned a shipyard.

Irene didn't seem to notice Blake's discomfort in her father's house. She was at home, she had everything familiar around her. Blake felt so out of place that he went often to see Mary Ann and Ralph. Occasionally Irene went with him but she looked so wrong there in her fine clothes with her pretty jewellery and her professionally cut hair. He knew that Mary Ann did not know how to talk to Irene any longer. He scarcely did himself. Sylvester invited them to Sunday dinner. Blake wondered whether that was just in case he might be tempted to change his mind and leave.

When Simon came home he laughed at Blake.

'Quite the boss, aren't you?'

'No,' Blake said quickly. 'You could have done it if you'd wanted.'

'Thanks very much, I couldn't stand it. Sitting very pretty now, aren't you? It was a good day for you when you married my sister. I underestimated you, David, you did know what you were doing. What a step up for a pitman and what a shame all the things you must have learned down the pits aren't any use in the shipyard, but of course you're not labouring in the shipyard, are you? You married the boss's daughter so you must have some special kind of ability. I wonder what that is?'

Since this occurred to Blake several times each day he didn't need to hear it from Simon. He felt foolish, he knew so little but he wanted to be there. He liked the smell and feel of it all, the excitement, the decision-making. He liked watching the skilled men and listening to the intelligent ideas of the designers and engineers. He didn't put forward any ideas, he didn't say anything much at all. He was just there, he was part of it. The shipyard became the object of Blake's fascination. He learned as quickly as he could at Sylvester's side. Best of all, the manager, Wilson Stokes, liked him and since Blake had respect for the man it pleased him that Wilson was prepared to put up with his ignorance not just because he was family but because he seemed to like him.

Sylvester was so pleased that Simon had come home that he was easier to bear but after Simon had gone away again he was less and less tolerant. At every meal he criticised Blake, censured everything he had done, every comment he had made at work, every move. He talked about Simon, how much better he would have been, how much he had wanted Simon in the business, how he wished that he had another son until Blake thought he couldn't stand it.

In the middle of one evening when Irene had gone for a bath he went off to the peace of his own room and stood drinking whisky. There was a balcony, and it was a nice night so he finally sat out there on his own. The room overlooked the big gardens at the back of the house and now it was quiet with the shadows beginning to fall across the garden.

There was a soft knock at the door and when he didn't answer Irene opened the door and said, 'May I come in?'

There had been no polite enquiries when they had lived in the pit town, Blake thought ruefully. Those days she was always flinging herself into his arms. Now it was like having antiques all over the place. He was always frightened he was going to knock something over or break it and that included Irene. She didn't look much like the girl he had married, she was too self-assured for that and now particularly, coming into the bedroom wearing a nightdress that made him stare. It was almost transparent. She was like another man's wife, a rich man's wife. He had a sudden longing for tea in the kitchen in Seaton Town and Irene in a remade dress. He looked carefully at her as she came out on to the balcony. The clinging stuff had thin straps over her bare shoulders and it was the palest cream like ivory. It showed every curve.

'Do you like it?' she said.

'I think it's disgusting,' he said and pulled her down on to his knee and kissed her. Irene laughed. She put her arms around his neck and looked at him.

'Are you very unhappy?'

'How could I be unhappy with you?'

'That doesn't answer the question. I'll put it another way. Do you hate it here?'

He smiled in recognition of the question he had put to her when she burned the dinner at Mary Ann and Ralph's.

'Yes, I hate it. I'm not a gentleman, Irene, and I'm never going to be.'

'I don't care. I adore you. I know that my father and Simon are impossible but Simon isn't here very much and Daddy . . . is awful. Do you want me to talk to him?'

'No, it won't make any difference.'

'You must admit,' Irene said, fingering the lapel of his jacket, 'that you do look very nice these days. Tailoring is so important. I'm frightened to let you out in case some woman steals you. Must you wear such dark suits and white shirts?'

'Why not?'

'Because, darling, it drives women wild.'

'Don't be daft, Irene.'

'Davy, I don't think you ever look into a mirror. Are you going to make love to me or am I to starve? I went shopping today and bought this ridiculous outfit so that you would slaver. Please?'

She called him 'Davy' in the bedroom. Blake liked it. He kissed her. Irene looked at him.

'You look like somebody else's wife,' he apologised.

'Adultery is meant to be fun.'

Blake carried her into the bedroom and put her down on to the bed and kissed her and then he took off his jacket and pulled at his tie and she sat up, said, 'I'll do that,' and then there was a knock at the door.

Blake glared at it.

'Go away,' he said.

'Mr Richmond says you're to go downstairs at once.'

'Tell him I'm busy.' Irene was undoing the buttons on his shirt now.

'He says it's important, sir.'

'Bloody hell. Don't move, Irene, I'll be back in a minute.'

He put on his jacket and pushed back his hair and followed the maid down the stairs. The door of Sylvester's library was open and Sylvester stood by the desk where the telephone was.

'What is it?' Blake said and as he did so all his impatience fell away. He shut the door. Sylvester was leaning on the desk as though he couldn't stand up. 'Are you in pain?'

'It's Simon,' Sylvester said.

Simon was still in training. He couldn't be hurt. Blake searched his mind for possibilities.

'What's happened?' he said.

'He's been shot.'

'Shot? How could—'

'It was an accident. Some boy . . .'

'Is he badly hurt?'

'He's dead,' Sylvester said.

Blake had met disaster often enough for his heart to encase itself in ice but even then he didn't know what it was like to lose a son. He thought that the nearest he had come was the loss of his grandfather. He knew that Sylvester Richmond no longer liked him, that he had not done so for a long time. Ever since they had met he had desperately wanted to be the son that Sylvester had wanted. Simon was not and now he never would be but he knew that Sylvester resented that he was there and Simon was not, that he had a fine natural ability for business which Simon had lacked. He could almost feel the way that Sylvester Richmond hated him and worst of all there was nothing he could do to ease the pain. There was nothing anybody could do. He had never been anything other than a source of amusement to this man and now he was a means to an end so that Sylvester could go on being powerful, having the shipyard. He was of use and that was all. Now he had another use.

'You can tell Irene,' Sylvester said as though he was conferring a favour.

Blake went over to the cupboard where the decanter stood and poured him some brandy. He didn't offer it to Sylvester, he was too afraid the man would dash it out of his hands. He placed it just within reach and then he left the room. He walked slowly up the stairs and into his bedroom. His wife was sitting up in his bed, naked, and she was smiling.

'That didn't take long,' she said and then she saw the look on his face. 'David? Tell me what's wrong, tell me quickly.'

He sat down on the bed and tried to find the right words before he realised that there weren't any.

'Simon's been hurt.'

'Badly hurt? He's dead.'

'Yes.'

He knew that her grief wasn't for the man that he knew or even the man that she knew, it was for the memories. It was for being children and growing up together and all those things which could never be tampered with now or destroyed and it hurt the more for that. He knew that she couldn't understand how they had grown so far away from one another, of how much she had wanted Simon to be the brother he had been when they were children and that he hadn't been for so very long now. She put on the ridiculous nightdress and covered it with a suitable wrap from her room and then she ran downstairs to her father. Blake went after her. The old man's mood was uncertain and he didn't want her hurt any more by these people who claimed her and then rejected her and then reclaimed her. Sylvester took her into his arms.

'You're all I've got now,' he said and the room echoed to Blake of the little hillside farm. He tried not to think too often of those days, it turned his emotions upside down. You could think too much about the things which had damaged your life. He couldn't bear to think of Alistair and Annie there. Mary Ann had told him that Annie had had a little girl. He thought of her being brought up there and playing outside and of how his mother had done the same thing and he shuddered.

Sylvester didn't go to the yard that week. Blake went alone. He knew so little without Sylvester that he felt like an intruder. Irene had wept over her brother. Blake had held her in his arms all night but after that first reaction with Irene Sylvester showed no emotion of any kind. He was silent and still, he didn't eat or sleep and there was the funeral and another week and still Sylvester wouldn't go to the shipyard.

The days went by and Blake kept on going alone until it became a habit. People began consulting him about the things they would have talked to Sylvester about and when he came home he would relate what had happened, hoping to awaken some kind of interest in the older man, but nothing happened and Blake was obliged to go to the experts that he had and delegate the responsibility as Sylvester had never done because he didn't know how to do anything else. To his surprise the men worked harder for their further involvement and the yard ran more smoothly. He held meetings so that they could voice their ideas. He was at work so often and for so long that Irene complained of neglect.

'It's like walking about blind being there without your father,' Blake said.

'I know that but I need you here at least sometimes,' she said. 'Especially now.'

'Why especially now?' Blake said, taking her into his arms in the privacy of her bedroom.

'We're going to have a baby,' Irene said.

Blake hugged her to him. 'Does your father know?'

'As if I would tell him before I told you.'

'Tell him now; it's the best thing he could possibly hear.'

'I love you, David Blake,' she said.

Twenty-five

It all happened as Annie had feared it would. Sunniside was sold and rather than go back and live with his father, when the war began Alistair joined the army. Annie went home to Grayswell with little Susan and left Charles Vane bemoaning the fact that the goverment wanted farmers to use their land to grow crops when he had concentrated mostly on dairy farming. Ploughing was the thing that first winter, and in the freezing weather in the fading light Annie left Susan with her mother and gave herself up to the task of ploughing as much of Grayswell as they could manage. What had been pasture became oats, barley and wheat. When the MinAg men came on threshing day to take the corn they took every last bag and there was nothing left to feed the hens on. Tommy was eager to join up and Frank, much to Madge's distress, had done the same. Mr Harlington taught Madge to plough and Elsie helped both at Grayswell and at Western Isle.

Alistair had joined the Durham Light Infantry and as Susan became a little older and was able to be left Annie sometimes got the chance to go across to Brancepeth for the weekend and see him there. In some ways it was better than being at home, his father was not forever wanting him to go to Western Isle and they spent time together, going dancing and meeting new friends and joining up with Madge and Frank and Tommy and Clara.

One Saturday night, and the summer of 1940 was glorious, Tommy and Clara, Madge and Frank went with them from Brancepeth to a dance in a Durham hotel and while they were standing at the bar waiting for drinks Annie saw two people walk in. Men not in uniform always stood out at dances these days but he would have stood out anyway, she thought. The dark suit was perfectly cut and he was tall with thick fair hair and there was something not just familiar but even nearer than that. It was Blake. The young woman with him made Annie stare and then made her envious and finally angry. She had copper-coloured hair which was swept on top of her head, pinned with what looked to Annie like a very expensive gold clip, and she wore gold earrings. She was perfectly made up and the dress she had on was pale caramel-coloured crêpe, long and simple to just below the waist where it veered gradually into soft tiny pleats. The neckline was not low but flattered her long neck and the colour of her hair, and the sleeves were just ruffles to show off the tops of her arms, ruffles which followed the line of the material almost down to her waist. Annie had never before seen such a dress. They didn't come near, they went to the other side of the room to meet other people, but Annie had to turn away.

'Did you see that?' Madge whispered. 'What wouldn't I give for just one dress like that? However do people afford it, especially now?'

'It was probably just an old thing she had in her wardrobe,' Clara said laughing. 'And wasn't he handsome? Who could resist a blond man? I wonder what colour his eyes are.'

'They're blue,' Annie said, looking at her husband who was talking quietly to Tommy. 'With a touch of grey in them.'

Madge looked at her.

'It was Blake,' Annie said.

'Don't be silly,' Clara said. 'Blake couldn't look like that in a million years. They must be very rich.'

'I think you're seeing things, Annie,' Madge said.

Blake chose that moment to look in their direction

and after a minute or two he and the beautiful woman got up and came across. Annie wanted to run out of the hotel and catch the next bus back to Brancepeth. Her dress was pretty, it was deep green, long with big puffed sleeves and a V-neck, but she knew that beside the other young woman's it looked like something cheap and secondhand.

Blake was actually smiling when he reached them.

'Good evening.'

Alistair said, 'Hello, Blake, how are you?' and Annie blessed him for his naturalness. Frank muttered hello and Tommy looked them both up and down and said, 'Well, well, don't you look prosperous? Wouldn't the army have you then?'

Blake introduced them and when he introduced Irene as his wife Annie went cold with jealousy. She couldn't believe it and she hated herself for the way that she felt. It was hard to see him with a woman so undeniably classy, wearing in her ears what Annie felt quite sure was real gold. She had on a wedding band and a ring warm with rubies. It glittered madly under the lights and worst of all Annie could feel the three men stare not just because Irene was so beautiful but because the dress that she wore merely hinted at the curves of her body.

She smiled and she had a flawless accent and when Tommy spoke she laced her fingers through Blake's fingers but he only smiled.

'You could say I'm more associated with the navy really.'

'Oh,' Tommy said, 'how's that?'

'I build ships.'

'What kind of ships?'

'Aircraft carriers, destroyers—'

'All on your own?'

'Not quite. Irene's father owns a shipyard.'

Annie thought back to Mary Ann. She had not mentioned Blake in a long time. Annie knew that he was no longer at Seaton Town but she had carefully not asked and Mary Ann was too tactful to say anything. Annie had not known where Blake was or what he was doing. She had not known that he was married or even in work.

Irene's other hand was clasped around a glass of champagne in which the bubbles were still working themselves to the surface.

Blake said one or two other polite things – his manners, Annie thought, had gone up several notches – and then he went back to his friends with his wife. Annie wanted to go off to the ladies' cloakroom and burst into tears but she couldn't and she happened to look at Alistair just then and that was another shock. Never before had they looked so much alike.

'That bastard,' Tommy said, when Blake had gone, 'I never liked him.'

'How did he come from nothing to something that fast?' Frank said in dismay.

'I expect he worked,' Alistair said. 'Who wants another drink?'

'He could work for fifty years and never get that far,' Tommy said as he went to the bar with Alistair.

They had to wait. From the bar Alistair could see Blake and Irene and their friends and he wondered as he had sometimes wondered before why he felt sympathetic towards Blake. They had nothing in common. He had always felt jealous that Annie had preferred Blake when they were younger. He thought it was because Annie and Blake were the same age and he was two years older. The gap was too much for him to have been friends with Blake until it was too late. He wondered what she felt now with Blake sitting across the room with the most elegant woman that Alistair had ever seen, looking so rich. He had stopped listening to Tommy going on about Blake. He took Annie's gin and tonic back to her.

She swallowed a third of it in one gulp and smiled brilliantly at him.

Later they danced and later still Annie met Irene in the ladies' room. She was sitting applying fresh lipstick when Irene came in and sat down beside her.

'That's a very beautiful dress,' Annie said.

'Thank you. It isn't new. Who gets anything new nowadays? I bought it just before the war. You have a little girl, don't you? Mary Ann told me.'

'You know my grandmother?'

'I lived with them for a while. She was very kind to me. She was kind to Davy too.'

'Davy . . .' Annie said.

'What's your little girl called?'

'Susan.'

'We're going to have a baby,' Irene said, smiling blissfully at her.

'It doesn't show.'

'Not yet.'

Irene went off and shortly after that they left. It was unfortunate that the others came out just in time to see Sylvester's silver Bentley pull out of the car park. Annie couldn't think of a thing to say all the way home.

'We ought to get rid of this damned car, you know,' Blake said as they turned into the street. 'It drinks petrol.'

'We never go anywhere. All we do is work. Besides, it's Daddy's second love after the shipyard.'

Sylvester was back at work, fired by the idea of helping the war effort, taking on a full workforce, designing and building the right kind of ships and making money. He and Blake were at work all the time except when they were asleep. At first there had been long gaps in Sylvester's concentration but he gradually got better and to Blake's surprise their roles became almost reversed so that he was doing the major part of the work while Sylvester sat beside him offering what was usually good advice. After Sylvester went back to work his criticism of Blake ceased and Blake felt guilty because he was enjoying the war when plenty of people he knew weren't. He tried to tell himself that he was doing a good job but to compensate he worked so hard that he lost weight and couldn't sleep and couldn't eat and was perpetually trying to turn out the work faster and better.

'Your farm girl's very beautiful,' Irene said now.

'Irene—'

'Oh, I don't mind. Why should I? She's married now with a child and we're having a baby. Her husband seems rather nice.'

'He always was,' Blake said.

'It's difficult not to hate people though when they've taken what you wanted.'

'I envied him so much. He had everything, parents, a public school education, a big farm just waiting for him because he was an only child . . .'

'The other two don't like you.'

'No.'

Irene smiled.

'They liked the look of your wife though.'

'I noticed.'

Irene sat back against the big leather seat and closed her eyes.

'Wait until I'm eight months pregnant. Then I'll really be something to look at. I might just close my eyes for a minute.' Blake took one hand off the steering wheel and gathered her in beside him. She smelled of the perfume she always wore. It was the most wonderful smell in the world. Often in the early mornings he could smell it on the pillowcases.

'I love you,' she murmured against his ear.

Blake thought that he had never been as happy in his life.

Twenty-six

Frank was captured at Dunkirk and taken prisoner and Annie moved to the Hall to give comfort to Madge. She took Susan with her and that helped to distract Madge, that and the work.

Mr Harlington had started drinking again when the war began and even more heavily after Frank's capture so he was not a lot of help. Elsie was mostly there too. The three of them ran the house together but keeping everything going was hard. The house had taken on a dusty neglected air which Madge wasn't very happy about but providing food for people was now the important thing. The house had to wait.

Tommy had gone into the RAF and was never at home during this time, being in the ground crew, keeping the aeroplanes in the air. Clara complained that Tommy was happy there, having managed to get away from farm work at last.

'He hasn't been this pleased with himself since he used to take the post round,' Elsie observed crisply.

Alistair was away. Annie had no idea where he was and spent a great deal of time trying to reassure his mother and putting up with his father's blusterings. Charles Vane was almost as little help as Mr Harlington except that he didn't drink as much. Only her own father, Annie thought fondly, went on just the same as he had always done.

One Sunday afternoon, when Annie had taken Susan over to Grayswell for tea, the tea was ready and her father was missing.

'It's always the way,' her mother grumbled mildly, 'the minute you put the tea on the table folk find something better to do.'

Annie went out into the yard and called his name but there was no reply and she thought of where she went when she wanted to be quiet and she walked down the field to the river. He was sitting there on a big stone.

'Daddy,' she said, 'what are you doing? The tea's ready. Mam's getting herself into a right state.'

She didn't say any more because he only smiled and she thought about how he had been quiet all the week.

'There's something the matter, isn't there?' she said.

'Aye.'

She sat down beside him. There were tiny fish among the rocks, flitting about under the water in the sunlight.

'You're going to have to tell somebody. Is it something serious?'

'It's bad enough. I've been called up.'

'You have? Whatever for? You're too old—'

'I'm not that old,' her father objected. 'It's a specialist thing you see. They want me to go as a small arms expert.'

Annie didn't say anything. She knew, though her father rarely talked about it, that he had gone away to the First World War when he was much too young to do so and had been a sniper, killing men when he was little more than a child himself, and married too. She knew also that her father was a brilliant shot from the days when he had taken her shooting. He had taught her to shoot by sitting her behind him and letting the barrel of the shotgun rest upon his shoulder. She had seen her father take a left and a right with pigeons and they were not an easy bird. He was what the other farmers called 'a pot man'. Her father killed nothing without good reason and she knew that her parents had never had much money so her father shot over his land and there was always meat of some kind on their table. She remembered coming down here when she was little and finding her father in mid-stream of a Saturday evening fishing. He would go out at teatime and come back after a couple of hours with fresh trout for supper. Her mother took it for granted. Her father never came back empty-handed like other fishermen. Freshly cooked trout in Grayswell butter was one of the delights of Annie's childhood.

Yet he loved nothing better than to watch fish or to have his dog put up a covey of partridges from a hedge though he would bring the dog to heel for fear it should touch them. He would never let poachers anywhere near and when he found them he always did what he called 'banging their heads together', which meant that they would be sent on their way staggering. Pheasants walked safely over the fields at Grayswell and her father was always bringing in injured kittens or hares or ducks. Her mother said it was sometimes more like the vet's than a farm.

'Frank's father wants to sell me the farm,' her father said now.

'I know. I overheard you and Mam talking ages back.'

'I can't afford to buy it. I'm frightened somebody else will.'

'Who buys anything in wartime?'

'We've lived here for a very long time. My grandfather farmed here. I promised myself that I'd get it for us if

Harlington could ever be persuaded to sell it but I can't raise the money.'

'Have you asked him not to sell it to anybody else?'

'He needs the money. We'd better go back. Your mother will be past herself.'

'Are you going to tell her about going away?'

'I'll have to. She will help you. You know how to run the farm.'

'I just don't want to do it without you.'

'It won't be for ever,' her father said.

A lot of people had sent their children to America, some had even gone themselves and the rich in the area had been the first to have shelters built in their gardens. Irene didn't say anything to them but she didn't approve, especially of those who lived inland with big houses and huge gardens who closed up their houses and left when both the houses and the gardens were needed. They were in America and the people left here were fighting for them when every foot of ground was needed to grow food and the inland houses were needed to evacuate the children. Irene did what she could, talked to the right people, tried to help.

Women were trained as men left the shipyards. When the bombing started the shipyards were targets for the

Germans and she knew that Blake expected daily that there would be severe damage to Richmond's yard but it escaped. One early afternoon in May 1941 the sirens sounded just after the midday break. The bombs which fell within a few minutes missed the shipyards completely but destroyed houses in various streets and two weeks later there was a six-hour raid.

Everywhere there were destroyed buildings, most of them houses, but nothing was untouched, the streets, the shipyards, the railway station. People died or were hurt or spent hours in musty shelters. Irene took in as many of those who had been made homeless as she could and was perpetually seeing to meals and finding clothes for them.

Irene and Blake's baby was a boy. She and Blake had talked about the child and she knew that he didn't care either way and neither did she but she thought that secretly her father wanted a boy although he was a more tactful man of late and would not for the world have said so. But when the boy was born she could see by the joy in her father's face that he was pleased and he came to the nursing home every day of the fortnight Irene was there to hold the baby and smile.

'What are you going to call him?' he said.

'Well, I don't know but not Sylvester,' she said laughing.

'I should hope not. It's the most dreadful name in the whole world,' her father said.

In the end they called him Anthony, which was an old family name, and added Richmond in the middle so her father was well pleased. Blake said that he didn't care what the baby was called, he just wished that it would shut up occasionally. Sylvester insisted on having a nanny for the child and although Irene would rather have done without she let him have his way and was very glad of it during the first few months because she was so tired and Blake was no help being almost always at work. Sylvester was there a great deal too; he seemed to glory in the ships they were building, he was so proud of them.

One summer day in 1942 when Blake was in his office at the shipyard his secretary came in, puzzled.

'I've got a young woman on the telephone,' she said. 'She wants to make an appointment to see you. She won't tell me what it's about and I've told her how busy you are but she's most insistent. Her name is Mrs Vane, Mrs Anne Vane. Shall I get rid of her?'

Blake stared into space for a few seconds and then he said, 'No, just see when she wants to come.'

*

It was a long way. It wouldn't have been nearly so far by car but Annie didn't want anybody to know that she was going so she said that she was going shopping, made sure nobody saw her and took the train.

She had never been to Sunderland before in her life and was quite surprised at how big it was. She had had nothing to eat that morning and wanted to have something before she went to the shipyard office but she found that she could swallow nothing, she was so nervous.

Only desperation had sent her to Blake. If there had been anybody else to help she would never have gone but there wasn't. She had tried to talk to her father-in-law but he wouldn't help her. He said that he had no capital and he managed to make her feel greedy. Alistair confirmed what Charles had said. Because her father had no money at all no one would loan him what he needed to buy the farm and she could think of no other way.

She found out where the shipyard was first and then walked the streets. She was not interested in anything, the shops held no pleasure for her. There was not much to buy in them anyway. She couldn't concentrate. In the end she was early and once she got there she only wished that she had stayed at home.

She was ushered through dark corridors and past doors with various names on them and then through a set of wide doors and up a big staircase where the linoleum had given way to carpet. The young woman with her was tall and blonde and well-dressed in a blue costume which Annie envied her. She did not talk as they mounted the stairs. The carpet was thick and there was silence. At the top of the stairs there were more doors. Everything was brass and mahogany, not modern at all, as though the company had been prosperous for a long time. There was the smell of lavender polish and cigars and leather. The corridor was a wide hall and at either side there were doors. The young lady finally stopped outside a door and ushered her into the office and left her.

Blake got up from behind a big leather-topped oak desk and came to meet her and Annie could have laughed for how strange it all seemed. This man, she thought, had never been a farm boy. His cuffs were perfectly white and had gold cufflinks, and his suit was so well cut. His smile was nicely calculated and he held out his hand to her and it was not a hand that did any work.

'Hello, Annie, how are you?' he said easily.

'I'm fine,' she managed.

The office had a big window which looked over the river and at any other time Annie would have been delighted to see the ships on the river and the town at the far side. The office itself had several inviting leather chairs none of which she felt capable of sitting in. The blonde came back in with a tray. The crockery all matched and was silver and blue and white and there were tiny dark chocolate biscuits.

'Have one of these. I don't know where Irene gets them from.' He sat her down and gave her tea and smiled at her.

'So. How's Alistair?'

'Fine.'

'And your little girl, Susan?'

How had he known about that and remembered her name?

'She's fine too.'

'We have a little boy,' he said.

'That's lovely. I didn't know.'

Annie had to concentrate on her tea because her hands wouldn't keep still and although the little biscuits looked delicious she was afraid that she would choke so she didn't have one. Her stomach rumbled emptily.

Blake leaned against the front of the desk in a friendly way that worried her and asked about her mother and father and the others and chatted a little about Irene and the baby. He even made her laugh once or twice.

'So,' he said finally, 'something's the matter?'

'I need help,' Annie said, trying to get the words out with them falling over one another. 'I need some money.'

'Money?'

'Yes. Mr Harlington is going to sell the farm. Dad is desperate to buy it. We have no capital. We're better off since Grandma died . . .' Annie stopped there. It sounded so heartless but the old lady had been so sour and so hard to keep. 'I thought you might help. Oh, I know . . .' Annie put down her cup and saucer here, glad, relieved to have got the words out and not caring what she had to say to get what she wanted. 'I know how you feel about me—'

'I doubt that—'

'I know what I did but I . . . I just thought that you might help because of Dad and Mam, that's all. They would pay interest, I'm sure they would.'

'How on earth would they ever do that?' Blake said and Annie's insides nearly hit the floor with disappointment. 'Look, Annie, I haven't got any money or I would give it to you. I know I look as if I have but I don't have anything. How could I have? I started with nothing and went down. I don't have a house or a car or anything to call my own. It all belongs to Sylvester. I just work for him like I worked for your father. I don't own anything.'

'But you – you look so rich.'

'I'm not rich. I married Irene, that's all. It just happened. She . . . it's a long story. Sylvester had a son and he died and he needs or he says he needs somebody with him. He doesn't really, he's perfectly competent, but he's getting old. I'm just his son-in-law, that's all, and for me to ask him for money on somebody else's behalf – well, I just couldn't do it.'

'I see.'

'I'm sorry, Annie, I wish I could help. I would if I could.'

'I'd do anything rather than have my father lose the farm; he's worked so hard for it and our family has lived there for a very long time.'

'Yes, I know. I know how you feel about it. I felt like that about Sunniside. Did you like living there?'

'Not much. It felt as though you were there.'

'I feel like that too sometimes.'

'I'm staying at home now that the men have all gone.'

'Couldn't Mr Harlington help? His son is married to your sister.'

Annie shook her head.

'They're in a bad way financially. There's nothing he can do. He needs to sell the farm.'

Blake saw her out. Annie wished that he wouldn't.

She wanted to go somewhere and quietly hate him and despise his civility and his calmness and his suit. Once out in the street she took deep breaths of air, thinking that the office had been stuffy. She didn't cry in the street. She didn't cry in the train on the way home. It wasn't until she reached the white gates of the farm and saw the big stone dog which her grandfather had carved there so many years ago that she finally gave in to her tears and stopped blaming Blake for something which was not his fault.

Twenty-seven

Not long after Annie had left there was a slight noise at Blake's office door. Sylvester moved softly for a big man and now he came in, hesitating slightly in case Blake was not there or had someone with him and when he saw that neither was the case he shut the door.

'I understand that you had a visitor,' he said.

Blake cursed Sylvester's active mind and his way of knowing exactly what went on in the building.

'Yes.'

'A young woman.'

'Yes.'

'And she wanted?'

'It's personal, Sylvester.'

'My dear boy, while you are married to my daughter nothing that you do with another young woman is beyond my curiosity. Enlighten me.'

339

'She wanted to borrow some money,' Blake said flatly.

'She thought you cared sufficiently to loan her some?'

'Yes, she did.'

'And?'

'I haven't got any money, Sylvester.'

'David, is this your polite way of asking for an increase in salary?'

Blake laughed.

'No,' he said, 'it isn't. You pay me very well, I know that. She needs a lot of capital.'

'I keep on telling you that you can have what you want—'

'No.'

'One of these days,' Sylvester said slowly, 'your independence will be the undoing of you, lad.'

'I'm hardly independent. I live in your house, drive your car and work at your shipyard.'

'You don't have to work at my shipyard. My rivals would be happy to filch you from me. As for the rest I don't like living alone. You don't want to deprive me of my grandson's rather noisy company, do you? What did she want the money for?'

'To buy a farm. Her father is the tenant. They've lived there for a long time. They have the chance to buy it. She's frightened that if they don't buy it somebody else will.'

'Do you want to buy the farm for her?'

'No, of course I don't.'

'For her family, then – these are the people who took you in?'

Blake looked straight at him.

'I don't owe them anything. I worked hard every day of my life while I was there and they treated me like a servant most of the time. I never had a single day off in all the years that I was there. I don't want to buy the farm for them, I don't want anything more to do with them and as long as I live I don't ever want to go back there.'

'You wish perhaps to take revenge?'

'What should I want to take revenge for, Sylvester?'

'I don't know. Passions take people that way. Perhaps you would like to buy the farm?'

'Do you know, Sylvester, you remind me slightly of that bit in the Bible where the Devil showed Him all the kingdoms of the world—'

Sylvester laughed.

'Let's keep the Bible out of it, shall we? Is it good land?'

'Yes, it has a river running through it.'

'The Wear in fact? God love it. Where would we be? Land is always a good investment. I'll buy it for your birthday.'

'No!'

'Tell me, if the owner is so pressed to sell and the tenants cannot afford it is it not the truth that someone else will very likely happen past and buy it at a very good price?'

Blake didn't say anything.

'I think we ought to buy it. I think it would be very sound.'

'Sylvester, I don't want the farm.'

His father-in-law was at the door by then.

'David, you lie like a gentleman.' He opened the door and hesitated. 'Did she cry when she left the office?'

'No.'

'You mustn't forget that money is just a commodity and such a useful one. I expect she cried a good deal when she got home,' and Sylvester left the office.

Joseph Harlington came to Grayswell. It had been such a good day too. Tommy and her father were both at home and Alistair was coming home. He was due to leave the country again; he did not know where he was going but Annie had the feeling that once he was gone it would be a long time before she saw him again. Even so she was trying to make the best of what time they had. Her mother and Clara had made a big dinner, it was Sunday and they were all as happy as they could be considering that Madge was alone. She had not come to Sunday dinner but that afternoon she and Mr Harlington had come to the farm.

Annie was surprised to see him, he rarely ventured anywhere especially in the afternoons since after the Sunday meal he had usually drunk enough that he was not capable of walking further than his armchair by the fire. He looked to her too sober for comfort and when Rose had made tea they sat around the fire and he said what Annie most feared.

'I've had an offer for the farm, Jack. I'm sorry.'

The blood drained from her father's face and Annie knew how hard this was for him.

'That's not fair,' Tommy said straight away and Jack put a hand on his arm.

'You know the situation, Tommy, if we could have raised the money we would. We couldn't so we have nothing to complain about. Try to behave like the man you think you are.'

'You can't sell it to anybody else,' Tommy said, almost shouting at Joseph Harlington. 'This is our home!'

'You'll still be living here. It probably won't feel any different, Tommy. That's all I can offer,' Mr Harlington said.

'Who's bought it?' Rose asked.

'A man called Sylvester Richmond.'

'No!' Annie said, brought to her feet. Mr Harlington looked vaguely at her.

'You know him?' he said.

'He's Blake's father-in-law.'

Tommy let out what was almost a howl.

'That bastard!' he said.

Tommy wouldn't wait. Annie didn't blame him. They got into the old truck and drove. It didn't seem to take long because Tommy made the truck go faster than was good for it. It was the finding of Sylvester's house that took the time and then Tommy halted the truck at the imposing building where the Richmonds lived.

'Is this it?' he said almost beneath his breath.

'It must be.'

'It's bigger than the Hall.'

Tommy drove in at the gates and up to the front door where he parked the truck and then he got out and hammered on the door and Annie stood there with him. A middle-aged woman opened the door. Tommy pushed past her and he went into the great wide hall and there he shouted Blake's name.

At first there didn't seem to be anybody about and

then she saw Blake coming down the stairs with a baby in his arms. He had the child held in against his shoulder as though it had been crying.

'Please don't shout like that,' he said.

'I'll shout as much as I like,' Tommy said. 'How could you do that to us, after all my parents did for you? You're a no-good bastard.'

'I haven't done anything,' Blake said.

'You've bought the farm, our farm!'

'No, I haven't.'

'Don't split hairs, Blake. Your father-in-law has bought it.'

'I can't help what Sylvester does with his money,' Blake said. 'It was nothing to do with me.'

From the depths of the house a very big man came into the hall.

'What is going on?' he said.

Blake's wife came down the stairs at that point and took the baby from him.

'You did it on purpose,' Tommy accused Blake, 'because Annie wouldn't marry you.'

Annie looked into Irene's eyes and wished herself anywhere else.

'I think you ought to leave, Tommy,' Blake said evenly.

'Why, what are you going to do about it?'

Sylvster roared with laughter at this point.

'You can tell the man's a farmer,' he said, 'he's like a little bantam cock.'

Tommy turned and glared at him.

'That farm is my home.'

'No one's disputing the fact. Nothing will change, except the shape of your face, I dare to predict, if you persist in calling David names. You don't look to me like you're much good with your fists. I should go home if I were you,' and Sylvester turned and walked back into the darkness of the hall.

'Take the advice, Tommy,' Blake said gently.

Tommy stood there for a few seconds as though he was going to hit Blake and then he turned and walked out.

'What I don't understand,' Alistair said afterwards, 'is how Blake knew the farm was for sale?'

Annie blushed.

They had gone back to Western Isle and were sitting by the fire. She hadn't wanted to go. She hadn't wanted to leave Grayswell, as though Sylvester Richmond might suddenly appear and throw them out. She knew that Alistair wanted her to himself, to take her to bed, but Annie couldn't think about anything but what had happened.

'You told him?' Alistair said in wonder.

'I went to see him. I thought he might help.'

'Whatever gave you that idea?'

'He's rich,' Annie said helplessly.

'Annie, he was desperately in love with you, he wanted to marry you—'

'He bought the farm anyway. How could he do that?'

'Why shouldn't he? You should be glad that somebody did—'

'I just wish it had been anybody else.'

'Why, what difference does it make now?'

'He told me – I went to his office – he sat there and told me to my face that he had no money and couldn't lend it to me or he would have.'

'That's the truth, surely. It isn't his money. I don't understand how Tommy could make such a fool of himself—'

'It's all right for you. You'll have Western Isle. We'll never have Grayswell now, not ever,' and Annie got up and ran out. She ran upstairs and when he followed her into the bedroom she turned a wet face to him and said, 'I'm sorry, Alistair, a fine homecoming this was.'

'It's all right. I know you're upset.'

'It wasn't for Tommy, it was for my father. He's worked so hard and he wanted to own the farm. I was only trying to help. Tommy was so angry when he realised I'd gone to Blake. I made things worse.'

'No, you didn't,' Alistair soothed and she went into his arms and hid there. 'I don't suppose Blake cares about the farm anyhow, why should he?'

'Why not?'

'He has other things now. He has a wife and a son and a good living. He'll have the shipyard after Sylvester. He got out of here.'

'You sound envious.'

'I am. It took the army to get me out.'

Annie laughed through the tears and then she kissed him.

'We won't talk about it any more, I promise,' and she kissed him again. 'Let me show you how much I've missed you,' she said.

Twenty-eight

Blake could not help feeling guilty about the buying of Grayswell. He had tried several times to talk Sylvester out of it and then had given up. Sylvester had decided that they would own the farm and own the farm they soon did. Blake felt betrayed somehow and that he had in his turn betrayed the Lowe family. He also felt threatened. He kept dreaming that he was at the farm or going to the farm and he spent time brooding about it. He had wanted to get away from the dale, thought he had managed and now it was as if the connection could not be severed. He had wanted to shut the past out of his life and it intruded over and over again. There was also a less than nice part of him that said there was no reason he should not own Grayswell since Alistair and Annie had owned Sunniside. He argued with himself that it was not the same thing but the wounds had not healed from childhood. He doubted that they ever would.

Sylvester did not make it easier. He had the deeds made out in Blake's name and presented them to him on the morning of his birthday. Irene was not impressed.

'Father, you are a meddler,' she said, presenting Sylvester with his ration of bacon and egg.

Sylvester picked up knife and fork and began to demolish the food with speed.

'You don't want me to die of boredom now do you, child?' he said.

Irene said nothing more. Blake said nothing at all. It was not until they were alone in her bedroom that night when she was sitting at the dressing table brushing her hair and watching him through the mirror that she was able to talk to him. He was lying on her bed, fully dressed, totally silent and apparently absorbed in his thoughts.

'Are you upset about the farm?' she said to him.

'I just wanted to pretend that it had all gone away.'

'The past doesn't go away,' Irene said, 'especially the nasty bits. Maybe facing it will help.'

'Tommy never liked me.'

'I hate to be rude but I can't say that I took to Tommy very much . . . or your farm girl either. I wanted to go over and pull her hair.'

Blake smiled.

'I'm glad you didn't,' he said.

'Sometimes dignity is all there is left.'

Blake said nothing to that. Irene got up and went to him.

'Don't worry about it. It wasn't your doing.'

'It's got my name on it, Irene.'

'Oh damn and blast them,' Irene said. 'They didn't appreciate you when they had you and I don't see why we should care about it now. I know my father is an interfering old bugger but there's not much we can do about that.'

'Irene, your language is awful.'

Irene laughed.

'There speaks the farm boy. If I were you I'd try to get used to owning things. You're going to own a great deal more than a farm one day.'

'What do you mean by that?'

'Davy, my father isn't going to live for ever, even though he thinks he is, and you are married to me. He owns a great many things. In time we'll inherit the shipyard, a chain of shops, a part-share in half a dozen ships, several houses and a fish and chip restaurant.'

'A fish and chip place?'

'It's the most valued thing he has. He was born there. His mother ran it.'

Blake laughed.

'I thought his parents had the shipyard.'

'They did but my grandmother liked having her own business. She had a pub too and a shop but they started out with the fish and chips. Such giddy heights as you have come to, a family who made their way frying fish. So you see, a farm is nothing. Besides, your farm girl deserved it.'

'That's not very nice, Irene.'

'I don't much care. I should think she's very sorry now.'

'Alistair Vane's all right,' Blake said grudgingly.

'He seems the best of the lot, not that that's saying much.'

'I always sort of liked him. I did go through a time when I thought Charles Vane might be my father.'

'Did you?' Irene said. 'Why?'

'Just talk.'

'But you don't think so now?'

'I don't know. I didn't want to think that a man like that could have been my father but he's Alistair's and Alistair isn't like him at all. He's rather nice really.'

'You're rather nice too,' Irene said and hugged him.

Afterwards there was not a way in all the rest of his life in which Blake could think about what happened that summer without pain. Not once in all the time that followed did his life ever quite recover. It was too much to absorb. To an extent he could accept that his grandparents had died because they were older, he could accept his mother's death because he had not known her and his father's absence but when Irene died the whole world stopped.

He always remembered every detail, every second about that day. The way that Irene was upstairs with the baby when he left so instead of kissing her goodbye he only shouted up to her, the way that he had not seen her, the silly quarrel they had had the night before because they were both tired. He remembered leaving the house, going to work, how he spent the morning. There had still been no bombing of Richmond's yard.

That morning when Blake and Sylvester were at work and the nanny was out with the baby in his pram because it was a fine day a single German aeroplane came in over the coast just above the town and a minute before the sirens sounded dropped three bombs.

There was nothing left of Sylvester Richmond's fine house and it was hours before they dug the bodies out of the rubble, among them two people Irene had taken in the week before when they had lost their own home, and Irene herself.

When Blake was summoned and went home it made no impression on him that other houses were ruined, that other premises were nothing but rubble, that other people had been killed. He could not believe that what was left had been a place where he and Irene had lived together with their child and Sylvester. He could not believe that anything had stood there other than what remained and he could not believe that Irene was dead.

Some friends of Sylvester took them in, Marjorie Philips and her husband, Neville. He was a ship owner. Sylvester had known them a long time. Blake remembered Marjorie from Sylvester's Sunday get-togethers, when she was always sidling up to him, smiling sweetly because her husband was away.

She didn't sidle up to him now, she was white-faced with concern and shock. She made sure that Hetty Forster, the nanny, was comfortable and could manage with the baby. She prepared rooms for them, she made food which they didn't eat and gave them brandy which Sylvester drank but Blake didn't.

He dragged himself to work day after day because there was so much to do and Sylvester was no help. Sylvester didn't go to work, he stayed at home and there Blake presumed Marjorie tried to entertain him with gossip. Blake even went to work on the morning of Irene's funeral.

He didn't sleep so there seemed little point in staying in bed, he couldn't eat and after the funeral the house was full of people making kind remarks. It seemed to him that things had to get better after the funeral but they didn't because he kept on having to get up after a sleepless night and carry on. He tried to find reasons for getting up.

With Sylvester not at work there was more to do. Blake didn't seem to get tired. He could be awake all night, eat nothing and work eighteen hours a day and not feel any worse. There was no way that he could feel any worse. The nights got longer and longer even though he was only in bed four or five hours. Lying there awake thinking of Irene was the worst torture that had ever been devised. He was frightened of how he felt as though he would never want to do anything again, as though he would never want anything or anyone again. He hated the sound of the baby crying because it reminded him of how happy they had been; he couldn't bear to have the child around him. Sylvester did nothing now, all day. He slept in the afternoons. Blake didn't know whether he slept at night, they didn't talk.

Even walking around the streets of the town reminded him of her all the time. The parks they had gone to, the shops she had liked. Everywhere was the sound of her laughter and her voice and she was nowhere.

One night about three months later when Neville was away from home and Sylvester had gone to bed he went to his room to find Marjorie there. She was not a bad-looking woman for her age, she had kept her figure, but there was something almost pathetic about the way she wore the seductive nightwear which was much too young for her. Her face was covered with make-up, subtle so that she looked younger than she was but the clinging material hinted that her body had long since given away its secrets and was starting to feel tired. He told himself that he must try not to offend her but he was so surprised that he stood back against the door inadvertently shutting it behind him, and himself and Marjorie inside.

'I thought you might be lonely,' she said.

'Marjorie . . . I don't want to be rude but . . .'

'Men are no good at being on their own,' she said. 'I know if anything happened to me Neville would marry again straight away. I just thought you might like a little bit of comfort,' and she began to take off the top layer of whatever it was she had on. Blake's first reaction was that he wanted to go and tell Irene because it would make her laugh. Instead he managed to get the door open and walk out.

He left the house. In the streets there were people.

They were determined to have a good time in case there was no tomorrow. The men and many of the women were wearing uniform. They were laughing loudly, singing. There was singing coming from the pubs and music from the dance halls. There were cinemas and clubs and it seemed like the whole world was out. Blake was comforted there because it was only the present. There was no past and no future here, there couldn't be.

He went into the nearest pub and had a drink. It felt so good, the first one always did. The second beer slipped down easily too and after the third things didn't seem so bad. There were lots of girls in the pub, some of them fair and one with red hair but nobody had the particular shade that Irene's hair had been. They were all young, not like Marjorie. He shuddered thinking of Marjorie, her body starting to give in to life, not firm any longer, tired. He was tired too. The other people in the pub didn't seem tired; they were making the best of things, the air was blue with cigarette smoke and the people behind the bar never stopped serving.

He lit a cigarette and thanked God for alcohol and nicotine and the fuggy warmth of the pub. He drank until he couldn't think any more and then he walked home and went to bed and slept.

*

He tried to persuade Sylvester to go to work with him but the older man had no enthusiasm.

'Sylvester, I need you there. I can't manage without you.'

'Liar,' Sylvester said mildly.

'I'm getting it all wrong, Sylvester. I'm incompetent, I'm ruining your company.'

'You can't, the whole thing is too well insulated for any one person to ruin it. Besides, you have more ability in your little finger than most men have in their whole bodies.'

They never talked about Irene. They couldn't talk about her in the past, she would be dead then. Nobody else talked about her either. Their friends never mentioned her.

After six months Blake was invited to a dinner party. He didn't want to go but he knew that his friends were trying hard and a dinner party was a rarity in these days of rationing. It meant that people had made sacrifices.

He thought of saying that he couldn't spare the time and it was true that he was working very hard but the idea of actually going to someone's house for food and conversation was too inviting so in the end he agreed.

He didn't have far to go, it was just along the road. Even in the blackout it was no real trouble. He was glad he had gone when he got there. The hostess, Phyllis, greeted him with a warm smile, her husband, Clive, provided him with a glass of beer. Several people there were known to him but after a while it became clear to Blake that Pauline Kington, who had been Irene's good friend, had been asked for his benefit. She was seated next to him at dinner. Her perfume wafted under his nose. Her dress showed off her pretty arms and neck.

Blake tried to eat and couldn't; he tried not to drink too much and that was nearly impossible too. Pauline talked. He didn't know what she was talking about because he felt sick. No one mentioned Irene. It was as if she had never been.

Blake excused himself and went to the bathroom. He felt faint. The big black and white room swayed and then he was sick. The dinner and the beer went down the toilet bowl and after that he washed his face and hands, swallowed some cold water thankfully and stood outside the front door in the darkness, taking big breaths of fresh air.

When he went back into the drawing room Pauline looked up and smiled. Blake knew that if he stayed at the other side of the room it might seem offensive so he went over and sat beside her, declined coffee, smoked a cigarette and listened to Pauline talking about books and films and politics. Around him the others discussed the war and business.

'The war was the saving of the shipyards, wasn't it, David?' Clive said.

'Was it?'

'Oh, come. Since 1935 you've been coining it in. I daresay Richmond and Dixon has never made as much money in all of its existence. Some people have done very nicely out of the war and you're one of them. A great many people have work now. Before the war many of them had nothing.'

Luckily Pauline was staying so Blake didn't have to be polite and offer to walk her home. He didn't think he could bear another second of her smiling sympathetic beautiful face or her intelligent remarks. It was not long before midnight that he reached his bedroom. There was no sign of Marjorie, no sound of any kind, just the thankful silence.

It was a long time since he had gone to bed sober and after the first few minutes he stopped being thankful for the black silence, began to resent his wakefulness and to wish to be drunk enough so that he could sleep.

He looked at the shadows in the room. He thought about the evening. He thought of how dinner parties used to be fun, going out with Irene, having her somewhere near all evening, coming home to talk everybody over. And then the best bit. Bed. Not necessarily sex but just being there, the joy of Irene's sweet body, to be able to turn over and know that she was there, the warmth, the comfort, the silky feel of her nightdress when she wore one, the smoothness of her body when she didn't.

He thought of her voice and her laughter and then he thought of the way that her coffin had been lowered into the ground with her name and age so bright in brass on its plaque on the top, never to be seen again.

They had offered him a double plot in the burial ground as though his life was finished and he had been horrified but now it didn't seem such a stupid idea. He did feel as if his life was finished.

He whispered her name to the room over and over again to try and keep her presence alive. There was no headstone at Irene's grave. Sooner or later people would remark on it. Sylvester would want that and then, when there was a stone with her name on it, then he would know for certain that Irene was dead.

After this wakefulness Blake made sure that he was drunk every night when he went to bed. He couldn't go through those nights where sleep was never a visitor. He couldn't go on pretending that he was sane during the day without sleep of some kind. If he was drunk he could sleep for three or four hours before the wakefulness claimed him again and those hours were enough to get him through the work and the day.

He was not afraid of dying now. He never worried personally about the war and every teatime he looked forward to the evening, to that first glass of beer. He wished that his whole life could be that first glass of beer, when anticipation was the important thing. The second and the third were good, the fourth was important, the fifth was vital and after that he moved into the kind of happiness where nothing else mattered.

He and Sylvester moved into a house. It was better, Sylvester said roughly, than watching Marjorie salivate every time Blake walked into the room. Marjorie had, unknown to Sylvester, been very off-hand since Blake had walked out of his bedroom.

The house was on the edge of town and made Blake think of the country. The gardens were dug up for vegetables but the house was empty. It was not a big place, just a kitchen and bathroom, two small reception rooms and three bedrooms. The previous occupants, the landlord told them with a grin, had died of a nasty disease.

'It doesn't surprise me,' Sylvester said, looking around

when the man had left. 'The plague, by the age of some
of this furniture.'

That made Blake smile.

Sylvester became absorbed trying to make some kind
of order in the house and the nanny, Hetty, seemed
determined to help. Hetty was not just the nanny any
more, she did the housekeeping and she managed all
by herself because the young women were away in the
forces or the factories. Hetty was not a young woman,
she was in her fifties. She seemed to like fussing over
Sylvester and to Sylvester's disapproval she had a brother
who got her things on the black market so quite often
there were real eggs for Sylvester's breakfast.

She fussed because Blake didn't eat. He took to going
out in the evenings because she didn't seem to approve
of him drinking in the house or maybe it was the quan-
tity. She didn't approve of the way that he never wanted
to see the baby either. If it hadn't been for the fact that
Sylvester liked Hetty so much – she was, Blake thought,
the saving of his sanity – Blake would have got rid of
her. So he left them sitting cosily around the fire with
the baby and went out. It was weird. It was like, for the
first time ever, having parents. Indeed, Hetty treated him
so much like a son that Blake would have been amused
if amusement had been possible. So he went out after

work no matter how tired he was and there at some bar he drank his worries away in a sea of alcohol.

The room was dimmed but not dark when he awoke that particular Thursday morning, as though beyond the curtains the day was trying out a pale sun for size. But that was unimportant. The important thing was that the miracle had happened, the thing he had most wanted in his life had actually occurred; the past few months were nothing but a nightmare and it was over. He was lying in her arms. He was naked and she was wearing the kind of nightie which he had loved best, with the satin feel to it which accentuated the curves of her body. He could feel the warmth of her beneath it, the swell of her breasts. She had her arms around him as though protectively somehow and she smelled of a perfume which was faint and all the more enticing for that.

And it was the perfume which broke the illusion. It was not Irene's perfume. He tried to hold on to the first awakening, the delight, the magnificent blinding relief that Irene was alive and that it had just been a bad dream, that nothing had happened and they were in bed together just as they had been so many mornings though never enough, but it was too late now, the illusion had gone and pressing behind it was the even more unacceptable idea that if she was not Irene then she was somebody else and although he didn't have a hangover, just a strange, rather pleasant lightheadedness, he didn't remember who she was.

She was apparently awake because when he tried to move out of her arms she let him. The bed was big enough for him to move back and look at her.

She was very young, eighteen or nineteen, and she had fair hair and blue eyes. She was extremely pretty.

'Good morning,' Blake said.

'Hello. Would you like some tea?'

Blake had the thirst of a perpetual drunk. He nodded.

'I'd love some.'

She got out of bed and Blake admired the outline of her figure before she put on a rather disappointingly shapeless dressing-gown and left the room.

He sat up. The bedroom was very ordinary. It had in it some dark heavy furniture, a wardrobe, a dressing table and the bedhead and foot, all depressingly dark and dingy, he thought. Nothing modern here, as though there was little money.

Sunlight was trying to get past the dark red and green curtains and here and there tiny shafts of it fell on the wallpaper. It was the kind of wallpaper which could be painted over and it was dark cream.

When she came back with tea and toast on a small mahogany tray Blake sat up. She put down the tray in the middle of the bed, there was plenty of room it being a double, and she sat with her feet under her and handed him a teacup.

'I ought to make you some kind of apology, I just don't know what to say,' Blake ventured.

'You don't remember?'

'Not even your name.'

'Helen, and you haven't anything to apologise for. You just passed out. I've never seen anybody drink like that. And then we came back here and you took your clothes off and . . . when you were unconscious I thought you'd died.'

'I'm sorry.'

'I know how you feel,' she said, picking up a small piece of buttered toast. 'I know exactly how you feel. My husband was in the merchant navy.'

'Dead?'

She nodded.

'Two months ago.'

She didn't eat the toast; she sat there with a cup of tea in one hand and the toast in the other as though she needed to give her fingers an occupation. In the next room a baby started to cry and she got up from the bed and came back shortly with a little girl in her arms. The child looked about six months old. Blake put down his tea, took the baby from her and the noise stopped.

'Magic,' Helen said.

After he had cuddled the baby she took her, sat back against the pillows and fed her and Blake sat and watched her just as he had done with Irene, the intent way that the baby sucked, its tiny hands on her breast and afterwards she changed it, her hands deft with nappy and pins and there was silence. It was the most peaceful silence Blake had heard in a long time. He lay down and closed his eyes and Helen put the baby between them and in a very short while as the room warmed with the morning sunshine Blake fell asleep.

Twenty-nine

When he got home late in the morning Hetty looked disapprovingly at him. Sylvester, sitting with the baby on his knee, looked surprised.

'I thought you'd be at work,' he said.

'I'm just going. I have to get changed.'

'Why don't you have the day off?'

'Can't.'

'I want to talk to you, David.'

Blake paused halfway to the stairs.

'Won't it wait?'

'You work all day and you drink all night.'

Blake went with him into the small sitting room where a fire burned high in the grate.

'Did you spend the night with a woman?' He caught Blake off-guard.

'Yes. I'm sorry, Sylvester, I—'

'Don't be sorry. You're killing yourself with work and drink, you might as well have something to enjoy.'

'I didn't . . .' Blake couldn't go on.

'Are you going to take Anthony?'

'Later.'

'He's lost one parent. Don't you think he needs you?'

'Sylvester, I have to go to work—'

'You'll damned well listen,' Sylvester said, raising his voice. 'Your son needs you and so do I. You're not more efficient for working the hours you do. How can you be with a bloody permanent hangover? The business will not fold up if you take the odd hour or even for God's sake the odd day. When was the last time you had a day off? You even went to work the day of Irene's funeral.'

'I had to.'

'I know you had to. Well, she's been dead over seven months now, David—'

'I know how long she's been dead—'

'I know you do but don't come back here drunk any more and be back for dinner.'

'I'll be back in time for Anthony's bath,' Blake promised.

Blake went to work but was back in time to eat with them and he put the child to bed and he sat with Sylvester that evening by the fire with nothing stronger than a cup of tea. He went to bed early because he was so bored and slept. When he awoke it was eleven o'clock in the morning and he felt wonderful. His head was clear, the day was bright and he was hungry. He ate a huge breakfast and then he and Sylvester walked Anthony in his pram in the park. It was Sunday.

'I didn't mean to push you around,' Sylvester said apologetically, stopping the pram as he spoke.

'Yes, you did. I'll make a bargain with you, Sylvester.'

His father-in-law eyed him with care.

'I'm not sure I like the sound of this.'

'I'll stop drinking if you'll come to work.'

'I can't come to work. I'm too old.'

'Too heartbroken?'

'That too. Both my children.'

'You have a grandson.'

'Thank God I have. Maybe he'll be the saving of us both.'

'I'll stop drinking for a week if you come to work for a couple of hours every day. Will you do that?'

'Two hours?'

'Yes.'

'I can do that.'

'Right.'

Sylvester held his gaze.

'What?' Blake said.

'It wasn't Marjorie Philips, was it? The other night?'

Blake laughed.

'No, it wasn't Marjorie Philips.'

'I am glad,' Sylvester said and he set off pushing the pram again.

Their life settled into a dull routine. Blake went to work every day but not for such long hours and Sylvester went with him for four or five hours. Anthony walked and talked and grew and kept Hetty very busy. Blake went nowhere. He turned down the invitations and stayed at home listening to the wireless with Sylvester or playing cards with Hetty or just reading. He also spent a lot more time with the little boy who soon became a person and not a baby. Blake bathed and took him to bed every evening and read him a story. At weekends and on summer evenings all of them or one of them took Anthony to the park to sail his boats. The little boy was nothing like Irene. It hurt Blake. To his dismay the child looked like the Vanes, he was dark, but the more time Blake spent with him the more the little boy responded to him.

It was a long time before Blake finally became

sufficiently bored to want to go out again. The first night that he went drinking with some of his colleagues from work he wanted to get drunk, the beer tasted so good, but he didn't. He had two pints and then went home. They managed to persuade him to a dance though he left early and occasionally afterwards he went out to eat but it was always such a relief to go home.

One summer evening after a day of very hard work he went with two friends into the country for a drink. They hadn't intended to go far, petrol was short and journeys weren't encouraged, but it was such a beautiful evening and they had not been anywhere in so long that they just kept driving for the sheer novelty of getting away from the streets and work of Sunderland.

Blake wasn't driving so he had no say in where they went. They stopped in Durham for a drink and went on and it was only when they ventured to within a few minutes of the dale that Blake's nerves got the better of him.

'Hadn't we better get back?'

The driver looked at him.

'It's early yet, Davy.' His friends at work had picked up Irene's habit of shortening his name after she started using it all the time.

'There's a pub up here that I used to know quite well, just down the bank here.'

It was a lot further than just down the bank and Blake's mind became a cinema reel of memories as they ventured nearer and nearer to his old homes. Finally they drove into the car park of a pub and there was a dance going on.

Inside the place was crowded and was as usual full of servicemen, in various stages of inebriation. They fought their way to the bar for drinks and Blake looked around. There were plenty of pretty women. One, coming towards the bar, rather drunk, cannoned into him and when she lifted her face in apology he saw it was Madge.

Blake had always wondered how they would react knowing that he now owned Grayswell and Madge hesitated.

'Blake! How lovely to see you,' she said nervously. The sweet smell of gin and tonic wafted over to him. 'How are you?'

'I'm fine. How are you?'

'Managing. Frank's still away, you know.'

'You must miss him very much.'

'It gets worse,' she said.

'Yes.'

'Tommy's here somewhere, and Annie.'

'Annie is?'

'Yes.' Madge waved vaguely. 'Across there.'

She excused herself and went off to the ladies' and Blake wandered around the room until he saw Annie. She was sitting on somebody's knee and he was not Alistair Vane. He was a big man wearing an officer's uniform. Tommy was sitting next to him. The music had stopped so Blake had no difficulty in hearing what Tommy said as he looked up.

'Well, well, if it isn't the owner. What are you doing, come to check that we're running your farm properly?'

Annie didn't speak to him at all. She had her arms around the man's neck. Blake had a grave desire to pull her off his knee and hit the officer and then hit her. He went away back to the bar to his friends.

Annie danced with the officer, close. Tommy and Clara danced together and Madge had some man. Blake's friends found women to dance with but he didn't want to dance. He went outside.

The dale never changed, he thought, and it was a perfect evening, the kind that never got dark. He heard somebody behind him and when he turned it was Annie.

'Did you call in at the farm to see my parents?'

'I haven't been any further up the dale than here.'

'I should think you haven't,' she said.

'Who's that man?'

'What man?'

'The officer you're with.'

'Oh, Johnny. He's just a friend.'

She was drunk too, Blake thought now, she was swaying slightly. Her black hair was shorter than it had been but just as shiny and her brown eyes were so cold on him.

'I'm surprised you have the nerve to come back here,' she said.

Blake said nothing. Annie's gaze faltered.

'I'm sorry,' she said, 'and Tommy's sorry too. He sent me out here. We just didn't know what to say to you, the abuse was easier than anything else. We're very sorry about Irene, Blake.'

Blake couldn't think of anything to say.

'Come inside and dance with me,' Annie said.

'No, thanks.'

He walked back inside and left her there.

He badly wanted to go home now, back to the safety of the house and the child and Sylvester. He didn't want to be here, there was nothing for him here, but his friends were dancing and drinking and seemed happy with the women they had found so he sat down in the corner of the bar and ordered beer.

After a few minutes Annie appeared at his elbow. 'Where's Alistair?' Blake asked.

'He's in Burma fighting the Japs.'

'And you're sitting on somebody else's knee?'

'I don't see what business it is of yours, or do you think you're your brother's keeper?'

'He's not my brother.'

'How do you know?'

'I just do.'

'Well, you're wrong.'

'How do you know?'

'There are ways of telling. He has exactly the same eyes as you. He kisses like you do as well.'

'You're drunk,' Blake said dismissively.

'It was one of the reasons I married him.'

'Oh, shut up.'

'Will you dance with me?'

'Certainly not.'

'I'll go back and dance with Johnny. Or would you rather buy me another drink?'

'You've had enough to drink.'

'Yes, Grandpa.'

They danced. The music was slow. Blake looked around for Tommy first, thinking he might object and cause a fuss but Tommy and Clara had gone. It was getting late. Johnny tried to cut in but Blake wouldn't let him.

'If he leaves I have nobody to take me home,' Annie said.

'I'll take you home.'

'Do you still have that big silver car?'

'I'm with other people.'

'Do you still have it though?'

'Sylvester won't get rid of it.'

'I don't blame him.'

'It's not much good when there's hardly any petrol.'

'I'm sorry about Irene. I envied her so much, you can't imagine.'

'That was only because you thought I was rich.'

'No, it wasn't.'

'Yes, it was.'

'She was so beautiful and classy. I always wanted to be like that. When I saw you with her . . . I felt such a yokel.'

Blake smiled at that.

'You were never a yokel. How long has Alistair been away?'

'A very long time.'

'Is that why you sit on people's knees?'

'I wish you would stop going on about it. It's none of your business.'

'I wish you wouldn't do it. It isn't fair to him.'

Annie stopped dancing and looked up into his eyes.

'You like Alistair, don't you?'

'Yes. I like him a lot.'

'I don't sleep with Johnny, you know. Or anybody else.'

'All right.'

He took her back to the farm. The night was warm and still. Blake patted the old stone dog on the head. It was so strange being there with Sunniside almost in sight, the village not far away and the churchyard. He wanted to be there, he wanted to run into the farmhouse with her and be fourteen again. He had never felt less at home here than he did now that he owned it. He wanted so much to be welcome here, to be able to visit, for it to be normal, for Rose to ask him in for tea and ginger cake. Annie reached up and kissed him briefly on the cheek and said goodnight and he watched her in at the white gates and down the cobbled yard and up the step and in at the back door. He imagined her bolting the doors, walking through the big kitchen and up the wooden stairs and along the hall. He thought of her parents and her child asleep and then he thought of his own child asleep in Sunderland and was glad when he could go home.

Later that week when Blake went out for a drink with the same friends, he spotted some people he knew. Pauline

Kington was with them with a man he didn't know and Blake excused himself and went over. Somehow after seeing Annie he felt lonelier than ever and as he reached Pauline he thought that she looked pretty. She greeted him with obvious pleasure and asked after Sylvester and Anthony. Blake went back to his friends but he rang Pauline and asked her if she would go to the cinema with him. It was an easy way to ask her out; there were plenty of cinemas within walking distance and the nights were fine and light. They went out to tea first. Blake didn't intend it but it was Irene's favourite teashop. Somehow he missed her even more being there with another woman. He tried to think what they had ever talked about and only knew that it had always been wonderful but Pauline was pretty and kind and she sat there smiling at him from across the table so Blake wasn't too unhappy.

He walked her home in the gathering dusk. It was good just to be walking with a woman again, to spend time, to appreciate her pretty face and her chatter. She worked in a shipyard office, her father owned the place, he was one of Richmond and Dixon's rivals, so they had plenty to talk about. Before he had always thought that women would be bored with his work but Pauline understood the intricacies of the business and was happy to talk about it. It was only when Blake got home that he thought Irene had hated talking about shipyards and shipping and work and it hadn't made any difference to their relationship.

Thirty

Long before the war ended, at least it seemed to Blake like long before and at least before other people thought the war was ending, things changed in the shipyards. By the end of 1944 the Admiralty began to cancel their contracts. Blake had an aircraft carrier almost finished when it was cancelled with two more cancelled which were just at the planning stage. By the early part of 1945 he had a good amount of non-warship orders and the pressure was off. The men gradually went back to working normal hours.

Sylvester had been of late very dissatisfied with the small house they were renting and as soon as the war was over he went looking for another.

They had no celebrations. They had lost too much to be anything other than relieved it was finished and to sorrow over Irene and Simon. Between work and house-hunting Sylvester tried to encourage Blake to go out more but he never wanted to now. He thought that perhaps it was the aftermath of war, the coming down. Some months before he had awoken in the night from some terrible dream he could not recall and had not felt the same since.

There had been a kind of fear, maybe even physical which he had not experienced before within the dream, of men shouting in another language and of open land somewhere that was not here and then there was a loud bang and after it silence, a complete silence such as he had not known, like a cushioning, a peace and when he had awoken it was strange to find himself in darkness in the small rented house and it was different than ever before. It was the strangest thing, as though there had been too much loss, as though there had been too much sorrow, as though nothing that went on in the world had anything to do with him now. The peace before he awoke had been an unimaginable relief.

The feeling passed when day came and the ordinary noises of the day began. He felt that he belonged again, there was the child and Sylvester and Hetty and there was work but there was too an almost physical pain which did not go away, it had to be carried around with him like a heavy parcel and it was as if only work and home were safe. Nothing made Blake happy. His friends introduced him to various women but other than being polite to them Blake didn't spend any time with them.

One day in the spring of 1945 he and Sylvester went to look at a house. It wasn't far from where they were living now and while they were there Blake began to think about Grayswell and the family.

'You aren't paying attention,' Sylvester said.

'What?'

'You aren't listening to me.'

'Sylvester, I spend a great deal of my life listening to you.'

Sylvester grinned.

'I know you do, my boy. I want to know what you think about the house.'

'I like it.'

'Good. I like it too. We must get some help for Hetty when we move here. The poor woman's managed all this time. She can't be expected to go on for ever doing everything herself.'

'Sylvester, would you mind if I sold the farm?' Sylvester looked at him.

'If you need money—'

'It's not that. I want the Lowes to have it. I thought

that if I give them a chance to repay me bit by bit it might work but you bought it for me, gave it to me. I don't want to upset you.'

Sylvester stood there grinning happily.

'I wondered how long it was going to take you,' he said.

'What do you mean?'

'Well, I did offer to lend you the money to give them in the first place, if you recall, but I don't think you felt sufficiently friendly enough towards them to help them and I wasn't going to push it. I don't mind what you do with it but I'm very glad.'

'Sylvester, you are a serious manipulator.'

'How else do you think I got rich?'

On the first Sunday afternoon that Blake could get away alone he drove Sylvester's Bentley up to the dale. He knew that it was the best time to catch Jack and Tommy straight after their Sunday dinner so he timed his visit. He drank in the views all the way. It was a sunshiny spring day and the world looked good. He parked the car a little way from the house and walked back.

The yard was empty. He opened the little side gate and went over and knocked on the door. To his surprise Annie came to the door. He had not thought of her there, he thought of her with Alistair, perhaps having dinner with his parents at Western Isle.

'Hello, Blake,' she said.

It was not the most overwhelming welcome Blake had ever had.

'Hello.'

'You'd better come in.'

They had evidently just finished eating. Rose was washing up in the back kitchen. Madge was not there, she must have been at the Hall with Frank and Mr Harlington, but Elsie was there with a young man he didn't recognise and whom nobody offered to introduce him to, and Jack and Tommy were there. Alistair was nowhere to be seen.

The room went silent as Annie ushered him in and she went straight back out again. Rose didn't even come out of the kitchen. They didn't greet him, they didn't offer him a seat. Blake stood in the middle of the floor and said to Jack, 'I want to talk to you about the farm.'

'As far as I'm concerned there's nothing to say unless there's something you're dissatisifed with.'

'No, it's not that.'

'You can't put us out—'

'No, it's not that either.' For some reason Blake couldn't get the words out. 'I want to sell it to you.'

Jack shifted in his chair. Tommy, for once in his life,

had nothing to say and Elsie got up with her young man and they went out.

'If I could have afforded to buy it I would have done when Mr Harlington offered. I haven't the money to buy it and I can't raise it. Don't tell me you need the money.'

'No. We could draw up a legal agreement and you could pay us back gradually like a mortgage.'

'At what price?'

'The same as Sylvester paid.'

'At what interest?'

'None.'

'It was a low price.'

'Yes, I know.'

'Why?'

'No reason. A farm isn't any use to me.'

'I don't understand why you bought it, or why your father-in-law did.'

'He was just trying to make a point.'

'Dear way of doing it.'

'Maybe.'

'I'm sorry about your wife,' Jack said shortly.

'Thanks. The solicitor will be in touch.'

Blake turned to go. Annie was standing in the doorway. She followed him out to the car.

'You haven't got rid of it yet,' she said.

'We will, sooner or later.'

'Make it later. It was nice of you to come. You didn't have to. You could have done it through your solicitor by letters.'

'I decided I did owe your parents.'

'And you'd rather it was the other way round?' she asked, smiling.

'Who bought Sunniside?'

'Elsie and her young man are going to live there. His parents have it. They own shops and picture houses.'

'That's nice.' Blake opened the car door. 'How's Alistair?'

Her face changed. Blake pushed the door shut.

'He is all right, isn't he?' Blake's insides were doing crazy things now as they had been trying to do for months. The black blinding feeling came down on him, the feeling he had been pushing away all that time. 'He's at Western Isle with his parents?'

She was shaking her head but she didn't say anything.

'He's not. He got hurt in Burma? I knew it.'

'The Japanese shot him. He's dead.'

'No. No.' He could remember the night, he could remember the shot, he could remember how it had felt since then. The loss, the sick feeling, the not wanting to go on, the not wanting to admit that something important was stopped and he knew then for the first time what he had not admitted to himself all these years, that he and Alistair were about as close in blood as it was possible to be. Alistair was dead and there was nothing in his memory that would make it any easier.

'I think you'd better come back inside,' she said.

'Never. Never again, never. I hate this place. I hate all of it,' and to his own consternation Blake leaned his arms on top of the car roof and started to cry but only for a minute or two. He turned wet eyes on her. 'And what did Charles Vane say when they told him his only son was dead?'

Blake hauled open the car door. Annie tried to stop him.

'Blake—'

He pushed her out of the way.

'Blake, stop it, you'll have an accident. Don't you think it's bad enough? Don't you think it's bad enough for me?'

He stopped, took a couple of deep breaths and said, 'You could have bloody well told me. You never write any bloody letters to me. Never.'

'I'm sorry. I just knew that you were going to feel like this about it and you'd already gone through it all with Irene and . . .'

'Why didn't you tell me? I could have come and . . . I

couldn't. Nothing helps, I know it doesn't. I knew that he was dead.'

'How?'

'I don't know. I just knew. I kept telling myself that I was just being stupid and that it hadn't happened, that I couldn't have known. Nobody could have been less close than Alistair and me.'

'I don't think that's quite true. He liked you a lot. Come back inside. I'll get Mam to make you a cup of tea.'

'No. I'm going home. Your dad will have the farm now. It was what he always wanted.'

He drove away. He drove for a couple of miles and then pulled in at the side of the road and gave in to the tears, tried to think of the few good times they had ever spent together and remembered the night before Madge's wedding, sitting in the ford at Stanhope, singing drunken songs with Alistair.

Thirty-one

'I need another drink,' Annie had said, waving her glass.

'We should go.' Madge looked uneasily at her.

'Stop worrying, will you? There's plenty of people to take us home.'

'I didn't want to be here in the first place.'

'You've danced every dance with a different man. What more could you want?'

'I could want a particular man,' Madge said and got up and walked away.

Annie watched her threading her way through the couples. She felt wonderful. The music blasted its way through the night, the gin and tonic flowed. She only hoped that Madge would not try to go home by herself. Home. She laughed out loud. Some home.

A tall man appeared beside her. She thought hard for

his name but couldn't recollect it and went off to dance with him.

Madge had not gone home and at the end of the evening there was a car and two men. They stopped on the way back, though she could hear Madge in the back objecting and she watched him look at her, turn towards her and then take her into his arms and then it was the moment before. It was the moment of hope when his lips came down on hers and he would be Alistair Vane.

She fought him off. She persuaded him to drive them home. She got out of the car laughing and reached in and rescued Madge and amid the protestations from the men she slammed the car doors and led Madge in at their gates and across the yard to the house.

'He had twenty pairs of hands,' Madge said. 'How could you make me get in with them?'

'It was a lift home and they're officers, aren't they?'

'I don't know how you could kiss him. He's married. They have two children. What about his wife?'

'I don't know his wife. Who cares?'

Clara had looked after Susan and was sitting up waiting for them. They often went out together and Madge would spend the night. Susan was crying.

'She's hardly stopped since you went out.'

Annie made no remark. She took her child and went

on upstairs to her room. She wasn't thinking about the child, she thought about the man in the car and the moment that his mouth touched hers and the cold-water kind of disappointment. It always happened and she always expected it and she hated the tiny part of her which told her in a silky voice that this time it would be him, that this time she would remember and forget and the world would come together again and he would be there.

She hated the going out to look for that this time and she hated the staying in that reeked to her of her youth finished. Alistair was dead and she had sworn to herself that her life was not over but that tiny silky demon voice purred its way through her consciousness and even her dreams and it was cruel.

He was there in her dreams, he was a dozen men and more and himself. He went away, he came back, he found her again and she had given herself to another man and yet she never did, not even in her sleep. She did not understand how her body could ache so much and yet whenever a man touched her she felt disgust. She wanted the ache to go away but it seemed that it was all that was keeping her alive and what she wanted more than anything in the world just then was for Alistair Vane's daughter to shut up. She had cried constantly for months now. Anybody would think that she knew her father wasn't coming back.

Susan did finally sleep and the gin and tonic soothed Annie. She thanked God for alcohol and silence and then she lost consciousness.

That was before, before the war ended. Now it was to some people as though it had never happened; they went on with their lives. Annie didn't know how to go on. Sunniside was long gone, she didn't feel at home here any more with her parents and Tommy and Clara and she couldn't go and live at Western Isle because now that Alistair was dead his parents had no interest in her and none in Susan.

She went often, mostly out of a sense of duty because they were Susan's grandparents, and Western Isle was still a wonderful place but there was a defeated air about it because Alistair was dead. His father no longer wanted to do anything. There were few visitors to the place now and Annie began to hate going so much that she put off her visits. It was as though the house and land had gone into mourning.

Charles dismissed what help they had and retreated to his study. What he did there Annie could never make out but Mrs Vane could not manage things by herself and the house took on a dusty neglected air.

One winter day when Annie had trudged up because it was almost Christmas she walked into the hall and stopped short. Usually there was a big fire with the dogs sitting around it but today there were no lights and no fire and no dogs – she could hear them howling from one of the outside buildings. Mrs Vane came out of the kitchen, she was making a meal, but there was no sign of Alistair's father. The place was freezing. She went thankfully to the kitchen with her mother-in-law and sat for a while but that day was just the beginning. It seemed to her after that that every time she went there things were worse.

The stone walls were allowed to fall down, the road to the house became covered in weeds and rubbish, the fences were in bad repair. Charles got tired of listening to the dogs howling outside with the result that they were allowed in all the rooms and there was mud and hair even in the bedrooms.

That winter Charles went out with the dogs shooting a lot when Annie visited. Dead pheasants lay outside on the stone steps until they were hung, a fox was left to rot by the back fence. Moles were strung up, and rooks by their necks. Inside there was always the smell of wet, muddy dog and Charles stormed about in his wellingtons complaining. Cracked windows were lashed with rain.

Alistair's mother gave up trying to keep things right and kept to the kitchen where it was warm. The once that winter when Charles came out of his study when Annie was there he took one look at Susan and said, 'Get that brat out of my house!'

'This brat is your grandchild,' Annie pointed out furiously.

'Do you see this house? Do you see it? There's nobody to inherit it.' He glared at his wife. 'All she could produce was one child. One.'

'It's only a house,' Annie said, not caring that it was the wrong thing to say.

'Only? Have you any idea how long we have lived here? How long this has been the home of the Vane family? Over seven hundred years and now because of her and because of the war there's no son. That's the first time.'

It seemed to Annie that she understood then what Western Isle meant to Charles Vane. It was more important to him than his wife or his son had ever been just because his family had stuck in one place for hundreds of years. It was quite ludicrous, she thought, that a piece of ground could be so important, and now that he was frustrated he was destroying it along with himself. He didn't understand that he and Western Isle were separate things, he thought that Western Isle was something to be possessed, that he could hold things. Now because the house could not go on being his reason for living he was abusing it, neglecting it. The house needed caring for, not like this but as a part of things which went on regardless of who lived and died, Annie could see. There was nothing she could do; she took her child and went back to Grayswell.

And there she had an idea. She telephoned Blake at his office.

'I want to talk to you. Do I have to make an appointment?'

'Of course you don't. Is there something wrong at the farm?'

'Do I have to come to Sunderland?'

He hesitated.

'I'll come there if you really want.'

'To Western Isle.'

'Why?'

'I just want you to come.'

'Annie—'

'It's important. I know you don't want to come over here but it'll take ages by train and there's Susan.'

'All right, all right. Just tell me when.'

*

Annie looked around her with great satisfaction that morning. It was pouring with rain and had been for several days. The crops were sodden and spoiled in the fields, the house was cold and smelled foisty, the yard was filthy. It looked even worse by the time Blake turned up in a brand-new car the colour of thick farm cream, a Bristol 400. He looked around him and then got out.

Annie ventured into the downpour.

'Do mind your shoes,' she said sarcastically, looking at his unsuitable footwear. 'Come in.'

Blake hesitated.

'Hurry up. Mrs Vane has the kettle on and you're getting soaked.'

She didn't spare him. She took him in through the front door. The hall was bare and cold. The kitchen was better. Alistair's mother chatted nervously and gave him tea. Annie watched him shudder over the tea which had been sitting on the Rayburn for some time and was mahogany coloured and stewed bitter. When the woman tried to drink hers her hands shook so much that the tea spilled into the saucer.

Blake didn't linger. Annie didn't blame him. Outside the rain had stopped but the sky was deep grey.

'Do you want a lift home?'

'This is my home.'

He didn't misunderstand her or pretend to.

'All right, you've made your point. It's nothing to do with me.'

'This is your inheritance. Look at it.'

'It's not mine.'

'Your family has lived here for seven hundred years.'

'No, my family lived at Sunniside. The fact that Alistair's father raped my mother does not make this my inheritance.'

'He raped her? How do you know that?'

Blake looked at her. 'Do you seriously think that a shy sixteen-year-old girl would have sex with a man like that willingly?'

'She might have done.'

'That's ludicrous, Annie, and you know it. He effectively killed her by what he did. He ruined my grandparents' lives and rather than do anything he let me lose Sunniside to go and work as a servant for other people. You don't really think I'm going to come here and play Santa Claus to help him?'

'It's not for him.'

'Isn't it? Who is it for then, you? You think I owe you something?'

'No.'

'That's good because that's how I feel about it. I hope the place falls to bits around his ears.'

'And what about your son?'

Blake laughed.

'You really are scraping the barrel now. My son will have everything. He doesn't need a broken-down farm in the middle of nowhere.'

'Oh, Blake, that really is awful. Look at it, Blake, look at the lovely mullioned windows, look at the stonework. People have lived here for a thousand years. You can't do it.'

'Can't I?' He turned away towards the car.

'What about Alistair? His father made him stay here because of this place. All that sacrifice for nothing. Have you any idea how he would feel if he could see it?'

'Well, he can't see it, can he?' Blake said roughly.

'You could do it for Alistair.'

Blake turned around and glared at her.

'Where are you with all this blackmail?'

'I don't care how I do it,' Annie said from between her teeth, 'I just want you to help,' and she thumped him on the shoulder.

The tears which usually behaved themselves when other people were there suddenly were uncontainable, brimmed and even fell, two or three.

'Will you stop crying?'

Charles Vane came out of the house.

'What the hell are you doing on my land?' he said.

Annie tried to control the tears so that she could speak. 'This is—'

'I know who he is. You have no right on my property, David Blake.'

'Don't worry,' Blake said, 'I'm leaving.'

Annie watched the cream car glide out of the yard. 'That was your chance,' she said.

'They were nobody,' Charles said. 'They never had anything,' and he turned around and walked away back into the house.

Thirty-two

It was all Sylvester's fault, Blake thought, guiding Pauline around the dance floor. He didn't want to be there. She was smiling at him. She had been to the south of France for the summer and had a deep tan. Her dress was low and her arms were bare and she was making intelligent conversation. The dinner had been perfect, beef and wine and cream, red wine, low lights, candles, music. All he really wanted to do was take her somewhere comfortable, haul down her knickers and—

'You're not listening, Davy.'

He wished she wouldn't; they all called him that now whereas once the only person who did was Irene. He couldn't even give Pauline a decent kiss without her thinking she was almost to an engagement ring. He had to go on dancing and hear her talking about politics, proving that she had a mind.

It had been Sylvester's fault, one Sunday afternoon after too much dinner and too much brandy. Blake had been seeing Pauline occasionally until then.

'It isn't good for you, you know.'

'What isn't?' Blake had been playing on the hearthrug with Anthony.

'I made the mistake. I don't want you to do it.'

'What?'

'Go through the rest of your days without a wife. That child needs a mother.'

'He has Hetty.'

'That's not the same thing and you know it. And he's an only child. It isn't good for him.'

'I was,' Blake objected.

'Precisely. Do you want that for him?'

In the end that was what had done it, the idea of Anthony growing up with only one parent, and no brothers and sisters as he had done. Blake began to go out socially and was asked to parties and dinners that summer. He went to picnics and dances. Sometimes he enjoyed them, he liked the conversation, the change, feeling like a person again and not just a parent, but all the time there was that pressure to try and find somebody. At first it seemed as if every young woman would do. They were all so nice, he liked them, they could make him laugh and they could talk to him and then he realised that he had no preference and therefore no feeling for any of them and he became bored.

The wanting of Irene became so bad that everything was a huge effort. Each day getting up was like beginning the climbing of an enormous mountain; each morning it was a bigger mountain. He had promised Sylvester that he would not drink and he thought of Pauline. Now he was dancing with her. One evening soon afterwards he took her home for Sylvester's approval.

Sylvester was his usual self while they had dinner, he made her laugh, he told stories, he got her to talk but when Blake had taken her home, come back and demanded, 'Well?' Sylvester frowned.

'It's up to you, David. She's very beautiful, very bright. Did you take her up to see Anthony?'

'Yes. He was asleep.'

'But you don't love her?'

'I can't love anybody, Sylvester. I love Irene. Pauline's the nearest I've got. I think I could care about her if I got to know her, if we spent some time, maybe.'

Blake tried hard. He took her out. One Sunday afternoon during the autumn he left Anthony at home for once with Sylvester and took her for a drive.

'Where do you want to go?'

'I want to go to the country and paddle in the river.'

It seemed stupid to stay away. There was nothing to stay away for any longer. It was a golden afternoon. They stopped at lunchtime and sat outside a pub and ate sandwiches and drank beer in the sunshine and then they parked the car in the village and walked. Blake deliberately didn't look up at the hills or think about the past, he took her by the hand and they walked from the village across the bridge and down through the wood to the river. There she slipped off her shoes and stockings and put her slender brown feet into the water. Blake sat on the river bank with her and when she turned to him laughing he took her into his arms and kissed her and a harsh voice behind him said, 'What are you doing here?'

Blake had long been stifling his conscience and as he turned and saw Annie it all came back to him, leaving her crying in the yard at Western Isle, pretending that none of it mattered, keeping the bitterness going in his mind so that he would not turn back or come back. He had felt safe at a distance in Sunderland and now he thought ruefully he shouldn't have come here.

She was wearing old trousers and a dirty shirt as though she had put in a long shift. She reminded him somehow of the grim determination of the pit lads in the old days.

Her face was smudged with dirt, her hair was pulled back
unbecomingly and there were shadows under her eyes
like great half-moons. She was thin and her hands were
red with work and she was a shock to Blake after all the
polite and well-bred town girls. Especially she was so
different from the elegant blonde girl beside him in her
expensive cream dress, with her brown skin and her hair
bleached from the French sun.

'We're not doing anything,' he said, getting to his feet.
'Why?'

'This is my land.'

Blake looked around him.

'Yours?'

'I'm farming Western Isle now and I can do without
people like you trampling down the corn.'

It was a big field of golden wheat and he had come
carefully around the outside of it to reach the river.

'We haven't trampled it down.'

'Somebody's come straight through the middle of it,'
she pointed out. 'Some stupid town type.'

'Well, it wasn't us. I do know better than that.'

'There's no right of way here.'

'Then how do other people get to the river?' the girl
said, speaking for the first time.

'People around here have better things to do than

paddle in the river once they're older than about twelve,' Annie pointed out.

Blake said nothing more. They left.

Annie didn't wait to see them. She made her way back up towards the farm and was soon gone from sight. Charles Vane had been taken ill with the flu and was so bad that Annie decided to go over to Western Isle when the doctor was there. She didn't go back to Grayswell, she stayed. First of all she looked after her father-in-law since Mrs Vane wasn't well herself and then she began on the house. She turned the dogs out, she spring-cleaned the upstairs rooms and shut the doors and opened the windows to clean air. Then she began downstairs. She lit fires in the foisty rooms, she blackleaded grates and cleaned cupboards and polished furniture. Mrs Vane got better and began to help. Charles got worse and stayed in bed. Annie made a start with the animals. She cleaned the dairy. She fed the hens properly so that they laid well. She made sure that the milk did not go sour and there was butter and cheese. She took on help, a girl from the village for the house and a boy to help her outside and then she began with the fields.

There was always too much to do. When Charles would not give her any money to help run the farm she went out and sold his car. That summer when she saw Blake down by the river there was still a great deal to do but Annie was determined not to give up. It was to her now almost as though Susan had lost her mother and not her father; Annie felt like a father towards her now, striding around the fields, making decisions, buying and selling. She enjoyed it. She worked from dawn to dusk and sometimes went back to Grayswell to put her child to bed. More often she didn't so in the end Susan went to live at Western Isle and then at least Annie saw her when they had meals together. It also gave Alistair's mother something important in her life other than the man grumbling upstairs.

In the end he got better. Annie had harvested the crops by then, she had the farm working but once he was downstairs again there was nothing to do but see all her work come to nothing. By Christmas it was as though she had not been there, as though she had struggled and achieved nothing. He shouted at her, he hurled abuse, he wouldn't let her do anything she wanted. In the end there was nothing for Annie to do but leave. She felt as though she was entitled to Western Isle, to do what she could for it because of Alistair and because she felt as though it was Susan's birthright. Charles Vane could not have been less understanding.

'This is my house, my farm,' he raged. 'Nobody's ever going to take it from me, in particular no woman will get the better of me. Get out and take that brat with you.'

She didn't want to go back to Grayswell. Her parents had moved out into another house just along the road because her father had been unwell the past few months so although her father officially ran the farm Tommy and Clara were doing most of the work. Annie felt like an intruder in the house even though Clara assured her that she was welcome to make her home there and especially because of Susan.

Annie got a job helping out at a café in Stanhope. She rented a small house for herself and Susan and there she lived that winter. It was not how she had ever thought her life would be. The house was so tiny after the farm-houses she had lived in and she was lonely. There was nothing but a back yard for Susan to play in. She went to school in Stanhope and Annie took her for walks when the weather was fine or up to see Madge and Frank or to visit Jack and Rose. She didn't go to Grayswell much; Tommy was not welcoming.

One day not long before the end of the winter – and Annie was looking forward to that very much, warmer weather and lighter nights – Paul Monmouth came into the café. He had never married. He had a cup of coffee and asked her if she would have dinner with him and Annie agreed but when they were seated in an expensive hotel one rainy April evening she realised now why she had not married Paul. He was boring. Even being out, getting dressed up and having Frank and Madge take Susan for the evening, even the good food did not compensate for the fact that Paul was not interesting. He talked at her rather than to her, he showed no interest in her life. He didn't once ask about Susan or how she felt being alone all this time. At the end of the evening she tried to force herself to see him again since the alternative was to stay at home but never had staying at home looked better. She tried to stop him from kissing her and when he insisted she was as polite as possible and escaped, running into the tiny house and shutting the door behind her. The peace and quietness in the little freezing house was so comforting.

She filled a hot-water bottle and went to bed, huddled there not able to sleep, lying in the darkness with her eyes open, wishing things otherwise.

All winter there had been parties and dinners. People asked Pauline and Blake out as a couple now. He had gone to meet her parents and it was obvious that they wanted him to marry her. Sylvester was tactful and when Pauline came to the house he was kind to her. Hetty was kind too. Pauline seemed to like Anthony. Sometimes they took him out for the day and Pauline bought him ice-cream and held his hand when they went for walks.

Late at night when he took Pauline home and kissed her goodnight her body invited his hands but Blake never touched her. It cost him; it was like turning down the first drink on a Friday night or one of Hetty's Sunday dinners when he was very hungry.

One Saturday night when he came home Hetty was still up. She made him cocoa. Blake hated cocoa but she always made it if she happened to be there so he drank it.

'And how was the beautiful Pauline?' Hetty asked.

'She's all right,' Blake said.

'I won't buy a new hat yet then.'

'What?'

'For your wedding.'

'I haven't asked her to marry me, Hetty.'

'No, but you will shortly.'

'What makes you think so?'

'I don't know.'

They were sitting in the kitchen at their new house. It was a brand-new kitchen with a cream Aga and neat cupboards, windows on two sides to let in the light, a wall-built refrigerator, a square wooden table – Hetty liked the house but she loved the kitchen.

'Don't you like Pauline, Hetty?'

'She's very nice. She's also very bonny and very clever, clever enough to get you to marry her.'

'I haven't decided yet.'

'Do you think men decide? She just has to play a waiting game, that's all, lovely girl like that. Sooner or later you're going to get tired of coming home to bed alone.'

'I'm tired of it now.'

'Yes, I know you are. You're too young to be by yourself and you had too good a wife to think it can't happen again.'

'Don't you like Pauline, Hetty?'

'Yes, I think she's a nice girl and you're a very eligible young man. You're a catch,' Hetty said and she put the cocoa mugs into the sink and went to bed.

Blake thought that Hetty was mistaken, Pauline really did care for him, and then he saw what the problem was: he didn't really care for her. She was beautiful and intelligent and she would make a good mother for Anthony and a good partner in that she was classy and presentable but he did not love her. In the end he had to tell her because he knew that it was unkind of him to make her think they might marry when in fact it was not going to happen.

'I loved Irene,' he said, trying to explain without hurting her later that week at her parents' home. 'I don't think I'm ready to love anybody else.'

She went to him, she did what Blake could bear least: she kissed him and put her arms around his neck and her lovely body close.

'I understand how you feel, I know how much you loved Irene. There's no rush, I can wait,' she said and she kissed him hard. 'Make love to me.'

'Pauline—'

'There's no one here.' She slid one hand down his shirt front. Blake stopped her.

'No,' he said.

'So you aren't going to marry her,' Sylvester said when Blake went home and explained.

'No.'

'Thank God for that.'

'What?'

'You'd be making a big mistake just for the sake of going to bed with her.'

'It wasn't just that—'

'I know it wasn't. Young Anthony liked her. You'll have to tell him something.'

'I will.'

Sylvester gave him a large brandy and then he said, 'What about the girl you had?'

'What, Annie? No.'

'I thought her husband had been killed. Has she married again?'

'Not that I know of.'

'Why don't you go and see her?'

'She doesn't care about me, Sylvester, I've known that for a long time now. She only thought she did in the beginning because I was a bit like Alistair.'

'Aren't you still "a bit like Alistair"?'

'Not sufficiently like or unlike him for it to work.'

Sylvester said nothing more and Blake tried to dismiss the conversation from his mind as he had dismissed her and Western Isle from his life but it wasn't that easy. He told himself that it was a waste of time. He concentrated on work and being with Sylvester and Anthony but there soon came a Saturday afternoon when Sylvester had taken the child to the park and he was not at work and suddenly he couldn't bear the silence any longer, and he shouted to Hetty that he was going out and left.

It seemed like such a long way, longer than ever

before; the car didn't eat up the miles, it just slowly chewed them no matter how fast he went and it was turning into a nasty day. Rain threw itself at the windscreen. The wipers made their little humming sound. He reasoned that she was still at Western Isle so he didn't stop when he reached Grayswell but when he got to the entrance a big For Sale sign swayed in the wind and he stayed there for a minute or so before turning the car in at the drive and it was worse than before. It was worse than he had anticipated. Nothing had been planted, the fields were full of weeds. He stopped the car in the big yard and got out. The lawn in front of the house was knee-high and even longer in the orchard. The animals had gone, the barns and byres were empty, some of the windows of the house were open. Its dark windows were covered in cobwebs and ivy had almost covered some of the upstairs windows at either end. There were no doves in the dovecots. There was no sign of any kind of life except for the cherry trees swaying in the garden. They were covered in pale pink blossom and every time the wind blew it rained pink on the lawns. The wind was the only sound, no lambs crying in the fields, not even a farmcat or a bird. The paint was peeling off the front door and the window ledges and rain had turned the windows grey with dirt.

Somewhere in the big yard a half-door swung open and shut and Blake's memory provided him with Alistair Vane as a big, dark, good-natured lad saying to Blake's tormentor, 'Leave him alone, Tommy, he's only a boy.'

Blake drove to Grayswell and Tommy came out of the byre, saying without rancour, 'What the hell do you want?'

'Is Annie here?'

'No. Nice car. You always have such nice cars, you lucky bugger.'

'Where is she?'

'Why, what's it to you?'

'Just answer the question, Tommy, for once.'

'Old man Vane died. Did you know? Heart attack the doctor said. Couldn't stand losing Alistair.'

'And Mrs Vane?'

'Annie took her in. 'Course she'll have some money when the farm sells. She'll be able to buy herself a nice little house in the village.'

'It was her home.'

'Not much good with nobody to run it and no money to run it with—'

'Charles Vane had money.'

'Not the last few years. He was never a good farmer,

415

you know, as my father says. Made a lot of bad choices. He couldn't hold things together, that's what he needed Alistair for. It would have been all right if Alistair had been alive. That's what my father says anyway.'

'Where's Annie?'

'She has a house in Stanhope. Nice little place,' Tommy said.

The house, as Blake shortly discovered, was down a tiny side street with no view. He banged on the door and Annie opened it.

'Well,' she said, 'look what the cat brought in,' but she let him in.

Blake hadn't realised that he had become used to luxury. The tiny house was a shock. It was very dark inside because there were houses all around it. A cheerful fire burned in the sitting room but there was no carpet, just a rug in front of the fire and net at the window for some kind of privacy from the people walking past. The chairs looked cheap. Annie offered to make some tea. He followed her into the kitchen but it was so small, there was barely enough room for two people and he could see the outside lavatory and the coalhouse through the net at the window and the tin bath hanging up in the yard. The kettle was on over the fire and she busied herself with cups and saucers and milk and sugar, saying without turning to look at him, 'Did you know that Alistair's father had died?'

'I went to Grayswell. Tommy told me.'

'I have Mrs Vane here. She's gone to Madge's for her Sunday dinner and taken Susan. I'm working Sundays you see over at the pub. I've just finished.'

'And Western Isle is for sale?'

'Yes, it's for sale. I just hope somebody buys it soon and we can move into a house big enough to swing a cat.'

'Tommy says he had a heart attack.'

'Do you care what he died of?' Annie said, suddenly quiet.

'Not particularly.'

'Then don't ask.'

'Annie—'

She turned around then.

'It finished him off when Alistair died and you damned well know it,' she said.

'Annie—'

'He fell all the way down the stairs, you remember those beautiful wooden stairs at Western Isle that had been there for hundreds of years? He fell all the way down them, Blake, and when he got to the bottom he was dead, or maybe even before. Are you satisfied?'

'Yes.'

'Right,' and she turned back and scalded the tea. She stood over the tea tray with the big brown teapot on it and she said, 'Did you go to the house?'

'Yes.'

'That was what you wanted, wasn't it? You wanted to see Western Isle like it is now, you wished it. Or maybe you even wish somebody had burned it down—'

'I don't wish that—'

'Don't you? You just wanted to watch it drop to pieces. You wanted everybody to be sorry. Well, there you have it. Everybody is and shall I tell you something else? I do wish I'd married you, I do wish it because I wouldn't have ended up in this pitiable bloody awful little house all by my bloody self!'

'I'm only rich because I married Irene.'

'You always say that,' Annie declared, frowning at him. 'I don't think it's true. You couldn't do the kind of job you do unless you were cleverer than other people. Somebody told me you own it now. Isn't that true?'

'Sylvester made me a partner, yes.'

'He would hardly have done that if he'd thought you couldn't manage.'

'All right then, except for one thing. You never cared for me like you cared for Alistair. Isn't that the truth?'

'Yes, it's the truth. I know you didn't believe it at the time and that it was partly because of you that I fell in love with him but I could never have loved you like I loved him.'

'How are you managing without him?' Blake managed after a little pause.

'I'm not,' Annie said. 'People don't understand, they think you get better after a while but it isn't true.'

'I know.'

'Of course you do. I'm sorry that you know. Do you still want some tea or are you going to storm out?'

'I never storm out.'

'You do it all the time,' Annie said.

She carried the tray through into the other room and put it down on a tiny table beside the fire. It was warm close to the fire but a draught howled in from the outside door. She handed him a cup and saucer. It was not a big cup of tea but it looked to Blake the size of a duck pond. He sat down on the edge of the sofa and it nearly tipped up and spilled his tea.

'You have to sit way back,' Annie explained.

Sitting back was not much better because the cushions displaced themselves and left him sitting on the springs.

'It wasn't a good buy,' she explained. 'I bought it for the colour. It's too short at the back as well. It gives you neck ache after a while and you can't lie down on it unless you're Susan's size because it's too short.'

'The perfect sofa,' Blake said, battling with his tea.

'Settee.'

'What?'

'It's a settee. Only rich people say sofa.'

'I wouldn't have said it was either.'

She smiled at him and drank her tea and put down her cup and saucer on the tray again and then she said, 'What did you come for?'

'I just came to see how you were.'

'You know what they say.'

'What?'

'You can take the boy out of the country but you can't take the country out of the boy. I saw Paul Monmouth again recently. He took me out for dinner. It was the worst evening of my life. He told me all about his shops, I mean all about them. Do you talk to that blonde woman about your shipyards?'

'I only have one.' Blake drank his tea and left.

That night he sat by the fire with Sylvester and told him what Annie had said about loving Alistair and about the farm.

'You should buy it,' Sylvester said.

'What would I do with a farm?'

'It's not what you would do with it, I think you're meant to buy it. If you don't then it goes the wrong way somehow and you've let everybody down, including your fair Annie.'

'She's not mine, she never was.'

'If you bought Western Isle you could put things right there. You could let the land; wouldn't Tommy want it and wouldn't it bring you closer? And we could go there at weekends—'

'It's not a cottage and I don't have much time at weekends.'

'I think if you let somebody else buy it you'll be sorry later,' Sylvester said.

Blake didn't answer.

'Won't you be sorry later?'

'I wanted not to have ties there, I wanted not to go back but casually, occasionally, I wanted to forget it all. I was happy with Irene; I thought it was all finished. Annie doesn't love me and I don't think I love her any more. I just want to stay out.'

'And can you?'

'No, I don't think so.'

Thirty-three

Blake bought Western Isle and very cheaply. Annie was furious. At least Mrs Vane then had enough money to buy a house in Stanhope. She didn't ask Annie to go there to live with her and Annie wished that she had. It was such a nice house, detached stone with gardens all around and enough room at the back for a garage and to keep hens. The garden was pretty with trees and roses and a lawn. It would have been just the place for Susan to grow up. Sometimes when she went to bed at night now she imagined herself living in the tiny house down the back street for the rest of her life. She wanted another job but work was difficult to find so she went on working at midday at the pub, struggling to keep everything going. Her parents tried to help but Annie's pride would let her take nothing from them. Hardest of anything, she was invited to the Hall to see how Madge and Frank were. All the farms had been sold off. Frank had given up working at the grammar school and they were quite prosperous. They gave dances there and Madge showed Annie the dresses she bought for these but Annie was never invited because it was only couples. On these evenings she sat at home and imagined what it was like to be a guest, to be invited to dinner at a house where there was a ballroom, to have company and good food and laughter, to dance with your husband and to be the other half of him, to plan for the future. When Susan was in bed she sat by the fire in the tiny house and tried hard not to think how happy she and Alistair had been.

For a long time there were workmen at Western Isle. Blake was never there. Annie would have known if he had been; she saw her mother every week and nothing escaped Rose's eyes.

'I don't know why he bought it,' Rose said sniffily. 'Did you know that he has Alistair's pictures up in the house?'

'What pictures?'

'Albert Morley went there the other day and he says in the sitting room there are paintings and drawings of Western Isle with Alistair's name on them.'

That weekend Blake came to the farm; Annie knew within hours. On the Saturday afternoon she left Susan with her mother and walked up to Western Isle. A big man opened the door. Annie didn't know what to say. She had expected Blake.

'I'm Annie Vane. I came to see Blake.'

'Do come in, my dear. I'm Sylvester Richmond and you are more than welcome.'

Annie didn't know how to refuse the invitation and as he took her straight into the sitting room she could soon see for herself some of the drawings and paintings which Mrs Vane said she had taken with her to the new house because Annie had no room in her small home.

'David isn't here, I'm afraid, but you will have some tea.' He didn't wait for her to say either she would or she wouldn't but shouted amiably along the hall, 'Hetty, bring some tea for the lass, will you?'

As he spoke a small boy came through the hall and into the room and Annie got a shock. He looked so much like Alistair.

'Yes,' Sylvester said, 'my daughter had the most wonderful-coloured hair—'

'I remember.'

'You met? And of course David has fair hair. So what do we get? A gypsy.'

'A Vane,' Annie said clearly.

'I beg your pardon.'

'That's what the Vanes look like. This was their home.'

A middle-aged woman came in shortly with a tea tray but Annie refused.

'I came for the paintings,' she said.

'What paintings?'

'Those. My husband painted them. They got left here by mistake when we moved out.'

'Oh. Yes, of course.'

There was the sound of the outside door. Sylvester looked relieved and as Blake came into the room said helpfully, 'We have company. Mrs Vane has come to tea.'

'Hello, Annie.'

'Hello. I came for the paintings.'

'What paintings?'

'The ones which Alistair did. They were left in the attic by mistake.'

'I assumed they went with the house. Don't you want them to stay here?'

'They're mine.'

'I'll have them sent down to you.'

'I'd rather take them now if you don't mind.'

'Of course not. Do you have a car?'

'No.' Annie hadn't thought about that or she could have borrowed one from Grayswell. She hadn't thought Blake would give in without a fight.

He proceeded to take down the paintings for her.

They were scattered through the house. Annie got to see each room and she couldn't help thinking how pleased Alistair would have been with what had been done. It was all so tasteful, expensive but comfortable, and it became clear to her long before the last picture was removed that each one had been carefully chosen for where it went, that Western Isle was a fitting setting for Alistair's work.

Blake handled the pictures like they were babies and he and Sylvester tore up cardboard boxes and wrapped and taped them so that they could not be damaged. While this was going on Annie sat very properly by the fire, wanting the tea which Hetty offered but afraid of her shaking hands. She began to wish heartily that she had not come, that she had not demanded the paintings of Blake. She had nowhere to put them. They loaded them into the car and drove to Grayswell to collect Susan.

He didn't go into the house with her though she asked him and all the way to Stanhope nobody said a word. He carried them into the house one by one and stacked them by the wall in her tiny sitting room.

'I thought his mother had them in her new house.'

'I thought you were going to live there.'

'She decided she'd rather be by herself.'

'That's it then. That's all of them. I have to get back.'

Annie saw him out of the house, thanked him, let him get halfway to the car and then she ran after him, got hold of his sleeve and said shakily, 'I want you to take them back.'

'Take them back? Annie, I've just spent the better part of two hours getting them here.'

'I didn't understand—'

'There's nothing to understand. Naturally, anything that was Alistair's belongs to you. I didn't think at the time.'

'But they should be there. He painted Western Isle because he loved it so much.'

'He painted very well,' Blake said.

'Yes, I know. You made such a good job of putting them in the right places and . . . I want you to take them back.'

'I don't think I should.'

'Please.'

'All right but there's a condition.'

'What's that?'

'You have to come and help me.'

'I don't think—'

'You have to, otherwise I won't take them.'

If Sylvester Richmond thought it strange they should bring the paintings back and unpack them and put them up on the walls so that everything was as it had been earlier in the day he was much too polite to say so and afterwards he insisted on introducing Annie to a particular dry white wine which he said he was inordinately fond of and after that it was time for dinner. After two glasses of wine Annie forgot about having the shakes and was even hungry. Full of dinner, Susan nodded off in the car on the way home and Blake carried her in and up the stairs to bed. She didn't wake up properly even when Annie undressed her. Blake kissed her and tucked her in and they went back downstairs.

'I'm sorry about today,' Annie said.

'Don't you like to see me at Western Isle?'

'Of course I do. It's what I wanted all along. I wanted you to have it, it's your inheritance. Anthony looks like the Vanes.'

'Yes I know. Like Alistair.'

'I didn't say that. He was a shock when I saw him. Alistair would have liked what you've done with Western Isle. He had taste.'

'Thanks. Goodnight, Annie.'

'Goodnight.'

When Hetty came into Stanhope to do some shopping the following Saturday morning she brought Annie a spice cake which she had made at home during the week. Annie gave her tea.

'Mr Richmond's having a dinner party next week,' Hetty said. 'He wants you to come.'

'I can't do that. I haven't anybody to bring me.'

'He'll send the car for you.'

'No, I meant I haven't an escort.'

'Oh, Mr Richmond's dinner parties aren't like that,' Hetty said scornfully. 'He only invites people he likes.'

'Will you be there?'

'I should hope so. I have it to make.'

'I could come and help you.'

'Could you? That would be a boon.'

When Hetty had gone it occurred to Annie that Sylvester Richmond was a clever man and had got exactly what he wanted – or was she sure what he had wanted?

The other people there were obviously house guests, Annie thought, when she arrived the following afternoon to find two other women helping Hetty in the kitchen. Sylvester was not there but came in later with two men, introducing them. They were all about his age and they went down to the cellar and came back with several different bottles of wine all of which were opened and tasted and everyone's opinion, hers included, was asked so that by the time the dinner was almost ready everyone

429

was laughing and she felt as if she had known them all for months.

'Where's David?' she asked. It seemed so disrespectful to call Blake anything else here in this house where his father-in-law and everyone else referred to him as David.

'He had to go to work. He shouldn't be long. He promised he would be back for the meal.'

That was when Annie realised that she had been asked to partner Blake because the others were so much older. She and Hetty were upstairs getting changed when Blake came home. She helped Hetty put Anthony to bed and they went downstairs.

After Blake said hello the first thing he said was, 'Didn't you bring Susan?'

'I took her to my mother's.'

'I told Hetty to ask you to bring her.'

'She must have forgotten.'

Blake went up to change and when he came back down they had dinner and Annie only wished that Madge could have seen her, wearing her only good dress and being among the kind of people she had always wanted to be among. They talked about books and paintings and they congratulated her on Alistair's work, saying how much Sylvester loved them and how good they were. The women were intelligent enough to ask her about Alistair and to say how sorry they were and that next time she must bring Susan. Annie soon felt a warm glow which had nothing to do with the wine. She nearly accepted the invitation to stay the night. Blake took her home and as he drove the car slowly down the narrow roads Annie remembered driving like this with Alistair, stopping and admiring the views and being glad she was here. She had rarely felt like that lately. She felt as though she wanted to get away. It was the first time in her life that she had wanted to leave and it was a strange sensation.

When Blake stopped the car she thanked him, hesitating.

'I don't know what to call you now.'

'You can go on calling me Blake if you want to. Everybody does around here.'

'But the people tonight didn't and Sylvester never does.'

'My friends call me Davy. At one time Irene was the only person who called me Davy.'

'Your grandmother used to.'

'How do you know that? I didn't tell you.'

'No, you didn't tell me.'

'So how do you know?'

'It was just – it was just sort of a guess.'

'No, it wasn't. It's too accurate. Tell me.'

'I heard her.'

'You heard her call my name?'

'Yes.'

'When?'

'The first night that we spent at Sunniside after our wedding.'

Blake said nothing.

'I'm sorry, Blake, I didn't—'

'You went on living at Sunniside thinking there was a ghost?'

'It wasn't a ghost and I loved the farm. We were very happy there in spite of . . .'

'In spite of what?'

'All the heartache and all the hardship that had gone on. There's always a bit of people left in the houses where they have lived. What's wrong with that?'

'I don't know.'

'Susan was born there.'

'I'd forgotten about that. It's strange to think of Alistair at Sunniside and me at Western Isle.'

'I like to see Anthony there.'

'Of course you do. He's more of a Vane than the Vanes.'

Annie laughed.

'You're pleased about it, aren't you?' Blake said.

'Not pleased exactly. The children could be taken for brother and sister. Thank you for the evening.'

'Bring Susan next time,' Blake said as Annie got out of the car.

Thirty-four

When Blake got back he thought that everybody had gone to bed, it was so quiet. He went around switching lights off until he came to the sitting room and there Sylvester was seated in an armchair before the fire with a brandy glass in his hand.

'Join me,' he said.

Blake helped himself to brandy and he reflected that this was probably the most enjoyable thing that Sylvester had taught him over the years. He sat down across the fire, only saying as he did so, 'Did you let the dogs out?'

'I did. I thought I might have had a long wait for you.'

'No such luck,' Blake said roundly.

'Is that what you want?'

'I suppose not. It was your scheming, Sylvester. You asked her.'

'I thought you were in love with the girl.'

'It was a long time ago.'

'Can you stop loving people when you have done so completely?'

'You can when they don't love you. I was always a very poor second best. Alistair was always first.'

'He's dead.'

'Yes.' Blake sat back and sipped his brandy and sighed. 'What competition. He'll never get any older, he'll never do anything wrong, his child is always there to keep his memory alive, he won't make any mistakes or betray anybody or fall over.'

'What was he like?'

'He was kind and good-tempered, loyal and talented . . .'

'That's a lot to like about a man who married the woman you loved.'

'He was my brother.'

'Ah.' Sylvester looked down into his brandy. 'I'm so sorry.'

'Annie didn't tell me when he died and when I found out . . .'

'You should have told me. When things hurt you I want to know. You don't stop loving people when they die, that's the hardest part. You go on loving them with nothing to sustain you until you dry out. I love Laura still and it's been such a long time. I dream about her often

435

and she's just as she was, young and beautiful, just like Annie. People should marry again. If you go on too long standing around on the sidelines it dehumanises you. You start being smug and thinking you know more than other people and despising them. I loved Irene so very much but I don't want you to give up your right to be part of things. I've asked Hetty if she'll be my wife.'

Blake laughed.

'Have you? Has she said yes?'

'Being a very sensible woman she has. It's a financial arrangement really. It means I won't have to pay her any more,' and Sylvester chuckled. 'Do you know what I'm going to do? I'm going to give her the best of everything. I'm going to buy her the biggest diamond I can find. I'm going to swathe her in furs and give her a Rolls Royce and take her to Paris for her clothes. What do you think about that?'

'I just hope she's going to go on doing the cooking, that's all. Cooks are harder to find than wives,' Blake said.

'You are not a gentleman, sir,' Sylvester said, grinning. 'Would you like some more brandy?'

'I'd love some.'

Sylvester poured the brandy and then sat down.

'Ask her to marry you,' he said.

'I can't. She'd only turn me down.'

'Can she afford to turn down a rich man? I thought she was living in a tiny house in a back street and had to work at some mediocre alehouse in order to survive. Does she know how rich you are?'

'I don't want that.'

'My dear boy, you really must try to live in the world. Women always marry men for their money, how else are they to survive?'

'She wouldn't have me the first time because I was poor.'

'Well then.'

When Annie had the invitation to Sylvester and Hetty's wedding she panicked. In the first place she didn't want to go and in the second she had nothing that she could wear among rich people. Her mother and Madge came to her rescue. Her mother said that she ought to go and Madge offered to loan her some clothes. Being left with no excuse Annie went.

Sylvester sent a car for her. No one, she thought, could accuse him of modesty. It was a Rolls Royce with a uniformed chauffeur. Annie wanted to take cover as they glided majestically down the dale. Susan was excited and stared out of the window.

They were to go to the house first. On the outskirts

of Sunderland they turned in at gates and there were big parklands on either side with trees and huge lawns and finally a big stone house where the drive swept up to the entrance.

Susan clambered out of the car before the chauffeur could reach her and dashed up the steps just as Blake came out of the house. He got down and swept her up into his arms and she shrieked with delight.

'Hello, Annie. My, don't you look fine.'

'Do you think so?' Annie said anxiously.

'Edible,' Blake said and he kissed her on the cheek.

Sylvester came out too and Anthony. The children went off to play and Sylvester ordered coffee for Annie but she wanted to see the bride and went upstairs. Hetty was wearing sugar pink and it suited her. Annie told her so.

'These clothes were so dear, you can't imagine,' Hetty said.

'I think I can. Are you nervous?'

'Terrified.'

'Sylvester is a wonderful man.'

'He's a bossy old soul but beggars can't be choosers,' Hetty said, smiling.

'Are there going to be many people at the wedding?'

'Annie, Sylvester doesn't know the meaning of the word small. He's invited everybody in Sunderland.'

'Oh dear,' Annie said.

She didn't have to worry. She was treated like one of the family. She went to the church with Blake and the two children and when it came to the reception she sat on the top table with them. Annie had difficulty in not feeling very important.

There was a dance at the house in the evening and it did Annie's soul good to note that the ballroom was bigger than the one at the Hall. Throughout the day there was crate after crate of champagne though she tried not to drink much and in the evening there was Anthony's nursemaid to put the children to bed. All Annie had to do was go up and kiss her child goodnight. Then she danced.

Dancing with Blake brought back memories of the village hall and of the first time that he had kissed her. His dancing was even better now. Perhaps, Annie thought, he got a lot of practice. It was a warm summer evening. People wandered outside. There were big ponds in the grounds and a stream some way from the house. Annie was asked to dance all the time and escaped to the garden late in the evening. She sat down on a low wall beside a formal part where there were lots of stones and crazy paving and intricate geometrical lawns and sharply cut shrubs.

Blake found her there, handed her a glass of champagne.

'I don't think I should have any more,' Annie said, taking the glass reluctantly.

'Would you rather have something else?'

'A cup of tea would be nice.'

'I'll go and—'

'No. Don't. I'm quite happy just sitting here.'

They hadn't seen each other for weeks. Sylvester and Hetty had been often to Western Isle and had Anthony with them but Blake had been working.

'How's the dale?' he asked.

'It never changes.'

'That's what I like best about it. Susan's grown such a lot since I've seen her.'

'She didn't forget you.'

'Are you still working at the pub?'

'Yes but I've got another job as well, in a café. It's just during the summer season but it helps.'

'What do you do with Susan?'

'She spends a lot of time with my parents. They like it – at least most of the time – but I wish I could see her more. It isn't easy.'

'Do you remember telling me that you wanted a nice house with a garden for the children to play in, a car and some decent clothes and a china cabinet and a piano and to talk to people who know things?'

'Sometimes I shudder for your memory,' she said.

'There's the shipyard and a chain of shops, a sizeable chunk of half a dozen ships and a fish and chip restaurant.'

'A fish and chip shop?'

'Irene's grandmother had it. She ran a pub too.'

'What happened to the beautiful blonde?' Annie said. 'The one you kissed down by the river.'

'It just didn't work out.'

'She turned you down?'

'You were the only person who turned me down.'

'Don't think I haven't regretted it,' Annie said flippantly. 'The night you walked into that dance with Irene, I could have scratched her eyes out. You looked . . . so rich, so classy.'

'But you had Alistair.'

'Yes.'

'Annie, look. I don't want my child to grow up like I did. I want him to have parents. I want him to have a mother. I can give you a lot. I can get you out of there, that little house and those awful jobs. We could buy a nice house and Susan could go to the best schools. She could be brought up at Western Isle, at least part of the time. You want that, don't you?'

'Yes, but—'

'Will you marry me?'

'No.'

The warm evening was suddenly full of sound, birds, the stream, distant passing traffic.

'Why not?' Blake asked.

'How could I marry you for reasons like that after what I did to you? I didn't marry Alistair for who he was, it was because I cared for him. I did care for you; I think it was something to do with being brought up together and having so much time and you were like Alistair even then. In a way I learned how to love him from you. How can I marry you now you live in a different world? You need somebody like Irene. I'm not like that. I don't think I could be polite to people at dinner parties, wear the correct dresses and be David Blake's wife. I'd hate it.'

'You'd rather stay in the dale in that tiny house and be a waitress?'

'No, of course I wouldn't but—'

'You wouldn't marry me when I was poor—'

'Blake—'

'You could always marry somebody else of course, somebody you won't confuse with Alistair.'

He would have walked away but Annie got hold of his arm.

'Don't be angry, please. Everything's changed. You

don't belong in the dale any more and I'll never belong anywhere else—'

'That's not true. You can be anything you want to be. You're not really going to turn me down? Not when I can give Susan all that. Tell me you're expecting a better offer any minute?'

Annie laughed shortly.

'In the dale?'

'Last time of asking.'

Annie hesitated and then nodded. It was for Susan, she consoled herself.

Thirty-five

Blake wanted to buy Annie an engagement ring. She always wore the diamond solitaire which Alistair had given her as well as her wedding ring and although she tried to talk herself into taking off these rings she couldn't so in the end she moved them on to her right hand and let him buy her sapphires. She felt quite sick in the shop in Newcastle. She could choose it all separately, whichever stones she wanted, all of them bigger than the single diamond which glinted on her right hand. In the end she couldn't do it, apologised and walked out of the shop. Blake didn't say anything to her, he bought her some tea but Annie spilt it into the saucer and the tears dropped and splashed. Blake gave her a handkerchief.

'I'm sorry. I didn't mean to be such an insensitive bastard. We won't bother.'

'No, I . . . no, I want a ring. I just don't want anything

big, if you see what I mean. Could we not just go into a shop and buy something – something modest?'

The sapphires she finally allowed him to buy her were very modest indeed. They were all that Annie could bear. Her family reacted just as she had thought they would. Tommy wondered if he had a magnifying glass and her mother thought Blake was mean.

'I thought he had money,' she said, letting go of Annie's hand.

Clara and Madge very delicately said nothing. It was the same with clothes and cars and fur coats. She wouldn't let him buy her anything. They were to be married very quietly in the village church and there was to be no honeymoon. Blake had wanted to be married in Sunderland with lots of people and a big reception but Annie's parents wouldn't hear of her being married anywhere but the village church where she had been christened and confirmed and been married to Alistair.

Annie didn't realise until too late that this was a mistake and as soon as she knew it she couldn't understand why she hadn't seen the problem from the beginning. By then Blake had stopped trying to persuade her about anything. The only thing he had insisted on was that they should go back to Sunderland after the reception to Sylvester's house and that Hetty and Sylvester would stay at Western Isle with the children. Annie hadn't the strength to argue.

If her first wedding day had been difficult her second was much worse. There were no guests except the family and since Blake had no family there was only Hetty and Sylvester and Anthony on his side. They had a small lunch at Western Isle and every second that she was there Annie expected Charles Vane's voice from the top of the stairs, shouting at her. In the middle of the afternoon she went out to the stables and cuddled one of the horses and cried. She was glad to be away. Nobody seemed to remember what to say to anybody.

She had worn a cream dress, wide and swinging with a neat waist and a big cream hat. The dress was pretty but it was nothing like the long white dress which she had worn for her first wedding. When they set off for Sunderland she couldn't look up at the track which led to Sunniside.

Nobody said anything all the way back to Sunderland. Annie felt as though she was going to the other side of the world. It was one of those wet foggy November days which are barely light. Annie had wanted to wait until the spring or at least Christmas but Blake had wanted to get married. The last leaves had dropped from the trees and lay in piles of mud by the roadside and the tyres swished wetly as he drove. Annie had changed. The dress was new to her, it had been Madge's, barely worn, but Annie thought now that it suited Madge and the weather, not her, it was all browns and greens. Blake had said nothing about the dress but she had no desire to know what he was thinking. He rarely said what he thought.

When the car swept to a halt in front of the big door the rain had stopped and night had fallen. There was a light on outside and although there was no one at the house it soon became obvious to Annie that careful preparations had been made and that people had been there up till a very short time ago.

There was a wonderful smell of lavender polish. The hall had freshly cut flowers and so did the rooms, cut-glass vases filled with big, bushy chrysanthemums, yellow and white. There were huge log fires as well as central heating and in the kitchen the refrigerator was full of food, some of it already cooked, ready to be heated. There were bottles of champagne in there too.

'Do you want champagne?'

'I'd rather have tea.'

'Something told me you would,' and Blake pushed up the lid on the Aga and put on the big shiny kettle.

'I'm sorry, Blake, I didn't mean to be awkward.'

447

'It's no bother.'

'No, I didn't mean about the tea. I know it isn't easy for you either. What happened with your other house? Couldn't it be rebuilt?'

'It was completely destroyed but I couldn't have gone on living there even if it hadn't.'

'I suppose not.'

'You don't feel like that about Western Isle?'

'Alistair loved it. He didn't die there, he died to keep it alive if you see what I mean.'

'Susan loves it. I'm going to buy her a pony.'

'You'll spoil her.'

'I want to give her everything I can. She's all there is left of him.'

Annie looked at Blake, leaning back against the Aga rail. He hadn't even kissed her when they became engaged, only in church just very briefly. There had been nothing. She wondered if he was thinking about Irene, missing her.

'What was your first wedding day like?'

He smiled.

'We didn't have any money. I was a pitman then. I felt so awful, I couldn't give Irene anything. We had a tiny little house which went with my job and she'd been so well off, she'd had everything, maids, clothes, no work to do. She ended up as a pitman's wife. She was very good at it eventually.'

'She didn't care about being poor?'

'Oh, I think she cared about it but we were young and . . . it didn't matter in the end.'

'Alistair's father got drunk on our wedding day. Tommy and Clara quarrelled and there was a huge snowstorm. We were meant to go to Blackpool. We never got there. We were snowed in at Sunniside all week. That kettle's boiling.'

There was an old silver teapot set out on a tray with sugar bowl and milk jug. Annie found the tea caddy and Blake got the milk out of the fridge and she remembered making tea for Alistair and herself rather in the same way because there had been nothing to do and it was so difficult.

Blake carried the tray through into the small sitting room; Annie had rejected the idea of sitting in the drawing room, it was so big for two of them.

'Do we have to buy another house?' she said, as they sat down.

Blake looked surprised.

'I thought you'd want your own house.'

'Do we have to decide?'

'No, I don't think so. I think Sylvester and Hetty would prefer to have us and more especially the children here.'

'It's not exactly cramped,' Annie said.

'If you change your mind let me know.'

They did have champagne in the evening and put on soft music, Mozart, and they sat in the dark by the log fire with a lighted candle or two. It made Annie think of being small when the farm had no electricity and they had candles in the bedrooms. They lay on the big sofa and Blake put his arms around her and drew her back against him. It was a long time since Annie had spent such a peaceful evening with a man. When he kissed her she turned her face towards him and then she waited for the way that it had been when other men had kissed her after Alistair died. She waited for that awful disappoint-ment, she set herself not to draw back because they were married now and she had not made things easy for him but it was not like that and neither was it the kiss she had been waiting for all that time and she was amazed and horrified because it made her feel over-eager and desperate. She didn't want him to know, she drew back and was confused. She wanted to laugh and cry and be glad but she couldn't, it seemed such a betrayal to both of them. He stopped and let go of her. The logs fell apart in the grate, the music was suddenly all wrong. Annie made an excuse and fled. She couldn't go back, her courage failed her. She went upstairs to her bedroom and stood by the window.

Blake followed her upstairs.

'Aren't you coming down again?' he said from the doorway.

Annie turned around.

'Don't you want to take me to bed?'

'Ever since I was fourteen. Have I done something wrong, I mean besides all the rest?'

'You haven't done anything wrong. I hate this dress, it doesn't suit me. I wish I hadn't worn it.'

Annie looked at him standing there in his expensive suit with a gold watch on his wrist which must have cost a fortune. She had never felt so poor or so stupid.

'Don't worry about the dress. You're just tired.'

'Getting married is tiring. I swore I wouldn't do it again,' Annie said, trying to smile and not quite managing.

'Look, why don't you get changed and I'll come back—'

'No.' Annie knew that she couldn't go through this again. In her haste to get rid of the awful dress she took it off swiftly, rolled it into a ball and threw it into the corner of the room. And then she felt so vulnerable standing there in her underclothes sure that she had made a terrible mistake. What was she doing here with a man she barely knew any more? She fastened her arms across her front and tried not to let the feelings overwhelm her. He was not Alistair, he was never going to be Alistair, he didn't even kiss like Alistair any more and she had kept telling herself that he would, that he would feel and taste and be just like Alistair but he wouldn't, she knew that already. He even smelled expensive, of good clothes and the kind of soap you bought in boxes that was shaped like lemons. His hands were fine with neatly cut nails and his hair was well-cut and so clean and shiny. Annie couldn't find anything left of what he had been.

He said her name and took a step towards her and she backed into the dressing table which was just behind her and knocked over all the little bottles of perfume and nail varnish and face cream which had been provided for her. The noise seemed magnified a hundred times in the silence.

She hadn't noticed before how modern the room was. Alistair would have loathed it, the furniture was all sharp and angled and colourless and the bed – the bed was enormous. There were white covers on it, so white they almost hurt her eyes. Annie had never before wished to be back in that awful little house in the side street in Stanhope but she did now. She had never been in a bedroom like this with anybody other than her husband

and she had never before been aware of how little like Alistair he was. He didn't look anything like him, he wasn't gentle and sensitive like Alistair. How could he have been after all he had gone through? Even the blue-grey gaze was not the same; there was something cool about it that frightened her. There was nothing of the boy left, nothing at all, he was a man now, rich and confident. He had hundreds of men working for him. She had missed the part of his life that had changed him from the boy who had loved her so much to this.

She felt as though he had bought her. She could not let him buy her jewellery or clothes or anything that would make her feel even more like something he owned. It didn't make any difference now when he put very gentle hands on her. All she wanted to do was run away.

Before now it had seemed to Annie very often that Alistair was not dead at all, that she belonged to him still, that she did not want to love anyone else because it would be a betrayal and that as long as she did not get close to anyone else they would always belong to one another. He could never betray her and she still felt married to him. After all there had been no fight, there had been no separation, no reason for him to leave her. It was all unfinished business with them. She felt that he had walked out halfway through their life. Sometimes when she saw people on the street she was convinced she saw him. Things were not over between them, they had a child, there must be some kind of a future for them.

Blake picked her up and carried her over to the bed and put her down there and he was so careful and so gentle that Annie's starving body clamoured for him. The bed was high and firm, nothing like the feather mattress she was used to. The room seemed to her big enough to lose half a dozen people. It didn't feel like anything to do with her. She felt as though she had been picked up off the street for use. The soft glow from the bedside lights seemed to mock her cheap pretty underwear. She felt like a rabbit caught in car headlamps. Under his hands and mouth her body began to ache and give and respond. And he knew, just by having been married for a number of years, how to take her clothes off her, how to undress a woman deftly, how to touch her and kiss her and what she wanted him to do to her. He knew too much, Annie thought savagely, some woman had taught him carefully and well how to do this. And she was so screamingly ragingly hungry. He peeled off his clothes and he held her against the warmth of him and his body began to satisfy the dreadful aching. Annie closed her eyes as she gave herself to him. It was in a way the nearest thing to somebody wiping a blackboard or painting a house or destroying a building. It was the devastation of her marriage to Alistair Vane, the complete annihilation of it. There was nothing casual or fumbling or inept about what he did to her and her body was completely out of control wanting more and more and clinging and eager and so grateful. Annie hated herself. She hated the person that had done this. She imagined that he ran his life like this, taking what he wanted, completely in control, so thorough, so clever, so good.

When he finally let go of her she didn't move for what felt like a long time but wasn't and then she turned over away from him and tried to find a cool place on the bed. In the silence she crept under the covers as far away from him as she could without falling out of bed. She closed her eyes. She couldn't think any more, she was exhausted.

Blake waited until she fell asleep and then he pulled on his clothes and went downstairs and opened the French windows which led into the garden. The night was freezing and clear and well-starred and his sharp mind gave him back in intimate detail each moment of his first wedding night just like a cinema reel, the shabby little house, the tiny bedroom, Irene laughing, the warmth, the cuddling, the whispers, the little moans of pleasure which she couldn't silence but should have because of the neighbours, her body generous and sweet, pressing herself into his hands. He didn't understand what he was doing any more, he didn't know anything. He had tried to get things right but it wasn't any good and tonight had confirmed his suspicions. Annie's response was only hunger, there was no love. She had married him because he could keep her and her child. She would give him her body and he would pay, like some terrible illicit arrangement.

He didn't want to go back in but he went in the end because the cold reached through his shirt on to his body and chilled him thoroughly. He locked the French doors and walked slowly upstairs. He nearly made himself go back to her but in the end he went into his own room and built up the fire and sat there with a glass of brandy while the night got older and finally greyed into morning.

Sylvester, Hetty and the children came home the next day. Annie was so relieved to see them. She had gone without breakfast rather than face him. She crushed Susan to her and afterwards had the dubious pleasure of watching her daughter throw herself into his arms. He carried Susan into the house, promising her jelly and ice-cream and all manner of other treats. Anthony chattered excitedly. Annie took him by the hand.

That afternoon when they had eaten a big Sunday dinner, at least some of them had, Annie could scarcely get food down, the children went off to play and Sylvester and Hetty went for a walk because the sun had come out though it was pale and low in the sky. Blake sat down by the fire in the drawing room with her on the big sofa there. Annie couldn't look at him.

'I want to talk to you about Susan.'

She had to look at him then.

'We haven't talked about schools,' he said.

'But it's all decided. The uniform's bought.'

'I mean for when she gets older. I've had Anthony's name down for a good school for years. We can do the same for Susan if you want.'

'A good school?'

'Boarding school.'

Annie stared at him.

'You want to send the children away?'

'I want a good education for them.'

'Alistair hated boarding school. Aren't there good schools here where they can come home every night?'

'I want them to have the best, all the things I didn't have, two parents, a good home, an education, a decent beginning.'

'Boarding school isn't a decent beginning,' Annie said

roundly. 'I think it's horrible sending little children away from home.'

'It didn't seem to do Alistair any harm.'

'That's because he didn't have a good home life or parents. I thought part of the reason we got married was to give our children that and now you want to send them away for the best part of their childhood—'

'No, I don't. They get long holidays and—'

'Well, you're not sending Susan away. I won't let you,' Annie said.

'I was only offering.'

'When are you going to send Anthony away?'

'I'm not sending him away. You make it sound like prison. He'll go when he's nine.'

'Nine? He's your only child, Blake, I don't know how you can.'

Susan appeared in the doorway.

'Why are you fighting?' she asked.

'We're not fighting,' Annie said.

'Yes, you are.' She went to Blake's knee and got on to his lap without asking. 'Daddy, will you—'

'David is not your Daddy,' Annie said immediately. 'We talked about it, don't you remember?'

'Aunty Hetty said that he's my new daddy.'

'You can call me Uncle David if you like,' Blake said.

'It isn't the same.'

'Go and wash your hands for tea,' Annie said and the child went off immediately.

'Does it matter?' Blake said.

'It matters to me. I don't want her to forget Alistair.'

'Does she do that by loving someone else?'

'You're not at a board meeting, Blake, don't try to be clever,' Annie said and she followed Susan out.

That evening Annie and Sylvester put the children to bed and when Susan had finally fallen asleep Annie said to him, across the bed, 'Did you know that Blake was planning to send Anthony to boarding school?'

'Yes. I did the same thing. Because I'd had a very hard time myself I wanted everything to be right for Simon and I sent him to Harrow. I wish I hadn't but there was the business to attend to and Laura was dead.'

'But you didn't send Irene?'

'It didn't seem so important. I thought she would marry well and have children.'

'And then she married Blake?'

Sylvester chuckled.

'Can't you talk to him, Sylvester? Don't let him send Anthony away.'

'I have tried.'

*

Annie went to bed early and was lying there reading a book when Blake walked into her bedroom. He didn't even knock. Annie looked severely at him. Blake pushed the door shut.

'You asked Sylvester to talk to me about Anthony.'

Annie put down the book.

'I thought you might listen to him.'

Blake walked over and sat down on the bed.

'The subject is not open for discussion. Am I making myself clear?'

'As crystal,' Annie said.

He took off his jacket and threw it at the nearest chair and pulled at the knot in his tie and swore.

'If you come here I'll do that for you,' Annie offered and when he went nearer she undid it. 'There's no need to be so angry just because people don't agree with you.'

'You tried to manipulate the situation to your advantage.'

'Did I?'

'I get that all day at work, I don't need it here.'

'Yes, master.'

He shot her a reproachful look and went off to the bathroom. Annie went back to her book. He came back some time later wearing the bottom half of a pair of black cotton pyjamas and said softly, 'Do you want me to go and sleep in my own room?' Annie put down the book.

'You did last night.'

'I didn't sleep, I just sort of sat there.'

'I didn't sleep much either,' Annie said. 'I don't know whether I can manage this, Blake.'

'Not even just to sleep?'

At some time in the night when Annie stirred she was curled up against him just like she used to curl up against Alistair. It was so much the same that she went back to sleep happy and didn't dream.

When she awoke in the morning he had gone to work. She and Hetty got the children out to school. Susan was smartly dressed in her new uniform. Afterwards Hetty announced that they were going shopping.

'You haven't forgotten the dinner dance on Saturday night,' she said.

'Hetty, I don't want to go.'

'You're his wife, you have to go,' Hetty said flatly. 'You might as well get used to it, from now until February there are parties and dances all the time. Some of them are even enjoyable.'

Annie laughed.

'Are you coming to some?'

'I wouldn't miss the chance of letting the old buzzard step all over my corns,' Hetty said.

Annie bought for herself a very expensive dress. It was black and halter-necked leaving her back bare to the waist and it was long. She bought black suede shoes and Hetty put up her hair and when she came downstairs Sylvester whistled.

Annie was fairly comfortable about going out with Blake. They were sleeping together every night though they barely touched and she was asleep when he left for work and once that week she had been in bed and asleep when he came home but it made it possible for her to smile at him now.

They drove to Newcastle and as soon as they got there Annie began to enjoy herself. They drank champagne. The people he introduced her to were interesting to talk to. She danced with all the men so it was late when they finally danced together. Annie thought that she only had to close her eyes to be sixteen again dancing with him in the village hall at home, except that she thought he danced even better now, and when it was late and they drove home it was just like coming home with Alistair had been, talking everybody over, discussing the dinner and the conversation and the night.

It was very late when they got back and everybody had gone to bed. They went into the drawing room where the fire was still on and after he had put a couple of logs on to it they sat down on the big sofa there and drank brandy together.

'Blake . . .'

'What?'

'The dress . . . it was very expensive.'

'Was it?'

'You don't mind?'

'It's a devastating dress. Every man who danced with you tried to reach as far as he could with his fingertips.'

Annie laughed.

'You noticed?'

'It was difficult to miss.'

He put down his brandy and he took her glass from her and then he pulled her into his arms and kissed her. It was a good kiss too, Annie thought greedily. And he reached up and undid the halter and the dress slipped down to her waist.

'You've wanted to do that all evening, haven't you?' Annie said.

'Wasn't that why you wore it?'

She was at home here. This was what happened after dances. During the war when Alistair was not at home so much the dance was just an interruption, just a way of delaying the feel and taste of him but it was not like that any more. There was plenty of time, time for him to inch down her clothes and kiss her all over her body and for her to talk to him softly into his ear and unbutton his shirt and slide her hands inside his clothing. It had always been good, it would always be, it didn't change like that and nothing else mattered now.

He eased her down on to the rug in front of the fire and by its light she caught a glimpse of his fair hair and the world crashed.

'Alistair . . .' she murmured and he stopped. Annie couldn't see him very well after that for the tears but she was aware that he went from passion to anger in a few seconds.

'No, it's not Alistair,' he said slowly. 'You never use my name when we're alone. Everybody else that I know does. Go on, say it.' He gave her a little shake.

'David.'

'You remember it? I am sick and tired of hearing his name on your lips. On Saturday night I just wasn't him and now you think I am!'

'It wasn't. It wasn't. It was just because . . . it was just with going out like that and dancing and having a few drinks and then coming back and . . .'

'Like this?'

'Exactly like this, yes. Exactly.' The tears spilled. There seemed to be a bucketful of them as though they had been welling there all week.

'So, I'm like my brother, too much like him for you to distinguish the difference tonight but not enough like him so that you would give yourself freely to me on our wedding night.'

'I didn't mean to . . .'

He looked at her in disgust and then he got up and picked up his clothes and went to bed and left her there. She thought she heard him slam the bedroom door, even from downstairs.

Thirty-six

Being Blake's wife was the hardest way that Annie had
ever lived. He was rarely at home and when he was he
worked most of the time and he was bad-tempered
except with the children. He left for the shipyard early
and came back late and they rarely spoke about anything other than mundane matters and they never slept
together at all.

Annie had hoped that they might go to Western Isle
some time in the first half of December but they didn't
because each weekend they were invited to go out and
at hotels and at other people's homes she was obliged to
wear expensive dresses and look her best and smile and
be nice and it was exhausting. She came to hate dinners
and dancing where people ate too much and laughed
too much and smoked and drank too much. Blake rarely
danced with her unless he had to and it seemed that

everywhere they went Pauline Kington, like Mary's little lamb, was sure to be there. It snowed early. Blake built snowmen and had snowball fights with the children. Annie starting drinking gin as she had done after Alistair died, to blot out the evenings. Her main desire at these times was just to go home and crawl under the covers.

She grew homesick for the dale and for the old life now that she knew she could never have it back and she was frightened in case it snowed too much and they would not be able to go to Western Isle for months. Blake wanted to buy Susan a pony for Christmas. Annie protested.

'I've already bought all kinds of things for her and she's having dancing lessons. Sylvester is talking about buying a piano in case she wants piano lessons. My daughter is about as musical as I am, she doesn't need all these things and I don't want you to buy her a pony. We never go to Western Isle.'

'I thought we'd go for Christmas or just after.'

'Promise me, Blake, no pony. I won't have you and Sylvester spoiling my child.'

'That's going to make life very awkward.'

'Why?'

'Because I'm buying Anthony one.'

'What makes you think he likes horses?'

'Everybody likes horses.'

'I think he'd rather have a train set.'

'He's getting a train set as well. Sylvester's buying it.'

Annie gave up. Every Friday and Saturday night they went out. She wore long dresses, low-necked, strapless and wide to show off her shoulders and neat waist. She had two fur stoles and half a dozen pairs of sandals. Annie was always dancing. But when they came home she went straight to bed. Whether he stayed downstairs and drank brandy by himself she didn't know.

He bought her rubies for Christmas. The stones in the ring were so rich that Annie felt obliged to take off the small sapphire ring and wear that instead. There was also a bracelet, a slender gold circle with a ruby and two diamonds, and a necklace, a gold chain with a single ruby and diamond. They were so beautiful that Annie hated them.

It snowed before they set off for Western Isle but nobody could deny the children the sight of their ponies that day. There was already quite a bit of snow which had fallen two days earlier and people had been pleased to have a white Christmas. The roads were clear at first but when they got past Durham and into the dale the snow began again. Nobody minded. They were planning to stay at Western Isle all week so being blocked in there didn't matter and when they arrived and it was a blizzard they tumbled into the house and lit the fires and had a drink and began the dinner. Hetty had cooked the turkey overnight and brought the Christmas puddings with her so all they had to do was the vegetables. Annie helped her with that. Sylvester was busy building a Meccano empire with Anthony, and Blake went out to the stables with Susan, promising that she should have her first ride as soon as the snow stopped.

It didn't stop and when Blake and Susan came in at last regretfully from the stable Anthony had been sitting by the fire for a long time with a pencil and paper. He had showed no interest in the pony, all he had wanted to do was stay inside. Blake had said nothing but Annie could feel his disappointment. She took the little boy in with her and she thought back to Charles Vane and Alistair and shivered.

When Blake did come into the drawing room she thought it a good idea to make a point.

'If you'd bought him charcoal pencils and a drawing pad for Christmas it would have been sufficient,' she said as the children ran into the kitchen for some of Hetty's trifle. She sat down on the arm of Blake's chair and shoved under his nose the drawing his son had completed.

'Look at that. Look how good it is.'

'He's only a child. Who can tell what he might be.'

'Are you denying that he has talent?'

'Annie, he'd be a lot better off getting some fresh air and exercise instead of sitting inside by the fire every day of his holidays, drawing houses.'

'It isn't just any house, it's Western Isle.'

'Don't you think we have enough drawings of Western Isle?'

'He doesn't need to go away, he can go to school here. Don't you want to watch him grow up, see him every day?'

'I don't want him to be like me.'

'He's not like you. Susan's more like you. He could go to art school—'

'Art school? Annie, I have half a dozen businesses—'

'Have you any idea who you sound like? You sound like your father,' Annie said.

'I am not like him. Don't say things like that to me. I thought you of all people would understand. People have to live, they have a living to make, they need money before they need anything else. Alistair could afford to indulge himself because his father was well-off, because his grandfather had been a clever man, but you know it's only one generation out of so many that can do it and do you know how they do it? With other people's sweat, that's how. They indulge themselves because other people have worked.'

'Alistair was good—'

'Lots of people are good, Annie, but it's a buyer's market. The world is full of people who are not quite brilliant. There isn't enough room up there for them all. Some of them have to work for their living instead, get their hands dirty—'

'I don't know how you can talk about Alistair like that.'

'I'm not talking about Alistair though as far as you are concerned it's all that matters, Alistair's child and Alistair's ability. Even Anthony looks like Alistair and is talented like Alistair and can't be sent away to school because he's sensitive like Alistair.'

'Stop it,' Annie said, getting up and moving well away. 'You think you're so clever but if it hadn't been for Irene how far would your cleverness have got you, eh? You could still have been a miner like a lot of other clever men who have brains and no opportunity—'

'That's why I want an education for my son so that he can go as far as his ability will take him.'

'He can do that without being sent away,' Annie said.

'I don't agree.'

'You can't send him away, you just can't.'

'Why can't I?'

'Because you've lost so many people you loved. You haven't had the time to spend with them. He loves you so much, Blake, and he's only a little boy. Don't send him away. Time is all we have, it's all we're meant to have. We're meant to know that, to see it, not take things for granted and think there will always be another time, another day. There won't. You should know that better than anybody. All we have is now. Please don't send him away.'

'What do you want me to do, leave him here with you so that you can make him into a mammy's boy?'

'It's one thing nobody could accuse you of, you cold bastard!'

She fired at him the first thing which came to hand from the small table nearby. It was a costly Chinese orna-ment. It skimmed past his face and broke against the wall. The telephone was ringing insistently.

Hetty came in just then.

'I thought you might like some . . .' and then she stopped because she saw the vase. 'What happened?' she said.

'Annie threw it at me,' Blake said and he got up and went into the hall to answer the telephone. Annie sank down into the nearest armchair and cried.

472

'Oh God, Hetty,' she said, 'he's just like the old man was. I'll end up like Mrs Vane, arranging flowers and doing as I'm told.'

'Oh dear,' Hetty said, cuddling her, 'I don't think it's quite that bad.'

'He wanted me to be Irene and I'm not and I wanted him to be Alistair and he's anything but. It wasn't a good idea, Hetty, this getting married. I can't love him and he certainly doesn't love me. Last time we went to a dinner dance he danced with every woman in the party except me, and he dances so well,' and Annie found a handkerchief in her pocket and blew her nose. 'I trod on everybody's toes I was so inept. And he wants to send Anthony away. How am I going to stop him?'

Sylvester came in then. He stopped and frowned at the broken vase.

'I'm sorry, Sylvester. I threw it at Blake.'

'Couldn't you have thrown something else at him?' Sylvester said. 'Something from Woolworths perhaps?'

'Do you have anything from Woolworths?'

'No, I don't believe we have,' he said, and put a comforting hand on her shoulder.

Blake came back in.

'That was Tommy on the phone. He wants me to go

up to Sunniside. Elsie and Ron have had to go to Alston, his father's not good, and they can't get back. He's got too much to do to go there himself. He just wants me to see to the animals. I'll not be long.'

Annie would have gone after him but Sylvester stopped her.

'He shouldn't go by himself,' she protested. 'He's never been back there. Tommy's so stupid, he doesn't understand.'

Before Blake got halfway there the snow had turned into a blizzard and the day was dark. He stopped when he came in sight of the house but only momentarily. The animals needed feeding, he didn't have to stay long, he didn't even have to go inside the house.

It took him quite a long time to get there, the wind behind the snow was against him and he was walking uphill. When he reached the house it was almost impossible to see anything and he was numb with cold. He couldn't have gone inside anyway, the house was locked up. Just getting inside the buildings with the warmth of the animals was such a relief that he stood for a minute or so to brush the snow off his face before he started the task he had come for. It took him a long time. He was almost finished when he heard a voice behind him and when he turned around a small snowman had walked into the barn. He could see nothing but her eyes.

'What the hell are you doing here?' he said.

'I was worried about you.'

'Worried about me?'

'I'm too cold to talk. Can we go inside?'

'It's locked up.'

'Elsie keeps the key under a stone.'

They found the key. Inside the little house the fire was banked down in the sitting room but Blake brought that to life and put wood on it. The kitchen was warm from the Rayburn. Annie found dry clothes for them and she gave Blake his and went off into the little sitting room to change. He made some tea and they sat by the fire and drank it gratefully.

'You shouldn't have come. You could have got lost in this.'

'I didn't want you to be here by yourself.'

'Why ever not? I used to live here.'

'I thought you might start thinking about things when you got here.'

'Like what?' Blake said roughly.

'Your grandfather and your grandmother and Bessie.'

Blake looked down into his teacup for a second and then he said, 'It was the hardest thing of all, leaving her. I found my grandfather dead in the top field and watched them take my grandmother away in an ambulance knowing that she probably wouldn't come back but leaving Bessie here, that was the hardest thing. Isn't that funny? I watched out of the back window of the car until I couldn't see her any more. I never saw her again. I couldn't even tell her. But Bessie was the only one who got to stay really, who never had to leave.'

'You came back.'

'I didn't want to come back but I couldn't tell that to Tommy—'

'Tommy's so stupid,' Annie said.

'Do Elsie and Ron like it here?'

'It's not big enough. Ron's father is going to help them buy something bigger – I'm sorry, I didn't mean to say that.'

'Why shouldn't you? It's true, it was never much of a farm. I should know.'

'We're going to have to stay the night, you know.'

'No, we're not.'

'Blake, it's a white-out, I cannot walk all that way in the blizzard.'

'I'm not staying here. You shouldn't have come.'

'I thought you might be upset about having to come back.'

'I was very happy here until my grandfather died.'

'Then why don't you want to stay the night?'

'I just don't, that's all. I want to go back and spend Christmas night with the children and Hetty and Sylvester. This place is freezing and there's only one decent-sized bedroom since you and Alistair crucified the other one for the sake of a bathroom—'

'We did not!'

'Yes, you did. I was born in that room. My mother was, my grandfather, God knows how many Blakes before that. What did you have to go and spoil it for?'

'It isn't your place!'

'It'll always be my place. I'll probably come back and die here.'

'That's horrible.'

'It isn't horrible at all, it's what things are all about, at least until the bloody Vanes spoil everything.'

'You're a bloody Vane.'

'I am not!'

'And your son is. I've never seen anybody look more like a Vane.'

'Don't talk about it,' Blake said, getting to his feet.

'We can sleep down here,' Annie said, 'we can take blankets and pillows off the bed.'

'There's nothing to eat and there's probably nothing to drink.'

'There's plenty to eat and there's a bottle of whisky in the kitchen, I saw it.' Annie went off to the kitchen and came back with the whisky and two glasses. She poured out the golden liquid and then looked at him.

'I'm sorry about earlier, shouting at you and about the vase.'

'It doesn't matter to me about the vase. It was Sylvester's.'

'I did apologise to him.'

'I really don't know how you missed me. You should learn to take aim before you fire.'

'I was too angry. I didn't think. Are you hungry?'

'Starving.'

'It's all the walking. I'll go and see what there is.'

Annie found half a cold chicken in the pantry and plenty of bread. The level on the whisky bottle went down steadily.

They sat on the sofa with pillows in the corners and blankets over them.

'Can I ask you something?' Annie said.

'What?'

'Are you having an affair with Pauline Kington?'

Blake started to laugh.

'Whatever made you think that?'

'You pay her a lot of attention.'

'I wouldn't do that.'

'Wouldn't you? I thought you might. I thought you might well before now.'

'It's not that easy. I'm just a country boy at heart, I have to live with myself.'

'But you have thought about it?'

'Yes, but I've never done anything about it.'

'You treat me as though I don't matter, like I'm just a doll all dressed up to look good beside you. I hate it.'

'I thought that was what you wanted.'

'No—'

'Yes, it was. That was what you married me for, so that you could be rich. It was all you ever wanted. So now you've got what you wanted, clothes, jewellery, furs, cars, a big house, the sort of people who know things, a good school for your daughter.'

'I thought I would be treated with respect.'

'Respect?' Blake put down his glass and laughed. 'Respect isn't an automatic gain, my flower.'

'I'm not your flower.'

'No, you're more like a nasty little thorn in the side. Just answer me one thing. If I'd been poor would you still have married me?'

'I didn't intend to marry you, Blake.'

'It was the money.'

479

'It wasn't just the money. Susan likes you. She has no father and you can give her such a lot.'

'I wish we were at home now.'

'What, Western Isle?'

'No, Sunderland. I haven't got a bloody home here any more. I know where I am there.'

'Who you are,' Annie corrected him. 'All-important David Blake.'

'At least I'm me there. I don't have Alistair Vane to live up to every time I breathe.'

'That's not true. You never had to.'

'Isn't it? Even that day in the barn just after I got to your place, the day I knocked Tommy down for you, it was Alistair.'

'Blake, I went out to the hayshed in the night for you.'

'But you went out riding with Alistair and let him kiss you.'

'How did you know that?'

'He told me. He told me he was the first person who ever kissed you.'

'I was impressed, that's all. He was older than me and he had a nice horse.'

'A nice horse?'

'These things matter when you're thirteen. It doesn't matter now.'

'It is the matter now. He gets in my way more now he's dead than he did when he was alive.'

Annie tried to hit him for that and he stopped her and the glasses and the whisky went flying.

'I hate you. You're horrible,' she said, struggling.

'I'm sorry. I didn't mean to say it. I just feel so awful about it, that's all. He has no right to be dead. I can't hate him now.'

'You hated him?'

'Of course I did. He took you and now look. I've ended up with his wife, his child, even his bloody farm. How do you think that makes me feel? I didn't even want Western Isle. I wanted to sit there and let it drop to pieces . . . and then I couldn't because of him. He never even knew, he thought I was just an upstart from a shabby little hillfarm.'

'You were,' Annie said and she took him into her arms and kissed him.

Blake pushed her from him.

'I suppose you think it's a proper house now it has a bathroom. You bloody ruined it.'

'We did not! Your family had done nothing to the house.'

'They never had any money to do anything. They barely survived and they never owned it either. You seem to forget that.'

'Then you should be pleased that somebody did more than that.'

'With Charles Vane's bloody money? You think that pleases me?'

'Why won't you let it rest, forget it? He's dead.'

'I can't forget it. He ruined my family.'

'Yes but you got the better of him, didn't you? You got exactly what you wanted and do you know why? Because you're exactly like him, that's why. Alistair was like his mother but you – you're just like him!'

'If I am then it's your fault. You did it. You took from me the only thing I had left that mattered. You went to Alistair because he was a better prospect than me—'

'I've paid for it then, haven't I?' Annie said and got up from the sofa and ran into the kitchen, crying over the Rayburn so that the tears sizzled on top. And when he followed her there she said, 'Yes, I loved you. When you went away I thought that the world had ended and the only thing that helped, the only person who made any difference was Alistair. I – I made him into you as best I could until I didn't need to any more. He was good enough all by himself and you – as far as I was concerned you were just a clerk in a shipping office and you were never going to be anything else and it mattered. Before you went away you were the only person who ever made me feel loved, right from the beginning, right from the day that you knocked Tommy down in the old byre. I thought you were the best thing that ever happened to the world.'

'But you let me go.'

'Yes. Yes!'

She would have run away up the stairs and into the freezing bedroom where she had spent so many nights with Alistair but he got hold of her when she tried to get past him and said gently, 'I loved you too, always. Don't run from me.'

Annie put her arms up around his neck and this time he kissed her and after that he kissed her again and they went back into the room by the fire and this time it was like it should have been all those years ago, before anybody got in the way. There was nobody now, no ghosts, no memories, no past, no future, nothing to spoil things, just the little house as it was, snowbound and quiet. They even went to bed eventually and slept in each other's arms.

In the middle of the night when Annie awoke he woke up too, asking sleepily, 'What are you doing?'

'Being thankful that Alistair and I put in a bathroom and I don't have to go down the yard,' she said and he chuckled a little bit and went back to sleep.

When she came back from the bathroom she stood for a few seconds beside the window. The snow had stopped completely and a large moon graced the sky, decorated with a few stars in a blue-black scene. The fields were covered, the trees were starkly white and drifts were leaning in curves against the stone walls. Annie thought she had never seen the little farm look so peaceful and there was not a sound of any kind in the still night.

When she got back into bed he put his arms around her again as if she had never left him, even though he was asleep.

The following morning the walk was all downhill to Western Isle though the snow was so deep it made Annie's legs tired. The roads had been ploughed by then and when they reached the farm it felt so civilised with its neat yard and buildings. The children tumbled out of the house. Sylvester and Hetty came to the door.

They were to stay at Western Isle for the full week but long before the week was over Annie was ready to leave. She didn't want to be there in the dale in the quiet, she wanted to get on with her life and her marriage. They left on New Year's Eve and it was such a relief to go that she didn't even look back to see any of the farms.

Sunderland was a homecoming. There wasn't nearly as much snow there to Annie's relief and the children's disappointment. The air seemed so fresh, she thought it must be the sea, and when Blake went back to work the following day and the weather was not so bad she took the car and drove to the nearest beach and walked a long way before turning back as the tide crashed halfway down the sand.

Blake came back when it was dark and he called Anthony into the drawing room.

'I bought you a present,' he said.

'But I already had my presents.'

'This is special,' Blake said and he went into the hall and came back with an easel, water paints, oil paints, drawing pads, charcoal pencils and everything else which a would-be painter might need.

The boy fell on it all exclaiming excitedly and Susan came in.

'Is it for me too?' she asked.

'Yes, of course,' Blake said.

The children went off, Anthony dragging the easel with him. Annie looked at Blake.

'Be careful,' she said, smiling, 'you're turning into a person.'

He sat down on the big sofa by the fire and she

brought him a glass of whisky. He pulled her down on to his knee and kissed her.

'I cancelled the boarding school,' he said.

Annie hugged him so hard that she nearly knocked the glass out of his hand. He put it down to appreciate the hug better and Annie kissed him all over his face.

Fifteen minutes later when she went into the kitchen to check the dinner she peeped in at the sitting room where the children had gone with their new art things. They were both drawing in front of the fire. Annie ventured nearer. Anthony was drawing a horse and making a good job of it but Susan's drawing was indecipherable.

'What is it?' Annie asked.

'It's Daddy's works of course. That's a ship about to be built and that's me helping Daddy. It's nearly finished. Do you think he'd like to see it?'

'I'm sure he'd love to.'

Susan scrambled to her feet and disappeared in the direction of the drawing room and Annie went off towards the kitchen, smiling.

If you enjoyed
Far From My Father's House,
please try Elizabeth's other novels in ebook

THE SINGING WINDS

UNDER A CLOUD-SOFT SKY

THE ROAD TO BERRY EDGE

SNOW ANGELS

SHELTER FROM THE STORM

Question & Answer
Elizabeth Gill

Where were you born?
Newcastle upon Tyne

What's your comfort food?
Smelly cheese like Stinking Bishop

Dog or cat?
I'm a country girl. You name the animal – I
love it and have probably kept it

What's your favourite holiday read?
Anything by Hilary Mantel or Peter Robinson

What would people be surprised to discover about you?
I can milk a goat

What is your favourite way to travel?
Orient Express

What are you currently listening to?
Bach, Beethoven, Brahms. I love opera. Favourites:
Madama Butterfly, Handel's *Giulio Cesare*. Live music is
so inspiring and fills me up and makes me happy

What are you currently reading?
Various books about women in medicine,
especially the first women doctors in
America in the 1860s

ALSO BY *Elizabeth Gill*

Miss Appleby's Academy

'Original and evocative – a born storyteller'
Trisha Ashley

'An enthralling and satisfying novel that will leave you
wanting to read more from this wonderful writer'
Catherine King

'Elizabeth Gill writes with a masterful grasp of conflicts
and passions hidden among men and women of the
wild North Country' Leah Fleming

www.elizabethgill.co.uk

www.quercusbooks.co.uk

@ElizabethRGill

AVAILABLE IN PRINT AND EBOOK